Blind Faith

Janet Clark

Blind Faith

Janet Clark

Published by 1stWorld Publishing
1100 North 4th St., Fairfield, Iowa 52556
tel: 641-209-5000 • fax: 641-209-3001
web: www.1stworldpublishing.com

First Edition

LCCN: 2006940375
SoftCover ISBN: 978-1-4218-9918-3
HardCover ISBN: 978-1-4218-9919-0
eBook ISBN: 978-1-4218-9920-6

This material has been written and published solely for educational purposes. The author and the publisher shall have neither liability nor responsibility to any person or entity with respect to any loss, damage or injury caused or alleged to be caused directly or indirectly by the information contained in this book.

The characters and events described in this text are intended to entertain and teach rather than present an exact factual history of real people or events.

REVIEWS: BLIND FAITH

Award-winning writer Janet Clark presents Blind Faith, a novel about the Roman Catholic clergy sexual abuse scandal as experienced through the eyes of young Jack O'Donnell and his family during the late '60s and early '70s... An involving story about the blind faith of a community manipulated, children betrayed, and the struggle to cope with hopelessly tangled emotions. Highly recommended.

—*Midwest Book Review* (Oregon, WI USA)

Janet Clark is passionate about giving a voice to those who suffer the terrorism of sexual assault. This book comes forth out of her desire to increase awareness, validate victims' pain, and encourage healing.

—*Arlene M. McColley Nicola,* MSW, LISW Licensed Independent Social Worker

Janet Clark has written a compassionate, enlightening, frustrating, believable, true to life novel...

—*Robert Charles Wolf*

A tale that offers hope... In Blind Faith, Janet Clark uncovers the secretive, frightening, abhorrent, and unfortunate world of a sexually abused child. It is a melancholy story of broken trusts, beliefs, and loyalties, and yet, is inspirational seeing how someone can find the strength to fight back against the powerful, rise like a Phoenix, and overcome seemingly insurmountable circumstances.

—*Dr. R. L. Ronconi*

A Recommended Read by the Online Review of Books and Current Affairs... "Emotionally charged."

"The world is a dangerous place to live, not because of the people who are evil, but because of the people who don't do anything about it."

—*Albert Einstein*

Prologue

Anger and shame swirled through the boy's soul, threatening to spiral into yet another outburst of rage. He'd promised himself he'd get it under control, but then a word or a sound or the suffocating smell of the man's aftershave would trigger another landslide, and he would felt his tenuous grasp on control slipping through his fingers like a mountain climber who loses his rope and then finds himself sliding helplessly down the rocky crevice of the mountainside.

But then the woman gave him a foothold, one of many she would give to him that would enable him to continue his steep and arduous journey.

"Write a letter to the man who abused you," she'd said.

The boy had looked at her like she was the crazy one.

"You want me to write a letter to *him*? All I want to say to him is, 'Go to hell,' he'd sputtered angrily.

"Then that's what you should write. Whatever you've felt toward him, put it down on paper. How he hurt you, how he damaged you with his actions. Get it out, all those feelings. You ever go fishing?" she said in an apparent non-sequitur.

"Yeah, a few times," he said. "What's that got to do with anything?"

"Did you ever get your fishing line all tangled up?" she asked.

"Yeah, I think that's why I hated it," the boy said, remembering the frustration of trying to untangle the wiry mess.

"Your emotions are a lot like that tangled-up fishing line," the woman told him. "Right now, they are so twisted together because of the abuse that you often find yourself becoming angry and you don't even know why. Then you have lashed out and harmed other people. Once you get clear on your true feelings and can associate them accurately with what caused them in the first place, you're going to find it a lot easier to keep yourself from behaving aggressively. You'll find that, once you get that line straight, your emotions are truly your friend, not your enemy."

"So, am I going to send this letter to him?" the boy asked.

"That will be up to you," she said. "This is something I want you to do for yourself, though. Why don't you start with writing down what happened."

Light

"Then God said, "Let there be light," and there was light. And God saw the light, that it was good; and God divided the light from the darkness."

—*Genesis 1: 3-4*

Chapter One 1964-1970

Jack looked hungrily at the bowl of sweet creamy oatmeal his grandmother, Lucinda, had placed in front of him, but even at six years old, he knew enough not to take a bite just yet, and not only because the cereal was still steaming. He watched his grandmother as she swiftly moved around the tidy little kitchen, pouring orange juice and coffee and bringing a plate of cinnamon toast to the table before she finally sat down with Jack and his older brother David.

"Ready, boys?" she said. Jack and David bowed their heads, folded their hands, and joined their grandmother in saying grace, an unbroken ritual in the O'Donnell house.

"Bless us, oh Lord, and these thy gifts, which we are about to receive from thy bounty through Christ our Lord, Amen," they chanted together.

Lucinda allowed herself a rare moment of reflection as she drank her first sip of coffee and looked proudly across the table at her two grandsons. With his light brown hair, broad face and cleft chin, David strongly resembled his father Mike, who had left for work at the cold storage facility hours earlier, while the rest of the family was still sleeping. Jack, however, looked so much like his mother that it sometimes broke Lucinda's heart. The gap-toothed smile, the even features, the eyes that couldn't lie, all reminded Lucinda of her only child, Rita, who had died just a few months after Jack's birth.

"Do you want Alan and me to take Jack to school with us, Grandma?" David asked as he reached for another piece of toast. "We can help him find his room and everything."

"No, thanks, honey," Lucinda said. "I'll walk with Jack today. Maybe next week he can start going with you boys." *I'm not ready to let go yet,* she added silently.

Lucinda's mind flashed back to the morning Rita had died. Only three things had kept Lucinda going the day she'd lost her only child. First was the relief she'd felt to know her daughter's pain had finally ended: Lucinda had watched helplessly as brain cancer had zapped Rita's strength and crippled her with crushing headaches that visited with ever-increasing ruthlessness during the last weeks of her life. If there was anything more torturous than losing a child to death, it had to be standing by and watching her suffer, unable to alleviate the pain.

The second thing that kept her going was her promise to Rita, that she would help Mike raise the two boys. When Lucinda and Mike had come home from the hospital after Rita had died, Lucinda had walked in the door and found their neighbor Rose Castani rocking Jack, who was contentedly drinking from his bottle. Lucinda had held out her arms and Rose, immediately understanding her need, had stood up and handed the baby to his grandmother. She settled into the rocking chair with Jack, who nursed on, barely missing a beat. As his little body nestled into her own, Lucinda's pain had lifted just enough to let her know that she would somehow make it through this ordeal.

It didn't seem possible that almost six years had passed since Rita's death, and that Jack, whom she had raised from infancy, was actually old enough to start school. But here it was, Jack's first day of kindergarten, and David was starting sixth grade. *Rita, baby, you'd be proud,* Lucinda thought, wiping a tear from her eye before the children could notice.

"Go upstairs and brush your teeth, boys," she said. "It's almost time to go."

Last but certainly not least, what had enabled Lucinda to

survive the loss of her daughter was her deep Catholic faith. For Lucinda, the Church was her lifeline. The Church was where she had taken comfort when her own mother had died when Lucinda was a young woman, just newly married. Her faith was what had strengthened her when her husband had left her and their daughter to start a new family with another woman. And her faith was what gave her the courage to go on after she'd had to bury Rita, her little girl, and the strength to raise Rita's boys.

A soft rap on the door jarred Lucinda from her reveries. She got up to open it. Alan Castani, his stubborn hair smoothed down and lying flat, at least temporarily, smiled shyly and shifted from one foot to the other. Alan and David had been best friends since before kindergarten, but the boy was still a little bashful, even more so as he approached adolescence.

"Hi, Mrs. Walters," he said. "Is David ready?"

"I'm coming," David called from the stairwell. He grabbed his jacket and hurried out the door. "Bye, Grandma, see you after school. Bye, Jack, have fun," he said to his brother, who had followed him down the stairs. Lucinda got the coats out of the closet in the hallway, then quickly cleared the breakfast dishes off the table before heading out the door with her youngest grandson.

Jack, like David and Alan, was dressed in neat navy blue pants and a tucked-in white shirt. He carried a sack with a box of crayons, a package of tissues, a pair of stubby scissors, a mat for naptime, and one of Mike's old shirts to use as a paint shirt. (Actually, Jack carried the sack for the first two blocks and then, finding it was a lot heavier than it had looked, he turned it over to his grandmother, who carried it the rest of the way.) As they approached the school, Lucinda felt a rush of apprehension, though Jack seemed to be taking it all in his stride. She walked him through the double doors, down the hallway crowded with lively children and anxious parents, to the door of the kindergarten room, and bent down to give Jack a kiss.

"Be a good boy, Jack, and remember, Grandma will meet you here after school to walk you home," she said.

"I will, Grandma," Jack said nonchalantly, then squared his

shoulders and walked into the classroom, a sunny room with big windows and bright posters displayed on the pale yellow walls. Jack's teacher, a fresh-faced young nun named Sister Marie Therese, greeted him warmly and seated him at a table with three other children, who were busy coloring.

Lucinda watched for just a moment, and then slipped out the door. It was a bittersweet moment. She had enjoyed having Jack all to herself for these past six years, but she also knew it was time for her to start letting go. A public elementary school was just four blocks from their home, half the distance as St. Maria Goretti's, but Lucinda trusted that the education and the surroundings would be superior at St. Maria's. Most importantly, she knew Jack would be safe here.

Established near the turn of the century, St. Maria Goretti's School was an attractive tan brick one-story building on the same site as St. Maria Goretti Church. The founders of the church had been eager to establish a place where their children would learn their Catholic faith right along with reading, writing and arithmetic. St. Maria Goretti School educated students from kindergarten to eighth grade, with two sections in most of the grades, drawing children from throughout the working-class neighborhoods that surrounded the school. The students' parents were shopkeepers, factory workers, railroad employees. Some families were a little wealthier, some a little less, but there were no great extremes at either end of the spectrum. The lack of economic disparity and the families' shared faith made for a solid, somewhat insular community at St. Maria's. Diversity meant some folks were Irish Catholic and some were Italian Catholic, with a few families of German extraction thrown in to the mix.

Students at St. Maria's followed a very structured routine. The subjects were standard: reading, handwriting, geography, history, language, math, religion, art, music and gym. Some of the teachers were nuns and some were lay teachers. Each Friday morning all the students gathered at the church for Mass. The carefully controlled atmosphere of the school provided a comforting rhythm to most of the students; though future educators would pronounce learning by rote and repetition to be stifling, the students at Maria Goretti's knew no other way and most of them were happy there.

Lucinda walked back to the school at noon, having spent a busy but strangely quiet morning cleaning the house. She joined the group of young mothers waiting in the hallway. Soon Sister Marie Therese opened the door, and the children rushed out excitedly.

"Grandma, look at my picture! We got to paint, and we played on the monkey bars at recess, and had treats, and I didn't spill my milk, Grandma," Jack assured her.

"Well, good job, Jack," Lucinda said, admiring the reds and purples and yellows splashed somewhat randomly over the page. The anxiety she had felt earlier was alleviated when she saw how well Jack was adapting to his environment. "Let's go home and we'll have some grilled cheese sandwiches," she said, folding his small hand in her own.

Later that evening David shared the news from his first day of school. He would begin serving as an altar boy this year, and practice started the following Thursday after school. Father Delanoit had chosen David to be in the first group of boys to serve, which Lucinda suspected was due to David's reputation for being responsible and trustworthy. She was very proud, and even Mike looked pleased when he heard the news.

"That's great, son. I used to be an altar boy myself, about a million years ago," Mike said. Mike was not an especially religious man himself, but he knew the Church had been important to Rita, as it was to Lucinda, and couldn't imagine bringing up the boys any other way.

That first month of school passed quickly. Jack flourished in the warm learning environment in Sister Marie Therese's classroom. He practically exploded with excitement the week it was his turn to take care of the classroom pet, a guinea pig named Betty. Lucinda chuckled to see his exuberance until she found out the student who cared for the guinea pig all week had to bring it home for the weekend. Lucinda, who took to heart the axiom that cleanliness was next to godliness, was not a fan of allowing animals in the house.

"Jack, you'll have to keep that creature in your room," she said. David had helped him lug the cage and sack of food home on Friday afternoon.

"I will, Grandma. Only she's not a creature. She's Betty, and she's a very good girl, aren't you, girl?" he said, carefully carrying her up the stairs.

When Jack still hadn't come back downstairs an hour later, Lucinda began to get worried, picturing the rodent roaming around the bedrooms, leaving a trail of droppings behind her. So she went up to check the situation out and found Jack sitting next to Betty's cage, clasping a well-worn copy of Mailman Mike and reading to the guinea pig, stopping after each page to hold the book in front of her cage to show her the pictures.

"And that's the story of Mailman Mike," he concluded. "Do you want to hear another story, Betty?" he asked, and then noticed his grandmother in the doorway, smiling at the sweet scene. "I don't want Betty to be scared, being in a new place, so I'm reading her some stories," Jack explained.

Lucinda gave him a squeeze and a quick kiss on his still baby-soft hair, and then went downstairs to fix supper. That boy never failed to lift her heart. Rita, she knew, was looking down from heaven at him, beaming proudly.

"You've got yourself two good boys, sweetie," Lucinda whispered. She wiped away a tear, picked up the potato peeler and got to work.

By the first Sunday in October, David was ready to serve at Mass, along with Alan Castani. Mike, Lucinda and Jack took their usual pew, right across from Rose Castani and her crew. Rose's husband had died in an accident at the John Deere plant two years before, leaving her with six children to raise on her own. Alan, the second oldest, sometimes seemed to get lost in the shuffle, Lucinda had noticed. That morning Alan was slouching, his eyes glued to the floor, as they waited for Mass to begin.

But David stood tall, a slight smile playing at his lips. He felt honored to be playing this role in the celebration of the Mass. As the time approached for David's confirmation, he was beginning to take more interest in the Church, in God. He felt a warm glow of peace every time he received communion, a sense of drawing near to the God who brought his grandmother so much comfort. He began to wonder if maybe God was calling him to the priesthood.

After church, Mike took the family to the House of Pancakes for breakfast to celebrate. The perky red-haired hostess escorted them to a booth, where Mike and David sat on one side and Lucinda and Jack on the other.

The waitress brought menus and coffee for the adults. After she took their orders, Lucinda said to David, "Honey, you really did a good job today. I was so proud of you!"

"That you did, my boy," Mike said. "You almost looked like you belonged up there," he added, then looked a little surprised, wondering to himself where that came from.

"Thanks," David said.

"Alan seemed awfully nervous or something," Lucinda said. "Is there a problem, do you know?"

"I don't know. He did seem weird today," David said. "Before Mass when we were putting on our robes and Father Delanoit came in the sacristy, Alan just about jumped out of his skin: he even dropped the chalice! I thought Father Delanoit was gonna be really mad, but he wasn't at all. He even gave Alan a hug and told him not to worry about it."

"That was kind of him," Lucinda said. Father Delanoit always seems to pay a little more attention to the kids like Alan, who need it, she thought. Boys who don't have a father of their own.

"I want to be an altar boy, too," Jack said. It must be a good gig, because David was getting a lot of attention.

"You will," David assured him. "All the boys get to be altar boys in the sixth grade."

"Geeze!" Jack sighed. Six years was a lifetime to him. "Were you ever an altar girl, Grandma?"

"No, Jack, there aren't any altar girls," Lucinda said. "Only boys get to serve that way."

"Why?" Jack asked, his dark blue eyes perplexed. "I don't think that's fair!" he protested, but the theological discussion ended when the waitress arrived with their breakfasts. Lucinda ate her pancakes slowly, savoring every bite. Food always tasted better when she wasn't the one to cook it, and that didn't happen very often. She sometimes wondered if Mike would ever remarry, and if he did, what her place in the family would be. There was no sign that was going to happen any time soon, though.

It had been over five years since Rita's death, but Mike didn't really date. At least not that Lucinda was aware of. He did spend a couple of nights a week at Dooley's or one of the other watering holes, and there had been a few occasions where he'd drunk enough alcohol that he could justify going home with a woman he'd met there, but no one could compare with Rita in Mike's eyes. Rita! He remembered the day he'd met her like it was yesterday.

Mike O'Donnell was a big, swaggering Irish-American, the first generation in his family to be born in this country. Like most men with a swagger, Mike's covered up a host of insecurities. When Mike was a little boy growing up in Cleveland, he had struggled in school. At that time, children weren't diagnosed as learning disabled or dyslexic, which Mike was; they were written off as stupid or shamed for not trying hard enough. After ten years of being labeled, Mike had had it with formal education. He dropped out of high school and, at his uncle's urging, moved to Hook's Point, Iowa. His uncle worked at the cold storage warehouse there and encouraged Mike to apply for a job when a position opened up. So he did.

He started working at the plant, making good money and enjoying the respect of his peers. Life was good—Mike got by just fine without the reading skills which had proven illusive for him. He worked hard, dated some girls and spent some time in the bars, though he vowed not to become the drunkard that his father was. After a few years of the single life, Mike grew tired of it: the loneliness and a gnawing empty feeling in his gut that only alcohol could alleviate. Until he met Rita.

One summer afternoon Mike received a message from his foreman to report to the office. When he got there, one of the secretaries, a forty-something woman whose mouth was set in perpetual scowl, handed him a paper.

"You didn't fill out your income tax form completely," she said accusingly, as if Mike had the power to single-handedly take down the entire United States fiscal system with his error. She thrust the paper at him and waited impatiently for him to complete it.

Immediately, Mike was back in fourth grade. He was standing at the blackboard, forehead puckered as he labored to diagram a complex sentence, his bitchy teacher ready to pounce at the first error. He blinked, willed himself into the present moment, and looked at the form.

Shouldn't be too hard, he told himself. He'd memorized a few tricks that generally concealed how inept he felt when confronted with the written word—Mike was an intelligent man, but his impaired reading ability made him feel ashamed, and the shame made him confused, which made it harder still to read. He took a deep breath to avoid getting stuck in that old cycle.

"I don't have all day, just because you want to waste time to get out of work. Would you mind hurrying up and finishing that form," crowed the harpy.

Mike's hands shook as anger battled with shame. He struggled to keep his temper: this job was too damn good to lose on account of that old bitch.

"What do you want me to do?" he said.

"Just finish the form! Damn immigrants, come over and take up all the jobs and they can't even fill out a simple piece of paperwork," she growled.

And then, when he was on the brink of walking out the door of Jefferson Cold Storage for good, an angel appeared. Only this one was a fiery little Italian angel.

"Cut it out, Dianne. Some of those tax forms, you have to practically be a Ph.D. to fill them out," said the dark-haired girl whose desk sat kitty-corner across from Attila the Hun, also apparently known as Dianne. The girl's angry expression changed to a smile as she looked up at Mike.

"Hey, it's okay. I work with these things and I can barely figure them out," the girl said, and suddenly his anger and shame were dissolving. She had moved out from behind her desk and stood next to Mike. "All we really need is your John Henry right here," she said.

Mike inhaled, breathing in deep the delightful springtime scent of the girl. As he lowered his six-foot two frame into a chair, he brushed against her. Their eyes met and he felt his heart filling up, not just with desire—although he definitely felt that—but something else, something even stronger. Mike smiled at the girl, his confidence restored, and whispered, "What's with the cob up her ass?"

Rita snorted, smothering a laugh, as Dianne managed to give them both a withering look while she answered the phone. "She's just getting warmed up. That woman's something else, I'll tell you."

"Hey, you saved my life there. Let me buy you dinner tonight at Moby's," Mike said. Moby's served steaks as well as seafood and had just the right ambiance for a first date; quiet enough to talk, but with enough action that there wouldn't be a big awkward silence to contend with if the date went sour. Although that didn't seem likely to happen.

Rita surprised him by blushing slightly before she said, "Sure. I get off work at five."

"I get off at three. That gives me time to run home and catch a shower, and then I'll swing back and pick you up," Mike said.

"How about I meet you there," Rita said, her feistiness returning. Later in their relationship Mike had learned that Rita's father had deserted the family when Rita was a little girl, forcing her mother to take work cleaning houses in order to provide a living for them. After watching her mother struggle all those years, Rita had vowed that she was going to be careful in love not to fall in love too quickly. But she and Mike had only dated a few months before they both knew it was the real thing. Mike had loved Rita with all his heart; he'd been a faithful husband throughout their too-short marriage and still missed her every day. The brief encounters with other women left him feeling even more lonely, feeling ashamed, feeling as if he had betrayed his wife.

Mike's real betrayal was deeper. Increasingly, whiskey was becoming his mistress. Not only did Mike drink in the bar every Wednesday and Friday, he was drinking at home now, also. He'd have a nip before bed to help him sleep and a few shots while he worked on his car in the garage. He was able to rationalize it by telling himself he never drank in front of the boys, like his old man had, and he wasn't getting shit-faced. And he wasn't. Mike was a quiet drunk, not an obnoxious one like his father. So it was easy for Lucinda to overlook the undeniable fact that Mike was an alcoholic.

And her denial was understandable, for there were moments where Mike did seem to be totally present with his sons, like later that afternoon when they watched the football game on television, David sitting on one side of Mike and Jack on the other, all three of them cheering whenever their team scored a touchdown. Then they drifted outside and had their own game. What Lucinda didn't see, nor did the boys, were Mike's occasional trips to the garage, where he'd have just a nip, then pop a breath mint to hide the smell.

And so far, nobody was the wiser. Nobody was hurt if he sipped a little whiskey now and then, Mike rationalized. He wasn't like his father, an out-of-control, raging bull, who had kept his family on a constant state of high alert. Mike was a good dad. Nobody could say that Mike O'Donnell's boys lacked for anything they needed, and he rarely laid a hand on them. Lucinda was more apt to deliver a swat to their butts than Mike was, for he feared turning into his old man. His boys would never know the pain and fear that he'd grown up with. Mike had promised Rita that he'd take good care of their sons, and he fully intended to keep that promise. His boys would come to no harm under his watch, that was for sure.

That year flew by in a blur, Lucinda thought. It seemed as if one day Jack was bringing home finger paintings and a permission slip to visit the fire station and the next day, she was enrolling him in the first grade. Now he was gone for a full day, and, while sometimes Lucinda got lonely, she did take the opportunity to stretch out for a nap in the afternoon on occasion.

Lucinda was now sixty-one years old. Most of her hair had turned white, the lines in her face were a little deeper every year, and, let's face it, she told herself ruefully, the old gray mare ain't what she used to be. She considered herself fortunate to have the good health to look after a house and raise two boys, but a lifetime of hard work had taken its toll. Hopefully, her health would last at least until both boys graduated from high school.

Lucinda had also begun taking one night a week off to go out for pie and coffee with a couple of other women from the church. While her life wasn't easy, it was peaceful. Mike took good care of the family financially, both of the boys were good-natured and obedient, and life rolled along fairly smoothly, one year evaporating into the next. Pappa, Lucinda's father, visited about once a month, and sometimes Lucinda tried to convince him to move to Hook's Point so she could keep an eye on him, in case his health began to fail, but he said no, he was perfectly happy in Chicago and she had enough to worry about without having an old man like him adding to her troubles. Lucinda had to admit, he really didn't need her help; although he was now in his eighties, Pappa still cooked all his own meals, kept his apartment scrupulously clean, and socially, the man got around a lot more than she did.

Tony Gargano, like so many others, had come to America in search of a better life for himself and his family. He and Lucinda's mother Gina emigrated from Italy in the early 1900s and joined Tony's brother in Chicago, where Tony worked as a tailor and Gina took in laundry while taking care of Lucinda. Lucinda remembered Pappa whistling as he walked up the stairs to their flat after work, sometimes surprising her mother with a bouquet of flowers or Lucinda with a carefully stitched addition to her doll's extensive wardrobe. Other nights he'd stroll in the door and, sweeping Gina into his arms, dance her around the little kitchen, twirling her around until she'd squeal, "Enough, Tony, you're making me dizzy!", and then he'd release her, turn to Lucinda and twirl her around, until both she and her mother dissolved in a fit of giggles.

Tony never made the fortune he'd dreamed about, but his little family lacked for nothing, especially love. When Lucinda married, she'd expected her life to be a replay of her parents', and it came as a shock to find out not all men were cut from the same cloth as Pappa. She still felt a wonderful sense of security whenever he was around.

And the boys were growing up. In 1970, David was a senior in high school and Jack was in the sixth grade. David and Jack, with six years between them, weren't exactly close, for they each had separate interests and friends, but Jack did look up to David as his big brother, and David stood ready to defend Jack if any neighborhood bullies tried harassing him.

David would much prefer talking it out to fighting it out, however. His boyhood faith had ripened into something deeper, and he was beginning to believe that he did indeed have a call to the priesthood. Whatever it was, David knew he felt a tug in his spirit away from the drinking and brawling and necking with girls that most of the boys at school were obsessed with, towards a higher purpose. Sometimes his buddies gave him a bad time because he didn't join in their crude talk and lusty appraisals of the girls in their class, but David considered their teasing to be pretty minor when he compared it with the torments which the great saints he'd studied about in religion class had to put up with. Getting boiled in oil, thrown into the lions' den, crucified upside down, now that was persecution.

Jack was looking forward to sixth grade, for this was the year he would get to serve as a patrol boy, helping the little kids cross the street before and after school, and as an altar boy. When he was in the lower grades, the sixth graders seemed like super-heroes: big, strong kids who could do just about anything an adult could, but not as dull and boring as grown-ups tended to get. Finally, his day in the sun had arrived. And, he lucked out—he got Mrs. Gardner for a teacher. Young, pretty, and upbeat, she was the teacher everybody hoped for. The other class got stuck with Sister Veronica, a stern-faced nun whose temper was legendary. But Jack had gotten lucky, it seemed. Sixth grade was shaping up to be a good year.

Chapter Two

On the first day of sixth grade, Mrs. Gardner handed out the assignments for patrol boys and altar boys. During September and October, Jack would serve as a patrol boy, and in November he would start practicing to be an altar boy. Every morning in October, Jack arrived at school twenty minutes early and every afternoon he stayed twenty minutes late, carefully guiding the younger students across the street. Since he was the youngest child in his family, it was a treat for Jack to play big brother to all those little kids. The time passed quickly, and before he knew it, Jack was trading in his patrol boy uniform for altar boy vestments.

"When are you going to serve at your first Mass, Jack?" David asked, as the boys and Lucinda sat at the table, eating meatloaf and baked potatoes.

"Father Delanoit has me on the schedule for the third Sunday in November," Jack said, drenching his meatloaf in ketchup.

"Doesn't it seem like just yesterday you were practicing to become an altar boy, David? It does to me," Lucinda said.

"It does. Me and Alan Castani. Whoah—that's been six years ago," David said. He ate several bites of meatloaf before he spoke again. "Alan dropped out of school last week."

"No! I'll bet his mother was fit to be tied," Lucinda said. "But that boy's been giving her trouble for a couple of years, now. I just don't get it. He used to be the nicest boy—I remember you two were such good friends when you were younger, David, why, if Alan wasn't over here, then you were at the Castanis."

"That was a long time ago, Grandma. Things change—people change," David said.

Almost imperceptibly the three of them glanced at Mike's vacant chair. Mike missed supper several nights a week now, often not getting home until after Jack's bedtime, weaving slightly as he walked in the door and then immediately heading to bed. And when he was home, Mike spent more and more of his time in the garage, supposedly working on his Chevy. But even Lucinda couldn't deny that his drinking was way out of hand.

Lucinda loved Mike as if he were her own son, and she hated seeing him waste his life this way. He was never loud or abusive, but neither was he truly present with his boys any more. He brought home most of his paycheck, he met all their material needs, he made it to all the important functions, but he wasn't really there for them on a day-to-day basis. David tried to fill in the gap for Jack, helping him with his homework, tossing the football, and offering guidance. But they all missed Mike. Increasingly, it seemed the boys had lost both parents, Lucinda thought sadly.

Jack's first altar boy practice was on a Tuesday. He and seven other sixth-grade boys marched over to the church after school let out, eager, excited and a little apprehensive. Serving as an altar boy was a high calling, Mrs. Gardner had told the class at the beginning of the school year, a service which put the boys in close proximity with the body and blood of Christ. She encouraged them to conduct themselves in a manner worthy of this honor, both while on duty and in their everyday lives.

For Jack, that really wasn't a stretch. He wasn't interested in raiding his dad's beer supply, like some of the boys did. Mike had given him a taste of the stuff a few times, and frankly, he'd rather have a grape soda. Beer tasted like crap. (And that's about as far as Jack went with cussing.) One time he had shoplifted a Hershey's bar at Roland's Market, and he'd felt like such a jerk that he swore he'd never do it again. He left a dime on the counter the next time he was there to make up for it. And he wasn't into looking at the girlie magazines. His buddy Brian Ludgate had shown him the centerfold from his brother's Playboy, and while Miss August was probably the prettiest girl he'd ever seen, looking at her that way made him feel funny, uncomfortable, excited but also ashamed. He was sure his grandmother would take one look at his face and know what he'd done, and more than anything, Jack hated to disappoint his grandmother.

He'd listened to the stories about his mother that Lucinda told —Dad didn't talk about her much, but Jack could see from the look on his father's face how he had felt about her—but Lucinda was the only mother that Jack had ever known. He called her "Grandma," like David did, but to Jack, Lucinda was mother. More than getting into trouble, what kept Jack from misbehaving was that he hated seeing Lucinda's face fall when he did act up. It felt like a knife to the heart.

Besides that, he just really wasn't drawn to all that junk. Jack probably wouldn't admit it to his friends, but he liked being a good kid. He liked helping other people, he liked knowing everybody could count on him to get a job done right, and he even liked going to church well enough—it made him feel light inside, warm and happy. Who knows, he might even end up going into the priesthood like his brother David was planning to do.

But for now, Jack was determined to do a good job serving as an altar boy at St. Maria Goretti's.

Father Delanoit met the eight boys at the door. His was an imposing figure, as he stood over six feet tall and had the build of an ex-football player, which he was; he'd started on his high school team thirty-odd years ago. Father Delanoit had brown hair, just graying around the temples, and piercing green eyes, which he fixed on his young charges, scrutinizing them. They felt as if they were up for inspection and not likely to pass.

"Good afternoon, boys," he said in his rich baritone voice.

"Good afternoon, Father Delanoit," the boys said in unison.

"Follow me," he said, turning and walking to the front of the sanctuary. He indicated that they should sit in the front pew, which they did after genuflecting to the Blessed Sacrament, a practice instilled in them since they were able to balance themselves on one knee. Jack sat in the middle of the group, right in front of Father Delanoit.

"Boys, what you are going to be doing as altar boys is both an honor and a duty," Father Delanoit said. "It is an honor, of course, to be in such close proximity to the body and blood of our Lord, and to be in service to His Church. It is also a duty, and an important one, because your role is crucial to the priest's ability to do what he is called to do. Some of you may find that you also have a calling. But regardless of that, you will always remember the years that you served as an altar boy as a pivotal part of your faith. At the end of the pew are instruction booklets. Pass them down," he said to Rob Myers, who was sitting at the end, "and turn to the first page."

"Each time, before you begin your duties, you must say this prayer, which is the same prayer the priest says when he puts on his alb, the garment he wears to say Mass," Father Delanoit instructed them. "Say it with me."

"Purify me, O Lord, and make me clean of heart," said the eight young boys and the priest, "That through Your graces I may serve at Your Altar with dignity and respect and that I may be worthy to receive Your Word at this liturgy, witness Your changing of our gifts of bread and wine into Your precious Body and Blood, and through Your gift, posses eternal joy."

"Very good," Father Delanoit said. "Now, we'll go over a few rules for proper decorum when serving a Mass, and then I will show you where to find the supplies you will need."

"First, remember always to bow to the altar as a sign of reverence and honor, and genuflect as a sign of adoration when you enter and leave the sanctuary and when you cross in front of the Tabernacle," he said. "Next, fold your hands in the appropriate position when walking or standing, unless you are holding something. The appropriate position is palms together, chest high, the right thumb crossed over the left," Father Delanoit said, demonstrating the proper form as he spoke. "Go ahead and do that, now, boys."

The eight boys brought their hands to their chests and folded them according to Father's instructions.

"Tuck your elbows in against your sides, more," he said. "That looks much better. Also, when you hand the elements of communion to the priest, give him a slight bow, for a bow is a sign of respect, and the priest is always to be shown respect. The reason for that, boys, is the priest is Christ's representative on Earth. When you show respect to a priest, you are actually showing respect to God," Father Delanoit said. Fixing his steely gaze upon them, he added, "And if you disrespect a priest, you are then showing disrespect to God Himself."

Father Delanoit paused a moment, allowing that to soak in, then said, "Follow me, boys, and I will show you where to find your supplies for Mass."

The boys followed him onto the altar, where the priest pointed out the ciboria, which were bowls for holding leftover communion wafers, the communion cups, the cruet of water, and the bowl and towel for washing hands. Then he led them back behind the altar to the sacristy, where the robes, or albs, were stored. Finally, they went back to sit down in the sanctuary.

"For practice, I'm going to divide you into two groups. The first group will meet on Tuesdays right after school, and the second group will meet on Thursdays, starting this week." Pointing to the boys sitting on his right, he said, "You four boys will start practice on Thursday, and the rest of you, next Tuesday." Jack was in the Thursday group. "You are dismissed."

Each boy carefully genuflected and made the sign of the cross, then walked quietly out of the church. Once released, their pent-up energy emerged and they ran en masse down the hill and around the corner to the end of the block. There they split up and headed towards their own neighborhoods. Jack and his friend Wayne Dutcher walked together, past the old but stately homes close to St. Maria's, and the simpler houses in their own neighborhood. They reached Wayne's house first, and Jack walked the rest of the way alone, mulling Father Delanoit's instructions over in his mind. Hopefully, he would get it right on Thursday. Father Delanoit didn't seem like somebody you'd want to have mad at you.

When the boys went to the church for practice on Thursday, Father Delanoit had them go directly to the sacristy, the small room behind the altar where the priest and his assistants prepared for Mass. He told them to put on their albs: the long white linen robes signified purity and self-denial. He also told them to recite the same prayer they had said on Tuesday—Father gave them each a palm-sized prayer card with the words printed on it and a picture of a dove descending to a man in a white robe.

Jack, who was of average height and weight for a boy his age, had no trouble finding a good fit. But Wayne, who at 5' 10" towered over all the other boys, had a bit of a problem. The longest of the white linen garments came to his mid-calf.

"We'll have Mrs. McGrevey lengthen this one," Father Delanoit said. Mrs. McGrevey was the housekeeper at the rectory. "Here, then, boys, tie the knot of the cincture on your right side," he said, demonstrating on Jack how to tie the cincture around the waist.

Father Delanoit led the boys back into the church, once again showing them the supplies for communion. He told them the proper procedure for lighting the candles and called on Wayne to demonstrate. He told them what would be expected of them during the different parts of the Mass, and how they should conduct themselves when waiting to perform their next duty. Then he led them through a trial run. Jack had communion duties: he had to get the paten, a round gold dish with a handle, and stand next to Father Delanoit and hold the paten under Father's hands, ready to catch any hosts that should fall.

"That's good for today, boys. I'll expect to see you all back again next Thursday," Father said. "You can put your albs away and go home."

"Thank you, Father," the boys said, bowing slightly before

heading to the back sacristy to change.

They quietly hung up their albs and prepared to leave.

"Go ahead and go out the side door, boys. We've got a few people who like to come to church about this time every day to pray, and I don't want you to disturb them," Father Delanoit said. He pointed toward a door that led down a hall and outside, opening into a courtyard between the church and the rectory.

The four boys left the church and walked home, Jack and Wayne went in one direction and the other two boys headed the opposite way.

That evening as Mrs. McGrevey served Father Delanoit and Father Schmidt, their supper of veal cutlets cordon bleu and rice with lettuce salad, Father Delanoit asked her what she could tell him about young Jack O'Donnell and his family.

"His mother died when he was just a baby, poor lad, and his grandmother's raised him ever since," she said in her Irish brogue.

"What about his father?" Father Delanoit asked.

"Well, Mike O'Donnell is a good, hard worker," Mrs. McGrevey said.

"But?"

"He's a bit of a drinker, Mike is," she said. It never took much coaxing to get Mrs. McGrevey to talk. "Ever since his wife died and left him with the two boys, he's not been the same. He goes to work every day, and Rose Castani said he brings Lucinda—that's the grandmother raisin' the boys—most of his paycheck, but he's got the one failing." Her own husband Patrick, God rest his soul, had been "a bit of a drinker" himself, until he drove his car off the road by Lake Camellia after his last fishing trip, so she hated to condemn the poor man.

"Two boys, you say? Is David his brother, then?" Father Schmidt asked.

"Yes, he is, and a better young man you'll not find," Mrs. McGrevey stated.

"I've got him in class this semester. He is a good kid," Father

Schmidt said. Father Schmidt, or Schmitty as his friends called him, taught at St. Anne's, the local Catholic high school. "He's actually considering a vocation. David was asking me some questions about the priesthood just the other day," he said, primarily addressing Father Delanoit.

"Oh, is he? We can always use somebody of that caliber," Father Delanoit replied. Schmitty recounted part of the conversation he'd had with David, and Father Delanoit nodded at all the right times, but he was actually still thinking about poor Jack O'Donnell. The boy was almost an orphan, it seemed.

Chapter Three

The phone rang at the O'Donnells' early Monday afternoon, just as Lucinda was coming in from the backyard, carrying the sheets she'd hung on the clothesline first thing that morning. She enjoyed the fresh smell of linen dried in the sun, and she knew she wouldn't have that luxury for much longer, since fall would soon give way to winter. Lucinda set the sheets on the counter and answered the phone.

"Mrs. Walters?" the caller asked.

"Yes," Lucinda said.

"This is Mrs. McGrevey from St. Maria Goretti Church. I'm calling to see if it would be convenient for you if Father Delanoit stops over next Thursday after Jack and the boys are done with altar boy practice."

"Of course, Father Delanoit can come over—he's welcome any time," Lucinda said. "But is there a problem with Jack?" Knowing her grandson as she did, the idea seemed quite implausible, but she was surprised that Father would be planning a visit for no discernable reason. He was a very busy man, Father Delanoit.

"No, he didn't say anything about a problem with your boy," Mrs. McGrevey assured her. "Sometimes he just likes to get to know the boys and their families, and he wanted me to arrange for a visit. If Thursday's not convenient…"

"No, no, Thursday's fine," Lucinda said, quickly calculating how much scrubbing she'd need to do to get the house up to her exacting standards for company, a priest even, by then. "We'd be honored if Father could join us for supper that evening," she added.

"Well, thank you, Mrs. Walters. I'll check with the father and call you back tomorrow morning," Mrs. McGrevey said. "Good-bye."

"Good-bye," Lucinda replied. She picked up the sheets and pondered what to fix for Thursday's supper as she remade all the beds.

When the family gathered around the table for supper that night, she told them about the plans for Thursday evening. Fortunately, Mike hadn't stopped at Dooley's, so he was there to hear about Father Delanoit's upcoming visit. Lucinda made a mental note to remind him again on Thursday morning, so hopefully he'd make it home on time and in decent shape.

"Father Delanoit is coming here for supper?" Jack said, somewhat incredulous. The priest's commanding presence made it seem that he didn't have the same need for regular sustenance as mere mortals do.

"Yes. Mrs. McGrevey said he likes to get to know the boys and their families, which I thought was nice," Lucinda said.

"That's right. Jack is going to be an altar boy now, too, isn't he," Mike said.

"Yes, Dad! I had two practices already," Jack said, a hint of exasperation in his voice. Lucinda shook her head ever so slightly, a reminder to be patient with his father.

"Of course you did. That's right, I knew that, my boy," Mike said. "Seems just yesterday that David was an altar boy. I don't remember the father coming for supper back then, did he, Lucinda?"

"No, he didn't. I do remember he stopped at Castani's a few

times, though, to see Alan. How is Alan doing, David, do you hear?"

"He signed up for the Army, last I heard," David said.

"Hmm," said Mike, still pondering Father Delanoit's visit. "Wonder why we rate this time." The idea of having a priest for a guest was less than pleasing, especially a cold fish like Delanoit. Something about that man always set Mike's teeth on edge. But he'd try to get along with him, knowing how important it was to Lucinda and maybe to Jack as well.

By mid-afternoon on Thursday, Lucinda had the entire house polished, scrubbed and practically glowing. Not that she ever let it get really dirty, but today she'd gone above and beyond her normal cleaning routine in her quest to make the simple little house look as appealing as possible. And it did. From the green and gold afghan she had crocheted and draped over the comfortable brown easy chair, to the shining milk-white dishes displayed in the plain wooden cabinet, to the carefully framed family photographs hanging on the wall, Lucinda had succeeded in making the house a haven for her daughter's family. She felt quite honored that Father Delanoit wanted to come into their home.

Next, she turned her attention to preparing the meal. Lucinda had bought a nice cut of beef, which she coated with flour and browned in shortening, then added tomato juice, beef bouillon, Worcestershire sauce and mushrooms. She brought the meat mixture to a simmer and let it cook while she tore iceberg lettuce and sliced carrots and onions for the salad. Then she added sour cream and wine to the meat and mixed it, and prepared some noodles. Finally, she took some rolls from the freezer and got them ready to heat.

With supper almost ready, Lucinda set the table and tidied up the already neat house. She gave her home an appraising glance, satisfying herself that everything was in order.

"Hi, Grandma. Do I smell beef stroganoff?" David asked as he walked in the door and threw his coat over a chair.

"Yes, you do smell beef stroganoff, and would you kindly hang that coat up, young man? I have been cleaning all afternoon, and we are having Father Delanoit over for supper," Lucinda said.

"Yes, ma'am," David said, bowing a penitent's bow, but with a twinkle in his eye. "I thought it looked awfully… sparkly around here. Not that it doesn't always, anyway. Of course. So when is everybody supposed to be here so we can eat?"

Just then, Mike walked in, his eyes slightly bloodshot but his gait fairly steady, and right behind him walked Jack, leading Father Delanoit.

"Father Delanoit gave me a ride in his Riviera," Jack said breathlessly. His nervousness over having the priest visiting his home was forgotten in his excitement about riding in the new Buick Riviera.

"You drive a Riviera, Father? You'll have to show me all the extras on that baby," Mike said, genuinely interested.

"I'd be glad to," Father Delanoit said. "My, it does smell good in here."

"Well, thank you, Father," Lucinda replied. "Everything is ready, so shall we gather around the table, now? Jack, would you take Father's coat for him?" As they sat down at the table, Lucinda asked, "Father, would you say the blessing for us?"

"Of course," he replied. "Bless us, oh Lord, and these thy gifts which we are about to receive through Christ our Lord, Amen."

"Thank you, Father," Lucinda said. She then passed him the beef stroganoff; he served himself a portion and passed it to Jack, who was seated at his left.

"You have a lovely home," Father Delanoit said. "Have you lived here a long time?"

"Eighteen years," Mike said. "My wife Rita and I moved here when we found out she was expecting David." He paused, and then added, "She died not long after Jack was born, and Lucinda, Rita's mother, moved in to help me with the boys."

There was a brief but awkward silence, which Father Delanoit broke.

"You're certainly doing a good job with them. Jack listens to directions very well at altar boy practice," he said, smiling briefly at the boy, "and I hear from Father Schmidt at the high school that David is considering a vocation. Is that correct, David?"

"I am thinking about it, Father," David said. "It's a big decision."

"That it is," the priest agreed.

"So, Father Delanoit, tell me, where did you serve before you came to Hook's Point?" Lucinda asked.

"After I got out of seminary, I worked at St. Mary's Parish in Chicago for several years. I was transferred to Christ the King in Atlanta, then later to the Holy Family Church in Peoria until I came here to serve at St. Maria Goretti's. That was almost ten years ago," he replied. "Mrs. Walters, this beef stroganoff is excellent."

"Why, thank you, Father. Jack, pass Father some more stroganoff, dear," Lucinda said.

"Thank you, Jack," Father Delanoit said, and served himself a second helping.

By the end of the priest's visit with the O'Donnells, he had learned a number of things which would prove useful. Mike O'Donnell had the ruddy complexion of a regular drinker, which indicated that the information Mrs. McGrevey had given him was not just idle gossip. (The woman was insipid and stupid, but she did generally know what was going on in the parish.) O'Donnell had, at best, a tenuous grasp on what was going on in his household. He provided for his sons, but beyond that, Mike O'Donnell probably had little influence in their lives. The man's status in the community was such that, if O'Donnell were ever to make any complaints, he would not garner much attention from anyone of influence.

Lucinda was clearly the hub of the family. She seemed to be a strong woman and could possibly be problematic, but Father Delanoit didn't think so. Lucinda was much sharper than Rose Castani, but she had the same blind faith in the Church that her neighbor did. People like her could be counted on to ignore any evidence that might test their loyalty. David, too, could be a problem. His affection for his little brother was genuine. But David was a senior in high school, and in addition to taking a full load of classes, he worked twenty hours every week at the grocery store. He would really be too busy to notice if there were some subtle changes in his little brother Jack.

Father Delanoit thanked Lucinda for the lovely meal, again complimented the O'Donnells on their comfortable home, and went home satisfied. His time had been well spent. Everything was in order. He looked forward to the next time he would see Jack, but waiting didn't bother him. It was an essential part of his plan, and Father Delanoit was an extremely patient man.

Next Thursday Jack, Wayne and the other boys hustled over to the church after school. They were becoming comfortable with the routine, though there was still an awful lot to remember.

"Do you light the candles on the right of the altar, starting from the left, or on the left of the altar, starting from the right?" Wayne asked Jack as they vested in their albs.

"You light the ones on the right first," Jack said. "Then you bow in front of the altar and light the candles on the left."

"Was it weird, having Father Delanoit eat supper at your house?" Wayne said.

"Not really," Jack shrugged. "It was okay, I guess."

"My father said the reason he went to your house is to check up on you. To make sure you were all right," one of the other boys said in a nasty, singsong voice. "Because your old man's a drunk," he added with an ugly smirk.

Jack's cheeks burned with shame. It wasn't the first time he'd heard the taunt, but for some reason, this time the anger erupted, burning hot like molten lava.

"Liar!" Jack shrieked, landing a punch on the other boy's face. He responded with a left jab, and at that moment, Father Delanoit walked in the room.

"Boys!" the priest thundered. Both combatants immediately dropped their fists and stared in horror at the priest as they realized they were fighting in the sacristy, an unthinkable sin up until just a few moments ago. "Just what in the devil is going on here?"

"He punched me first, Father," said Ronny, the boy who had taunted Jack, managing to look about as innocent as possible under the circumstances.

When Father Delanoit fixed his glare on Jack, the boy burst into tears, completely undone by the public shaming and his own behavior.

"Jack, follow me," he said in an ominous tone, as he walked down the corridor. Looking over his shoulder, he said to Ronny, "I'll be back to talk to you. Don't think you're off the hook."

Jack followed Father Delanoit down the hall and out the door. He was frightened, of course—what did they do to you for fighting in church? Send you to reform school? But he was also relieved to get away from the other boys. He hadn't cried in front of the other kids since second grade, when he fell off the jungle gym and broke his arm. He hated to think how they were going to razz him.

Why had he blown up like that? Jack wasn't stupid. When his dad didn't get home until after eleven o'clock at night and then could barely make his way upstairs to bed, Jack knew what was going on. A lot of times when Mike was working on his car in the garage and Jack went out to talk to him, he smelled whiskey on his breath and saw that his father's eyes were glazed over, so Jack just made an excuse and went back to whatever he'd been doing, because he knew his dad had been drinking and wouldn't really hear what Jack had to say, anyway.

Grandma never talked about it, and Jack hated to make her upset, so he didn't ask a lot of questions, but David had told him their dad had started drinking more after their mother died. That always made Jack feel a little queasy if he thought about it; after all, his mom was carrying him when she found out she had cancer, and then she died when he was a baby, so in a little corner of his mind, Jack wondered if it was his fault that his mother had died so young. Which would make it his fault that his dad drank too much.

David, seeing the worried look in his brother's eyes once when they were talking about their parents, reassured Jack that their mother's illness had nothing to do with Jack. It was just God's will. (Why God would take a mother away from her family, Jack didn't know. David said it was a mystery.) And David said that Dad drank too much because he missed their mom. At that point in the conversation, David sighed and looked down, so Jack knew he missed their mom, too, and he quit pestering him with questions.

Jack loved his dad in spite of his drinking problem, and it made him sore to hear anybody say anything bad about him. So, while he really hoped he wouldn't get sent to reform school or anything, Jack was a little glad that he'd socked the other kid. He'd had it coming.

"He had it coming, didn't he, son?" Father Delanoit said. Jack almost jumped out of his skin. Did Father read his mind, like the gypsy woman who charged a quarter to read your palm at the carnival? "I heard what he said, Jack. About your father."

Jack gulped. Shame battled with relief as he looked at Father Delanoit's face, which for once showed a softening. His eyes were warm and kind as he said, "Jack, while I don't condone hitting someone in church, this is one case where I think a physical response was warranted. I know you care a great deal about your father, in spite of his—problem, don't you, son?" Father Delanoit said, putting an arm around Jack's shoulders and gently squeezing the tight muscles there.

"Yes, Father. I…I am sorry, though, Father. I never meant to hit a guy in church," Jack said, tears welling up again in response to Father Delanoit's unexpected kindness.

"I know you didn't, son," Father said, continuing to rub Jack's shoulders as he spoke. "You've been doing a good job. I know your grandmother is extremely proud of you. And your father, too," he hastily added. "So I think the best thing to do for us is to keep this our little secret. You won't do anything like this again, will you, Jack? No more fighting in the sacristy?" he said, almost smiling as he spoke, like they were sharing a joke, but Jack didn't really see how it was funny. He was awful glad that Father wasn't going to call his grandma, though.

"No, I sure won't, Father. Thank you for not telling my folks," he said. Jack couldn't believe how lucky he was.

"And now, Jack, you can head home. I'm going to have a talk with Ronny, and I don't think he'll be bothering you any more," he said kindly. "I want you to come to the church tomorrow after school, and you can make up the practice then."

"Okay, Father Delanoit. I'll be here tomorrow," Jack said. As he headed for home, Jack's heart was light. Father Delanoit was a lot nicer than he had thought. He may seem strict and all, but he was really an okay guy.

On Friday, Jack walked over to the church after school let out at three-thirty. He'd told his grandma that he had an extra practice, which technically was sort of true and sort of not, since he didn't practice yesterday, but at least it wasn't an out-and-out lie. Lying to his grandmother made him feel like a real jerk. He'd only done it a few times, usually to avoid getting into trouble, and he hated it. Jack didn't think this would count as a lie, anyway.

Jack would have been nervous, working alone with Father Delanoit, but Father had been so nice to him yesterday, so he felt comfortable. He walked back to the sacristy to vest in his alb, and was surprised to find Father Delanoit waiting for him. Usually he met up with the boys in the sanctuary.

"Hello, Jack," Father Delanoit said. "How are you doing today?"

"Fine, Father. Thanks again for giving me another chance, Father Delanoit," Jack said. He took the alb he usually wore from the hanger, put it on, and then took the cincture and began to tie it around his waist. Father Delanoit stepped behind him and tied the cincture, reminding him to make sure it went on the right side. Which Jack always did, anyway, but he knew that Father Delanoit liked things to be just so, like his grandma did with things around the house.

Father Delanoit led Jack through his practice, which went really fast, because nobody else was there and Jack pretty much knew what he was supposed to do. He knew how to light the candles and carry the offering, when to genuflect and when to bow, when to stand and when to sit. So after about fifteen or twenty minutes, Father said that was it, he'd done a good job and he could quit for the day.

"Jack, I'd like you to come over to the rectory," Father Delanoit said then. "I'll wait for you there."

Jack went back to the sacristy to hang up his alb and cincture, then walked down the hall and out the door and headed to the rectory. He wondered if Father had something he wanted Jack to take to his grandmother, or maybe wanted him to run an errand. But, when he reached the rectory, Jack discovered that wasn't what Father Delanoit wanted at all.

Chapter Four

Jack walked home from the rectory in a daze. What had happened—what Father Delanoit did to him and made him do—was so totally outside of his experience that Jack never knew such things even existed. He felt like he was floating outside his body, and he didn't ever want to get back inside it. Father Delanoit had told him that he was special, that he was lucky to be chosen, and that it was to be their secret.

Like he wanted anybody to know. In a rush, his mouth filled with vomit, and Jack found himself puking his guts out, right there on the street. He began to shake, and more than anything he just wanted to wake up and find out this was all some weird, horrible dream. He took a deep breath and began running toward his house. When he got home, Jack opened the door, hung up his coat and began walking upstairs to his room.

"Hey, Jack, where are you going so fast?" Grandma Lucinda appeared in the doorway between dining room and the living room, wearing her beige apron with the rooster print, her hands white with flour. "How was practice?"

How could she simultaneously be the one person Jack most wanted to see in the world and also the very last? He longed to rush into her arms, yet he felt so repulsive that he just wanted to disappear. He could not look his grandma in the eyes.

"Okay, Grandma. But…I don't feel very good. I'm gonna go lie down," Jack said.

He looked pale and weak. Lucinda walked towards him to see if his forehead was hot.

"I'm okay," Jack said, his voice rising. "I just need to lie down, okay?" Then he bolted up the stairs and into his room, slamming the door.

Lucinda stood in the middle of the living room, feeling somewhat taken aback. It was so unlike the boy to speak sharply. She walked toward the staircase, then hesitated. Perhaps he just needed some time to himself. He was approaching those teen-age years, and even a good-tempered boy like Jack would experience some ups and downs as he went through all the changes that adolescence would bring. Lucinda decided the best thing to do was to leave Jack alone.

Jack lay down on his bed and stared at the ceiling. That out-of-body feeling was wearing off, unfortunately. Right now, he would rather be anywhere in the world but inside his body. He still could feel where Father Delanoit had touched him, and it made him gag. He ran to the bathroom and vomited again, then sunk to the floor, resting his face on the cool slate gray linoleum. He was still lying there, hands holding on to his stomach, when his grandma knocked on the bathroom door.

"Jack, did I hear you throwing up?" she asked.

"Yeah," he replied weakly.

"Did you feel sick at school today?" Lucinda asked.

"Yeah," he lied. The first of many lies he would need to tell, he sensed. Jack sighed deeply and pushed himself up and leaned over the toilet again as bile filled his throat.

"I'm sorry, kiddo. There must be a flu bug going around," Lucinda said, the concern evident in her voice.

"Must be."

"Well, honey, I'll leave you alone unless there's something I can do for you."

"No, thanks, Grandma."

Lucinda walked into Jack's room and straightened out his bed for him, then went downstairs to check on supper for the rest of the family and to see if they had any Seven-up for Jack.

He stood up and looked in the mirror. Jack was surprised to see that he looked exactly the same as he had that morning, because he felt like an entirely different person. But, other than looking a little pale, he looked just like he always did: short brown hair just starting to get little shaggy, dark blue eyes, a slight gap between his front teeth. Jack rinsed his mouth out with water, then brushed his teeth for a long time. He filled the bathtub with steaming hot water, as hot as he could stand, hobbled weakly to his room and got his blue striped pajamas, and then went back into the bathroom, stripped and got into the tub. The hot water stung and soothed at the same time.

Jack could not get his mind around what Father Delanoit had done. He couldn't even have imagined such a thing. Father Delanoit said it was all right because he was God's representative, Christ on Earth, but that Jack shouldn't tell anybody because they wouldn't understand.

Jack didn't understand.

Then Father Delanoit said he especially shouldn't tell his grandma or his father. After all, Father Delanoit had kept it quiet about Jack's fighting with the other altar boy in church. It would be a shame to have to report that to the authorities, because they would have no choice but to send Jack to reform school. But he needn't worry—that could be their little secret, Father said. He knew that Jack hadn't meant to lose control that way.

Jack couldn't stand to think about it for another minute. He grabbed the bar of Ivory and scrubbed himself all over, then got out of the tub, drained the water, and dried himself off. He put on his pajamas and then wiped out the tub. Grandma hated a dirty bathtub. Jack threw his clothes in the hamper and went to his room, pulled back the covers and crawled into bed.

"Jack, I brought you some Seven-up. Maybe a little later you can have some soup if that stays down," Lucinda said.

"Thanks, Grandma. I just want to go to sleep now," Jack said.

Lucinda put her hand on his forehead, which felt warm, but that was not surprising after a hot bath. He shrugged off her hand, turning his face to the wall. Lucinda pulled the curtains and closed the door, then went downstairs. She and David ate their supper alone—it was Friday night and Mike was down at the bar. Later in the evening, Lucinda checked on Jack and found him sleeping. He'd thrown off his blankets, though, and a cool October breeze was blowing through the open window, so she covered him up, gently tucking him in like when he was a little guy.

Immediately Jack shot up, his hands flailing wildly.

"Don't!" he cried in a strangled voice.

"Jack! You're having a bad dream, honey. It's me, Grandma. I was just covering you up," Lucinda said. She wondered if perhaps Jack was running a fever. "I'm going to take your temperature. I'll be right back with the thermometer."

She went to the medicine cabinet and found the thermometer and returned to Jack's room.

"Under your tongue, lips tight," she instructed.

"No! No!" he said. "I mean... I'm okay. I don't have a fever, Grandma. I... I just had a bad dream. Would you stay with me a little while, please?" he said, sounding on the verge of tears.

"Of course I will, honey. Move over a little bit," Lucinda said, sitting on the edge of his bed. Her heart filled with sympathy for her youngest grandson. Puberty was tough, and she had a feeling that was more responsible for Jack's mood than this bout with the flu. He'd make it through just fine, she knew. He was a good, strong boy, and she often liked to think about what he and David would do when they were grown. Something good, no doubt.

But now, Lucinda tried distracting him from his discomfort with a story of her parents, how they had planned and saved to come to America from Italy, leaving behind the village and family they'd loved for a chance to build a more prosperous life here. She told him how Pappa would take time out of his busy day to make special outfits for her doll, and how he would dance with her mother in the kitchen. As she spoke, Jack rolled over onto his stomach and gradually his breathing became more peaceful. She put a gentle hand on his back for a moment, and if she heard him softly crying, she didn't say a word.

The next morning Jack stayed in bed until mid-morning, when Lucinda heard him running water for another bath. Eventually he came downstairs, looking a little pale but much better than the day before.

"Want me to make you some breakfast, Jack?" Lucinda asked.

"No, thanks, Grandma. I'll just make a couple of pieces of toast," he said.

"Wayne Dutcher stopped over to see if you wanted to play football over at the schoolyard. I told him you weren't feeling too great, but he could check back later," Lucinda said.

"Hmm," Jack said as he rummaged through the cupboards, getting out the bread and butter and cinnamon sugar. He prepared his food and sat down at the table, where David was finishing a bowl of cereal and reading the sports page.

"You feelin' better today?" David asked, his eyes still on the newspaper.

"Yeah," Jack answered, grabbing the comics and beginning to eat. "Where's Dad?"

"He ran to the store. Said he'd be back in an hour," David said. "You need something?"

"No, I was just wondering." Jack had determined that the best thing to do was to try to put this whole thing behind him. That, and try to stay away from Father Delanoit as much as possible. Eventually, maybe this would all seem like a bad dream. Every time he thought about it, he felt sick, so he resolved to push it out of his mind. Maybe he'd see if he could find Wayne, throw the football around for a while. Anything to get his mind off Father Delanoit.

"When do you serve your first Mass, Jacko?" David asked, using the nickname he'd given his brother.

"Who cares!" Jack yelled, shoving his plate of toast towards David. "And don't call me that stupid baby name anymore!" he added, glaring at his brother.

"Jack! You don't need to use that tone, young man," Lucinda reprimanded him. "Your brother just asked you a simple question, and the least you can do is give him a civilized answer." Lucinda knew that Jack didn't feel well, but she also knew that coddling bad behavior only brought out more of the same.

Jack felt ashamed. He hated making his grandma mad. And, he actually had always liked when David called him "Jacko." He could see that trying to put this stupid thing out of his mind was going to be harder than he'd thought. He resolved to try harder.

"I'm sorry, Grandma," he said. "You, too, David. I... I still feel a little bit sick, I guess," he said.

"No big deal," David said. He remembered what going-on-thirteen felt like. He grabbed his cereal spoon, balanced it on the end of his nose, and crossed his eyes. "No problem, Jacko," he squeaked in a falsetto. "No problem." Jack grinned weakly, and then finally broke into a spasm of giggles as David went through his repertoire of loony facial expressions. Lucinda's mind was eased as she watched the boys clowning around.

"Hey, you finally decided to get out of bed!" Mike said as he walked into the kitchen from the back door. "Are you feeling back to your normal ornery self, Jack?" he said, ruffling his youngest son's hair.

Jack, his spirits somewhat lifted, replied, "You bet I am." Although his "normal self" was not especially ornery, he always enjoyed his dad's spiel.

"What do you have up your sleeve today? Do you want to ride over to Hays to look at some cars, or are you hanging out with the boys?" Mike said to Jack, for David would be heading to work at noon.

"Sure, Dad, I'll come along," Jack said. He actually felt happy. Maybe things were going to go back to normal after all. Maybe everything was going to be all right.

Chapter Five

By the time Jack went back to school on Monday morning, he felt quite a bit better, although still numb. He had managed to put the creepy incident inside a box, put the box on a shelf in his mind, keep it in there and not look at it. He and his dad had a good day on Saturday, riding over to Hays, a larger city sixty miles south of Hook's Point. They sang "99 Bottles of Beer on the Wall," working their way down to 50 bottles before they both got sick of it and turned on the radio, listening and occasionally singing along with the top 40 hits, like "Sweet Caroline" and "A Boy Named Sue." His dad had a good singing voice and Jack hoped he might take after him with that. After they looked around at all the snazzy new cars on the lots—Mike's pipe dreams, he called them—they stopped at a restaurant and ate cheeseburgers. Jack only at about half his, but it was still fun to be with his dad.

That evening Grandma made her good homemade chicken noodle soup, with even the noodles homemade, and some of her honey wheat bread. David got off work in time for supper, and so they all ate together. It really felt good, almost normal. Jack did go to bed shortly after supper, telling his grandma that he still felt a little weak. That way he got to skip Mass in the morning. He didn't want to think about going back inside the church. So he put that thought in the box, too.

Sunday passed pleasantly, a lazy day of reading the newspaper and watching the football games on television. His dad took a few trips to the garage, but overall, he stayed pretty sober. Wayne stopped over to see if he wanted to ride bikes, but Jack told him he didn't feel too good. Wayne told Jack to pick him up tomorrow for school.

So on Monday morning Jack found himself sitting in his classroom, listening to Mrs. Gardner explain how they were going to start reading Mark Twain's classic, Huckleberry Finn. He loved to read, and he was eager to get going, not only because he wanted to read the story, but also because he found if he kept himself occupied, there were fewer intruding memories of what had happened at the rectory last Friday. Jack made it through the day all right, between reading about Huck's adventures and studying his new spelling words and struggling a little bit with math, his least favorite subject. At lunch, he ate with Wayne and Mark Richards, just like always. Mark entertained them with a story about how he and his friend from public school, Brett Davis, hopped a freight train on Saturday and rode from one side of town clear to the city limits on the other side of Hook's Point.

After school, the three boys tossed a football for a while. Wayne had wanted to play at the schoolyard, but Jack talked them into playing closer to home, telling them he wanted to check in with his grandma because she thought she might be coming down with the flu herself.

He was surprised how easy the lies came to him, now that he had started. Jack had always been an honest kid, but he was discovering he could lie just about as well as old Huck Finn. He did feel a little bad about it, but he didn't want to risk running into Father Delanoit, and if they stuck around the school, he might. Of course, he'd see him on Thursday at practice, but for right now, he was able to push that inevitability out of his mind. By Thursday, Jack would have a plan.

But Tuesday and Wednesday came and went, and by early Thursday morning Jack still didn't know what he was going to do. He thought about telling his grandma that he was sick again, but he knew that would only work for so long. He was scheduled to serve his first Mass the Sunday before Thanksgiving, and he didn't see how he could get out of going to practice. As much as he hated the thought of seeing Father Delanoit and remembering what he'd done, Jack figured he'd be okay today, with Wayne and the two other boys right there. He had to face the priest eventually, and today might as well be the day.

Jack was trembling on the inside when he and Wayne walked into the sacristy to vest. The other two boys were already there, and Jack had steeled himself in case there were any more nasty cracks, but today Ronny was quiet and subdued, making Jack wonder what Father Delanoit could have said to him. But he'd just have to keep wondering, because he wasn't about to ask.

They all went into the sanctuary, where Father Delanoit was waiting for them. He was sitting in the Celebrant's chair, his head bowed and lips moving slightly. Jack hurried in so he could stand as far away as possible from the priest. He felt nauseous, like he had on Friday, but he fought it off by concentrating on his duties. First, Father Delanoit again led them in a prayer: "Purify me, O Lord, and make me clean of heart," they chanted. *Will I ever feel clean again*, Jack wondered, his cheeks flaming as he remembered that awful day.

After they finished their practice, the four boys went back into the sacristy to change. Jack was dressed and out of there so fast that Wayne had to run to catch up with him.

"Where's the fire, man?" Wayne asked.

"Nowhere. But my grandma's making lasagna tonight and I want to get there before my brother and dad eat it all," Jack lied. Again. "What's the matter, can't keep up with me?" he taunted, grabbing Wayne's stocking cap and running down the street. Wayne took off after him and caught him at the end of the block.

"Turd breath!" Wayne said, grabbing Jack in a playful hold and wrestling the cap away from him.

Jack had to fight back a feeling of panic when Wayne touched him, but he remembered his resolve, to keep what had happened in that box in his mind, so he didn't let on what he was feeling. Instead, he punched Wayne in the arm, a little harder than he intended but still in the spirit of the game. He shoved the hat back on Wayne's head.

"You don't want your wittle eaws to get cold, Wayney," Jack mocked.

Wayne looked down at the ground, and then glanced quizzically at his friend. Wayne had a slight speech impediment, and while some of the kids teased him about it, Jack never did. That was a sore subject, like Mike's drinking was to Jack, and the boys were good enough friends that both understood those were not topics to kid each other about.

Jack immediately felt ashamed. Why did he say that? He felt about as bad as when he'd disappointed his grandma.

"Just kidding, buddy," he said. "I…I'm sorry."

"Forget it, man," Wayne said. They continued home, and tried to act as if nothing had happened. But they were both relieved when Wayne turned toward his house and they each went their own separate ways.

Jack felt doubly relieved that he had this first encounter with Father Delanoit behind him. Father Delanoit had hardly even looked at him. While Jack was glad, it was weird in a way. He almost wondered if the whole thing had been some horrible dream, but no, the memory was way too real. He had never even thought of such things. And he never wanted to think about it again. Maybe he wouldn't have to.

But on Friday after school, Jack's heart dropped when he approached his house and saw Father Delanoit's Riviera parked on the street in front of his house. His hand trembling, Jack opened the front door and found Father Delanoit sitting on the couch in his living room, drinking a cup of coffee with his grandma, who was sitting in her rocking chair and looking like she was entertaining the president or something, she was so proud.

"Jack, look who stopped over to see us," Lucinda said, beaming.

"Hello, Jack," Father Delanoit said.

"Hi," Jack managed to squeak. His heart was in his mouth and he could barely breathe.

"Jack, Father Delanoit said that you've been so helpful at church, doing extra work and being such a good example for the other boys that he wants to take you out to Tony's for pizza," Lucinda said. "Isn't that nice of him?"

Jack felt like he was melting. This couldn't be real. He blinked, and there sat his grandma and Father Delanoit, smiling and waiting expectantly. Some sort of reply seemed to be expected.

"Oh. That's… real nice, Father Delanoit," he said, feeling like he was speaking from under water. "But I… I don't feel too good."

"Oh, go on, Jack," his grandma urged. Father Delanoit rose as if to leave. "You'll have a good time. It's really quite an honor, you know," she said with a hint of exasperation in her voice.

Jack looked at her, pleading silently that she would somehow understand. Father Delanoit put his hand (oh god his hand!) on Jack's shoulder and gently ushered him to the door.

"I'll have him back by eight o'clock, Mrs. Walters," Father said as he ushered Jack out the door. "Thank you for the coffee."

"Of course, Father. No big rush, now. You two have fun," Lucinda said. She watched from the doorway as they got into the Riviera and drove off, her feelings a mixture of gratitude and shame.

What she had told Jack had been only half the truth. Father Delanoit had said that Jack was doing a very good job and that he was an exemplary altar boy. But he'd also told her there had been an incident with one of the other boys, who had teased Jack about Mike's drinking problem. Father Delanoit wasn't angry with Jack, he assured her. But he was concerned about the effect Mike's drinking was having on the boy. He'd made her an offer. An incredibly generous offer.

Father Delanoit wanted to spend extra time with Jack, outside of altar boy practice. Just some one-on-one time, where he could help fill in the gaps left by Mike's negligence. Lucinda had winced to hear him say that, and Father Delanoit was quick to add that he knew Mike was a good provider and that he did face many hardships, losing his wife at such a young age, but that didn't change the fact that Jack was missing out on much of the guidance that a father should give to a son. Why, he knew that Mrs. Walters didn't want to risk seeing Jack turn delinquent and getting into more serious trouble.

Lucinda, of course, did not want to see that happen. She sadly thought about Alan Castani and what a good little boy he had been. Father Delanoit had tried to intercede with him, but evidently, all his efforts were to no avail. But she knew it would be different with Jack. Jack was like a thirsty plant, eagerly soaking up the little bit of attention Mike did give him. If Father Delanoit was willing to take Jack under his wing, why, it could make a world of difference.

Lucinda took the coffee cups into the kitchen, then returned to the living room and stretched out on the couch, covering herself with the afghan. Mike never made it home for supper on Friday any more, David was working until ten at the grocery store, and since Jack was with Father Delanoit, she decided to take a little catnap, then make herself a simple supper. She felt a slight tug in her heart, as if she had misplaced something of value, but Lucinda pushed the feeling aside, resting assured that Jack was in good hands. She had enormous respect for the priests who served the people so faithfully, and Father Delanoit was known to be intelligent and very effective in the community, held in high esteem by Catholics and Protestants alike. She just felt very fortunate that he was taking a special interest in their family. It was normal that Jack might be a little nervous, but she was sure that would wear off quickly enough.

Jack scrunched as close to the door as he could, clutching the handle and trying not to panic. He felt like he was trapped in a nightmare and couldn't wake up. He tried to take a deep breath, but his throat felt like it was closing up, especially when it became obvious that Father Delanoit was driving towards the rectory, not the restaurant. When Father stopped the car, Jack briefly thought of making a break for it, jumping out of the car and just running, it wouldn't matter where, but then Father reached over and put a hand on his shoulder. Jack felt a sense of impending doom.

"Jack, I know the other day was… difficult for you," Father said, his voice soft and tender and much more frightening than if he were yelling at him. "Tonight will be different. You know what to expect, for one thing."

"I… I… I don't want to do that. I don't like it," Jack said, dangerously near tears, which he instinctively knew would not help his position any. Father Delanoit was like any other predator: any whiff of weakness simply made him more threatening.

"Come inside, Jack," Father said. The gentle tone was gone. "You know I've kept your little secret, fighting with Ronny in the sacristy. If I told your grandmother about that, you would be in an awful lot of trouble."

Jack knew that was true, but getting in trouble with his grandmother or even with the cops couldn't be any worse than what Father Delanoit had done to him last Friday. It couldn't.

Emboldened, he spoke up. "I don't care. I'm not going in there!" Jack said, with all the dignity a twelve-year-old boy could muster. He looked Father Delanoit right in the eye.

Father's face darkened with anger and Jack couldn't help pulling back. He wondered if Father was going to hit him, but instead he said, "Jack, if you think anybody is going to believe you if you try telling them about our little secret, you're wrong. Why, I'm one of the most respected men in the community, and you, well, Jack," his voice again softening, as if filled with sympathy over the boy's plight, "why, everyone knows you're having problems. Three boys saw you lose control in the sacristy. Not that anyone blames you for that. After all, everyone knows how difficult it is for you. Here, your mother got so sick when she was pregnant with you," he said, emphasizing the word you, "then died when you were a baby. And your father… well, everyone knows about your father, Jack." Father Delanoit sighed, as if deeply saddened by the situation.

"So people really wouldn't be surprised if you made up some wild stories. Though they would be angry, a boy from a family like yours, defaming a priest." Father Delanoit fell silent, letting his words soak in. He had hit pay dirt with his remarks about Rita, and Jack's head was reeling. Once again, he felt as if he were not in his body.

"You don't really want anyone to know about our little secret, anyway, do you?" said Father Delanoit, sounding incredulous. Jack's cheeks burned with shame at the thought of his father, or David, or God forbid, his grandma, finding out what the priest had done to him. Jack didn't even have the words to tell them what had happened if he'd wanted to.

"Come on inside, Jack," Father Delanoit said. "There's a good boy."

Jack felt like a robot, something from one of those space age movies that Wayne liked to watch, as he helplessly opened his door and followed Father Delanoit inside. He got through the next hour by pretending he was somewhere else. In another galaxy, far away.

Afterwards, Jack was amazed when Father Delanoit actually took him to Tony's Restaurant. He couldn't believe how the priest was acting like nothing had happened.

"I don't want to go in there," Jack said. He felt sure everyone would be able to see what they had done. He only wanted to crawl into a hole and pull the ground over himself.

"Oh, come on. Growing boys have to eat," Father Delanoit said. "Besides, so do I. Friday night is Mrs. McGrevey's night off and Father Schmidt's night to play cards with his sister, so I'm on my own. Come now, let's eat."

Jack followed him into the restaurant, a small corner pizza parlor that was always busy on the weekends. The lights seemed too bright, and Jack focused his eyes on the floor as the waitress led them to a booth. Sitting down, Father Delanoit indicated that Jack should sit opposite him, which he did, squeezing himself as far into the corner as he could. Father Delanoit ordered Jack a cola and a beer for himself and a pizza with the works. Jack couldn't stand the thought of food, but he was thirsty and he guzzled down his soda.

Somewhat revived, Jack glanced around the restaurant. Horrified, he saw his teacher Mrs. Gardner with her husband and their little girl walking in the door. Mrs. Gardner saw Jack and Father Delanoit and came over, a big smile on her face as she greeted them. Jack mumbled a small "hi."

"Well, hello, Mrs. Gardner," said Father Delanoit, all charm and geniality. "I heard that Tony's has the best pizza in town, so I thought I'd bring Mr. O'Donnell here with me to try it out."

"Sounds like fun, right, Jack?" she said, smiling. She couldn't help but notice how uncomfortable the boy looked, but her students often found it awkward, running into a teacher after hours. "Well, here comes your pizza—I'll see you later, Father Delanoit, Jack," the young teacher said. As she rejoined her family, she thought how admirable that the priest was willing to take boys like Jack under his wing.

The waitress put their pizza in the middle of the table and Father Delanoit served a piece to Jack and one to himself. "Will you get the young man another soda, miss," Father said. He was still nursing his first beer: no one could ever say that Father Delanoit was a drinking man. The occasional cocktail at a social gathering, a glass of wine or a beer with his meal, that was the most he ever imbibed. He liked to keep a clear head at all times.

"Eat up, Jack, my boy," Father Delanoit said cheerfully.

The thought of eating made him want to throw up, but to avoid an argument, Jack nibbled on his pizza. Anything to make this all pass by a little faster. When the waitress brought his soda, this time he sipped on it, and gradually his stomach felt a little better. He managed to have a bite of pizza in his mouth the next time somebody came up to greet Father Delanoit, so he didn't have to speak. The priest seemed to know half the people in town, Jack thought.

Finally, Father Delanoit was done eating, and, after he left a generous tip for their waitress and paid the bill, they left Tony's and headed toward Jack's house. The ride seemed endless, but eventually they reached his street. Jack was ready to jump out of the car the minute that Father pulled up to his house, but Father Delanoit put a restraining hand on his shoulder. Reluctantly the boy turned to face the man.

"We'll be getting together again soon, Jack," Father said in that hideously caressing voice. "But first, you'll get to serve your first Mass, this Sunday, I believe. That's quite a milestone. Why, I remember serving my first Mass as if it were yesterday." While Jack puzzled over this non sequitur, Louis Delanoit briefly remembered something else: Father Brockman, who had done exactly to him what he was now doing to Jack, when Louis was just eleven years old. But that memory made Father Delanoit feel small and vulnerable, two things he'd sworn long ago he would never allow himself to be, so he successfully squelched that memory before it barely reached his conscious mind.

"Good night, Jack," he said.

Jack wordlessly exited the vehicle and ran to his front door. He found his grandma sleeping on the couch, quietly snoring. He went upstairs and took a scorching-hot bath, put on his pajamas, then came back downstairs and curled up on the floor by Lucinda. Quiet shuddering cries racked his body, but he didn't make a sound.

Chapter Six

Lucinda watched proudly as Jack lit the altar candles one by one, starting at the right side, then moving to the left, carefully bowing as he passed the center. He looked so grown up in his alb, moving conscientiously from one task to the next. *Rita, baby, you gave the world a good, good boy*, she thought proudly. Mike sat on one side of Lucinda and David on the other. All three were more focused on Jack than on the Mass itself, but Lucinda was sure that God would understand just this once, at least that's what she asked the Blessed Virgin to intercede for on their behalf, as one mother to another.

Jack brought the wine and water to Father Delanoit. He brought the priest water, a basin and a towel for the symbolic washing of his fingers, an ancient sign of purification, then put them all away. Jack rang the bell during the prayers, and he also rang the bell three times as Father Delanoit elevated the communion host. Again, he rang the bell three times when Father elevated the wine. After Father Delanoit had given the people the Eucharist, Jack brought the water, basin and cloth, and poured water over Father Delanoit's fingers again. He executed all his duties perfectly, his solemnity a perfect disguise for the disgust he felt each time he had to approach the priest.

Lucinda, Mike and David waited for Jack in the back of the

church. When he met up with them, Mike put an arm around Jack's shoulders and pulled him close.

"You did a good job, Jack, my boy," he said. Rarely did Mike show affection now that the boys were getting older. Jack looked pleased, embarrassed and vaguely troubled all at the same time, Lucinda thought.

"You really did, honey," Lucinda said. "We're very proud of you." And David solemnly shook his hand, as if welcoming him into a brotherhood.

"Well, come on, people, let's go eat," Mike said. So they all got in to the car. Mike flicked on the radio, filling the airwaves with music from The Supremes. "So shall we have us a pizza at Tony's today, Jack? This is a cause for celebration, after all."

"No!" Jack yelled. "I mean… let's go to the House of Pancakes, like we did when David was an altar boy. Gotta keep the tradition going," he added sheepishly.

"You're the boss today," Lucinda said, and they drove to the House of Pancakes, where they spent an hour or longer, eating, laughing and talking. Jack felt almost good. They all watched the Minnesota Vikings whip the Chicago Bears on television that afternoon, then talked about their plans for Thanksgiving over supper. Mike's sister Sheila, her husband John and their twin girls Meghan and Peggy were coming to Hook's Point, and so was Pappa, so they would have a full house.

Thanksgiving came and went in a flurry of activity. Although Pappa was still in amazingly good health, he was starting to slow down. Lucinda brought it up to Mike that maybe Pappa should move in with them when David went away to college in the fall. Mike concurred. Either Pappa could bunk with Jack, or maybe they could remodel the space above the garage into an apartment for him.

Jack completed his practice and was now a full-fledged altar boy. Every other Friday evening Father Delanoit appeared at the house to take him "out for supper," and, while sometimes Jack was able to feign illness and get out of it, more often than not he had no choice but to go with the priest, each time coming back home and feeling like a chunk of his soul had disappeared. He grew quieter and more pugnacious: Lucinda chalked it up to adolescence, sighed and did what she'd always done when trouble appeared: she put one foot in front of the other and hoped things would eventually get better.

One Thursday afternoon in late February, Mrs. Gardner sent all the boys across the hall to Sister Veronica's room. It was time for "the talk," circa 1970. Nervously waiting for Father Schmidt to arrive, the boys fidgeted and whispered and poked each other. Somebody in the back row scraped his shoe on the linoleum floor, creating a noise which sounded similar enough to a bodily function that the room erupted in snorts and giggles. Even the perpetually pursed lips and wrinkled brow of Sister Veronica couldn't contain them.

Fortunately, Father Schmidt made his appearance, just in time to prevent a showdown with the volatile Sister Veronica. The boys rose from their seats, greeting Father Schmidt in unison as had long been their practice.

"Good afternoon, Father Schmidt," they said, a chorus of male voices in various stages of puberty. Jack's was still fairly high, though once in a while it broke into the embarrassing squeak that meant change was underway.

"Good afternoon, boys. Take your seats," Father Schmidt said kindly. "Schmitty," as his friends and co-workers called him, taught history and sociology at the high school. His was a genuine calling, demonstrated by the respect and rapport he shared with his students. Most of the kids tried to take as many classes with Father Schmidt as possible.

"Boys, you know today I'm going to talk to you about the virtue of purity, and how a Catholic man ought to conduct himself," he said. "Let me begin by telling you the story of St. Maria Goretti, for whom our school and church is named. Maria Goretti was born in Italy in 1890 to a devout Catholic family. She was just a simple little child, but today St. Maria is honored world-wide as an example of someone who valued her purity and pleasing God more than anything else, even her life."

"Maria Goretti was born in the late 1800s. Her father was a sharecropper who moved to Ferriere, Italy, to look for work. The Gorettis moved in with another family in order to save money. Maria was baptized, confirmed and had her first communion, just as all of you have done. She was just a normal little girl, but she was known for her love of God and her good character."

Father Schmidt paused and pushed up his glasses, which had slid down towards the tip of his nose. He had been walking back and forth, telling the story, as was his usual lecture style, but now he stopped and stood still, looking at the class as if to gauge their reaction to his next words. He cleared his throat and continued.

"The other family that the Gorettis had moved in with, the Serenellis, had a son named Alessandro. Alessandro, unfortunately, was not known for his good character. Quite the contrary. Alessandro was given to indulging impure thoughts and reading impure literature."

Jack thought of the magazines the boys had passed around and how embarrassed he'd been. Those days seemed a lifetime ago. He wished that was the only thing he had to be embarrassed about.

"Alessandro, who was 20 years old, began to try to get Maria, who was only 11, to engage in impure activities with him. She always told him they could not do what he wanted to do, that it was a sin and God would be angry."

"Boys," Schmitty continued, "our bodies are a temple of the Holy Spirit. While it's normal to have certain feelings as you get older and start to become a man, you must not act on those feelings until you are ready to get married. Until that time, it's best not to even think about things like that. Keep busy, play basketball, help your folks—anything to keep your mind occupied. Some of you may even have a call to the priesthood, and we make a vow never to marry, to remain celibate all of our lives. But most of you will someday marry. Keep yourselves pure until then."

Jack had felt his cheeks begin to burn as soon as the lecture's purpose became evident. He was afraid that everyone was looking at him, that they knew what had happened to him. He kept his eyes fixed on the groove at the top of the desk, where somebody had left a stubby green pencil with little bite marks on the side. He forced himself to focus on it.

"Back to the story about St. Maria," Father Schmidt continued. "One day Alessandro again began to try to convince Maria that they should touch each other in impure ways. Maria refused, telling him it was a sin, so Alessandro attacked her. He stabbed Maria forteen times." He paused again, and the boys' ghoulish imaginations pictured a bloodied Maria and a brutish Alessandro, battling it out over her virtue. "Maria died the next day from the wounds she'd received while protecting her virtue. Before she died, she forgave Alessandro and prayed for his soul. In 1950 Pope Pius XII declared her a saint."

"Boys, guard your purity," Father Schmidt said urgently. "Guard the purity of your sisters in Christ by treating them with respect. Don't let anything steal your soul, like Alessandro did. Stand firm in the faith."

"We won't all be declared saints, like little Maria Goretti, but we can all aspire to have the same desire to serve God faithfully, just like she did, right up to the end of her life. Most of us will never face the difficult struggle that Maria did, but we can still stand strong and be pure for God."

Pure for God. Pure for God. Purify my heart, Oh, God. Had it been a lifetime ago since Jack had felt like purity was a possibility, or only a few months? Whichever, Jack felt filthy most of the time, and even more so right now, after hearing the story.

"Boys, let's join together in a prayer," Father Schmidt said. "Dear Heavenly Father," he prayed as the boys bowed their heads and clasped their hands together, "please keep these boys pure in heart, in mind, in soul, as well as in their bodies, so they may be pleasing to you, your precious son Jesus, and the Blessed Virgin Mary. If they must walk in the valley of evil, be at their side. Help them to turn quickly to you to avoid temptation, we pray," he said. Then he pronounced a blessing over the boys before leaving to go back to the high school.

Sister Veronica, who'd been sitting outside the door correcting math papers, came back into the classroom. She found the boys much more subdued than when she'd left them.

"Jack," she said, "Go to Mrs. Gardner's room and see if she is ready for her class to come back."

"Yes, Sister," Jack said, relieved to have a chance to get out of the room and away from the others. He ducked into the boys' room on his way to Mrs. Gardner's. He looked in the mirror. The person staring back at him had dark brown hair and dark blue eyes. He was neither tall nor short, fat nor skinny. Just a regular kid. Why, then, he felt like such an alien? Jack splashed cold water on his face, stepped back into the hallway and drank from the fountain, then hurried to Mrs. Gardner's class so Sister Veronica wouldn't get mad.

For the remainder of the day, Jack had a hard time focusing on his work. Mrs. Gardner handed back their book reports on Huckleberry Finn; usually the big red 'A' at the top of the page would have made Jack proud, but not today. He toyed with the idea of running away from home, floating down the river like Huck had done when he couldn't take his pa's beatings anymore; the closest river to Hook's Point was iced over, though, so that wouldn't work, but maybe he could hop a train, like Mark Richards and Brett Davis, but instead of riding back to town on the next freight like they had done, Jack could just keep on going.

"Good job on your paper, Jack," Kelly, the girl who sat behind Jack, said quietly.

Jack looked at her blankly for a moment before responding.

"Thanks," he said a small sigh escaping. Increasingly, Jack felt as if he was living in two worlds, and it was getting harder and harder to maintain his involvement in the "real world" of school and friends and family. The hideous Friday nights with Father Delanoit overshadowed everything else, coloring the rest of his life a dull shade of grey.

"Do you want to study the spelling words with me?" Kelly asked.

"Ah… okay," Jack said. He turned around in his seat and faced the red-haired girl. Kelly was easy on the eyes, with small features, a smattering of freckles on her nose and cheeks, and big blue eyes laced with a thick fringe of lashes. Jack felt his spirits rising ever so slightly. "Do you want to go first, and I'll read them off for you?" he asked.

"Sure," Kelly said.

Jack reached for his blue folder where he kept his list of spelling words and pulled out the current week's list.

"Measure," he said, reading the word from the top of the list. He watched as Kelly wrote the word down, her handwriting small and neat. When she was finished, she looked up at him and smiled. He sat up a little straighter in his seat.

"Pharmacy," he said. "Official." Jack continued until he'd read all twenty spelling words. Kelly set her pen down and took the spelling list from Jack.

"Your turn," she said.

Jack opened his notebook and balanced it on his lap, writing each word as Kelly read them off.

"That's it," she said. "Let's see how we did." They each compared what they'd written with the master list, circling their errors.

"Three wrong," Kelly said. "Not too bad. I'll get them down before the test. How'd you do?"

"Just one wrong. Who'd think there's a 'p' in 'pneumonia?" Jack said ruefully.

"Well, thanks for studying with me," Kelly said.

"Sure," Jack said, wishing he could think of something clever to say. Since he couldn't, he smiled at Kelly and turned around in his seat. Looking at the clock, he noticed it was almost time for the bell to ring. Jack began to gather up a few books to take home, just math and geography today, and put the spelling folder back into his desk.

"Don't forget, your paper on the American Revolution is due tomorrow," Mrs. Gardner said. Jack wasn't worried about that, since he'd finished his paper the day before, but several students, including Kelly, let out a groan of dismay.

"Oh, no," Kelly said. "I've had to baby-sit my little brother every night, and I forgot all about that paper being due! I'm only about half way done!"

"I can help you," Jack said. "History's pretty easy for me."

"Like spelling? Everything's easy for you, Jack," Kelly teased. Then, seeing Jack's face cloud over, she said, "Thanks. I'd really appreciate that. Do you want to come over to my house after school?"

"Sure." Just then, the bell rang and the room filled with commotion as twenty-five sixth graders hustled to get out of school as quickly as possible. "Just a minute, I'll tell Wayne I won't be walking with him today. I'll meet you outside," Jack told Kelly.

Jack picked up his books and headed to the hallway, where he found Wayne by his locker.

"Hey, Wayne, I'm gonna go over to Kelly Ryan's house and help her with her history paper," Jack said.

Wayne lifted his eyebrows and looked at Jack significantly.

"No, it's nothing like that, man," Jack said disgustedly. "Kelly's okay, for a girl." Romance was the last thing on his mind. After hearing that creepy story today on top of everything that had happened to him, Jack didn't know if he'd ever want to be with a girl 'that way.' Jack was like most boys his age; he'd experienced occasional stirrings, enough to view girls as less offensive than he did a couple of years ago, but that was it. He looked at Kelly as a kind friend, nothing more. And Jack could really use a friend.

"So, see you tomorrow," Jack said.

"Not if I see you first!" Wayne replied, giving Jack a friendly shove.

Jack opened his locker and got out his coat. Bundling up against the harsh February winds, he walked down the stairs and out the door, where he found Kelly waiting for him. She smiled and they began walking quickly toward her house, which was right on the edge of the area where the more privileged students lived.

Kelly's mother was a widow. Her father had owned a bakery, but when he died of a sudden heart attack, her mother had been forced to sell the bakery in order to pay off the house. She worked as a nurse at the hospital from seven to three, and a few nights a week she earned extra money as a private duty nurse. On those nights, Kelly was responsible for watching her ten-year-old brother Bill until their mother got home, which was usually by nine-thirty. Their mother would hurry home from the hospital, throw together a simple casserole for Kelly to heat up for supper, and go off to take care of old Mrs. Quimbly, who suffered from dementia. It was fairly easy money: Mrs. Quimbly slept most of the time anymore, and Kelly was such a responsible girl that Mrs. Ryan felt comfortable leaving her in charge.

Kelly *was* responsible. She wanted to lighten the load for her mother, so she made sure the dishes were washed and put away, her brother had taken his bath and the house was picked up before Mrs. Ryan got home from work. And she tried to keep up with her schoolwork so her mother wouldn't have to worry. But somehow, that history paper had escaped her attention.

"Well, here's my house," she said as they turned the corner. It was a modest two-story brick building with lace curtains in the big picture window, where a yellow cat lay, indolently sunning herself. They went in the side door, which opened into the kitchen. Mrs. Ryan stood at the counter, putting together a tuna and noodle casserole.

"Mom, this is Jack O'Donnell," Kelly said. "He's helping me with my paper I have to finish on the Revolutionary War."

Mrs. Ryan turned to greet them. She was a pretty redhead like Kelly, though fine lines fanned out around her blue eyes, and her hair was beginning to fade. Her smile was warm and friendly.

"Hi, Jack," she said.

"Hello, Mrs. Ryan," Jack said, blushing slightly. He had never been self-conscious until Father Delanoit came along. Now he found it hard to meet new people. But Mrs. Ryan seemed to be as nice and accepting as Kelly, so that made things a little easier.

Kelly led Jack into the dining room just off the kitchen. They sat down at the gracious oak table, putting their coats on the chairs behind them, and got out their books and papers.

"How much do you have done already?" Jack asked.

"I finished writing about how Washington's army spent the winter at Valley Forge, and how they didn't have any shoes or warm clothes," Kelly said.

"Then you'll want to start with how France joined our side and helped us win the war," Jack said, flipping his book open. "That's on page 252."

Jack guided Kelly through the next sections of her paper, reminding her of the key points Mrs. Gardner said should be included. She was further along than she had thought, and was just putting the final touches on the Treaty of Paris when her mother came in the room with glasses of milk and a plate of cookies. The cookies weren't homemade like Jack's grandmother's, but they looked good anyway.

"Thanks, Mom," Kelly said, smiling.

"Yes, thanks, Mrs. Ryan," Jack said.

"Enjoy," she said. Slipping on her nurse's cape and pinning her hat into place with a practiced hand, Kelly's mother prepared to go to her second job. "The casserole's ready to go in the oven, Kelly. Just set it for 350 and cook it for half an hour. Remind Bill to wash his hands!" After giving Kelly a quick kiss on the cheek, Mrs. Ryan hurried out the door.

Jack was starting to feel at ease in this place. He looked around the dining room, noticing the gallery of family pictures on the wall by the kitchen. There was Kelly and Bill's school pictures—Jack thought Kelly looked pretty in a powder blue sweater, since he normally just saw her in her plaid uniform. Next to the school pictures was a wedding picture. The younger version of Mrs. Ryan looked even more like Kelly. She was holding hands with a man who was slightly plump and already balding. They both looked really happy. A picture of the whole family hung next to that. It looked like it had been taken about two years ago.

"Was that your dad?" Jack said, and then kind of regretted it. Of course it was her dad, you dummy, he thought.

"Yes," Kelly said. "We had that picture taken right before he died. Mom had been trying to get him to take time off work to have a family picture taken for a long time, and he kept putting it off, but finally he did. Mom said that was God's gift. She said every time God takes something away, he gives a gift to ease the pain."

Jack didn't know about that. He wasn't really comfortable thinking about God ever since Father Delanoit… he shook off the thought and said, "He looks like a nice guy."

"He was," Kelly said. "The best baker in Hook's Point."

"My mom is dead, too," Jack said. He didn't usually talk about his mother, but somehow the words just fell out of his mouth. "She died when I was a baby. I don't even remember her."

"That's too bad, Jack," Kelly said solemnly. "But she's watching you from heaven. My mom said that now Dad is like our guardian angel."

Jack felt his face begin to flush again. Did his mother see what Father Delanoit did to him? Would she hate him? He hated himself when he thought about it. He started gathering up his books to go.

"I'm sorry if I made you sad, Jack," Kelly said, sensing the change in her friend's mood.

"No, you didn't do anything wrong," Jack said. "I just… well, I just wish I had a mom, sometimes. But my grandmother lives with us. She is really nice."

They sat at the dining room table for a few minutes in a companionable silence, these two children who had each lost a parent, and then Jack said, "I'd better get going home, or my grandma will be mad." He stood and put on his coat.

"Thanks for helping me with my paper, Jack," Kelly said. Just then, they heard the door open and Bill walked into the room. The chubby, pleasant-faced boy looked as much like their father as Kelly did like their mother.

"What's for dinner?" he asked.

"Tuna and noodles," Kelly said. "But not for a little while yet."

"I'm starving!" he protested.

"I'll see you tomorrow, Kelly," Jack said, heading for the door.

"Bye!" Kelly called out, then turning her attention to her brother.

As Jack walked home, the warm glow he'd felt at Kelly's house began to fade away, and his mind again turned to the story that Father Schmidt had told them about Maria Goretti. Tomorrow would be the night that Father Delanoit picked him up for the biweekly outing. Slowly a plan began to form in Jack's mind.

He was nervous on Friday, as he always was when Father Delanoit was coming over. Usually he alternated between concentrating so hard on his classes that he couldn't think about anything else and going numb, drifting off to the place he went when Father Delanoit touched him, somewhere above his body, just somewhere else. Jack could only lose himself in his studies when it was a subject he really enjoyed, like English or history. During math class, he'd look at the numbers and then they would fade away, his mind floating into another sphere. Somewhere that grown men didn't do disgusting things to little kids. Anywhere but here.

"Jack, I asked you, what is the answer to problem four?" Mrs. Gardner said. "You're off in space somewhere this afternoon."

"I don't know the answer to problem four and I really don't care!" Jack shouted, knocking his book to the floor.

Everyone, including Mrs. Gardner, looked in amazement. Jack was usually a fairly even tempered kid. Sure, this year he'd been a little grouchier, a little touchy sometimes, but never one to sass a teacher. That was a serious offense at St. Maria Goretti's in 1970.

"Jack, pick your book up and calm down," Mrs. Gardner said.

Jack picked up his book, his face still sullen with anger.

"I will talk to you after school," Mrs. Gardner said. Math was the last class of the day, and shortly after Jack's outburst, the final bell rang. Students gathered their books and papers, and then poured into the hallway to get their winter jackets out of their lockers. Jack sat silent as a stone, looking intently at his desktop. The desk was shiny, burnished from scores of students opening and closing it, writing in their workbooks on it, occasionally sitting on top of it when the teacher was out of the room.

When the hallway grew quiet, Mrs. Gardner approached Jack, her arms folded across her chest and her pretty face puckered with an uncharacteristically stern expression.

"Well, Jack, what do you have to say for yourself?" Mrs. Gardner said.

Still looking at his desk, Jack mumbled, "I'm sorry, Mrs. Gardner." The brick in his chest moved slightly. He liked Mrs. Gardner, he really did, but sometimes he just got so angry that he hated the whole world, including her.

"Jack, this really isn't acceptable behavior," she said. "If you act like that again in class, I'm going to have to have your father in for a talk."

"I won't. I promise," he said.

"Okay, then, you can go home," Mrs. Gardner said.

Jack stood and walked to the hallway. He turned a minute, wishing that he could take back the last hour. Mrs. Gardner was really a nice teacher, and Jack hated for her to think he was a bad kid. She was busy grading papers at her desk, and Jack didn't really know what else to say, so he just went on his way.

When Jack turned the corner onto his street, he saw that Father Delanoit's Riviera was parked in front of the house. He usually stopped over and drank a cup of coffee with Lucinda before picking Jack up. Jack inhaled deeply. He knew what he had to do. His face was resolute as he walked into the house.

"Hello, Grandma. Hello, Father Delanoit," Jack said.

"Hi, Jack," his grandmother said warmly. "Father Delanoit is taking you to a new restaurant tonight. He said it got four stars in the Daily Tribune. How do you rate, huh?"

"Wow. Sounds great."

"We'd better head out, Jack," Father Delanoit said, slipping on his long black coat. "Thank you for the coffee, Mrs. Walters."

"Certainly, Father. My privilege," Lucinda said as she walked the priest and her grandson to the door. "Have a good time, now."

The ride to the rectory was silent, as it usually was, unless Father Delanoit turned on the classical music station. Jack's stomach was normally twisted into knots by this point, but this time he felt calmer. He knew what he was going to do.

Father Delanoit pulled up in front of the rectory. They walked up the cracked cobblestone sidewalk and through the front door into the hallway, where Father hung his coat up in the closet. Jack kept his jacket on, his hands dug into his pockets.

"Hang your coat up, Jack," Father Delanoit said, a hint of impatience in his voice. He put his hand on Jack's shoulder, which is the moment Jack made his move. He launched a kick into the priest's shin.

"NO!" Jack roared. "I'm not going to let you touch me again. It's wrong and you know it!"

Father Delanoit yelped, briefly losing his balance. As Jack threw a punch at the priest's gut with all the force his ninety-pound body could muster, Father Delanoit quickly regained his advantage and effortlessly pinned Jack's arms behind his back. Falling to his knees, Jack cried out in pain. Gradually, Father Delanoit released his hold.

"Now, Jack, that really was kind of silly," he said, as if he and Jack shared some kind of inside joke. "Really, now, what were you thinking? What were you hoping to accomplish with that move?"

"This is wrong," Jack said, his voice quaking. "I don't want to do this. God wouldn't like it." So far, this was not going like he'd envisioned.

"Jack, Jack, my boy," Father Delanoit chuckled. "I am here as Christ's representative, am I not? Surely, I can better vouch for what God would and wouldn't approve of than you can. Now," he said, his voice deepening, "don't ever try that again, do you understand me? I could make life very difficult for you, Jack." Again adopting that hypnotic, caressing tone, Father Delanoit said, "It would break your grandmother's heart, after all she's been through. Losing your mother, right after you were born… raising you and your brother, and then, there's your father she had to contend with. Come now, Jack," the priest said, putting his arm around the boy and leading him into his study, where he always took him. Jack wanted to keep fighting, but the moment the priest touched him, he felt himself floating away. The last thought that Jack was aware of that evening was that he was such a loser, he was weaker than a little girl like Maria Goretti.

What Jack wouldn't realize for many years: the problem was not that he wasn't as brave as the Italian saint, but instead, that Father Delanoit was a greater monster than Alessandro Serenelli ever dreamt of becoming.

Chapter Seven

Lucinda poured herself a cup of coffee, took it into the living room, and eased herself gingerly into the rocking chair. Helping with two moves in two weeks was a little strenuous, she had to admit. The family had finally convinced Pappa to give up his apartment in Chicago and move to Hook's Point with them, so they had spent one hot, sweaty weekend in mid-August clearing out Pappa's apartment, taking most of his furniture to the Salvation Army and bringing the rest, including the old iron bed he'd brought over from Italy, loading it into a rented trailer that Mike hitched onto the back of his Chevy, and moving him into the garage apartment they'd had built for him. The apartment had a bedroom, bathroom with a shower, sitting area and small kitchenette. The plan was, Pappa would eat supper with the family, and lunch if he wanted to, but still be able to maintain the independence he treasured.

Just ten days after they finished moving Pappa to Hook's Point, the clan followed David to Benedictine University in Hays, Iowa. David actually packed most of his possessions into his beat-up old Ford Galaxy, but the family wanted to see him settled into his room at the college. Mike was practically bursting with pride, because David had won a full-ride, four-year scholarship by maintaining a 4.0 grade average all throughout high school. His son would be the first O'Donnell to go to college. Mike's pride was only slightly diminished by the fact that David was seriously planning to enter the priesthood. That would not have been Mike's choice for his son, but he knew that was a decision for David to make. Mainly, Mike was just proud that he, a man who could barely read, had produced a kid this bright.

Lucinda, on the other hand, was delighted with David's choice. She realized it would be many years before David actually took his vows, if indeed he stuck with his plans, but she really felt blessed. David had never given the family any trouble during his adolescence, and she felt he truly was suited for the priesthood.

Lucinda reflected on these recent changes in her family. Her father had adjusted remarkably well to the move. She found she enjoyed his company as much as ever, and sometimes wished he'd spend more time in the main house. But he was just as sociable as ever, taking walks around the neighborhood and making friends with the neighbors. Yesterday he'd popped in at lunchtime, and then informed her that he would be eating supper with the Castanis that evening. The ninety-year-old man was bent and shriveled, and his vision was fading, but his mind was as sharp as a private eye's. His hearing was not what it used to be, yet he caught on quicker to whatever was going on around him than many people half his age. And he seemed to be a calming influence on Jack, who certainly needed it.

Jack's entrance into adolescence gave every indication that his would be a stormy one. Even toward the end of sixth grade, he was becoming belligerent, arguing with his teachers and getting into fights after school. Mike told Lucinda it was nothing to worry about, and even seemed to be a little proud. Although Mike was definitely pleased with David's accomplishments, he was a little baffled by his oldest son's choice of a vocation. Having one son who was a holy roller was enough for Mike; if Jack turned out to be a bit of a scrapper, well, boys would be boys, he reasoned.

It worried Lucinda, though. Jack had always been a good boy, just like David had been, and while Lucinda saw an increase in moodiness during David's early teen years, she had never seen the kind of angry outbursts which Jack displayed. Even more than his outbursts, Lucinda was troubled by Jack's secretive behavior. She had the distinct impression that Jack was hiding something from her, and she'd caught him lying to her on several occasions. Lies about homework assignments, lies about where he was going. She almost felt like she didn't know him anymore, and that bothered her. Lucinda had a vague feeling that she had failed Jack in some significant way. Occasionally she would see a sad, wistful look on his still-childlike face, but as soon as she spoke or looked directly at him, Jack's features fell into a mask of indifference.

Lucinda sighed and took a drink of her coffee. She was almost seventy years old, way past the time when most women tangled with moody adolescents. But Lucinda had never wasted any time on self-pity, preferring to take action when she had a problem. Perhaps she should discuss this with Father Delanoit. He might have some ideas as to how Lucinda should handle her concerns about Jack. Maybe this Friday, before he took Jack out to supper.

After his summer vacation, Father Delanoit had resumed taking Jack out every other Friday evening. Usually he stopped over for a cup of coffee before hand, unless he had too many appointments that afternoon. What a fine, godly man Father Delanoit was, taking time out of his busy schedule to spend time with Jack. Lucinda's admiration for the priest was tremendous, bordering on a sense of awe. He was not a friendly, man-of-the-people priest like Father Schmidt, who had guided David's decision to enter the priesthood; instead, Father Delanoit was more formal in his approach to people. He was a very efficient manager of the parish funds, well known for his ability to hobnob with the wealthier citizens of Hook's Point and encourage them to give generously to church causes. To Lucinda that made it even more impressive that he took an interest in a boy like Jack.

Jack didn't seem very fond of Father Delanoit, though. In fact, Lucinda had the distinct impression that Jack had hoped Father Delanoit was going to discontinue his visits after the summer break. The Friday before last, when Jack came home and found Father Delanoit here, ready to take him out for supper, he looked upset, and the next day he was terribly moody. Lucinda was disappointed that Jack didn't have more appreciation for the priest and his efforts. She was afraid that Jack was drifting away from the

Church. His attitude seemed more like Mike's than David's.

And, while Pappa was a good influence in so many ways, Lucinda had to admit that he wasn't any more interested in religion than Mike was. His attendance at Mass since her mother's death had been sporadic, and he seemed to have a slightly suspicious attitude towards the Church that Lucinda found a little troubling. No, since David had left for college Jack really didn't have a good male role model to aid his Catholic development. Thank God for Father Delanoit, anyway.

"Thank God for Father Delanoit," said Regina Lewis, secretary to Bishop Groat. A morning spent going over the receipts from the churches in the dioceses revealed that giving had taken a nosedive in many of the parishes last month. Bishop Groat was not going to be pleased, she fretted. At least she'd be able to show him the numbers for St. Maria Goretti's in Hook's Point. Giving was at an all-time high, and Father Delanoit had successfully convinced several of that town's movers and shakers to contribute a large, one-time gift to the diocese to pay for their new organ. You could always count on Father Delanoit to bring in the sheaves, Regina thought. The man had a way of persuading people to do what he asked.

Jack, however, was not thanking God for Father Delanoit. Sitting in his seventh grade classroom, listening to Miss Hightower drone on about where the commas belong in compound and complex sentences, Jack's mind drifted back to the first Friday after summer vacation had ended, when Father Delanoit came back into his life.

After school let out for the summer, Jack had spent two weeks in Chicago with Pappa. It had been great. They'd taken in a couple of Cubs games, seen all the tourist attractions: the Navy Pier, the Museum of Natural History, the John Hancock Center. They'd eaten at some of the best pizzerias on Taylor Street. And Jack had helped Pappa do some heavy cleaning in preparation for his move to Hook's Point. The edginess that engulfed Jack when he was home began to dissipate, and when he got back to Hook's Point and learned that Father Delanoit was traveling overseas for the summer, Jack felt like he'd won a death-row reprieve. He got into some pick-up games of baseball with Wayne and the other guys and entertained them with stories about watching the Cubs play at Wrigley Field; he went over to Kelly's house a few times and sat on the front porch swing, drinking lemonade and talking to Kelly and her family; he helped his dad paint the apartment they were preparing for Pappa; and he swam at the local swimming hole with the boys, swinging over the water on an old knotted rope that somebody had tied onto a long branch of the oak tree that grew near the water's edge, holding tight until he swung out over the deepest part and then letting go, experiencing the icy delight of plunging into the water and slowly surfacing to meet the hot sunshine.

He spent a little time with David, joking around like the old days and going out for burgers, but Jack didn't feel as close to his brother as before. He was actually relieved when the family dropped David off at college. Anymore, Jack felt tainted, unclean, and being around his brother the soon-to-be seminarian sometimes brought those feelings to the surface.

David sensed Jack pulling away, and he asked him once or twice if something was wrong. As if Jack's embarrassment wasn't enough to keep him quiet, Father Delanoit's warning not to tell anyone assured the boy's silence. He replied irritably when David questioned him, so David let the matter drop, chalking Jack's attitudes up to puberty.

And Jack was in the midst of puberty. He had shot up four or five inches since last winter, and while his face was still somewhat child-like, the baby roundness was gone. There was a slight definition to his muscles that wasn't present last year, and a few hairs had sprouted on his armpits and genitals. Besides the height increase, impossible to ignore when his jeans would no longer cover his lower legs, Jack took little note of his body's changes, because he couldn't stand who he saw when he looked in the mirror.

After summer vacation, though, Jack was feeling better than he had for months. He still lost his temper way too often, he knew, especially with his grandmother. Ever since Father Delanoit had first taken him into his study at the rectory, Jack felt cut off from his grandmother, from her love and protection, which had been a constant during all his life until that point. He sometimes felt like she'd have to hate him if she knew what had happened, and other times he was furious that she kept sending him off with the priest. The feelings were so uncomfortable and overpowering that Jack avoided his grandmother as much as he could; when he had to be at home, he hid out in his room, reading books and building model cars.

But even that situation had been getting a little better. Pappa joined the family for supper almost every evening, providing a buffer between Jack and Lucinda and keeping the tension at bay. Jack enjoyed listening to the two of them talk, occasionally lapsing into Italian, and reminiscing about their life in Chicago and all the people they'd known there. Pappa taught Jack a few card tricks and began teaching him how to play poker: five-card stud, draw poker and Texas Hold'em.

Then school started up. Jack's seventh grade teacher was Miss Hightower, whose name was a perfect fit with her appearance. She was tall and thin with a receding hairline and a beak of a nose, known for being strict and unyielding, but also fair. Jack was pleased to discover that Kelly was in his homeroom again this year. She smiled shyly at him from her seat two aisles over, and he felt his heart lighten, just like it did every time that he talked to her. But that Friday the emotional uplift he'd enjoyed over the summer crashed when he found Father Delanoit's Riviera pulled up in front of the house when he got home from school. When he opened the door, there was Father Delanoit, sitting on the couch in Jack's living room, drinking coffee with his grandmother, who couldn't have looked more pleased if she were entertaining the Queen of England.

So this year was going to be as rotten as last year, Jack thought. Stupid of me to think it might be over. Stupid.

Jack felt filthier than ever after Father Delanoit took him "out for dinner." He was in a foul mood all weekend, and the mood carried over into the next week. Monday was a struggle to keep his mind on his work, and Hightower corrected him sharply: she had called on him twice and both times, he had no idea what page he was supposed to be on. They were studying St. Petersburg in Russia, but for all Jack knew or cared, they were all stuck in Siberia. Even seeing Kelly didn't cheer him up. She had looked over at him and smiled, and Jack ducked his head, staring intently at a crack in the brown linoleum floor. By the time the bell rang to signal the end of the day, Jack's stomach was churning and his head pounding. He hurriedly finished his English assignment, then jumped out of his desk and flew to the hallway. He couldn't wait to get out of there.

But first, he had to get his coat out of his locker. The weather had been unseasonably cold this morning, and his grandmother had insisted Jack wear a jacket. Jack worked the combination for his locker too quickly and it refused to open. Breathing in sharply, he tried again. Nineteen to the right. Turn to the left, passing fourteen, then pausing there the second time around. Then thirty-six to the right. No luck. Jack tried it a third time and it still failed to open. Jack hung his head, feeling dangerously close to tears.

"What's the matter, Jackie forget his combination?" mocked a boy passing by, using a falsetto voice that set his two companions into fits of laughter. Jack, nearly blinded by the pain that was throbbing in his head, looked up to see his old nemesis Ronny Slater, the boy who'd tormented him about his father's drinking last year. The boy he'd punched in the sacristy. The fight Father Delanoit had agreed to cover up for him. The price of the cover-up. The price!

"Bastard!" Jack snarled, flying at his tormentor and pushing him into the lockers on the opposite side of the hall.

Taken off guard, Ronny lost his footing and began sliding to the floor. Jack grabbed him by the collar and rammed his head into the grey steel locker. Blood from the back of his head began running down Ronny's face as he slumped forward. Jack drew back, horrified. Horrified, partly by what he had done and partly because all he really wanted to do was to keep going, keep banging the bastard's head against the locker until his brains were a bloody pulp.

"Knock it off, man!" said one of Ronny's friends. "Are you crazy?"

At that moment Miss Hightower, who had walked downstairs to grab a cup of coffee to drink while she graded papers, appeared at the top of the staircase. Ronny was already on his feet. He only had a small cut where his head had hit the edge of his locker, but blood continued to seep from the wound, making it look much worse than it actually was.

"What happened up here?" she demanded. "I heard a scuffle when I was downstairs. Just what's going on?" She looked from Ronny to Jack and to the two other boys. No one spoke for a moment.

"Nothing," Ronny said. "Nothing's going on, Miss Hightower. We were just goofing around, and we got a little carried away, and I fell and hit my head." He looked steadily at Jack. "Jack here was just helping me up."

Jack, squinting, looked carefully at his opponent. What would be the price for this, he wondered. But he couldn't turn down an opportunity to escape what would surely be a harsh punishment, with calls to his father and grandmother, possibly even the police.

"Sorry, buddy," Jack said, the aftertaste of his words like meat gone bad. "We'll be more careful next time, Miss Hightower."

Looking at the boys, the veteran teacher instinctively knew there was a cover-up of sorts going on. But she also knew the power of the code, the code that said to tell was the worst offense a boy could commit. She wouldn't get any more information from these boys, that was certain.

"Go wash up in the restroom, Ronny," Miss Hightower said. "The rest of you fellows need to head home."

Ronny stood in front of the mirror, washing the blood off his face with a wet paper towel. As he looked in the mirror, he remembered the look on Father Delanoit's face after he and Jack had fought the last time, the priest's tightly contained anger more frightening somehow than Jack's out-of-control rage just now. Father Delanoit's warning not to torment Jack ever again was still fresh in Ronny's mind; that was the reason he had kept his mouth shut today, even though it would have been fun to see Jack get in trouble with old Hightower. Ronny had a predator's instincts and he knew better than to go against an adversary like Father Delanoit. For some reason Delanoit had taken a liking to Jack, the little weasel.

While Ronny's buddies waited outside for him, Jack hastily departed, leaving his coat in the locker. He really couldn't believe his luck. He felt relieved, but his relief was clouded by fear; he didn't like the fact that Ronny had some leverage over him and he didn't like to think what kind of pay-off he might want. Jack had learned that goodwill sometimes carried a hefty price tag. Whatever Ronny's price, though, it wouldn't be as high as Father Delanoit's.

Jack's greater fear was of his own fury. He never wanted to feel like that again. Over the past year, he had lost his temper with increasing frequency, but he'd never hurt anybody like that before. Jack felt like a raging beast was caged up inside him, and he resolved never again to let that beast out.

"Where's your coat, Jack?" Lucinda asked when Jack got home.

"I left it at school, Grandma," he said, fighting to keep the irritation out of his voice. "I'll get it tomorrow, okay?"

Lucinda noticed the edge in Jack's voice and looked at him more closely. She didn't like what she saw. He looked so agitated and unhappy. She longed to ask him what was the matter, but she knew he would only resist what he would see as her prying. She wanted to fold him into her arms like she had when he was small, but she knew he would pull back if she tried to touch him.

Suddenly, she had a brainstorm.

"Jack, run over and get Pappa, okay?" Pappa had told her he planned to stay home this afternoon and take a nap, but she knew he would be up by now.

"Sure," Jack said, and then headed out the back door. Ten minutes later, Jack and Pappa came in together. Lucinda saw that Jack looked more relaxed already.

"So I hear I got a summons to the big house," Pappa said. "What's up?"

"Well, I'll tell you," Lucinda said. "I thought we'd have just enough time before supper for a few rounds of poker."

"Always have time for poker," Pappa said. "What's the stakes? The winner gets out of dish duty?" Since Pappa had moved in, he and Jack alternated washing the supper dishes.

They gathered around the table, where Lucinda had set up cans of Coke and a bowl of chips along with the cards and a cup full of pennies, saved for such occasions. Whether he won or lost, Jack always seemed to feel better after a few rounds of poker with Pappa. So did Lucinda, for that matter.

"Deal the cards, Princess," Pappa said; Jack snickered whenever Pappa called Lucinda by one of her childhood nicknames.

"Ah, so you think it's funny, my boy," Pappa said, picking up his cards as Lucinda dealt them out. "Don't you know your grandmother here comes from royal lineage? The only living granddaughter of King Victor Emmanuel? Why, if it weren't for that foul Mussolini, we'd be sitting pretty right now."

"We'd be rolling in the do-rae-mi!" Lucinda chimed in.

"Are you in, Jack," Pappa asked.

Studying his cards, Jack nodded. He had three kings, a decent hand. "I'm in," he said, throwing a penny in the center.

"I'll see your penny and raise you two," Pappa said, his eyes gleaming.

Lucinda shook her head as she looked at her cards. "I dealt myself a fat lot of nothing," she said in mock exasperation. "I'm out already."

Jack threw four more pennies in. With three kings, it was worth a shot.

Pappa studied his cards a moment. He looked quite confident as he pitched six pennies into the pot. "Raise you two, Jack."

"I'm folding," Jack said. "Whaddya have, Pappa?" Evidently it was better than three kings.

With a Cheshire-cat grin, Pappa laid out his cards: a ten of spades, eight of clubs, three of hearts and two aces. The little old man looked so pleased with himself, Lucinda and Jack burst out laughing, in spite of the fact that they'd been hoodwinked.

"I couldn't believe you only had one lousy pair of aces," Jack said, laughing. He picked up the cards and began shuffling them for the next round. "Geeze, Pappa, from the look on your face I thought at least you had a flush or two pairs or something worthwhile!"

"From the look on my face, huh? The look on a man's face may tell you many things, Jack. Maybe half of them are true," Pappa said. Lucinda recalled how Pappa could sometimes pack more preaching into a poker game than the priest did in a Sunday sermon. "If you want to know the truth, you don't just look at a man's face. You watch his actions."

"And, if you were watching my actions, you'd know that just now I swiped a jack off the top of the deck you're shuffling and stuck it up my sleeve!" Pappa proudly produced the card, and then placed it back into the deck. "Watch the actions, Jack. Note the consequences. Faces can deceive and words can lie, but actions speak for themselves."

Even though Lucinda and Jack heard Pappa's advice, he still managed to skunk them for three more hands. Just when Lucinda dropped out to make the meatballs to go with the spaghetti sauce that had been simmering on the stove all afternoon, Mike came in, so he took her place. Pappa was on a winning streak and beat them twice more.

"Humiliated in my own home, and by an old man at that!" Mike ribbed him good-naturedly.

"You boys will catch on," Pappa said. "Eventually."

"All right, you guys are going to have to move so I can set the table," Lucinda said. They moved into the living room, laughing and talking. Maybe a man's face could lie, she thought, but Jack was still a boy, and whatever he was feeling tended to show up on his face. And now Jack's countenance was relaxed and peaceful, Lucinda noticed with satisfaction. As they gathered around the table, summoned by the aroma of spicy spaghetti and garlic bread, Lucinda had to congratulate herself just a little bit. Her instincts were still pretty good sometimes. It seems that Pappa's were better yet, though.

Chapter Eight

The following Friday, a crisp day in late September, Father Delanoit drove up to the O'Donnell house. Turning off his Riviera and getting out of the car, he inhaled the sweet autumn air, filled with anticipation and self-satisfaction. Father Delanoit always found it a bit amusing, spending time with dear old Lucinda Walters right before he took Jack for their little outing. The woman was like so many women in the parish, a little awe-struck in his presence and so eager for any attention he bestowed upon them. Why, he thought bemusedly, that must be how Elvis Presley or those very attractive boys from England felt when all their annoying little teenyboppers paid them homage with their shrieks and fawning gazes. Not that Father Delanoit had much use for modern music—he much preferred classical—but one couldn't help but notice modern trends, regardless of how lacking in taste those trends may be.

Humming a bit from Beethoven's Fifth Symphony, Father Delanoit knocked on the O'Donnell's door. He was somewhat taken aback to hear a man's voice inside. Mike O'Donnell was never around at this time of day; Father had heard from Mrs. McGrevey that he was spending more and more time at the bars. He supposed even drunkards took a day off now and then, though. Father Delanoit didn't really foresee any trouble from Mike O'Donnell. Throw around a few four-syllable words and the poor man positively shrank into himself, he had noticed. Yes, he knew how to handle the unfortunate Mr. O'Donnell.

"Why, Father Delanoit, I'm so glad to see you," Lucinda bubbled as she opened the door. "And I'm glad my father finally gets to meet you—I've told him what a godsend you've been with our Jack. This is my father, Tony Gargano."

Stepping into the living room, the priest extended his hand to the old man.

"I'm pleased to meet you, Mr. Gargano," Father Delanoit said. He took in every detail: the old man appeared quite slim and frail, standing just a little taller than his diminutive daughter. His hand was soft, but his grip stronger than the priest expected. Thick lenses covered the old man's eyes, yet they shone with a clarity and quickness that belied his advanced age.

"Pleased to make your acquaintance, I'm sure, Father Delanoit," the old man said. His thin, aged voice carried a trace of old Italy. "Please, let's sit down and visit," he said, taking a seat in the rocking chair.

"I'll get our coffee and cookies," Lucinda said. She disappeared into the kitchen to prepare a tray.

"Are you visiting Hook's Point from… Chicago, is it, Mr. Gargano?" Father Delanoit asked as he sat down on the couch.

"No, I've moved here. Lucinda's been after me for years and she finally won," said the old man. "They fixed up a little apartment for me over the garage, and, so here I am. For the rest of my days, most likely. So, Father," the old man said, leaning forward slightly, "Lucinda tells me you've been taking Jack out for supper for almost a year, now." He looked at the priest somewhat quizzically.

"Yes, I have. Jack's quite a fine young man, but I had noticed a… well, should we say a certain gap in his upbringing, in spite of the wonderful job your daughter has done with him." Looking appropriately saddened, he said, "First, the boy loses his mother just shortly after he was born, and his father… his father has certainly had a lot to contend with, hasn't he? I do consider it part of my pastoral duty to step in when a family has a need, and I did see that this family had a need."

"Of course. How kind," the old man said. For some reason Father Delanoit felt apprehensive, off guard somehow. Strange that a wizened old fellow like this would have that effect.

"So, are you finding the quieter pace of life in our little town to be dull, Mr. Gargano? Or perhaps this is just what one likes at your stage of life. A slower, simpler pace," Father Delanoit said. Wouldn't hurt to remind the old man that's what he was. Put him in his place.

"I've never found life to be dull, Father Delanoit," the old man replied. "You see, I'm a great observer of people, and people may be many things, but dull is seldom one of them. Wouldn't you agree, Father?" he asked, his brown eyes steady behind his thick glasses.

"Never dull, no, are they," Father Delanoit agreed.

Lucinda came out from the kitchen carrying a tray laden with a steaming coffee pot, cups and saucers, and a plate of her oatmeal-raisin cookies. The cookies were Jack's favorite. She placed the tray on the coffee table, her movements more graceful and poised than many women half her age. Lucinda poured Father Delanoit's coffee first, handed it to him and then poured her father's before serving herself.

"Have some cookies," she urged. "I baked them just this morning. So Father Delanoit, how was your overseas trip? Father Delanoit went on a mission to India, Pappa," Lucinda explained.

"It was an incredible experience. How amazing that a land so rich in natural resources has so many people living in poverty," Father Delanoit said. He sighed as though deeply troubled, when in fact he was recalling several exciting interludes with the street children he had had while overseas.

As Father Delanoit was expositing on the situation in India, Jack walked in the door. The expression on Jack's face reminded Pappa of someone much older, a soldier heading off to fight in a war or a man who'd resolved to carry out a difficult but necessary task, like Frankie Ronaldo had looked the day his children's much-loved cocker spaniel ran out into the street and got hit by a delivery truck. Pappa had seen the truck driver come barreling down the street, driving too fast and not even bothering to stop when he ran over the dog. The poor creature was mangled and bloody, its back legs completely crushed, but still alive and whimpering when Frankie reached her. Frankie knew there was no way that dog could survive, so he braced himself, found a brick sitting in a pile of junk in the alley, and swiftly hit the suffering dog on her head, crushing her skull and ending her misery as quickly as possible—he'd owed her that much, Frankie told Pappa later; she was the best damn dog anybody ever had.

The expression on Jack's face reminded Pappa of how Frankie had looked when he came back to the street, the brick in his hand. Not at all like a kid who looked forward to going out for supper with his parish priest, Pappa thought.

"Hello, Grandma, Pappa. Father Delanoit," Jack said, his tone somehow bordering on insolent, though Pappa also heard a trace of fear.

"Jack, here, have some oatmeal cookies," Lucinda said, lifting the plate in his direction. As Pappa looked at her, he noticed she seemed oblivious to the boy's mood. She'd been consumed with getting the house in order for Father Delanoit's visit and showing him the hospitality due to someone in his position. Lucinda must have picked up that reverent nature from her mother, Pappa mused. To him, all men put their pants on the same way. He held no one man in higher esteem than another, be he priest or politician, dogcatcher or doctor.

"No, thanks, Grandma. I'm not hungry," Jack said.

"Well, Jack, I hope you find your appetite soon," Father Delanoit said as he stood. "Tonight we're going to have pizza at Tony's. And I'd suppose we'd better get going if we want to beat the crowd. Mrs. Walters, as always, thank you for your kind hospitality; and a pleasure to make your acquaintance, Mr. Gargano," he said.

As Jack followed Father Delanoit to the door, he gave Pappa a backwards glance. Pappa thought the boy looked embarrassed or slightly wistful, he wasn't sure which. What he was sure about: the boy was not happy to be going out for supper with Father Delanoit.

Lucinda placed the cups and saucers on the tray and carried them into the kitchen. Pappa rocked back and forth in the old rocking chair, contemplating Father Delanoit and Jack's reaction to him. Was the priest given to ponderous lectures, maybe? Did the boy just find him boring, their get-togethers a tedious chore he had to endure twice a month, or was there something more ominous going on?

He walked into the kitchen and, picking up the faded yellow and red dishtowel, began to dry the dishes Lucinda was washing.

"Lucinda, our Jack is not fond of the good Father, now, is he?" Pappa asked.

"Pappa, he's not. The boy gives me fits sometimes. Wouldn't you think he'd appreciate the time Father Delanoit gives to him, not only the time but a nice meal in a restaurant? God knows that's not something we'd be able to afford. I just don't understand him anymore, Pappa," Lucinda said.

Pappa sighed. His daughter was not a stupid woman, by any means. Yet, like everyone else, she had her blind spots. And one of her blind spots was this overly deferential spirit toward religious authorities.

"Have you talked to the boy about it?" he asked.

"I've tried, Pappa, but he just gets angry and says nothing's wrong. I don't understand," she said again.

Pappa looked through his thick glasses at Lucinda, her loose grey curls, the lines on her face. Life had marked her with its joys and its sorrows. Here they were, father and daughter, both old now, but still he saw traces of his little girl in the face of the old woman she'd become. Lucinda had worn just that same troubled expression years ago, sitting at the kitchen table and working on her lessons. It was a look that said, 'I've tried my best and it still isn't working,' a combination of hurt and puzzlement. Back then, Pappa had hated the fact that his own English skills weren't strong enough to help his daughter succeed. So he had bartered with one of his customers. Pappa would do all her family's alterations free for one year if the woman, a second-generation American, would tutor Lucinda. The woman had four daughters, so it sounded like a bargain to her. Lucinda finished out that year near the head of her class; as far as Pappa was concerned, he was the one who came out ahead.

And Lucinda had looked the same way when she'd come to him shamefaced and repentant with the news that Doug Walters had left her, abandoning his wife and his daughter to run off with a woman almost half his age. Her face betrayed her every emotion: hurt, betrayal, confusion over what she had done to bring this disaster down on herself and her little girl.

"Nothing! You did nothing wrong," Pappa had told her, silently adding, except for marrying a man who wasn't worthy of your precious love. Lucinda had refused to move back home with her father, reluctant to face the judgmental stares and whispered accusations of the neighbors, but Pappa had helped her financially as much as he could, tucking five-dollar bills inside his weekly letters, and more when he could manage it.

Pappa felt the same determination to take care of his daughter that he'd felt back then. Not only that, but he was concerned about Jack. The boy had definitely changed over the past year or so, and not just the normal changes all teenagers went through. Jack was a troubled young man, angry and secretive, there was no denying it. Pappa drew himself up to his full height of five foot five inches and puffed out his chest a bit. Let no one ever say that Tony Gargano didn't take care of his family. Pappa would find out what was going on with Jack. Moreover, he had a hunch that Father Delanoit was somehow involved.

Later the next week Pappa paid a visit to Rose Castani. Rose urged him to join her for a cup of coffee and fresh pecan rolls. As they sat in her worn but scrupulously clean kitchen, Pappa turned the conversation to her second oldest son, Alan. He remembered hearing that Father Delanoit had started spending time with him not long after the boy's own father had died.

"Your Alan," Pappa said gently. "Didn't I hear that Father Delanoit took a special interest in Alan after Mr. Castani died, if you don't mind me asking?"

"Why, yes he did, Mr. Gargano. Father Delanoit—the man is a saint," Rose said. "Always running around, raising money for the church, but still taking the time to help a fatherless boy like my Alan. For all the good it did," she added. "But at least he tried. I'll always be grateful for that." Alan had quit high school, joined the Army and managed to get himself kicked out for insubordination, then more or less dropped out of sight altogether. Rose sighed, putting another sweet roll on her plate.

Pappa patted her hand.

"How did Alan... get along with the good father?" Pappa asked.

"Well, it's funny you should ask that," Rose replied. "Alan really didn't seem to like Father Delanoit very well. I don't know if he resented him for some reason, maybe he thought that Father Delanoit was trying to take his own father's place. Alan adored my Jimmy, and Jimmy loved all his kids. He and Jimmy, Junior, our oldest boy, though, they were too much alike, those two—they were always butting heads. But Alan and his dad were really close. Jimmy's death hit him hard—it did for all of us, but Alan more than the others. That's why I was so pleased when Father Delanoit began to take Alan under his wing. I thought it would help him get over losing his father like that. But it really didn't."

Pappa sipped on his coffee, taking it all in. The priest didn't seem to be terribly successful with these boys he tried to help. You'd think a busy man like that would quit throwing good money after bad. Strange.

"Did Alan ever tell you why he didn't like Father Delanoit?"

"No. He got upset one day and told me he just didn't want to go with him anymore. I told Alan that he was being ungrateful, that he needed to show some appreciation for what people did for him. Well, he went with Father Delanoit that evening. But he didn't come back. Father Delanoit dropped him off about eight o'clock, the same as he usually did, and Alan didn't even come in the house. He took off, met up with some hoodlums over on Fourth Street, and got himself drunk. Finally made it home about two in the morning."

"I was going crazy with worry. Then Alan comes in the door, so drunk he could barely walk. He started talking crazy, said he was going to take Jimmy's rifle and shoot Father Delanoit and maybe shoot himself. Finally he calmed down, well, passed out is more like it. I decided then and there not to let him go with Father any more. I don't know what Alan's problem was, but I have five other children, Mr. Gargano, and I couldn't afford any trouble. So I called the rectory and told Father Delanoit the next day. I said I really appreciated all he'd done for Alan and our family, but I needed Alan to stay home and help out with the younger kids. Father Delanoit was very understanding. He's a class act, that man is."

"He's something, isn't he," Pappa said.

"I see he's been taking an interest in your Jack, now," Rose said. "I hope Jack has the good sense to appreciate his efforts more than my Alan did."

"Jack's a boy with good sense, that's for sure," Pappa said. "Well, Mrs.Castani, I don't want to keep you," he said, rising. "That pecan roll was delicious. Your husband was a very fortunate man."

Rose blushed like a girl on her first date. Pappa, even as old as he was, always had that affect on women.

"You'll have to come again, Mr. Gargano," she said, walking him to the door.

"Oh, I most certainly will. Have a good day, Mrs. Castani," he said, bowing slightly and then heading back to his apartment above the garage. When he got there, Pappa took the footstool from the kitchen into the bedroom, opened his closet door, and carefully stepping onto the stool, reached onto the top shelf of his closet. One by one, he took down the boxes that he had stored there. There were close to a dozen, filled with photos and mementos. He placed the boxes on his bed and then put the footstool away. Then, winded from the exertion, he went into the living room and laid down to rest.

After he'd rested a bit, Pappa walked over to the main house. He found Lucinda in a cleaning binge, humming happily as she scrubbed down the kitchen cupboards.

"Hey, Pappa, come on in!" she called out.

"Oh, no, you don't," he said, standing in the doorway. "I know you, Lucinda. If I come anywhere near you when you're in this mood, you'll be putting me to work. And I'm an old man! That's why I'm here. Would you send Jack over to the apartment when he gets out of school? I need help putting some boxes away."

"Sure, sure, I'll send him over. Do you want to come over for lunch, Pappa? Or will you be okay till supper?"

"No, I'm fine. I'll be over tonight. Make it something simple—you're not exactly a spring chicken yourself, you know," he teased.

"Get out of here!" Lucinda called as he headed back down the walk.

Shortly after three-thirty, Jack knocked on the door of Pappa's apartment.

"Come in, come in," Pappa said. "Hey, is your grandmother still on her cleaning rampage over there?"

"Yeah," Jack said, ducking his head. He relied a great deal on monosyllables these days, it seemed.

"Well, I wanted to see if you could put some boxes away for me. I got them off the shelf in my closet, and I guess I'm getting to be an old man, Jack, because I can't quite get the oomph to put them back up there."

"Sure, I can help you," Jack said.

Pappa showed Jack the boxes and where he wanted him to put them. As Jack began placing them on the shelf, Pappa brought up the question that had been on his mind.

"So, Jack, Father Delanoit takes you out for supper every now and then, huh?" Pappa said.

"Every other Friday night," Jack said, sounding grim.

"You don't like the man," Pappa said. It was a simple statement of fact, with no implied recrimination or even request for explanation, and because of that, Jack felt no pressure, besides the inevitable knot in his stomach whenever he heard the priest's name.

"No," Jack replied.

"I don't either," Pappa said candidly. He waited a moment, and then softly asked, "Why don't you like him, Jack?"

Pappa watched Jack, observed his facial muscles twitch and his brows furrow. He moistened his lips before answering.

"I don't know. I just… don't like him."

"Have you ever told your grandma or your father how you feel?" Pappa asked.

"She thinks he's God!" Jack yelled. "And Dad… Dad is not around very much," he added wistfully.

"Jack," Pappa said. "Would you rather not go with Father Delanoit any more?"

Jack turned around and looked at him. The look on his great-grandson's face nearly broke the old man's heart. It was as if a mask had fallen off and he was seeing the real Jack for the first time in more than a year. The boy's sweet, hopeful expression strengthened Pappa's resolve to remedy the situation. As quickly as it had vanished, the mask slipped back over Jack's features, replacing the boyish sweetness with a look of moody insolence.

"Yeah, I'd rather not go with him," Jack said sarcastically. "Not that what I want matters. All the boxes are done, Pappa. Can I go home?"

"Sure, Jack. You can go home," Pappa replied, noting the sarcastic tone but choosing to ignore it. "Thanks for helping out an old man. I'll see you at supper, then."

Jack grunted in reply and went back to the house, leaving Pappa to ponder his next move.

Pappa's opportunity came that evening after supper. Mike was home for supper and if he'd been drinking, the effects weren't noticeable. He was alert and lucid, complimenting Lucinda on the roasted chicken and asking Jack about his schoolwork. When the meal was finished, Mike went out to the garage to work on his car and Jack began to help Lucinda clear off the table. It was his night to help with the dishes.

"Here, now," Pappa said. "You helped an old man today. What do you say I take over with the dishes and you go see if your father wants any help with in the garage?"

Jack shot Pappa an appreciative glance, then made a beeline for the garage. He still soaked up his father's attention when he was there to give it, and besides, who wouldn't welcome an opportunity to skip out on the dishes?

Pappa scraped the plates, discarding well-picked chicken bones and the last few bites of mashed potatoes into the garbage, then rinsed the dishes and stacked them. Lucinda finished wrapping up the leftover pieces of chicken, put them in the refrigerator, and filled the dishpan with hot soapy water.

"Nice of you to take over for Jack, Pappa," Lucinda said as she slipped on a pair of rubber gloves and began washing.

"Well, the boy helped me out this afternoon. Gotta give as good as you get, right?" Pappa waited until they were well into their dishwashing rhythm before broaching what he knew would be a tough subject. But then he got straight to the point. "Lucinda, I don't think Jack should go on any more outings with Father Delanoit."

Lucinda dropped the glass she'd been washing (fortunately, plastic) and looked at Pappa in surprise. The tone in his voice was one she seldom heard. He'd used the same strong, authoritative tone when he'd told her he didn't think she should marry Doug Walters.

"Why on earth would you say that, Pappa?" she said in amazement. She knew he was not an especially religious man, but this seemed most peculiar.

"Because, Lucinda, the boy is very unhappy, as you can plainly see."

"Well, Pappa, you know as well as I do, you can't always allow children to do whatever they please. Spending one-on-one time with the priest, that is such an honor, and a help in developing the boy's faith," Lucinda said.

"Lucinda, be honest. Has Jack's faith grown since this Father Delanoit began taking such an interest in him? Is he more religious? Is he better behaved?"

Lucinda had no reply.

"Jack has been in more trouble this past year than in all the first twelve years of his life combined. Jack is not the happy boy he used to be, Lucinda, and it's not just growing pains. Spending time with Father Delanoit is not doing Jack any good, and it's time we put a stop to it."

"Pappa, I know Jack has been a little testy lately, but maybe if Father Delanoit could just work with him a little bit longer, he'd …"

"He'd what? Go completely crazy, like Rose Castani's boy did? Lucinda, you have to look at the facts. Jack is miserable when he goes with Father Delanoit. He is even more miserable when he comes home. The time to end this is now," Pappa said.

"But why on earth would he so much dislike Father Delanoit?" Lucinda asked, genuinely perplexed.

Though Pappa had begun to form a shadowy suspicion, he kept silent. For now.

"That doesn't matter," he said. His voice softened as he added, "What matters is that we do what's best for our Jack, Lucinda. And what's best for our Jack is that these dinners, these meetings with Father Delanoit end."

Once, over fifty years ago, Lucinda had balked at Pappa's advice, choosing to believe that she was in love, choosing to believe that Doug loved her as much as she loved him, and that their love would never die. Ignoring Pappa had proven to be a huge mistake, although she at least did get her beautiful Rita out of the deal. But this time, Pappa's words resonated with something deep inside her, and she realized that she had never really been at ease with sending Jack off with Father Delanoit, although she couldn't imagine why.

"What will we tell Father Delanoit?" she said, somewhat fearfully.

"Simple enough, Tell him your old, doddering father is taking up more and more of your time, and you need Jack at home to help you out, so thanks but no thanks to the good Father Delanoit and his generosity," Pappa said, taking a page from Rose Castani's script. If it were his call, Pappa would favor calling up the priest and telling him to jump off a cliff. He didn't know what was going on, but he did know that something was wrong, something far more serious than adolescent angst or rebellion against authority. But Pappa knew that Lucinda would need a tactful way to end the Friday night outings, so he offered her one.

"Well, I guess that would work. Maybe we should have Father Delanoit over for supper so I could explain it to him," she said.

Pappa's initial reaction was to tell her just to call him on the phone and be done with it. But maybe this would be better, Pappa thought. He would like to have the opportunity to watch Delanoit when Lucinda told him their decision so he could gage the priest's reactions. While Pappa didn't want Jack to have to be around the man any more than necessary, if he could watch their interactions, perhaps he could figure out what was going on.

"Yes, invite the good Father over," Pappa said. "But stay strong, Lucinda. He may try to get you to change your mind. Remember, we need to do what's right for Jack, not try to make Father Delanoit happy."

"Honestly, Pappa, you make it sound like he's....like he's practically the devil," Lucinda said worriedly.

"I don't know what the man is, Lucinda. All I know is, I do not want him taking my great-grandson anywhere again," Pappa said with finality.

Chapter Nine

Lucinda hung the new green guest towel in the bathroom, tossing the slightly tattered everyday towel into the wicker hamper. Then, with a practiced eye, she surveyed the room and nodded, satisfied. Every stray hair had been banished, the toilet, tub and sink sparkled, and the mirror was shiny. Since this was the last room she needed to clean, Lucinda decided to give herself the luxury of sitting down for a cup of tea before she began to cook supper.

As the water heated, Lucinda went over her mental checklist for the evening's meal. She was serving beef stroganoff, just as she had the first time Father Delanoit came to dinner. Yesterday she'd washed her perfectly clean good china and glassware and polished the silver, so all she needed to do was set the table. Mike, who agreed that Jack's visits with the priest should come to an end, had promised to be here for dinner. And Jack… Jack's relief was palpable when Lucinda had told him of the decision to terminate his Friday night get-togethers with Father Delanoit. Lucinda thought Jack might want to get out of tonight's gathering, but he seemed to be almost looking forward to it. More and more, Lucinda knew that they had made the right decision. Why, then, did she feel so apprehensive about telling Father Delanoit?

She had actually rehearsed what she wanted to say in front of the mirror.

"Father Delanoit, we are so grateful for all that you've done for Jack," she had practiced, but then a voice inside practically shouted, "Quit fawning over him, you sap!"

"Okay, okay then," she had mumbled to herself. Try it again, Lucinda, she thought. "Father Delanoit, we appreciate the time you've given to Jack, but since my father has moved here with us and David is off to college, I really need Jack to stick around home a little more and help me out. We've decided to keep Jack home on Friday nights now. But we do thank you for your kind interest in our family."

Sounds reasonable, she thought to herself.

The copper kettle whistled and steamed. Lucinda poured the boiling water over her tea bag and mentally re-rehearsed her speech. After a couple of minutes, she set the tea bag onto a saucer to use again the next day, then took her tea into the living room and settled into the rocking chair.

Relax, Lucinda, she told herself. Like Pappa said, Father Delanoit is just a human being like everybody else. She took a deep breath and released it. Slowly sipping her tea, she deliberately turned her mind to other matters: David's visit home next week, their upcoming trip to Cleveland to visit Sheila and her family, her plans to wash the windows the next day if the warm weather lasted.

Four hours later, Mike, Pappa, Lucinda, Jack and Father Delanoit gathered around the old wooden table. Mike had brought home a bottle of wine, but at least he had started out the evening sober. Pappa was entertaining them with stories about growing up in the village in Italy, and Father Delanoit was listening attentively. And Jack looked happier than he had in a long time, though he still put on a mask of casual indifference when anybody addressed him directly.

"So Father Delanoit," Pappa said, "where did you serve before you came to St. Maria Goretti's?"

"I served at Holy Family Church in Peoria, and before that I was in Atlanta, Georgia," he replied as he helped himself to another one of Lucinda's buttery crescent rolls. "But I've been here in Hook's Point for almost ten years now."

"Didn't you tell us that you were at St. Mary's in Chicago, Father?" Lucinda asked. "I remember when you told me that, I was thinking I'd have to be sure and tell Pappa you had a Chicago connection."

Father Delanoit drew his grey-flecked eyebrows together and frowned. His eyes looked angry, only briefly, but long enough for Pappa to notice and file that reaction away.

"Yes, I did serve at St. Mary's. I'm afraid I wasn't really there long enough to make many connections, though. You know, the diocese likes to keep the priests moving, especially when they're young."

"Father Delanoit, you may have wondered why we asked you to supper tonight," Lucinda began. "I just wanted… we wanted to tell you we really have appreciated the interest you've shown in our Jack."

Pappa saw Jack's mask of indifference slip ever so slightly. The boy cringed, and then quickly arranged his features into their usual look of apathy. 'I'm not here,' his face seemed to say. 'You can't touch me.' Pappa wondered why that particular phrase struck him in the gut when he looked at his great-grandson.

"But now with David away at seminary, and Mike works late so many evenings, and my father living here now, well, I need Jack to stay home a little more. We're going to have to cancel your Friday evening get-togethers, I'm afraid," Lucinda said apologetically.

"Of course," Father Delanoit said smoothly. "Family matters take precedence, that's natural. Jack and I have had some very interesting talks, and I hate to see that end, but I fully understand. Perhaps, Jack, you can stop by the rectory occasionally. If I'm available, I'll give you a ride in the Riviera," he said, smiling beneficently like a loving uncle. For some reason, Pappa felt like striking the man.

Jack blushed, then felt furious with himself for betraying emotion. Almost there, he reminded himself. It's almost over. He saw no reason to reply, for it really wasn't a question. He just looked down at his plate and pierced a piece of beef with his fork, though he didn't bring it to his mouth.

"About that Riviera, Father: can I ask how much you gave for that?" Mike said, steering the conversation into a more comfortable territory.

Father Delanoit and Mike talked cars while Lucinda began to clear the table. Jack picked up the almost-empty bowl of stroganoff and the cleaned-out salad dish and followed her into the kitchen. As they stood together by the sink, Lucinda put her hand on Jack's shoulder. Since his latest growth spurt, she had to reach up to touch him, for he towered over her by a good four inches, not that she attempted to very often because he usually shrugged her hand away. But this time he just smiled, a look of gratitude sweeping over his face.

"Thanks, Grandma," he said softly.

If Lucinda had any doubts about her decision, Jack's actions dispelled them. She quickly hugged him and just as quickly, released him, not wanting to push her luck. As soon as they walked back into the dining room to finish clearing off the table, Jack again cloaked his face with that mask of indifference. At least now, Lucinda knew that the boy was still in there, behind the mask, and occasionally reachable.

After they'd finished clearing the table, Lucinda brought out apple pie and coffee. They discussed all the news at St. Maria's, the Chicago Cubs and their latest win against the St. Louis Cardinals, and the upcoming city council elections. Finally, Father Delanoit pushed back his chair.

"Mrs. Walters, that was a delicious meal. I thank you all for inviting me to your home," he said.

"Well, you are most welcome, Father," Lucinda said.

"And Jack, be sure to help your grandmother, won't you," he said, without really waiting for an answer. "I've certainly enjoyed our Friday evenings, but I know you need to be there for your family. I'll see you all on Sunday at Mass," he said as he rose to leave.

Mike walked him to the door, engaging him with another question about his Riviera. He closed the door behind Father Delanoit, and then rejoined Pappa at the table. Lucinda and Jack had retreated to the kitchen, and Mike heard the sound of clattering dishes and running water.

"What do you make of that guy?" Mike asked Pappa.

"Cold. Very cold. He's got all the right words, but there's something funny about the man," Pappa said. "I wouldn't want to play poker with him. He'd rob you blind and never bat an eye."

"That's kind of my impression," Mike said. "Well, he's out of our lives now." Rising, he added, "Hey, I'm going to go out and work on my car awhile. Thanks for convincing Lucinda to do this, Pappa. I… I never could quite put my finger on why I don't like the man. But I don't."

While Lucinda and Jack were washing the dishes, Mike was sipping whiskey in his garage, and Pappa was going over the evening's events in his mind, Father Delanoit was on his way back to the rectory, driving a little too fast. The Hook's Point police force was familiar with his car, though, and knew who was behind the wheel. They weren't about to pull him over for any minor violations, he knew. As he sped down the road, Father Delanoit silently cursed the O'Donnell/Gargano clan, especially the old man, Lucinda's father. They weren't aware of his special arrangement with Jack, the priest recognized, or the evening would have unfolded quite differently, he knew from instinct as well as experience. But the old man suspected, Father Delanoit was sure of it, and the old man wielded more influence in that family than the boy's father did.

Disgusting drunkard! Why, Father Delanoit had done the boy a favor. No one ever showed Jack any affection or paid him any attention until he came on the scene. The boy should be grateful, instead of acting like a whipped puppy.

Maybe it was just as well. Since he had first gotten to know Jack, the boy had shot up a good six inches and completely lost that look of child-like innocence. Now Jack's face was slender, his body beginning to fill out, his voice deepening. It was somewhat disgusting, really.

Father Delanoit was ready to move on. And he would be training a new group of altar boys very shortly, anyway. No doubt a suitable substitute for Jack would enter his life before long.

Chapter Ten

When Jack entered the eighth grade, he was the tallest boy in the class. He looked sixteen instead of barely fourteen, and he bore a striking resemblance to Rita, with the same strong, attractive features. He could have his pick of any of the girls in class, and many of them tried hard to get his attention, but he wasn't interested. The only girl who mattered to him was Kelly.

Kelly had remained a steadfast friend throughout all the turmoil of his seventh-grade school year. While Jack was incredibly relieved not to have to spend time alone with Father Delanoit any more, he had no illusions about his life going back to normal.

Jack was a different person, and he knew that. No longer did he look at the world with a child's hopeful innocence. He knew full well what kind of monsters lurked behind the most benign exteriors, and he knew just how ugly life could be. Worst of all, there was not a soul he could share these things with. Who would understand? Who would even believe him? Sometimes he felt as if there were a monster inside of him now. Not that he wanted to do to anybody what Father Delanoit had done to him. He didn't. What Jack wanted to do, sometimes, was to blow up the whole world and everyone in it. The depth of his rage terrified him.

Jack got into several smaller skirmishes and three real fights during seventh grade, one of which he provoked with an eighth-grader just so he could release some of the rage he felt without risking doing any real harm to anybody else. The eighth-grader, a big streetwise boy named Mark Malone, hadn't really wanted to fight him, but Jack had goaded him until he had no choice but to fight or lose face. Jack went home with two black eyes, but at least he felt some relief.

And at school, Jack got into trouble with Miss Hightower on a fairly regular basis. He would space off in class and, if she spoke sharply in an attempt at getting his attention, Jack often responded with an edge in his voice which was simply unacceptable to the strict teacher. Sometimes he had to stay after school and a couple of times, Mike had to come in and talk to Miss Hightower and reassure her that he would make Jack behave better. In fact, these meetings with school personnel were so uncomfortable for Mike, bringing back memories of his own difficult school days, that he would usually stop at the bar afterwards. By the time he made it home, any admonishments Mike might have given Jack were long forgotten.

But through it all, Kelly had been like an anchor for Jack. He drifted into deep, muddy waters and thrashed about in the turbulent waves, but because of her, he managed to stay afloat, though just barely at times. Jack could be sitting in class, ready to explode because of some nasty remark that Ronny Slater or one of his buddies made under their breath, or because Miss Hightower was getting ready to chew him out, but then he'd catch a glimpse of Kelly's face, all sweet concern, and his anger would dissipate. He hated to disappoint Kelly even more than he hated to disappoint his grandmother.

Jack still went over to Kelly's house so they could work on school assignments together. He'd been afraid that Kelly's mother would hear about all the trouble he'd gotten into and make Kelly stay away from him, but so far she hadn't. She still acted just as nice as always, greeting Jack and asking how his family was, sometimes bringing out a plate of cookies for them to munch on. Kelly's little brother Bill had started to hang out with them sometimes, too. At first, Jack thought he was a little annoying, but it was obvious that Bill fairly adored Jack. When Jack grew his hair longer, Bill pestered his mother until she let him grow his out, too. And when Jack mentioned that the Cubs were his favorite baseball team, Bill soon began sporting a Cubs jersey, though until then, he'd been a diehard Minnesota Twins fan. Jack soon warmed up to the little guy. Evidently, Bill missed having a father figure in the house, and if Jack could help a little bit, he was glad to do it. Though he had a hard time believing that anybody would look up to him, Bill clearly did, so Jack tried to live up to his expectations.

That's why Jack got worried when Kelly told him that Bill was slated to start altar boy practice with Father Delanoit in October. Jack had always figured he was the only kid that Father Delanoit had done what he did to, that there was something wrong with him, some reason he'd been the one targeted. But the possibility occurred to him that Father Delanoit might do the same thing to Bill that he'd done to Jack, and he couldn't ignore it.

That fear was in the back of Jack's mind as he and Kelly sat at the table in her dining room on the first Thursday in October, working on math, which was one class where Kelly had a definite advantage. She was patiently explaining how to add fractions with different denominators when Bill bounced into the room, looking for all the world as if he might explode.

"Hey, look what I got in the mail from Uncle Tim! A Yogi Berra!" For Bill, an avid baseball card collector and New York Yankees fan, this was indeed manna from heaven.

"That's neat, man!" Jack said.

Bill raced off to his room to put the card into his folder.

The two eighth-graders smiled at each other, remembering how it was when they were younger and hadn't yet learned to hide their enthusiasms under the cover of being "cool." Jack's smile faded, though, as the fear again entered his mind that Bill could become Father Delanoit's next victim.

Maybe he won't be, Jack reasoned. Maybe it'll be okay.

But then Bill came back downstairs, carrying part of his card collection in a long, narrow box.

"I won't be home right after school tomorrow, Kelly," he said.

"Father Delanoit wants me to stop over at the rectory and show him my cards. I was telling some of the guys about my Yogi Berra after altar boy practice, and he heard me. Father's a Yankees fan, too," Bill said with his usual enthusiasm. But when he saw Jack glaring at him, his face red and contorted, Bill dropped the box, scattering his cards all over the floor and then staggered backwards in shock. Jack looked like a raging bull.

"Jack, what's wrong?" Kelly said.

"He is NOT going to the rectory to see Father Delanoit! He can't!" Jack shouted, rising up in his chair and pounding the table with his fists.

Bill burst into tears and ran from the room, not even pausing to pick up his treasured cards. For the first time in their relationship, Jack saw Kelly look at him with anger.

"What's the matter with you, scaring my brother like that, Jack?"

"Scaring your brother! Scaring your brother? If that bastard gets his filthy hands on Bill, then he'll find out what being scared is all about!" Jack yelled. His lips trembled treacherously as he tried to gain control over himself. "Kelly, you can't let Bill go with Father Delanoit. You just can't."

Kelly looked at him, more puzzled than angry. Jack had a bad temper, she knew, but he'd never shown that side to her before. Why was he so upset? What was he talking about, calling the priest a bastard? (Wasn't that some kind of special mortal sin?)

"What's going on, Jack?" she asked him. "What is it about Father Delanoit that makes you so upset?" She'd seen it before, when Father Delanoit would visit their classroom and Jack would tense up. It was on those days, after he'd seen Father Delanoit, that Jack would often get in trouble with Miss Hightower for some minor transgression, mouthing off to her if she corrected him. And she'd noticed the look on Jack's face when he served Mass with Father Delanoit, a mixture of fear and revulsion. What was the deal?

"I...I..." Jack stared at the table. He spoke so softly that Kelly had to strain to hear him. "Father Delanoit... he touched me, Kelly. And he... he made me touch him." He looked up at Kelly, terrified of what his revelation would do to their friendship, to the way Kelly felt about him, but even more afraid of what would happen if he didn't tell her.

"He... he touched you? You mean, uh, *there*?" Kelly was incredulous. This was so out of her sphere of knowledge.

"Yes." Then the tears which Jack had been holding back for almost two years began to seep out. He sat down at the table and wept, his shoulders shuddering. After a moment, he struggled to regain control. Kelly had left the room, and Jack was afraid that she was so repulsed by what he had told her that she couldn't stand to be in the same room with him, but then she came back with a tall glass of water and some tissues, which she sat in front of him.

She looked at him gravely.

"So that's why you hate Father Delanoit," she said simply.

"That's why I hate Father Delanoit. And that's why Bill can't go with him. He can't, Kelly. You've got to get your mother to say he can't go. But don't tell her about me," Jack urged. "Don't tell anybody, Kelly. Please."

Jack looked so miserable at the possibility that his secret would get out that Kelly agreed not to tell anyone. She was still in shock, trying to come to terms with what had happened to Jack and how close her own brother had come to suffering the same fate.

"Oh, Jack," she said, suddenly aware of how costly this revelation had been for him. She got up and put her arms around him, gently kissing his forehead the way her mother did when she or her brother was sick. "I'm so sorry this happened to you."

Then Jack began to cry in earnest, great ugly sobs that racked his body. He clung to Kelly like a drowning man holding on to a life raft. Kelly held him while he cried, and when Bill stuck his head in the doorway, she shook her head and motioned for him to leave them alone. Finally, Jack's sobs subsided, and Kelly sat down in the chair beside him. He took a tissue, wiped off his face and blew his nose.

"It's the worst thing that happened to me in my life, Kelly. I....sometimes, I just hate myself and want to die," he said, his voice so low she had to strain to hear him. "I've even thought about killing myself. I... I couldn't just stand there and watch Bill go through the same thing."

"No," Kelly said. "I know you couldn't. Jack, please, don't say that ever again."

"About Father Delanoit touching me?" he asked, again afraid he'd ruined their relationship with his disclosure.

"No. About killing yourself. About wanting to die. Jack..." This time it was Kelly's voice that broke. Tears ran down her cheeks as she continued, "Jack, I... I love you. I couldn't stand it if you...you weren't here."

Jack looked at Kelly in amazement. Her blue eyes brimming with tears shimmered like a lake reflecting the sun's light. As soon as she spoke those words, the boulder that had covered Jack's heart for almost two years was pushed away, and he felt a rush of light, of hope, of love even. He turned to her, looked into her eyes and saw himself reflected back, not as the damaged, worthless piece of junk he felt he was, but as a whole person. He put his arms around her and kissed her full, pink lips. She tasted of strawberries. He kissed her again, and she kissed him back. Then they pulled apart and laughed, both struck giddy by the strange turn of events.

"What the heck is going on in there?" Bill demanded.

The sight of Bill standing there, confusion all over his chubby, earnest face, set them off again into fits of laughter. They laughed until tears ran down their cheeks, but finally the laughter subsided and Kelly remembered the problem with Bill and Father Delanoit.

"Bill," she said, "Jack didn't mean to scare you before. It's just that... well, Father Delanoit treated Jack badly, and he doesn't want you to get hurt the same way. I'm going to tell Mom, and I'm telling you now, I don't want you to go to see Father Delanoit tomorrow. You can't be alone with him, Bill."

"Why not! He just wants to look at my baseball cards, Kelly. What's the big deal about that?" he insisted.

"You just can't, that's all," she said. "Now, go to your room for a little bit, or go outside and play. I need to talk to Jack alone a minute."

"I'm sorry I yelled at you, buddy," Jack said. "I… I didn't mean to scare you."

"That's okay. But I still don't see what's the big deal about me showing the priest a few baseball cards," Bill said.

"Well, you're just going to have to trust me on that," Kelly said. Still looking confused, Bill grabbed his jacket and headed outside. Kelly waited until she heard the door close behind him to speak again.

"Jack, I don't know what to tell my mother," Kelly said. "She's going to think my not wanting Bill to go to the rectory is just as strange as Bill did. Jack… I really think you ought to tell somebody about this. Somebody in authority."

"No!" he said loudly. Determined not to lose control again, Jack took a deep breath. "I can't. I can't stand having people know about it, Kelly. Not everybody's going to be like you, Kelly. Father Delanoit always told me that nobody would believe me, and he's probably right."

"No, he's not! I believe you!" Kelly said. "And I'm sure my mother would, too. So would your family, Jack."

Jack felt dizzy, light-headed. Having his family learn about this had always been his biggest fear. What would his father say? His grandmother? No, Jack couldn't face his family if they knew what Father Delanoit had done to him.

"No," he said firmly. "I can't tell my family. If you think the only way to make sure your mother doesn't let Bill go with that bastard, then you can tell her, but only if she won't tell my family, Kelly. Otherwise, we're going to have to make up some story." Jack had gotten to be pretty good at that over the last two years, he reflected ruefully.

"But Jack, even if we keep Father Delanoit away from my brother, what about the next little kid out there, some kid who doesn't have anybody to warn him about Father Delanoit?" Kelly spoke the truth that Jack had, up until this point, been able to push out of his consciousness.

"I…I know, I know," Jack said miserably. "Last year, when Pappa convinced my Grandma to quit letting me go with Father Delanoit, I was so relieved. But after a while, in a little corner of my mind, I thought… maybe there was some other kid going through what I had. But I didn't know what to do."

"Jack, I really think you should tell your family. I'll go with you. You won't have to do this alone. But I really think you should tell them."

Jack studied his hands. Maybe Kelly was right. But he still couldn't stand the thought of people knowing what had happened to him.

As if she'd read his mind, Kelly said, "Your family is not going to think any less of you because of this, Jack. I don't, and neither will they. Father Delanoit should not be getting away with this, Jack. He should have to pay for what he's done to you."

Justice meted out to Father Delanoit: how many times Jack had imagined that very thing, delivered in any number of ways, most of which involved a lot of blood and guts. Jack's lips twisted in an angry smile.

"Yes, he should pay. But, even if my family believes me..."

"They will!" Kelly insisted.

"Even if they do, nobody else is going to take my word over a priest's. That's what Father Delanoit always told me, and I'll bet that's true. He's a big man around town, always schmoozing with the rich people, the guys that own the town, Kelly. Half the people at St. Maria's think he's the next thing to God. And who am I, Kelly?"

"You're Jack O'Donnell," she said. "You're just as good as anybody else, Jack. That's one thing my mother made sure that Bill and I both understood: there may be plenty of people with more money than we have, but we're just as worthwhile as anybody else. She always told me nobody's better than anybody else in the eyes of God."

"In the eyes of God, maybe, but most people don't think that way," Jack said. "Money talks in this town."

"Still, Jack, I think you need to do the right thing. I think you need to speak up," Kelly said.

"Kelly," Jack began, again struggling to maintain control, "that's easy for you to say. You aren't the one he did it to. You aren't the one... I...I can still feel his hands on me... it makes me sick to think about it. Let alone tell anybody."

"Maybe if you tell, it'll help make those thoughts go away," she said softly. "At least, he won't be able to do it to somebody else."

"I know," Jack said. He sat up straight and squared his shoulders. "Let's do it, then. Let's go now, while I have the guts to do it."

"I've got to watch Bill... but, wait, I'll see if he can play at his friend Tom's house until I get home. Okay, I'll call over there and then I'll go with you," she said. She quickly dialed their number and spoke to Tom's mother, who told her that was fine, Bill was no trouble at all. So Kelly grabbed her coat and Jack gathered up his books, and they headed outside to tell Bill to stay over at Tom's until Kelly came home. Then they walked the seven blocks to Jack's house, the silence broken only by the crunching of the leaves under their feet and the occasional rush of the wind.

When they approached the house, Jack looked at his home and shuddered, dreading what he had to do. Kelly took his hand and squeezed it. Strengthened by the warmth of her hand in his, Jack proceeded to the front walkway. Then he turned to Kelly and spoke for the first time since they'd left her house.

"Kelly, thanks for coming with me, but this is something I've got to do by myself," Jack said. He bent down to kiss her softly on the cheek.

"Are you sure, Jack?" she asked.

"Yes. I am. But I'll call you later," he said. Then he strode determinedly up the sidewalk and in the door before he had the chance to change his mind.

Chapter Eleven

When Jack walked in the door, he found his father, his grandmother and his great-grandfather gathered around the table. They were just about to begin eating a simple supper of chipped beef on toast and canned peaches. The three of them looked up, surprised.

"Jack, I thought you were eating at your friend Kelly's house," Lucinda said. "Sit down, dear, I'll set you a place," she said as she stood.

"No, Grandma, I don't want anything to eat. I… I came home because I have to tell you all something," Jack said.

Mike put down his fork, startled by Jack's tone. Pappa noticed that the boy appeared much older all of a sudden and realized he was catching a glimpse of the man Jack would one day become.

"What is it, Jack," Lucinda asked, fearing his answer.

"It's about Father Delanoit. I've got to tell you something. When I first started as an altar boy, Father Delanoit…. Well, he acted real nice at first, like he was my friend and then… and now, he's acting the same way with Kelly's little brother Bill, and I can't just stand by and let him…" Jack's courage faltered and Pappa saw he no longer looked like a man, but a little boy weighted down with something too heavy for him to carry.

"What is it, son?" Pappa encouraged him. He stood up and

began to approach the boy, but Jack took a step backwards.

"No! Just let me say it! He molested me, all right? Father Delanoit molested me!" Jack shouted.

"He did what?" Lucinda said, incredulous. This was impossible! Child molesters were leering men in trench coats who hung out in the alleys, not respected members of the community. Not men of the clergy. Not Father Delanoit.

"He molested me, Grandma! He...he touched me, and he made me touch him," Jack said. He began shaking, tears running down his face. "Every time he took me with him. Every time! He said not to tell anybody, or I'd get sent to reform school, because I punched Ronny Slater in the sacristy."

"You hit Ronny Slater at church?" Lucinda said. She realized as she spoke that this was the least important part of what Jack was telling her, but she simply couldn't get her mind around the rest of it.

"Yes, I hit Ronny Slater, because he called Dad a drunk."

Mike and Lucinda exchanged shocked glances while Pappa listened, quietly taking it all in.

"So Father Delanoit caught us, and he was real nice and said Ronny deserved it, but later he said I'd get sent to reform school if anybody found out. And he said nobody'd believe me, anyway. But you... you have to believe me, because now he's going to start in on Bill if you don't," Jack said.

"I believe you, son," Pappa said gravely. "Something about that man seemed suspicious the first time I met him."

"So that's why... that's why you didn't want to go with him on Friday nights, Jack?" Lucinda said, the horrible truth meeting the spot in her soul where she'd always known that something was wrong with Father Delanoit's interest in Jack. "He was doing this to you all that time, and I never knew! I made you go with him! Oh, baby!" Lucinda moved over to him and folded him into her arms, their tears mingling as she wept with the knowledge that she had been complicit in her grandson's abuse.

"Jack, I'm so sorry! I should have seen something was wrong, I should have known," she said, wracked with guilt. "I knew you didn't want to go, and yet I made you go with that… that monster!"

They clung to each other for a moment, then Jack said softly, "You got mad at me when I didn't want to go. After a while, I just…kind of gave up."

"Oh, Jack!" Lucinda wept, appalled at her blind faith in the man who had abused her grandson. Her boy.

Mike finally spoke.

"You're acting like all this is your fault, Lucinda," he said. "But I'm the boy's father. It was up to me to protect him, but I… I failed him." Mike remembered his promise to Rita, to take good care of their sons, and his heart filled with shame when he considered how he'd neglected to live up to his words, more concerned with anesthetizing his own pain than being the father his boys needed. David had somehow gotten by unscathed, but Jack had fallen prey to a monster, and all because Mike had been negligent. But no more, he vowed.

"That son of a bitch is going to pay for this, I swear to God!" Mike headed for the back door.

"Wait, Mike! What are you going to do?" Lucinda cried.

"What I should have done a long time ago. Take care of my son." With that, he walked out the house and jumped into his car.

Driving cautiously, Mike kept his anger at a low simmer, determined to maintain control over himself. Even though he hadn't been drinking much yet that day, his vision was blurry and his temples were pounding. Jack's words were a broken record, playing over and over again in his mind. He longed for the obliteration that only alcohol could provide, but Mike had taken his last drink of booze. He was dead serious this time. Never again would he fail to protect his children because he was too inebriated to see the danger that was befalling them, he swore it. Whatever it took, Mike O'Donnell had taken his last drink.

The sunset was spectacular as he drove up to the rectory, the sky ablaze with orange and pink and dusky purple light. As Mike parked in front of the building, the thought flashed through his mind that this was where it had happened, where that bastard in a frock had worked his perversions on his son. The revolting realization brought his simmering anger to a full boil. Mike grimly approached the rectory and pressed the doorbell. A full three minutes passed before Mrs. McGrevey opened the door.

"Yes?" she said, suspiciously looking at Mike. She'd never seen him at the priests' home before, and seldom enough at church, even. Her squinty eyes looked small in her round, flushed face. She used her considerable bulk to block the entryway, but Mike was not about to be deterred.

"Excuse me, ma'am," Mike said, carefully but firmly pushing his way past the housekeeper.

"Wait just one minute, now!" she sputtered. "You can't come bursting in here like that! Why, the priests are having their dinner, now!"

Mike walked down the hallway, glancing into the comfortable living area and into the study, continuing to the end of the hall. On the left was the kitchen and on the right he found Father Delanoit and Father Schmidt sitting at opposite ends of a dining room table, plates of steaming food in front of them. Both men looked up in surprise at the unexpected visitor.

"Mr. O' Donnell," Father Schmidt said, recognizing the father of David O'Donnell, who was planning to enter the priesthood. "Is there some kind of a problem?" he asked, genuine concern on his kind young face.

"Yes, Father, there is some kind of a problem alright," Mike said, his voice dangerously low, deceptively calm. "But maybe your good friend here would like to tell you just what kind of problem we have," he said, his eyes revealing the depth of his anger as he glared at Father Delanoit.

"Why, no, Mr. O'Donnell, I'm not sure that we have a problem at all," Father Delanoit said. "Oh. Oh, my," he said, his voice dripping with sympathy, "did Jack get into some more trouble, now?" Turning to Father Schmidt, he said, "You know David's younger brother? The boy does seem to like to settle matters with his fists. Not quite the boy for the books that his brother was. School seems to frustrate him, poor boy." As he spoke, he gave Mike a sympathetic look which seemed to say, 'like father, like son.' Mike felt that old shame rise up automatically, but he pressed ahead.

"No, Father, Jack is not in any trouble at school. As a matter of fact, the boy is very good with the books—brought home three A's on his last report card," Mike said. Not that he recalled seeing Jack's last report card, but if the boy hadn't gotten three A's, Mike was sure he was capable of it. He wasn't about to allow this wily bastard to sidetrack him or scapegoat his son. "No, the trouble is not with school. It's you," he said, standing squarely in front of Father Delanoit, who had turned to look at Mike when he came in the room.

"I'm sorry, Father Delanoit, the man just burst in here, pushed right around me, he did, actin' like he owns the place," sputtered Mrs. McGrevey, who'd followed Mike into the dining room, her chin stuck out like a pugnacious bulldog.

"You filthy son of a bitch!" Mike roared into the priest's face. "My family welcomed you into our home, my mother-in-law looked at you like you were the next thing to God Almighty, and all the while you were using my son to satisfy your sick perversions! And you, a man of the cloth!"

Father Delanoit sat, unnaturally calm under the circumstances, Father Schmidt would later note. The younger priest, however, was shocked. What in heaven's name could Mr. O'Donnell be talking about? He'd known David's father to be unreligious, but to come into the rectory and actually curse at a priest? And what did he mean, perversions? A cold dark fear, a realization, began to form in Schmitty's heart.

"Talkin' to a priest in that vile manner! My God, man, what's wrong with you? Do you want me to call the police, Father?" Mrs. McGrevey asked.

"By all means, Father!" Mike fairly spat the words out. "Have your bodyguard here call the police, and we can tell them how you put your filthy hands on a twelve-year-old boy!"

Finally, Father Delanoit looked as if he was engaging with the situation. An uncharacteristically kind expression spread over his cool features, and he finally spoke, his voice soft in contrast with Mike's belligerent shouting.

"I think I do know what this is all about now, Mr. O'Donnell," he said. "Some time ago Jack got into a fight in the sacristy with another boy, Matt Slater's son. I agreed to give the boy another chance, but Jack keeps getting into fights, provoking problems with his teachers. We try to consider the boy's background, losing his mother so young, and, quite frankly, we're concerned about the effect your drinking has had on Jack. Sometimes he's just not very truthful. Often times boys will tell the most preposterous tales to get the spotlight off themselves."

"You! You call yourself a man of God!" Mike bellowed. "Trying to turn this around… what you are, Delanoit, is a devil!" And with that, Mike pulled the priest out of his chair, drew back his fist and punched him in the face.

Mayhem descended as Father Delanoit stumbled, caught himself and responded by throwing a punch to Mike's midsection, Mrs. McGrevey again threatened to call the police yet stayed rooted to where she stood in the doorway, her eyes gleaming at the unexpected excitement, and Father Schmidt moved towards the two men, pleading for them to stop.

Mike doubled over, then stood up and pushed Father Delanoit against the wall.

"I ought to kill you for what you did to my son, but I'm not going to, because you're right about one thing, I've not been the best example, but that's changing. And I'll not risk going to jail over the likes of you!" Mike said. "I just want you to know, if you ever come near Jack again, you ever touch him again, you will regret it. And that's a vow, Father Delanoit," Mike said, then spat on the floor. He turned and walked out of the rectory, leaving the three others standing together in stunned silence.

Father Delanoit was the first to break the quiet.

"The man has obviously gone over the edge, ruined his brain with all the booze he's consumed," he said. While he was trying hard to regain his usual cool, detached stance, Father Delanoit's face looked pinched and his voice was shaky.

"What in God's name was Mike O'Donnell talking about?" Schmitty said. "Perversions? Touching his son? What's this about?"

"Surely you don't mean the man's convinced you to go along with his insane ramblings, do you?" Father Delanoit said, glaring at the younger priest, his eyes blazing.

"I just want to know what the devil he's talking about, that's all," Schmitty said. "I know you befriended Jack O'Donnell a couple of years back, right around the time I was counseling his brother about entering the priesthood. Didn't you take the boy out for meals, riding in your car?"

"I did what I've tried to do ever since I entered the priesthood: taken a boy from an underprivileged background and given him a little bit of interest and attention, which is more than his drunken father ever does. I don't like the tone of this conversation, Father Schmidt," the older priest said.

"I don't like it either, but you really haven't answered my question. What is Mike O'Donnell talking about?" Schmitty insisted.

"I don't have the faintest idea," Father Delanoit replied. "Just as I told Mr. O'Donnell, perhaps Jack is lashing out because he wants to deflect attention from himself and the trouble he's been getting into as of late. Now, if you'll excuse me, I'm going to the washroom, and then I'm going to come back down and continue with the meal that was so rudely interrupted." He walked to the doorway, and then turned to address Father Schmidt again before he left the room.

"I've had the distinct impression that you were trying to interrogate me just now, Father Schmidt. Kindly recall that I am your superior and that certain standards of behavior are expected from you. Including loyalty," Father Delanoit said. "This discussion is closed. And, my dear Mrs. McGrevey, I would like to request that this incident not be brought up outside of these four walls. We don't want a scandal breaking out in the church, especially right before the annual fundraising drive. No point in driving down the donations, all because of some ridiculous accusations."

Mrs. McGrevey, still stunned into an uncharacteristic silence, busied herself by straightening the table settings, picking up a picture that had been knocked off the wall during the skirmish, and fetching a wet washrag to clean the spot on the floor where Mike had spat.

"Nasty stuff," she muttered to herself as she wiped the floor, and Schmitty wondered if she was talking about the sputum or the allegations.

The young priest was shaken to the core of his being. His vocation was driven by a desire to serve God by sacrificially loving his people, and the possibility that someone would use his position to harm a child was totally beyond his comprehension. While he'd much rather think that Mike O'Donnell was deluded, as Father Delanoit insisted, Schmitty knew that he had to find out for himself what really had happened. He would say no more tonight, but tomorrow he would look into this. He would start by talking to Jack himself.

Father Delanoit carefully washed his face and hands at the bathroom sink, looking at his reflection in the mirror as he scrubbed himself. He noted his impenetrable look of dignity, only slightly marred by the angry red mark appearing on his cheek where Mike O'Donnell had hit him; he observed the even, handsome features, the well-groomed graying hair, and he was reassured. No one of any consequence was going to believe Mike O'Donnell's story. He was quite sure of that. Father Delanoit had been down this road before.

He recalled the angry sputters, the hysterical outbursts of a widow in Atlanta, the divorcee in Peoria, the unwed mother in Chicago. While the situation in Chicago had been a little dicey for a while, eventually it had all worked out. For Father Delanoit, that is. A grim frown crossed his face as he remembered "the situation," as he'd come to call it. A boy dead at 15. Hanged himself. A shame, but then again, there was no room in this world for weakness, Father Delanoit had reasoned. Still, he sighed deeply, remembering Charles. Let it never be said that Father Delanoit was a cold-hearted man.

Yes, he knew some people probably thought of him that way. He was a very skilled administrator, and as such, Father Delanoit didn't always come across as particularly warm. But he needed to preserve that cool facade in order to do the business of the Church, in order to make the difficult decisions that needed to be made on a day-to-day basis.

And he was good. That was one of the reasons that Father Delanoit wasn't especially worried about the recent turn of events. He was very good, a priest who consistently kept his parish afloat financially when all around him, others were flailing. He had a knack for being in the right place at the right time and bringing the right people together, successful men in the community who knew how to get things done. He was good at convincing the elderly members to leave a generous bequest to the Church, he was good at impressing on young families the need to give on a steady basis, he was good at seeing opportunities and grabbing them. What the fallout would be of Jack O'Donnell coming forth remains to be seen, Father Delanoit thought, but regardless of what it was, his future was secure.

He was surprised, however, that Jack had spoken to his family about their special relationship. He really hadn't seen that coming, especially since he hadn't had anything to do with Jack for almost a year now. He wondered briefly what had provoked him to speak out now. Not that it really mattered. It wasn't likely that anyone was going to believe the word of a troubled youth, a known alcoholic, and two elderly people who were probably half-senile, all from the wrong side of the tracks.

The really unfortunate aspect of this turn of events, the priest thought as he dried off his face and hands, was the impact it would all have on his plans for his latest protégé, young Bill Ryan. Father Delanoit had hoped to get better acquainted with Mr. Ryan this very Friday evening, and now, he realized, it would be extremely unwise to proceed with that plan. Most unfortunate.

Father Delanoit rejoined Father Schmidt at the dinner table, where they ate their meal in silence. After they were finished, Mrs. McGrevey cleared the dishes off the table, taking them into the kitchen to wash them. Father Delanoit followed her into the kitchen, closing the door behind him.

"Mrs. McGrevey, I'm sorry that you had to be a part of that unpleasant scene with Mr. O'Donnell," he said, a look of concern warming his patrician face. "I do hope you know that I'd never harm a child, or engage in the activities that man alluded to. To dishonor my vows in such a manner would be unthinkable!" he said, managing to sound both outraged and offended.

"Oh, Father Delanoit, I'd never want to think such a thing of a man of the cloth," Mrs. McGrevey said. "Yet Mike O'Donnell was surely angry about something, wasn't he, Father?"

Father Delanoit had known hundreds of people like Brigit McGrevey, people who just needed the slightest of reasons to believe what they wanted to believe, even if all their senses were telling them the polar opposite was true. She needed a bit of encouragement, a bit of stroking, and then she would be his staunchest defender.

"Yes, indeed he was. You know, Mrs. McGrevey, that man's had a heavy burden, and there are some who can't carry a burden as well as others," he said, bending his head toward her and speaking softly, conspiratorially. "Alcohol's the way that man has chosen to deal with the hardships of his life, and I believe it has seriously affected his mind."

"I don't know if perhaps someone did harm poor Jack in the unspeakable way that Mr. O'Donnell described, but I can assure you, my dear woman, I would no more harm a child in my pastoral care than I would desecrate the Holy Eucharist," Father Delanoit said.

"You know, I wouldn't be surprised if this is all Jack's way of drawing attention away from himself and whatever the latest scrape he's managed to get himself into," he added. "The boy's been courting disaster for quite some time now, getting into fights, being insubordinate with his teachers. Don't quote me on this, but I did have my suspicions that Jack was experimenting with drugs," he said, raising his eyebrows and nodding significantly. "I tried to talk to him about it, but he became very angry, insolent even. He even implied that he would get back at me if I confronted him any further about the issue."

"There's no telling what those kids will say or do when they start taking those drugs," Mrs. McGrevey said. "Why, my sister's boy Patrick—you remember Patrick, Father, you took him on a day trip to Chicago a few times—well, that boy got into the stuff, and he got so bad he'd steal the grocery money out of his mother's purse. Lie, steal, why, they've no morals whatsoever," she said, shaking her head.

"So you do understand," Father Delanoit said. In an unusual gesture of affection, the priest put his arm around the housekeeper's shoulders. "I thought I'd be able to count on you, Mrs. McGrevey. You have always seemed to me to be an intelligent woman, not one to be easily deceived, and it looks as if my impression was correct."

The woman beamed under his rare praise. There were those who said Father Delanoit was cold, but she's always known it wasn't coldness so much as class. When she first heard Mike O'Donnell's cockamamie story, she'd been half-tempted to believe it, but now that she and Father Delanoit had talked, she knew better than that. Why, she thought, I'll bet the boy is on drugs! That would explain the whole thing. Excitedly, she remembered the ladies of the parish were going to be gathering tomorrow morning to prepare the mailings for mission week. Mrs. McGrevey knew just who she could ask: Thelma Dalvey. The woman knew everything that was going on in Hook's Point, she did, and she was only too happy to share it. She'd ask Thelma tomorrow.

"Why, thank you, Father Delanoit," she said. "Now, if you'll excuse me, we've had quite a night. I'll just finish cleaning up in here and then get to bed. Tomorrow I'll need to be up early to get the coffee on for the ladies' meeting, and I'm just about all in."

"Of course, my good woman," he said. "And, although I don't probably say this as much as I should, you certainly do a wonderful job for us here, preparing delicious meals and keeping everything spotless. By all means, you do deserve a rest. Good night, now," he said, and again gave her shoulders a friendly squeeze.

"Good night, Father Delanoit," Mrs. McGrevey said. "It'll all work out, it will," she added, feeling almost maternal toward the dear man. Yes, she'd get the scoop tomorrow about poor mixed-up Jack O'Donnell.

Chapter Twelve

The next morning when Jack awoke, the first thing he noticed was a strange sensation in his chest, a sense of lightness, as if letting his secret out had removed some of the hard crusty shell that had grown around his heart, a protection from the abuse that Father Delanoit had perpetrated. Now that he had told Kelly and his family, that shell had cracked open, and light was finally penetrating his heart again.

Before he'd gone to bed, Jack had called Kelly and told her everything that had happened, how he'd told his family and how concerned they'd all been, and how they regretted not catching on to the situation earlier. He told her how his dad had gone over to the rectory and blasted Father Delanoit. Kelly had been as deliciously shocked as Jack had that his dad had told off the priest.

And he'd told Kelly how his dad had returned home from the rectory stone cold sober. Mike had asked Jack to come out into the garage with him, and he'd retrieved all the whiskey that he'd stashed in various nooks and crannies: in a small hole in the wall behind some loose plasterboard, inside his tool chest, six bottles in all, and the two of them took the booze into the kitchen and poured it down the sink.

He didn't tell Kelly how his dad looked him square in the eye and said, "Jack, if I'd been the dad you deserved to have, none of this would have happened. I can't change that now, son, but I promise you this: from now on, you'll have the father that you need. I made a promise to your mother, and God forgive me, I broke it, but I'll not be breaking this promise, I swear on her life," then hugged him. He didn't tell Kelly about that, because he'd almost broke down crying when his dad did that, and he figured he'd cry if he told the story, and he'd already cried more that day than he had in practically his whole life.

After Jack told her about all the events of the evening, Kelly suddenly became quiet. Again, he was afraid that he'd scared her off with his confession; maybe now that she'd had time for the whole ugly story to sink in, she was so grossed out that she wouldn't want any more to do with him, and who could blame her? Jack's fears were dispelled with her next words, though.

"Jack, I can only imagine how hard this has been, having somebody do something like this to you and having to keep it a secret for so long," she said softly. "For you to come out and tell me about it, just to protect Bill, was so brave. I said it before at my house, and I meant what I said: Jack, I love you."

"I love you, too, Kelly," he said.

"I'll see you tomorrow at school."

Jack didn't think he would sleep at all that night, but almost as soon as his head hit the pillow, he fell into a deep, restful sleep, undisturbed by the troubling dreams that often plagued his nights. He woke early the next morning, took a bath and got dressed, then headed downstairs. Although it was early—only a little after 6:30—Lucinda was already up, sitting in her rocking chair and drinking a cup of coffee. Jack hadn't expected to see anybody at this hour: Mike left for work about six and usually Lucinda arose at seven to prod Jack into getting ready for school.

"Grandma, I didn't think you'd be up so early," Jack said.

"Couldn't sleep," she answered. Lucinda had aged overnight, it seemed to Jack. The lines in her face looked deeper, her skin seemed to hang more loosely, her eyes even looked older than yesterday. Before. "Jack, I let you down. I knew you didn't like Father Delanoit, and that you were miserable around him, but I let my respect for the priesthood overrule what my heart was telling me: that the man was up to no good. Never in a million years would I have thought he would do such a thing, but I did see that you didn't like him, and I should have found out why that was. Instead, I sent you off with him just like a lamb to the slaughter," she said with tears in her eyes. "Can you forgive me, son?"

Jack responded by enveloping his grandmother in a hug.

"Of course, I forgive you, Grandma," Jack said. He was surprised at how small she seemed when he hugged her. 'Small but mighty' is how the family always described Lucinda, but right now, she just seemed old and frail.

They heard the creaking sound of the back door opening, and then Pappa's voice calling out, "Anybody up? I saw the light on and thought I'd invite myself over for coffee."

"I'll do you one better, Pappa," Lucinda said, rising and heading toward the kitchen. "Nobody ate much for supper last night, so how's about I make bacon and eggs for breakfast?"

Pappa gave her a quick kiss on the cheek, poured himself a cup of coffee and then sat down in the living room with Jack.

"How are you doing today, son?" he asked. His eyes lacked their usual humorous twinkle, but not the warmth.

"I'm okay, Pappa," Jack said, and he meant it. He felt better than he had for a long time.

"That's good." Pappa looked into his cup, studying the steaming coffee as he tried to decide how to approach the next subject. "Jack," he said finally, "as time goes on, you may find that some people will hear about this, what that so-called priest did to you." He paused, then continued. "Some people will be on your side, and some won't be. Just remember this: we—your family—we're always on your side. Just remember that, okay, son?"

Jack nodded. He knew it was probably too much to hope for, that nobody else would ever hear about what Father Delanoit had done to him. But his family's support had both surprised and strengthened him, and Kelly's faith in him made him believe that he could handle whatever was coming next.

"I know you are, Pappa," Jack said. The two sat enjoying a companionable silence as the smell of sizzling bacon drifted into the room. Soon the silence was broken as Lucinda called them to come out and eat.

They gathered around the table together. Their plates were loaded with eggs and fried potatoes and bacon and toast. Lucinda had been right; no one had eaten much the night before, so they were all hungry.

"Looks great, Grandma," Jack said, enthusiastically digging in to his eggs. He quickly polished off the meal, then excused himself to go brush his teeth and finish getting ready for school. Then he grabbed his jacket, gave his grandma a peck on the cheek and a salute to Pappa, and headed out the door.

As he breathed in the crisp October air, Jack was aware of his senses in a way that he'd not been for a long time. He could feel the cool air filling his lungs. The red and golden leaves on the maple tree in his front yard looked more vibrant than yesterday, and the crunch of the leaves under his feet filled him with child-like pleasure. He sprinted for a block or so, just for the joy of running.

But as Jack approached St. Maria's, anxiety replaced his elation. He knew nobody could have heard anything yet, but he still felt self-conscious. What if he ran into Father Delanoit? He determined to push those thoughts out of his mind and try to regain the cheerful feelings that he'd started out the day with. When he spotted Kelly standing by the entry door, talking to a couple of other girls, that task got easier, especially when she smiled at him.

Jack motioned to her to come and talk with him, so Kelly left her friends, who were trying mightily to look cool, but couldn't help breaking into giggles at what seemed to be a budding romance. Jack and Kelly definitely had "the look," a soft, doe-eyed expression that skeptics might scoff at as dopey, but not those who were in love.

"Hi," Jack said. He was surprised to find himself tongue-tied. Usually he had no trouble talking to Kelly, but all of a sudden he felt like they were beginning a new relationship, and he didn't know what was supposed to come next.

"Hi, Jack," Kelly said. She looked a little bashful herself, a slight blush on her cheeks making her eyes look even more blue than usual.

They were relieved when the bell rang, sparing them from an awkward silence. They joined the throng of students jostling and talking as they walked up the stairs and cracked open their lockers, storing coats and getting out the books they'd need for the morning classes, the girls pausing for a surreptitious glance into the mirrors they kept in their lockers, then heading into their classrooms.

While the students at St. Maria's were beginning their day, a group of ladies from the parish were gathering in the basement of the church to prepare the mailing for mission week. About a dozen women usually gathered, ostensibly to prepare the mailing, but also to catch up on the parish gossip: who was ill, who was pregnant, who was up to no good. Mrs. McGrevey had come a little early to prepare refreshments. As the coffee began percolating, the women started their task, stuffing the envelopes and addressing them, one for each family in the parish. As they settled into the rhythm of their work, they began to talk.

"Marilee, did I hear that your Ronald was going to have to hip surgery?"

"Yes, I'm afraid he is, and I just hope he doesn't have to go on disability, because I don't know how we'd make it."

"Did you know the Nooneys are moving to California? I heard he's going to work for Rockwell Aerospace."

"You remember Linda Berry lost her breast last year to cancer? Well, it's come back: spread into her lungs, now."

"You'll never guess who's going to have a baby! Kathy Fitzgerald!'

"No! Her youngest one's going off to college!"

In the midst of the chatter, Mrs. McGrevey tried to discreetly capture Thelma Dalvey's attention. She spoke in a low voice, just a little louder than a whisper.

"Thelma, what have you heard about Mike O'Donnell's boy taking those drugs that are all over the place?"

"What! Isn't Mike O'Donnell's boy studying to be a priest?" she said, looking puzzled and a little annoyed. Thelma Dalvey wasn't used to being out of the loop when it came to parish gossip.

"No, not that one, not David, but the younger one, Jack," Mrs. McGrevey said, her volume quickly increasing until she was speaking in her normal booming voice. "Jack. You know—the one who's been getting into so much trouble lately. Is he on drugs, have you heard?"

"Well, I wouldn't be surprised," Thelma said. She hated to be the last to know anything. "Seems like about half the kids are all doped up these days, smoking that marijuana and popping pills and God knows what all."

"Jack O'Donnell? Lucinda's grandson?" questioned Harriet Moore, whose sister had coffee with Lucinda every Wednesday.

"Yes, that's the one," Mrs. McGrevey said, any intentions toward discreet investigation thrown to the wayside. "That one is trouble from the word go. Looks like he's taking after his father, the boy is."

"Oh, Mike O'Donnell," Evelyn Ricardo said, her disgust apparent. "I saw him at the grocery store at ten o'clock one Saturday morning, picking up a twelve-pack of beer and looking like he'd already put a few away."

"Like father, like son, they say," Thelma added.

"Say, did anybody hear if the McKenzies are going ahead with the divorce?"

And so it was settled. By the next Friday, thanks to the good ladies of St. Maria Goretti's, almost fifty people—members of the church, their friends and neighbors—would learn that Jack O'Donnell was taking drugs. A few would embellish the story and claim that Jack had sold dope to some younger kids at the school. Several folks claimed to have seen it all coming.

But that morning Jack was blissfully ignorant of the chatter. In fact, it was the best day he'd had in a long time. He aced his English exam, scored a high B on a pop quiz in history, and even did pretty well on his math assignment. At lunch, he munched on fish sticks and listened to the guys making plans for the weekend.

"Jack, do you want to meet us at the football game?" Wayne asked. Jack's friendship with Wayne had changed since Father Delanoit began abusing him. He often found himself pushing away his old friends, fearful they'd see what had happened to him and despise him for it. Plus, their parents had heard about Jack getting into trouble for fighting and for being insolent, and they restricted their children from spending too much time with him, fearful that he would be a bad influence. But Wayne had remained a faithful friend and made it a point to include Jack in their plans as much as possible.

"No, I can't," he said. "My brother David is coming home for the weekend. It's the first weekend he's come home since he went to college, so I guess we're going to hang out." What he didn't tell them is that he knew his grandmother and Pappa and his dad were going to want Jack to tell David about Father Delanoit, before he possibly heard about it from another source. Feeling shame arise at the thought of telling his brother, Jack looked down at his lunch tray and pushed the green beans around with his fork. At that moment, Kelly approached the table.

"Hey," she said, smiling at Jack. The other boys exchanged glances and snickered. The bell rang, signifying it was time to go outside for a brief break before starting the afternoon classes.

"Hey, yourself," he said. "Come on." They carried their lunch trays to the counter, scraped the leftovers into the garbage can, and stacked their trays. Then they walked through the lunchroom, down the hall and out the big double doors. The afternoon sun felt warm on their skin, and the breeze mild. It would be hard to go back to class.

"So, are you going to the football game tonight?" Kelly asked.

"No, David's coming home. I'm going to tell him about Father Delanoit," Jack said. Not wanting to get bogged down in the whole mess again, he said, "How about tomorrow afternoon? Can

I come over to your house?"

"Sure, that sounds good," she answered

"Is Bill doing okay? I really didn't mean to scare him," Jack said.

"Bill's fine, Jack. When I think of what would have happened if you hadn't spoken up, it makes me sick," Kelly said.

Jack's heart fell a little at that statement. He was still scared that Kelly would find him repugnant because of what Father Delanoit had done. God knows, he'd felt that way about himself.

"Jack, it wasn't your fault," Kelly said, quickly recognizing his fear. "It was all Father Delanoit's fault. You were just a little kid. When I say 'it makes me sick,' I mean it makes me sick that somebody could do that to a child. To you, Jack. You could never make me sick. I… you know how I feel about you," she said.

"I know," he said. "I'm just not used to anybody knowing about it. I've kept it a secret for so long, it feels weird, having it out in the open."

"Nobody in their right mind is going to blame you or think any less of you for this," Kelly said.

"Yeah. Hey, let's walk around some."

They strolled over to the playground area and stood behind the chain link fence, watching the younger kids swing on the swing set, take turns going down the slide, and climb on the jungle gym. A group of sixth-graders played kickball in the field. Watching the children play reminded Jack of when he was in the sixth grade, so innocent and totally unaware of the turn his life was going to take. At least it won't happen to Bill, he thought. At least some good is going to come out of this. He tried to let the bad memories go and concentrate on being with Kelly for the last few minutes of recess. When moments later the bell rang, they walked back to the school and filed into the building.

The afternoon passed quickly. After class, Jack met Kelly in the hallway and they walked part of the way home together. When it came time to part ways, Jack gave Kelly a quick kiss and squeezed her hand.

"I'll see you tomorrow afternoon about one, okay?" he asked.

"I'll be there," she said before smiling and heading toward home.

When Jack reached his house, he walked in and found two navy blue suitcases sitting in front of the door, along with a pair of size twelve jogging shoes. A jean jacket was flung over the chair. For Lucinda to have allowed this state of disrepair to exist meant only one thing: David was home. Then he heard the sound of voices coming from the kitchen.

"Hey, little brother!" David called out. Then he was standing right in front of Jack, and then surprising him by catching him up in a bear hug. Jack felt all his worries melting away. David wasn't going to look down on him, not for this, not for anything. That just wasn't his style.

Looking at his older brother, Jack saw he looked much the same as when they'd taken him to college six weeks ago. His hair was a little shaggy and he was possibly trying to grow a beard—or else he just hadn't shaved in a couple of days—but overall, he was the same old David. As Jack saw the look of compassion on his brother's face, he realized that he must have heard about Father Delanoit from their grandmother.

"You know?" he asked simply.

"Yeah. Grandma was filling me in about it just now. Jack, buddy, I wish... I wish you could have told me," David said. "I'm your big brother, I would have helped you. That's what big brothers do."

"I... I couldn't, David. Father Delanoit told me I'd get sent away to reform school if I told anybody. What did I know? I was just a little kid," Jack said. "Besides that, it was just too creepy." He hung his head, hating like hell for his brother to know about this, even though at the same time, he was relieved that he did.

"Damn right, it's creepy," David said, as Jack looked up, shocked. Rarely if ever did he hear his brother swear. "It's creepy that a grown man, a priest, for God's sake, would do this to a little kid." David's face was contorted in anger, something Jack didn't see very often.

"I guess Dad really gave him hell," David said. "Told him off and even took a punch at him."

"He did?" Jack said incredulously. Mike had told Jack that he'd confronted the priest, but he hadn't told him the whole story. Like most abused children, Jack had viewed his abuser as an unstoppable force. The idea of his father taking Father Delanoit down a notch or two filled Jack with a delicious combination of awe and vindication. The brothers looked at each other a moment, then both began snickering. Before too long they were laughing out loud at the thought of their normally peaceful father punching out the priest. Their laughter cut through the tension and brought a blessed sense of normalcy to the situation. Gradually their laughter subsided, and David gave Jack the next piece of news.

"Father Schmidt is coming over, Jack," he said. "He wants to talk to you about what Father Delanoit did."

Instantly Jack's defenses went up.

"No! I'm not talking to him!" he yelled. "Who do you think he's going to believe? Me or his buddy, Father Delanoit?"

"Jack, I talked to him on the phone already, and I'm pretty sure he's going to be on your side," David said. "You know he's the one who's been counseling me about becoming a priest. I know him, Jack. He's a good man. Besides that, why would anybody make up a story like that?"

Jack hung his head again, suppressing a shudder.

"I'll be right here with you, Jack. Nothing bad is going to happen. And, if he proves me wrong and turns out to be a jerk, well, the O'Donnell men will just have to deliver justice to another priest!" David said.

Jack snickered again at the thought of his brother hitting anybody. What on earth had he started, telling his story about Father Delanoit? The only thing Jack had wanted to do was make sure Father Delanoit couldn't get a hold of Kelly's brother. This thing just keeps getting bigger and bigger, he thought.

Just then, they heard a knock at the door. Glancing out the window, the brothers could see Schmitty's modest Ford sedan parked in front of their house.

"It'll be okay, buddy," David said as he walked to the door.

"Hi, Father Schmidt," he said, ushering the young priest into the living room.

"Good to see you, David," Schmitty replied. "I'll be looking forward to hearing how you like college life. But today we have more pressing business to deal with. Jack, I'd like to ask you a few questions about Father Delanoit, if I may."

The priest's tone conveyed concern, but Jack was cautious. After all, Father Delanoit had sounded nice in the beginning, too. He had about as much enthusiasm for this discussion as he'd have for facing a firing squad, but he supposed he might as well get it over with.

Lucinda came into the living room, followed by Mike and Pappa.

"Jack, we just want you to know we're all here for you," Mike said, seeing the look of alarm on Jack's face at the sight of the whole crew descending on him. "If you want, you and David can talk to Father Schmidt here alone—we'll give you some privacy. But if you want us, just give a holler. We'll be right here in the kitchen."

Tears filled Jack's eyes at this uncustomary show of support from his father. He'd cried enough yesterday to last him a lifetime, though, so he just nodded and blinked away the tears.

Father Schmidt sat in the rocking chair and David sat next to Jack on the couch. The three of them stared uncomfortably at their feet for a moment, and then Schmitty cleared his throat and began to speak.

"Jack, your father made some pretty serious accusations against Father Delanoit last night," he began. Instantly Jack tensed up, feeling as if he were being accused of making it up. "Would you mind telling me when this all started?"

David looked at Jack encouragingly, easing some of his tension.

"When I was in sixth grade," he said. "It was when I practicing to be an altar boy, before the first time I served Mass."

Schmitty tried to hide his shock, but was only partially successful. My God, he thought. Had he been living with a monster all these years?

"When did he do this, Jack, and where were you when it happened?" he said, trying to keep a level tone.

"Every other Friday night, he'd take me into the study in the rectory," Jack said, his voice dead as he relived that awful time.

When Mrs. McGrevey and I were both out, Schmitty thought.

"And he… touched you? Your private parts?" he asked quietly.

"Yes," Jack said, so softly Father Schmidt had to strain to hear him. "He touched me. And he made me do it to him. He said if I told anybody, that I would get into big trouble and have to go to reform school. Right before he started, I'd gotten into a fight with Ronny Slater. Slater said my dad was a drunk, and I got mad and punched him at altar boy practice. At first, Father Delanoit was really nice about it, but then he always held it over my head. He said nobody would ever believe me, anyway."

"I believe you, Jack," Schmitty said solemnly. All the pieces fit. "Why did you decide to break your silence?"

"Because of Kelly's brother. Kelly is my… my friend. Her little brother Bill is starting altar boy practice," Jack said. His face darkened as he continued. "Father Delanoit told Bill to come over to the rectory on Friday night and show him his baseball cards. Well, I knew what that meant," he said, laughing mirthlessly. "I told Kelly not to let Bill go there, and I told her why. Then she convinced me to tell my folks the whole thing. So I did. And then I guess Dad came over to the rectory and let Father Delanoit have it." Jack sighed with relief. As incredibly difficult as it was to tell his story, every time he did, it seemed as if toxins were being drained from his soul.

"Yes, I know Bill Ryan is on the roster of altar boys," Father

Schmidt said. "Jack, what you did was incredibly brave. I don't know if I could have been half as brave if I were in your situation. Also, I want to tell you... how very sorry I am that a member of the priesthood could do something this despicable, this evil, to a child. To you. I am so sorry, my son," he said, and there was no mistaking the genuine sorrow, the humility, in the man's voice.

"Thanks," Jack said simply. He knew it would be a long cold day in hell before he ever again trusted another priest, but if he did, Father Schmidt just might be the one.

"Father Schmidt, what this had done to Jack, to our whole family, is devastating," David said. "Ever since Delanoit started abusing him, Jack has changed. We've all seen it, but none of us knew why until he told us about the abuse. Right around the time that Delanoit—I won't ever call the man 'Father' again, to me he's not worthy of the name—did this to my brother, Jack started getting into trouble, mouthing off to teachers, even to our grandmother. And that's not Jack. He was always a good kid."

"And Grandma—she looks like she's ten years older since the last time I saw her. She's got it in her head that she should have known, should have been able to stop it. But why would she? All her life, she's been taught to treat the clergy with a special respect, to put them on a pedestal. This is tearing her up," David said.

"I never should have told her," Jack said miserably. "I just didn't want Bill to..."

"No!" Schmitty interrupted. "None of this is your fault, Jack. The entire blame for this situation lies with one person, and that's Father Delanoit. No one else is responsible for what he did to you and how he disrupted your life and your family. Now, I'd like to bring the rest of your family in here and talk about our next step."

"What do you mean, 'our next step?" Jack asked as David went into the kitchen and signaled the others to come out in the living room and join the discussion. They all filed in and sat down, looking expectantly at Father Schmidt.

"The next step, as I see it, is to bring this assault to the attention of the diocese. Father Delanoit should not be allowed to remain in the priesthood after an incident, no, multiple incidents, of this magnitude," Schmitty said.

Silence prevailed as everyone considered the ramifications of following the priest's advice. Pappa, for one, had little confidence that alerting the diocese would help the situation any. He had seen too many powerful people retain their positions even after committing the most heinous offenses. Besides, it could bring unwanted attention to Jack, and that's the last thing the boy needed right now. Lucinda thought that if the bishop knew what Father Delanoit had done to Jack, he would surely take action and Jack would be vindicated. Yet it would be awkward for the boy, and God knows he'd been through enough. Mike was initially all in favor of the idea—anything to make that bastard pay. But, on second thought, what's to say the muckety-mucks were going to take the word of people like the O'Donnells over their boy wonder Delanoit? They weren't about to kill their cash cow, that was for sure. David was hopeful that, if notified, the diocese would do the right thing. How could he consider joining the priesthood if they wouldn't look out for the children under their care? But he knew Jack wouldn't want any more people to know about this than necessary. Taking care of Jack was what was most important now. For all Father Schmidt's talk about nobody being to blame but Father Delanoit, David still felt responsible. He should have seen something, known somehow. If it took him the rest of his life, he'd make it up to his little brother for not being more vigilant, David swore.

Jack was torn. Here he had been so sure that no one would believe him that he'd kept the terrible secret for two years, and now, everyone was being so nice: Kelly, Grandma, Dad, Pappa, David, and even Father Schmidt. But not everyone was going to be as full of good will as they were, Jack knew. Father Delanoit knew how to bullshit better than anybody he'd ever seen, and if people started asking Jack a lot of questions, he was afraid he'd get confused and lose his temper. And another thing: Jack couldn't face the thought of all the kids at school hearing about this. He'd rather die.

"No," he said firmly. "I don't want to tell anybody else. I don't want anybody to know what he did to me."

"Jack, I'm not going to tell you that I understand how you feel, because I don't," Schmitty said. "Nobody could unless they experienced it themselves. But I would like you to at least think about reporting this to the diocese, for the same reason that you told your family in the first place. Right now, because you spoke up, Bill Ryan is safe. But there's nothing to prevent Father Delanoit from doing the same thing he did to you to another boy, and we really have no way to stop him. If you should decide you're willing to allow me to report this to the bishop's office, I would do my best to keep you as far away from the limelight as possible."

"You heard the boy, Father," Mike said belligerently. "He doesn't need to play Superman. It's the Church's job to police their own, not a 14-year-old kid."

"Wait, Dad," Jack said. "I'll…I'll think about it. I hate to let him hurt any more kids. And, besides that, I'd really like to see him get what's coming to him."

"The hottest seat in hell is what he's got coming to him," Mike said.

"Take your time. You think about it, talk about it as a family, and then let me know what you want to do. And no matter what you decide to do, if I can help you, day or night, just give a holler. I'm here for you," Schmitty said, rising to leave.

"Thank you, Father Schmidt," Lucinda said, her faith bolstered to see that not all the shepherds were wolves in sheep's clothing. "We do appreciate your coming over."

As Jack and his family gathered around the table for supper, Schmitty drove back to the rectory, reflecting on all what he'd heard. Although they'd lived together for ten years, he'd never really felt he knew Father Delanoit. Sure, he knew that his housemate liked his coffee black and his eggs over easy, that his favorite football team was the Chicago Bears, that his penchant for neatness was extraordinary and occasionally a bone of contention between the two of them, because Schmitty's own style of living definitely leaned toward the casual. But he'd always felt there was an unbridgeable gulf between himself and his brother priest. He'd been disappointed when he first moved to St. Maria's and discovered that Father Delanoit was not really interested in building the type of mentoring relationship the younger priest had hoped for. Delanoit's faith was genuine, he had no doubt, but cerebral in nature and not open to sharing.

He'd always respected Father Delanoit, though, and viewed him as a decent, upright, if somewhat cold, person. Never in a million years would Schmitty have imagined he was capable of harming a child in the hideous way that Jack had described. He had gone to the O'Donnell house half-hoping that Jack would recant his story or prove himself an unreliable witness. But his story rang true in every respect. The Friday nights, the mildly obsessive interest Father Delanoit had always had about the altar boys which Schmitty had ascribed to his compulsion to have everything done perfectly, the part about Bill Ryan, all of the pieces fit together. Most convincing, however, was Jack himself. His pain and shame were palpable; no 14-year-old kid was that good of an actor. Schmitty knew with every fiber of his being that Jack was speaking the truth.

He pulled his car into the driveway at the rectory. Mrs. McGrevey had the night off, as she always did on Fridays. But Father Delanoit's Riviera was here. Schmitty grimly approached the rectory door, walked in and found his fellow priest sitting in his study, reading the text for Sunday's sermon.

"Father Schmidt," he said, his greeting typically cool and reserved, a signal that he did not want to be disturbed. Too bad, Schmitty thought grimly.

"I've been to the O'Donnells," he said, entering the study despite the dirty look Father Delanoit shot him. "I talked to Jack."

Father Delanoit calmly arranged the papers on his desk and marked his place in the Bible before replying.

"Poor Jack," he said, his voice sympathetic. "What a confused young man he has become."

"Surprisingly clear-minded is more like it," Schmitty said. "Jack is no more confused than I am. Although I am a bit confused, Father, I'll admit that. I am confused as to how anyone, let alone you—a priest—could do such a terrible thing to a child, a child in your care. Would you care to try to enlighten me, Father?"

"I don't like your tone, Father Schmidt," Father Delanoit replied coldly, pushing his glasses up and looking intently at his interrogator. "Do I need to remind you again that I am your superior, and as such, not accountable to you. I don't need to explain anything to you, let alone try to decipher the drug-induced ramblings of a troubled youth."

"Jack O'Donnell may be troubled, but if he is, it's because of what you did to him. You abused that young man, that boy, and you abused the office of the priesthood. What you did sickens me," Schmitty said, his voice shaking with anger. "To take the trust of an innocent child and misuse it that way... my God! What were you thinking?"

"We are not having this discussion," Father Delanoit said. 'It's clear that the O'Donnells have gotten to you somehow. I've always suspected you were too soft, too naive to be much use. It's one thing to help the people with their problems, but to get sucked into all the little dramas that some of them like to create in their pathetic little lives..."

"Little dramas? We're talking about the sexual abuse of a minor, here," Schmitty said. "Not hardly a 'little drama.' An abomination. A crime, in fact."

"Are you threatening me, Father Schmidt? Because if you are, you'd better have more than the word of that twisted boy," Father Delanoit said.

"No. I am not threatening you. I am trying to find out just how in God's name you could have used that boy to satisfy your own sick desires," Schmitty said.

"I don't know what on earth you're talking about, Father Schmidt. If you don't mind, I have a sermon to finish," Father Delanoit said, as calm as if they had been discussing the weather.

Schmitty turned and left the room, astonished by the man's lack of concern, if not for the boy, then for his own reputation. Wasn't he at least worried about the repercussions? The young priest retreated to his quarters, where he turned for solace and guidance to the God he'd always known to be faithful. Unfortunately, no answers seemed to be forthcoming.

Across town at the O'Donnells, the clan had assembled around the table. Jack noticed two unusual things about this gathering. First, rare was the night that Lucinda served a simple meal like this, ham sandwiches and potato chips, on paper plates at that. Jack assumed she had been so involved with telling David the news that she hadn't had time to cook a real meal. Secondly, Jack couldn't remember when was the last Friday night that Mike had been home, stone cold sober and sitting down at the supper table with the family. He looked a little pale and his hands were shaky, but so far, he was sticking to his promise.

The conversation moved away from the situation with Jack and Father Delanoit as the family peppered David with questions about college life. Were his subjects hard? How did he get along with his roommate? Was he taking time to have some fun? Was he eating well (Lucinda's major concern when anybody moved out of the sphere of her influence)?

David was adjusting well to college life, it seemed. He thought he was doing pretty well in his classes and, yes, he was taking time out from studying to go to the football games and see the city. His roommate, Mark Otis, also planned to become a priest, and the two young men sometimes talked long into the night, bouncing theological questions off one another and sharing their hopes and concerns about life in the priesthood. And, yes, Grandma, he was eating well, though he sure missed her homemade cookies.

After supper, Mike pushed back his chair and said he was going to go out for a while. Everybody looked at him, apprehension and disappointment clearly visible on their faces. They had hoped Mike would make good on his promise to quit drinking.

"No, it's not what you're thinking," he said. "I meant what I said last night. I've taken my last drink. But I know I can't do it on my own. I…I've tried before and never made it more than a week or two. There's a guy at work, he used to be one of my drinking buddies, then he got himself arrested one too many times and his wife left him, took his son and moved in with her parents. So he decided to get sober. Went to A.A. and really kicked it. He's asked me a couple of times if I wanted to go with him to a meeting, but I always brushed him off. I told him I didn't have any problem with drinking, I could stop whenever I wanted to. But that was a lie." Mike paused, looking down at the table.

"Before your mother died, boys, I made her a promise," Mike said. "I told her that I'd take good care of you and not turn to drinking like my father did. Well, I failed. I failed her and I failed you. Especially you, Jack. If I hadn't been drinking, then maybe that bastard would never have… done what he did to you." His voice grew husky and tears filled his eyes. "I'm sorry, son. I let you down. But that's not going to happen again."

Jack didn't dare speak, or he would have found himself crying yet again. He felt such a cacophony of emotion: joy that his father was going to quit drinking and be the father he'd wanted for so long; grief that it had taken so long and so much suffering for Mike to make this decision; fear that these would be empty words, another broken promise; hope that maybe life would be different now. Better. Maybe even good.

"So I talked to Scotty today and told him I wanted to go with him to a meeting. He's going to pick me up in about five minutes here. For a little while, Scotty said I should probably go to meetings every day, until I get used to not drinking. Then I can cut back to once or twice a week, and spend more time here at home."

"I always knew you were a goomba, Michael O'Donnell," Pappa said quietly.

"A goomba?" David questioned.

"Yes, a goomba. A real man," Pappa said. "We're going to have to work with you boys, get you up to speed on your Italian heritage."

"Yeah, just don't pick up the worst parts of your Irish heritage and I'll be happy," Mike said "Boys, if you keep away from the booze, it'll be the smartest thing you ever do." Just then, they heard a car horn honking. "Okay, that's Scotty. So I'll see you all after the meeting."

He headed out the door, and the family exchanged glances across the table. Would he, could he? Each hoped fervently that Mike would make good on his promise. But Mike had always relied on booze to get him through tough times. And for all the foreseeable future, tough times were the only thing in sight for this family.

Chapter Thirteen

Kelly had been upstairs cleaning her room, as was her normal Saturday morning routine, when her mother received the phone call from Reenie Walsh. Reenie Walsh had gotten a call from Thelma Dalvey, filling her in on all the latest about the people at St. Maria's, and when she heard about the trouble that Jack O'Donnell had gotten himself into, well, Arlene Ryan was the first person she thought of. Reenie knew that Arlene's little girl Kelly was going around with the O'Donnell boy, and she couldn't very well stand by and let that sweet little thing go down the drain with him, so she knew she'd better call Arlene first thing in the morning. Not that she wanted to—who wants to spread bad news—but she felt it her duty.

"Kelly, come over here and sit down," Arlene said gravely when Kelly came downstairs, startling her daughter into wondering if maybe her grandmother, who lived out of town and had been in poor health for a long time, had taken a turn for the worse.

"What's wrong, Mom?" Kelly asked.

"I just had a phone call that was very disturbing, Kelly," she said. "It was about Jack. Some people are making some pretty disturbing allegations."

"Well, it's all true, Mom," Kelly said. "And you can just thank

Jack for telling me about it, because Father Delanoit was going to do it to Bill."

"What!" Arlene said. "What's this got to do with Bill?"

"Father Delanoit told Bill to come over to the rectory and show him his baseball cards," Kelly said. "But Jack said that was just a trick to get him over there. He said if Bill went over there alone, Father Delanoit would... would molest him, just like he did to Jack. Jack saved Bill, Mom. Even though he hated to tell anybody what happened to him, even though he knew people might not believe him, he stuck his neck out for Bill."

Arlene quickly realized they were discussing two totally different topics. It seemed the second topic was even more pressing than what Reenie Walsh had told her.

"Father Delanoit molested Jack? And Jack thinks he was going to do the same thing to Bill?" she asked.

"Yes, he did, Mom," Kelly said. "Don't you believe me?"

"Kelly, this is the first I've heard of it," her mother said.

"Then what 'disturbing allegations' were you talking about?" Kelly asked, thoroughly confused.

"That was Reenie Walsh on the phone. She said she heard that Jack was on drugs and may be even selling them to younger students, and she wanted to tell..."

"That's a lie!" Kelly shouted. "Jack has never done drugs. He doesn't drink or smoke or anything, Mom! Reenie Walsh doesn't know what she's talking about."

"No, she usually doesn't. She said she hated to be the one to tell me, but she sure sounded pretty damn excited about it," Arlene said. "I needed to ask you, of course. I couldn't let you be around Jack if he were into that stuff. I do believe you, Kelly. I know I can always count on you to tell me the truth. That's why I'm really disturbed now. When did Jack tell you about Father Delanoit? Is that why you were so adamant that Bill couldn't go to the rectory yesterday? When were you going to tell me about this?"

"I was going to tell you, Mom," Kelly said. "I was going to tell you soon, but I wanted to give Jack a chance to tell his family first. He just told his grandparents and his dad the day before yesterday, the same day he told me, and then he was going to talk to his brother on Friday."

Arlene sat quietly, trying to process all this information. As a nurse, she knew that sexual abuse of children was much more common than most people realized, and not confined to any one social class. Child abusers weren't always the shifty-looking characters in the trench coat. They came from all walks of life; although this was the first time she'd heard of a priest sexually abusing a child, Arlene had known of doctors, teachers and other professional people who had done some pretty despicable things.

Sexual abuse of children was a topic people preferred not to talk about, but she had witnessed its tragic aftermath when she had worked in the emergency room at the hospital during her training. There the most violently injured children received medical care, but her teachers had informed her that most abuse victims were not as severely physically injured and so never came to the attention of any medical professionals. Their scars were emotional and often lifelong.

To think that Bill had come this close to being sexually abused made Arlene feel physically sick. Thank God that Jack had spoken up! Lord, that poor kid, she thought.

Jack had been quite shy the first few times Arlene met him, but as he became more comfortable around her, he had opened up more. He struck her as a good boy, maybe a little tense sometimes, but good-hearted. More importantly, her daughter liked him, and she was an incredibly levelheaded girl. Arlene sometimes felt guilty for counting on Kelly as much as she had since her husband Pat had died, but even when she was small, Kelly had seemed more like an adult than a child. If she thought Jack was all right, then Arlene wanted to believe that he was. And she owed the kid a huge debt of gratitude for not letting that pervert get a hold of Billy.

Still, she had to admit she was concerned about Jack's stability and how his situation would affect Kelly. Reenie Walsh was an idiot, no one could deny that, but not everything she'd said was untrue. Jack had been getting into trouble for fighting, Kelly had even told her that. Arlene didn't believe that Jack was on drugs, but she was worried about what direction he might end up going, with all the problems that he'd had to contend with. She didn't want Kelly to get dragged down with him. While Kelly was very reliable, she was also so warm-hearted that Arlene was afraid that her daughter could allow her desire to see Jack's good side overrule her common sense.

She couldn't very well forbid Kelly to see Jack after he had risked so much to protect Bill. But Arlene's instincts told her she would need to keep a close eye on her daughter's relationship with the boy.

"Is Jack coming over today?" she asked.

"Yes, he said he'd be over about one o'clock," Kelly said. "What's going on, Mom? Aren't you going to say anything about all this?"

"Have you ever seen Father Delanoit acting strange around the kids?" Arlene asked her.

"Not really. But I'm not around him that much. Well, he does seem to watch the boys awfully close, sometimes. Last week Bill said he was making him nervous at altar boy practice because he kept looking at him. Bill was afraid that he was doing something wrong. Then when Father Delanoit invited him to the rectory to show him his baseball card collection, Bill was all happy," Kelly said.

Arlene shuddered and shook her head.

"Good God!" she said. "Well, this family owes Jack a heck of a debt. And I will tell him that when he comes over."

"Mom, he's really embarrassed about it," Kelly said. "Don't make too big of a deal about it. He really hates to have anybody know about this."

"Don't worry, I'm not quite as stupid as all that," Arlene said. "I'll be discreet. What does Bill know about all this, anyway?"

"Nothing. We just told him that Father Delanoit was mean to

Jack and that's why he couldn't go over there."

"Good. That's plenty for him," Arlene said. The longer Bill could retain his sweet innocence, the better. Nothing was going to rob him of that prematurely if she could help it.

"Are you okay, Kelbell?" she asked, using Kelly's childhood nickname. "This has been quite a shock for you, hasn't it?"

"Oh, Mom, I just feel so bad for Jack! He carried this secret for two years and it's filled him up with so much…stuff… that I don't know how he can handle it. He talked about killing himself, Mom," Kelly said, her voice low.

"Kelly! I'm really sorry about all this," Arlene said, drawing her daughter close. "Maybe now that this is out in the open, things will start getting better. It's a hell of a thing for a young boy to have to go through. You've been a really good friend to him."

Kelly and her mother were always close, and even more so after her dad had died so suddenly. They'd always been able to talk freely. But Kelly wasn't ready to confide to her mother that her feelings for Jack went beyond friendship. She wanted to hold on to that awhile longer. She blushed as she remembered the feeling of his lips on hers, and she wondered if he would kiss her again today.

"I'd better go upstairs and finish getting ready, Mom," she said.

Her mother looked at her, noting the fact that she was already dressed neatly in jeans and a nice yellow top, her shiny hair hanging down her back in soft waves. Her girl was growing into a woman, she realized. Yes, Arlene would definitely need to be vigilant in the days and weeks ahead.

Promptly at one o'clock Jack rang the doorbell. Kelly, who had been studying her English assignment and glancing at the clock every few minutes, hurried to answer it. He came into the living room and, seeing that no one else was in the room, gave Kelly a quick kiss on her cheek.

"So did your brother make it home?" Kelly asked. They sat down on the couch side by side, close but not touching.

"Yeah, David's here. He was great. The whole family was. You were right, Kelly," Jack said. "I am really glad that I told them about it."

"I knew they'd want to help, Jack," she said.

"Father Schmidt came over, too. At first I didn't really want to talk to him, but I did, and actually he's a pretty okay guy," Jack said. "He wants me to report Father Delanoit to the diocese. I think I'm going to do it, too. I really want to get that … get him out of there."

"He should never be around little kids again," Kelly said.

"No," Jack said. "Hey, that's not all! I think my dad is really going to quit drinking. He went to a meeting last night at some church. This friend of his from work said they help people who want to quit drinking, and he came over and picked up my dad. I think he's really serious."

"That's good news," Kelly said Jack had never discussed his father's drinking much, but it had come up in conversation a time or two, and Jack always sounded a little sad, a little resentful, of the way his father spent more of his free time drinking than with his family.

Arlene came into the room and perched on the arm of the couch by Jack, her face reflecting the gratitude she felt towards him.

"Jack, I know this situation has to be hard for you. If there's ever any way that I can help, please let me," she said. "I could never thank you enough for what you did for Bill." Then she disappeared into the kitchen, not wanting to add to the boy's discomfort.

"So, are you still stuck on that English assignment?" Jack asked after a moment or two of awkward silence.

"Sort of. I'm still trying to figure out which ones are parenthetic expressions and which ones aren't," Kelly said. "But I'm done with math."

"Good, you can help me, then," Jack said, glad for a distraction. He was tired of focusing on all the drama of the past few days. Amazingly, homework was a welcomed diversion. The two of them spent a little over an hour working on their assignments. Then, by mutual agreement, they decided they'd spent enough of their Saturday inside with the books.

"Let's go to the park," Kelly said. "I feel like a mole, all holed up inside here."

"Sounds good to me," Jack said.

"Mom, Jack and I are going for a walk," Kelly called out as they headed toward the door.

"Okay, be back by four," her mom called back.

Jack and Kelly walked slowly at first, soaking up the autumn sun on their faces, enjoying the crunching of the dry leaves underfoot. Gradually they picked up their pace and soon found themselves approaching Goshen Park, a rambling 120-acre park in the center of town. They meandered past some picnic tables, painted green last spring but already beginning to peel, and stopped at the swing set. For a while they swung side by side, legs pumping as they went higher and higher. Then Jack jumped off his swing and pushed Kelly, loving the way the sun painted streaks of gold in her long red hair and how it flew behind her like a magic cape.

A group of kids who looked like they were probably ten or eleven ran over to the swing set and took the rest of the swings, shouting and laughing, so Jack and Kelly walked on, following a trail that led past the chaparral deep into the woods. A dead tree formed a bridge between the two sides of an engulfment. Jack stepped nimbly across it, but Kelly hesitated; it looked like a good ten-foot drop to the ground below, which was hard and rocky.

"You can do it," Jack said, holding out his hand as he walked back across. "Just don't look down." Kelly took his hand and crossed the log bridge, releasing a sigh of relief when she reached the other side.

"We can do anything," Jack said expansively, still holding her hand. "As long as we're together."

Kelly, her heart still beating fast, suddenly felt shy and a little uneasy. She squeezed Jack's hand once and then broke away.

"I'd better get home," she said. "I think it's getting late."

For a moment, a shadow came over Jack's heart, a feeling of abandonment and then an unreasoning but familiar anger, which frightened him. He would really rather die than to ever hurt Kelly, though the urge to lash out was once again arising within him.

"Yeah, we'd better get going," he said. "Go up to the right. That's the shortcut." The trail wound through the thicket, back up the hill, and ended at the park's entrance. They walked the rest of the way home in a comfortable silence, Jack's momentary anger having passed like an errant storm cloud on a sunny day.

When they reached Kelly's house, she turned to him and smiled.

"See you at school Monday," she said.

"Okay," Jack replied. "Kelly?" he said, touching her shoulder gently as she began to turn to go inside.

She turned around to face him again and he tenderly pulled her towards him and kissed her.

"I love you, Kelly," he said.

"I love you, too," she said. Then she turned to go in, and this time he let her go. He hurried home, running part of the way, not because there was any big rush, but simply because he was fourteen and full of life.

There would be no sandwich supper tonight, Jack realized as he walked into the house. Delicious smells wafted from the kitchen: roast chicken and sage dressing, apple pie with cinnamon, and yeasty rolls. Around the table Mike, Pappa and David were engaged in an animated game of five-card draw. As usual, Pappa's stack of pennies was piled high, easily dwarfing Mike and David's slim pickings.

"Jack! Just in time for the next hand," Pappa said. "Pull up a chair."

"Yeah, the old man is getting tired of taking advantage of the reformed drunk and the college kid, guess he needs a new victim," Mike said. Then he looked apprehensively at Jack, regretting his choice of words.

Instantly, Jack felt stupid and shameful. Would it always be like this, he wondered? People feeling like they had to walk on eggshells around him, or else saying something careless, something that reminded Jack of what Father Delanoit had done to him? Emotions churning, he turned and ran up the stairs to his room, only wanting to escape the pitying eyes of his family.

He slammed the door and flung himself onto his bed. All he wanted was for life to go back to normal, like it was before Father Delanoit ever laid a hand on him. And he'd briefly hoped that it would, after he'd told everybody and they'd all been so nice and everything. He'd thought maybe they could all go back to the way they were, even better than they were before if his dad really did quit drinking. But, no, it seemed like this was just going to go on forever. He'd always be the kid that got abused by the priest. Forever.

Someone was knocking at the door. Jack tried ignoring it, hoping whoever it was would give up and go away.

"Jack, can I come in?" David asked.

After a moment, Jack replied, "It's your room."

David entered the room and sat at the foot of Jack's bed.

"Everything is all fucked up," Jack said quietly. "Nobody's ever going to treat me like I'm normal. Because I'm not. I'm a freak, a sideshow freak, and that's all I'm ever gonna be."

"Bullshit!" David yelled, momentarily at least shocking Jack out of his despair. "You are just the same person you always were, Jack. Yes, this happened, this awful thing happened, and it's going to take awhile for everybody to know how to handle it. Remember, we've only known about it for a short time. It's going to take some time, that's all. We'll get through this, Jack, I promise we will."

Looking into his brother's eyes, David said, "If you want me to, I'll stay home, Jack. I can go back to college next semester. Or next year. I'm here for you, buddy."

“No, I don’t want to screw up your life, too,” Jack said. But he felt good that David was willing to do that for him. “No, I was just upset. I’ll be okay, man.”

“I know you will, little brother,” David said. “Hey, do you want to go play some cards? Show those old men who’s boss?”

“Sure,” Jack said.

They rejoined Mike and Pappa at the table, and they did show ‘the old men’ who was boss. It was still Pappa. Each of the others won one hand to Pappa’s four. As they played cards, the awkwardness that was present earlier evaporated—for the most part, anyway. The rest of the afternoon passed pleasantly enough, Lucinda’s roasted chicken and dressing tasted even better than it smelled. It felt good to have the family together. But Jack was becoming very aware that his life was not going to go back to normal any time soon.

Chapter Fourteen

At the O'Donnell house, nobody skipped Sunday Mass unless they were truly ill: only vomiting, diarrhea, a severe cold, or worse would suffice as a reason to miss church. Not a little case of the sniffles, not a headache, not even, in Mike's case, a hangover (which may have been why he did his more serious drinking on Friday night.) Lucinda always tried to make sure the entire clan gathered in their usual pew, and it was only the most unusual of circumstances that didn't find at least most of the family at St. Maria Goretti's on Sunday. That's why it was so remarkable that, by unanimous agreement, this Sunday the family stayed home.

Even Lucinda felt it best to stay away that first week after Jack's revelation. She really didn't know what she would do if she saw Father Delanoit right now, and the thought of receiving the Eucharist from that man's hands filled her with revulsion. She had not yet begun to grasp how the fact that this priest had molested her grandson would affect her faith. Right now, the only thing on Lucinda's mind was how best to help Jack get through this. Not having to confront his molester right now seemed fairly obvious.

Also, there was an unspoken agreement within the family that a decision needed to be made about reporting the abuse to the diocese. Yesterday they had left the matter on the shelf, because after all the intensity and drama of the two previous days, it seemed best to focus on other things, everyday matters. But now, with David needing to head back to school, it seemed necessary to come to some kind of conclusion and establish a plan of action.

So Sunday morning Lucinda rose early, whispered a prayer asking for guidance and begging forgiveness for deliberately staying away from Church. This was a mortal sin, punishable by eternal damnation. But what exactly was the punishment for stealing a little boy's innocence, she wondered. The God Lucinda had always known and loved surely valued the life of a child more than he valued adherence to every rule and regulation established by man, she thought. Anyway, she simply couldn't stomach seeing Father Delanoit, so that must qualify as a legitimate sickness.

She dressed quickly, running a comb through her mostly-white hair and splashing some cold water on her face before heading down to the kitchen and brewing a big pot of coffee. Her spirits lifted as the smell of fresh coffee filled the room, and she began gathering the ingredients for coffeecake, one of David's favorites. As she measured flour and sugar and cinnamon, Lucinda weighed the family's options in her mind.

They could say nothing about the abuse and transfer to a different parish. Hook's Point had another Catholic church, St. Augustine's, which served mainly the upper-middle class part of town. Lucinda didn't like the idea of Father Delanoit getting away with what he'd done, but this might be the easiest course for Jack, for all of them, just to leave St. Maria's and have a fresh start at another church. They could report Father Delanoit to the diocese and hope that appropriate action would be taken: that the bishop would see that the priest was severely punished and turned over to the civil authorities, and a new priest assigned to St. Maria's. The most important thing, however, was to do what was best for Jack.

Jack! Lucinda's heart broke anew every time she thought of what her grandson had gone through. The fear, the horror of a child being used to satisfy an adult's twisted sexual desires, an ordeal that no child should ever experience. The hopelessness when Jack had realized that he was trapped in that situation, and the sense of betrayal when nobody, nobody, even his family, saw what was going on and stopped it. What was this going to do to

Jack over the long term? How would it affect his adult life?

Lucinda pushed those thoughts from her mind as she poured the batter into a pan and placed it in the oven. They had enough to worry about without fretting about the future. Hopefully, Jack would be able to put this whole thing out of his mind after they decided how they were going to handle it.

"Morning, Grandma," David said, filling up the kitchen with his long, lanky form. Lucinda had become so accustomed to David's absence that she forgot how much smaller—and fuller—the house felt when he was home.

"Good morning to you," she said, reaching up to kiss his cheek before she wiped off the counter. "Does it seem strange to you, not going to Mass today? I've got to admit, while I couldn't possibly go to St. Maria's today, I feel a little bad about skipping."

"Yeah, it seems strange. But there's no other choice we could have made, Grandma," David said. "I'd feel like I was stabbing Jack in the back if I went into that church while Father Delanoit is there."

"So would I," Lucinda said. She poured herself a cup of coffee, and was surprised when David got himself a cup of the stuff.

"Since when did you start drinking coffee?" she asked.

"Since I started pulling all-nighters," David said. "Schoolwork, Grandma," he said in reply to her quizzical look. "No, I'm not interested in the party scene. Becoming a priest is still what I want to do, and as far as I'm concerned, that means living a holy life even now, before I'm ordained."

"Too bad all of them didn't see it that way," Lucinda said.

Just then, Mike strolled into the kitchen, and minutes later, Pappa rapped on the door, opened it up and joined the others. He and Mike each grabbed a cup of coffee and proceeded to divvy up the newspaper, Pappa taking the news and Mike the sports section. They read quietly for a while, and then Pappa pushed the paper aside and asked the question that was on everybody's mind.

"What are we going to do about the man who assaulted my

great-grandson?" he said.

"I think we should turn him in," David said. "The man is not fit to wear the collar."

"I agree with David," Lucinda said. "We really can't let him get away with this."

"All I care about is what's best for Jack," Mike said.

"That's what we all want, Mike. We want to do what's best for Jack," Lucinda said. They all grew quiet when they heard the sound of footsteps coming down the stairs.

"Do I get a vote? I heard you all talking," Jack said as he entered the kitchen. "Because I've decided what I want to do."

"What do you want to do, son?" Pappa asked.

"I want to turn him in," Jack said. "Nobody else should have to go through what I did. And besides that, I want him to pay for what he did to me."

"The bastard," Mike said automatically.

"When Bishop Groat hears about this, Father Delanoit will be out. I wouldn't be surprised if he gets removed from the priesthood," Lucinda said.

"I'm glad, Jack. I think you're doing the right thing," David said. "This way, not only will you be able to get some justice for what he did to you, but you'll know that you've protected the other kids, too.

Pappa listened to the others, but kept his thoughts to himself. He had seen too much in his life to assume that the next step would go smoothly. After all, the diocese had nothing to gain and much to lose by taking the word of a young boy over that of the priest. He had seen far too much to assume that they would be motivated by conscience instead of by the desire for power and money. Yet, he did not want to discourage Jack. He had the feeling that reporting the abuse was important for the boy to do, regardless of the outcome. So when he finally spoke, he kept his doubts to himself.

"Whatever you want to do, we're right there with you,"

Pappa said.

"I wanna do this," Jack said. Since he had decided to report the abuse, Jack had felt stronger, and more hopeful than he had since the first time Father Delanoit had abused him. Surely if they told the bishop what Delanoit had done to him, he would be punished. Then maybe Jack could have the normal life that had so far eluded him.

"When are you going to call them?" David asked.

"I don't think we should call them," Mike said. "I've got some vacation days due to me. I think we ought to drive to Mobile and tell the bishop about it in person."

Jack looked down at the floor and trembled at the thought of facing the bishop: as much as he wanted to do this, he was frightened.

"Jack, you don't have to come if you don't want to," Mike said. "I can go there myself and talk to them. Grandma can come with me, or I'll go alone, and fill you in on what they're going to do when I get back."

"No, I want to go, too," Jack said. "I'm the one he did it to, I want to turn him in."

"We'll all go," Pappa said decisively. "I want to ask them if anyone else has ever reported that man for abusing a child."

"You think he's done this before?" Lucinda asked.

"Of course he's done it before," Mike said. "The man is 50-some years old. He didn't just get up one morning and decide he was going to molest a little kid. I'll bet if you look in Father Delanoit's closet, you'll find a whole shitload of things you'd rather never see."

This just keeps getting worse and worse, Lucinda thought despairingly. She had been so focused on what had happened to Jack that she had not even considered that Father Delanoit had likely done the same thing to other children. She shuddered to think of how many times she had sat drinking coffee with the man, totally unaware of what was lurking behind his holy facade.

"I'll come with you," David said. "I can afford to miss a day or two of classes."

"No, for crying out loud, we don't need to take a whole caravan," Jack said.

"Jack is right, David," Lucinda said. "You stay at school. We'll call you as soon as we know anything."

"When are you going to go?" David asked

"I could call them first thing tomorrow and see when they can see us," Lucinda said.

Mike was more inclined to drive straight to Mobile and storm the gates, but he supposed it would be wiser to make an appointment. That way, he could arrange to take the time off work and Jack could get caught up on any schoolwork he'd miss while they were gone.

The timer beeped, so Lucinda took the coffeecake out of the oven and placed it on a potholder in the middle of the table. David set the table and poured orange juice, then decorously announced, "Grub!" before cutting himself a generous chunk of coffeecake.

"Hey, how about if you leave some for the rest of us," Jack said, though there was still plenty left in the pan.

"You guys get to have Grandma's cooking every day, what are you complaining about?" David said. "I'm just a poor starving college student."

"Is that why your belly's sticking out over the top of your jeans, because you're a poor starving college student?" Jack said, poking his brother in the stomach, which provoked David to give him a jab in return.

"You boys cut it out, now," Lucinda said, yet actually, she was delighted. Things might actually get back to normal, she thought, her characteristic optimism springing to the surface.

Later in the day David's roommate Mark picked him up to head back to college. Before he left, David reminded Jack of the promise he had made to him on Saturday.

"Just remember, little brother, I'm here for you," David said. "Even if I'm away, I'll be back in a flash anytime you need me. Just give a holler." He gave his brother a quick squeeze, then kissed Lucinda and shook hands with his father and Pappa.

"Arriverderci, il figlio," Pappa said, then grabbed David and hugged him.

Jack went upstairs and lay down on his bed, looking out the window at the clear blue autumn sky. He felt strangely full, like the little pieces of his soul that Father Delanoit had stolen from him were gradually being restored. His family's support, Mrs. Ryan and the way she'd treated him like he was some kind of hero or something, and Kelly, especially Kelly, all this love was like a balm on a wound so big and so deep that Jack had thought it would be impossible ever to heal it. But after this weekend, he really felt hopeful. Maybe it was going to be okay after all.

Chapter Fifteen

During second period the next day, Jack sat hunched over in his seat in the last desk in the third row, his chin resting on his hands, struggling to stay awake enough to absorb what Mrs. Bergerson was explaining about prime numbers. The steady drone of rain beating down on the windows didn't help the situation any. Jack's eyelids felt so heavy; maybe if he could close his eyes for just a moment, he would feel more alert… sometimes sitting toward the back of the room did have its rewards.

"Mr. O'Donnell, you aren't doing so well in this class that you can afford to sleep through it," Mrs. Bergerson said, sounding only mildly irritated. Frankly, if she were sitting down right now, she wouldn't mind taking a little catnap herself. There should be some kind of a law against rain on Mondays, she had always thought.

"Sorry, Mrs. Bergerson," Jack said.

"Party too hard this weekend, Jack?" Ronny Slater said. Several students turned to look at Jack and snickered.

"Ronny, we can do without your editorializing, thank you very much," Mrs. Bergerson said. "Now, who can explain how to find the greatest common factor for fifteen and twenty?"

Jack's drowsiness evaporated, replaced with embarrassment. Slater still seldom missed an opportunity to torment him, and generally his verbal digs had a hidden, or not so hidden, meaning. Jack realized that, even before Slater's comment, some of his classmates had been giving him the covert glance, the inquisitive look that made him think his name had appeared on the rumor mill. His cheeks burning, Jack feared that somehow word had gotten out about what Father Delanoit had done to him. When Andy Rhykkus, who sat in front of him, turned around and glanced at him while they were working on their assignment. Jack snarled under his breath, "Mind your own business, Rhykkus!"

"Sor-ree! I was just gonna see if you could lend me a pencil. Geez!" Andy said angrily.

Jack struggled to keep his own anger in check. Maybe nobody knew about it, maybe Slater was just being his usual asshole self. He felt a little bad, too: Andy never bothered anybody. He had no right to snap at him.

"Here," Jack said, reaching forward and setting a pencil on Andy's desk. "Sorry."

"Maybe you are on drugs, man," Andy said. "That would explain why you're all hyper half the time."

"Drugs! What are you talking about, drugs," Jack said, incredulously. He didn't even know anybody who did drugs. Some of the kids he knew had stolen a bottle or two of booze from their parents, but that's as far as their experimentation went, and Jack hadn't even tried that: he'd seen up close and personal what alcohol did to his father, and he wanted no part of it.

"Teresa Ricardo told everybody at the football game on Friday that you were doing drugs," Andy said. "I wasn't there, but Dan Hubert was, and he told me the next day."

"I'm not doing drugs, man," Jack said. "Teresa Ricardo doesn't know her ass from a hole in the ground."

At that point, Mrs. Bergerson shot them a warning look. Andy turned around and began working on his assignment, but Jack just looked blankly at his textbook, the numbers swimming over the page in meaningless combinations. Who would start a stupid rumor like that, he wondered? Still, he'd rather have people think he was on drugs than know about Father Delanoit…Father Delanoit! It made perfect sense! If he could convince enough people that Jack was taking drugs, then they would think that Jack was lying about the abuse. A thumping, throbbing pain began behind his eyes, slowly spreading into his forehead and temples. Jack felt the familiar desire to break something, to hit someone, anything to transfer this pounding pain from inside his head to something else. Or someone else.

Jack walked up to Mrs. Bergerson's desk and asked if he could use the restroom.

"Yes," she replied, then took another look at him. "Are you feeling okay, Jack?" she asked kindly. "You look a little pale."

Her kind words dissipated some of Jack's rage and brought the pounding in his head to a more manageable level.

"Yes, I'm okay," he said. He wanted more than anything to go home, but then he would look like he was running—and he would be. Then it would be twice as bad tomorrow. "I just want to use the restroom and get a drink of water."

"Go," she said, turning her attention to the pile of papers she had been correcting.

Jack walked down the corridor and into the boys' room. He opened the door to one of the stalls, used the toilet, then came out and splashed his face with cold water. Think, think, he urged himself. At least nobody knows about Father Delanoit. This is nothing compared with the shame he'd feel if that got out. What to say? If anybody else said anything to him, he'd just tell them the truth—he wasn't taking drugs, never had taken drugs, didn't even know where he'd find them if he wanted to. Try to focus, he told himself. Just get through the day.

He took a long, cold drink from the water fountain before he went back to the classroom. Then he kept his eyes firmly glued to his math assignment so he wouldn't notice if anybody was looking at him funny or not. By the time the bell rang, Jack had his temper under control again. He picked up his books and walked as quickly as he could to his next class, not looking at any of the faces in the hallway so he wouldn't have to contend with what he might see looking back at him.

At the same time that Jack was struggling with the fallout from the lies that Father Delanoit had planted in Mrs. McGrevey's mind, which she had gladly converted into rumors, Lucinda was setting up an appointment for the O'Donnells to talk to someone at the diocese. She called the diocese office in Mobile, first speaking to a secretary. Lucinda explained that she needed to talk to someone regarding a serious problem her family had with Father Delanoit, the priest serving at St. Maria Goretti Parrish in Hook's Point. The secretary, who sounded as if she was nursing a cold, connected Lucinda with the Bishop's assistant, the vicar general, Father Novak.

"Yes?" A terse male voice picked up the phone next.

"Hello, is this Father Novak?" Lucinda asked, reluctant to repeat the story again if she was simply going to be passed on to the next person in line.

"Yes, it is. What is this concerning?" he said.

"Father Novak, my family has experienced a very serious problem with Father Delanoit, the senior priest at St. Maria Goretti's Church here in Hook's Point," Lucinda said.

After a brief pause, Father Novak said, "What seems to be the problem?"

"We would like to make an appointment to come and talk to Bishop Groat about this in person," Lucinda said. "It's really a very serious matter, not something we want to discuss over the phone."

"This is a very busy time for Bishop Groat," he said. "I need to know in greater detail what the matter is that you want to discuss here."

"Father Delanoit has harmed a member of my family," Lucinda said. "That's going to have to be enough detail for you. This is a personal matter, and I want to talk to the bishop in person. That's why I'm calling, to set up an appointment."

The prelate was quiet for so long that Lucinda wondered if they'd been disconnected.

"Hello?" she said.

"You will have to wait a moment," he replied, clearly annoyed. "I will check the bishop's schedule and return your call. What is your phone number?"

Lucinda told him the number, and then asked, "When can I expect your call?"

"As soon as I check the schedule," he said, then hung up.

Lucinda sat holding on to the phone receiver, feeling dismayed. She had hoped for a little more interest in her concerns than what Father Novak had displayed. The prelate hadn't sounded concerned, or even surprised. Lucinda feared their allegation might be met with disbelief, but she hadn't anticipated disinterest. After all, it wasn't every day that a parishioner called the diocese claiming that the senior priest had injured a member of her family. The sinking sensation in the pit of Lucinda's stomach told her that maybe Pappa and Mike were right when they said the diocese might not offer them the help that she was expecting. Surely not, she thought, shaking off her fear. The man she'd spoken to just didn't have very good people skills, she told herself. Too much time with the books.

I probably have time to clean up the kitchen before he calls back, Lucinda thought. Don't want to start the laundry yet, though—I don't want go to all the way down in the basement and then have the phone ring. Lucinda had reached the stage in life where her knees did not appreciate multiple trips up and down the stairs. He will probably call back by the time I have the kitchen scrubbed up, she thought.

Three hours later, the breakfast dishes were washed and put back into the cupboards, the kitchen was sparkling, the living room dusted, and two loads of laundry washed, dried and folded, but still Father Novak hadn't called her back. Lucinda's irritation had move into anger about forty-five minutes before, when the phone had rung and she had rushed up from the basement to answer it, only to pick it up and hear a high-pitched voice squeal, "Martha? Is that you, Martha?"

Lucinda dialed the number again for the diocese. Again, the

secretary answered, and Lucinda struggled not to unleash her anger at the woman, who had nothing to do with the delayed phone call. The secretary connected her with Father Novak.

"Yes?" he said, sounding no more pleasant than the first time.

"Yes," Lucinda said. "I've been waiting for you to call me back."

"As I indicated before, the bishop's schedule is very busy. It's going to be quite difficult to find a time for him to meet with you this month," he said.

"This month I'm not interested in," Lucinda said. "This week we want to see him. Listen," she said, fueled now by her anger, "My son-in-law was all for driving right down there without an appointment and parking it in your reception area until the bishop decides to see us. I wanted to make an appointment, but maybe he had the right idea there."

"Hold on," he said. "It looks as if Bishop Groat could see you Thursday morning eight o'clock. He has to go out of town that afternoon and really had a lot of business to attend to before that, but if you can be here at eight, he could meet with you and your son-in-law."

"Eight o'clock Thursday morning. We'll be there," Lucinda said.

"Your name?" the prelate asked coolly.

"My name is Lucinda Walters, and my son-in-law is Mike O'Donnell," she said, not inclined to tell him that Jack and her father would also be there. Lucinda had played poker enough times with Pappa to know that sometimes it was best to keep your cards close to your chest, and this seemed to be one of those times.

"I have you on the schedule. Good day," he said, sounding not one bit sincere. But Lucinda didn't care. As long as the meeting was set up, that's all that mattered. Her faith in the Church told her that, even if this guy was a jerk, surely Bishop Groat would want to help them once he found out how Father Delanoit had broken the trust this family had placed in him, and the unspeakable things that man had done to Jack.

While Lucinda was trying to contact the bishop, Pappa was using the phone in his apartment to call his contacts in Chicago to see what they could tell him about Father Delanoit. He still had phone numbers for two old neighbors and a friend he'd played cards with, all of them long-time members of St. Mary's Church. Smoothing out the paper where he had written their numbers and laying it down on the table, Papa made his first call.

"Pronto," croaked a deep smoky voice, using the traditional Italian phone greeting.

"Sol? Sol Martino?" Pappa asked.

"Yeah. Who's this?"

"It's Tony Gargano! Sol, how are you?" he asked, surprised by the rush of emotion he felt at the sound of the crusty old fool's voice.

"Tony! Who'd have thought you were even still alive! You old fart, moving out of town on us. How are you doing?" Sol said.

"When you're as old as I am and you can still get out of bed every day, then you're doing pretty damn good. Sol, I need to ask you a question."

"Fire away. But I gotta tell you, the old brain isn't as sharp as it used to be," Sol said. As Pappa recalled, his former neighbor didn't miss much. Now, if he was just willing to share what he knew.

"Father Delanoit, Sol. Louis Delanoit. He was the priest at St. Mary's Parish about twenty years ago. Tell me about him: what did the people think of him, how long was he there, why did he leave. Anything you might have heard about the man," Pappa said.

"Let me see, Tony; Father Delanoit. That name rings a bell, but it's been a long time… oh, yes, I remember. Big, good-looking guy right out of seminary. He wasn't the fiery speaker that some of them are, but he was a smart one. And he started up a youth program at the church, trying to keep the kids from getting into trouble on the streets. Wasn't here very long, though," Sol said.

"Anything else? Did you ever hear anything about any trouble he may have gotten into while he was here?" Pappa asked.

"No, I don't remember anything about any trouble, Tony. Now, if Regina was still here, she would remember. The woman knew everything that went on at the church. And in the neighborhood, and in the family. But I never paid that much attention. Gossip's for old women, in my book," Sol said.

"Hey, Sol, you take care of yourself, you hear," Pappa said.

"You, too," he croaked. "Bye, Tony."

Pappa sighed. He had hoped that Sol could give him some information. But if he knew anything, he wasn't talking. The next call was no more helpful than the first one. His loquacious former neighbor, an elderly woman named Maria Barstinova, was no longer living in her apartment; her daughter, who was not exactly a youngster herself, said she hadn't been able to take care of Maria after the older woman had taken a fall the previous winter, so she had moved her mother to a nursing home. Pappa tried the last number.

"Pronto." Vince Barone sounded just the same as the last time he and Pappa had played a round of poker over two years ago. Pappa could picture him instantly: the thick white hair, the handlebar moustache, the jolly, harmless grin that belied Vinny's sharp native intelligence.

"Vinny! It's Tony! How are you doing, old friend?" Pappa asked.

"Tony! I was just thinking about you today. It's been a long time since I've heard your voice, too long," Vinny said. "How are things going for you in Hook's Point?"

"It's good to have family, isn't it, Vinny? My daughter spoils me rotten with her good cooking, just like her mother did. I'm happy there. But I've gotta say, I miss getting together with the old gang," Pappa said.

"Old is right, Tony. You moved away, Bobby can't make it out anymore—bum ticker—and you know that Lou passed away in April?" Vinny said.

"Yes, I heard, I heard," Pappa said. The two old friends observed a moment of silence, remembering their comrade and knowing their own time on Earth was drawing to a close. But not yet, Pappa thought. Not yet.

"Vinny, I've got to ask you something," Pappa said.

"Anything. You can ask me anything, you know it," Vinny said.

"I need you to tell me if you know anything about Father Delanoit, Father Louis Delanoit. He was at St. Mary's about twenty, twenty-five years ago. I need to know if there was any trouble of any kind, anything at all, that you heard about him," Pappa said. "I know it seems strange, but I have my reasons for asking."

Vinny hesitated. Pappa heard him take a deep breath before he replied.

"Father Delanoit was here a long time ago, Tony," Vinny said, his voice slightly cooler.

"Something happened, didn't it, Vinny? Something bad. Please, I wouldn't ask if it wasn't important," Pappa said urgently.

"Nothing happened, Tony. Father Delanoit came here right after seminary. He served here a few years, like they do, and then he got transferred. That's all. Why do you ask a question like that, Tony?" Vinny said.

"Because, Vinny, I told you, it's important. I'm asking you to tell me what happened," Pappa pleaded.

"Nothing happened, Tony. Leave it. Don't go stirring things up, causing trouble," Vinny said angrily. "Nothing happened. I've got to go now, Tony. Hey," he said, his tone softening, "Call me again sometime. We'll talk about old times. Not all that garbage about stuff that happened twenty years ago." He hung up the phone.

Vinny knows, Pappa realized, exhaustion and depression setting in. He knows, but he's not saying. Father Delanoit had done something at St. Mary's, just like what he did to Jack. Pappa had the feeling it was somehow even worse.

He was disappointed by his old friend's reaction. Disappointed, but not especially surprised. Sexual abuse of any kind, but especially of children, was something that people just didn't talk about. They operated under the "see no evil, hear no evil, speak no evil" rule, especially when it came to clergy members abusing children. While Pappa was grief-stricken when Jack came out with the truth about what Father Delanoit had done to him, he wasn't totally surprised. At some level he had known from the first time he saw the priest with his grandson that there was something unsavory, unwholesome, about Delanoit's interest in Jack.

Pappa had heard rumors, even back in Italy, stories about priests with boys or young girls, spoken in whispered innuendos with fearful backward glances lest the speaker be overheard by the wrong ears. Speaking evil of the clergy was practically viewed as blasphemy. Why, a person could be excommunicated and lose all hope of heaven. While Pappa was disappointed in Vinny, he did understand the mindset that kept him from opening up and telling him what he knew.

While Lucinda had been cleaning and doing laundry, waiting for the Father Novak to call her back, and Pappa had been placing his calls to Chicago, the vicar general had been making a phone call of his own. After a quick conference with Bishop Groat , who was dismayed but not surprised to hear that Father Delanoit had apparently slipped back into his old habits, Father Novak called the errant priest to find out just what had gone on down in Hook's Point that this woman was so upset about. Although, unfortunately, he had a pretty good idea already.

"Father Delanoit, please," he had said when Mrs. McGrevey answered the rectory phone.

"Who shall I tell him is calling?" she said. Sounded like someone official.

"Father Novak in Mobile," he said.

"Just a minute, Father, he'll be right with you," Mrs. McGrevey said, pleased with herself that she'd correctly identified this as an important call, worthy of interrupting Father Delanoit while he was working in his study.

"Father Delanoit, Father Novak is on the telephone," Mrs. McGrevey said through the study's closed door. "He's calling from Mobile," she added.

Where else would he be calling from, Father Delanoit thought to himself, though all he said was, "I've got it. Hang up the other phone, please."

"Father Delanoit here," he said. He had been expecting this call ever since Mike O'Donnell had burst into the rectory.

"What's going on down there?" Father Novak said in his usual abrupt manner. "We had a woman calling here, insisting on an appointment with the bishop. Said you'd hurt a member of her family."

"What's the woman's name?" Father Delanoit asked, not yet decided on what tactic he would use this time.

"Lucinda Walters. She and her son-in-law Mike O'Donnell are coming to the diocese on Thursday morning at eight o'clock. What the hell have you gotten yourself into this time?" the prelate asked, his voice simmering with anger.

"O'Donnell is an unfortunate man in our parish, an alcoholic; one of those folks who can't control the members of his own household, so he blames other people for his problems," Father Delanoit began.

"Cut the crap, Delanoit," Father Novak roared. "You've done it again, haven't you? Is there going to be another dead body lying in your wake this time?"

"Nobody's been hurt here," Father Delanoit said. Nobody of any consequence, he added silently.

"What the hell is the matter with you? When we covered up for you after that fiasco at St. Mary's, you gave your word that you were going to keep your nose clean," Father Novak hissed.

Father Delanoit wondered if the vein on the old man's face was throbbing about now, the one running down his forehead that twitched so remarkably whenever he was inflamed. Surely the man was going to give himself a stroke one day.

"You've been at it again, haven't you?" Father Novak demanded. "Answer me!"

Father Delanoit discreetly cracked open the study door and

looked to make sure the housekeeper wasn't lurking nearby. He heard her banging about in the kitchen—the woman had no more grace than a water buffalo—so he shut the door again, reassured that he would not be overheard.

"There was a young man, yes," he said softly. "We had a special relationship."

"Relationship!" Father Novak snorted. "How old was this one?"

The gig was up. No point in trying to lie about it now.

"Twelve."

"My God! You make me sick!" Father Novak said.

This was not Father Delanoit's first trip to the woodshed. He would have to listen to a certain amount of castigation, but really, very little was likely to change in his life as a result of the O'Donnells' trip to Mobile. He thought he'd done enough damage control with Mrs. McGrevey, convincing her to spread the story about Jack's alleged drug problem around the parish, so there really wouldn't be any major fallout here in Hook's Point. In his experience, the boys and their families didn't want anyone to hear about the incidents any more than Father Delanoit did. The only consequence that he might face would be a transfer to a new parish, and that was not really a problem. Although Father Delanoit was comfortable here, the situation with Father Schmidt was becoming somewhat difficult. The man was insolent, given to shooting daggers in his direction when he thought the older priest wasn't looking. He was aware of it, though: very little escaped Father Delanoit's attention. Maybe a move would be in order.

"I…I am sorry," he said. Like the boy caught with his hand in the cookie jar, he was indeed sorry, sorry that he'd gotten caught, and he knew the words that were expected. "I am usually a strong man, Father Novak. But I do seem to have a weakness in this area."

"I'm not interested in your sob story. I just want to know what in the hell am I going to tell Bishop Groat?" Father Novak said. "Is there any chance, the remotest chance in hell, that you could convince this family not to come to Mobile on Thursday? Any possibility that you could persuade them somehow to back off?"

“I’m afraid not,” Father Delanoit said, rubbing his chin as he recalled the blow he’d taken courtesy of Mike O’Donnell. “No, I’m quite sure not.”

“Damn!” the prelate roared. He was silent for a moment, then spoke with bitter resignation. “Well, then, that’s that. I’m sure you’ll be hearing from the bishop, Delanoit.” With that, he slammed down the phone and the line went dead.

Father Delanoit placed the receiver in its holder. The other priest’s words had little meaning to him; they passed by like dandelion seeds floating in the summer breeze. He had never been impacted by threats from people in authority, ever since Father Brockman had initiated him into this perhaps strange lifestyle. Any fear he had felt, Father Delanoit had buried long ago, along with any sadness or grief or shame. Since he kept his emotions so deeply buried, they never troubled him. Too bad Jack hadn’t seen his way to handle the situation in a like manner, he thought. Instead, it looked like things were going to get messy.

Chapter Sixteen

Rather than get up before six o'clock Thursday morning and make the two-hour drive to Mobile, Mike thought they ought to drive into the city on Wednesday and spend the night in a hotel. So, late Wednesday afternoon the four of them piled into the Chevy, Mike and Lucinda in the front seat, Jack and Pappa in the back.

The day was warm and sunny for late October, with a temperature approaching seventy degrees, but the pleasant weather did little to ease Jack's fears. He had looked forward to telling his story and hopefully getting Father Delanoit put away where he couldn't hurt any more kids, but as the time drew closer, Jack became more apprehensive. What if nobody believed him? What if he had to tell the whole sordid story again for nothing? He chewed his fingernails and stared out the window, not really noticing as they drove past empty fields and the small towns dotting the Iowa landscape as they made their way to the city.

By six-thirty, they had checked in to their hotel; it wasn't fancy, but at least, it looked clean and reputable. Mike and Jack would stay in one room and Pappa and Lucinda in the room next door. Right after they checked in and deposited their bags in their rooms, they went looking for a place to eat and settled on a restaurant a block down the street from the hotel, a quiet place called

Aunt Nelly's. As the family munched on burgers and fries, they deliberately kept the conversation light. But after everyone had finished eating, they began to discuss the trip's true purpose.

"Tomorrow we'll want to give ourselves plenty of time to get to the bishop's house. Probably should leave here about seven thirty," Mike said. "That morning traffic may be hectic."

"I am glad the bishop is going to hear us out," Lucinda said. From the tenor of her telephone conversation with the vicar general, she had feared he might not even give them the opportunity to talk to him at all.

"And why wouldn't he? His time is no more valuable than anybody else's," Pappa said. "The man is supposed to be the shepherd of his flock. Surely he ought to take time to listen if a member of that flock has been harmed by the guy who was supposed to be in charge."

Jack crunched on the ice left over from his cola. He wanted to tell the bishop what had happened, yet he also hated saying what Father Delanoit had done to him, he hated dredging it all up. More than anything Jack hoped that he could tell his story, that Father Delanoit would get what he deserved, and then he could go back to normal, like none of this ever happened. As he shifted the ice around in his mouth, he bit down hard on his tongue.

"Damn!" he cried out, louder than he'd meant to but surprised by pain so sharp it brought tears to his eyes. "I bit my tongue," he said when everybody at the table looked over at him.

"How are you doing with all this, Jack?" Lucinda asked, putting a warm, wrinkled hand on his, giving a gentle squeeze.

"I just want to get it over with," he said grimly.

"I don't blame you, son. Tomorrow at this time, it will be," Mike said. "And hopefully that bastard will be gone for good from Hook's Point. Well, folks, we have us a big day tomorrow. I think we'd better turn in."

Pappa nodded. He was worn out from the trip and the emotional roller coaster of the past few days.

"Good night, son," Pappa told Jack. "We're going to get through this together, remember that," he said, rubbing his great-grandson's tense shoulders a moment. Then they all went up to their rooms.

Lucinda unpacked her fuzzy faded pink bathrobe, her flannel pajamas and her toothbrush. After asking Pappa if he needed anything, she went into the hotel's postage stamp-sized bathroom to shower. She was in and out in ten minutes.

"You look all in, Pappa," Lucinda said worriedly. Her father had been the rock of Gibraltar through all this, and she drew considerable strength just from knowing he was here with her, and that he was here for Jack. How long could she expect that to continue, though?

"I'm alright, Princess," he said, as if he'd read her mind. "I don't plan on going anywhere until we've seen this thing through and gotten our Jack to the other side of it. I'm going to wash up and hit the sack now." With that, he took the pajamas and toothbrush that Lucinda had laid out for him and went into the bathroom.

In the room next door, Mike and Jack stretched out on their beds, watching television. The baseball playoffs were on. They welcomed the normalcy of it, watching the intense focus of the batter as he swung once, twice and then finally hit the ball into the outfield, running to third base and allowing three of his teammates make it to home. The announcer's enthusiastic voice and the cheering of the crowd alleviated the quiet tension which enveloped the hotel room, neutralizing it, making this seem like just a nice family vacation. As soon as the ball game was over, the two of them, by silent agreement, crept under the covers and tried to get to sleep while the illusion of normalcy was still with them.

The morning traffic on the drive to the diocese was not as heavy as Mike had expected, so they arrived at the bishop's headquarters at quarter to eight. Mike whistled as he looked at the magnificent old edifice.

"I thought these folks had to take a vow of poverty," he said. "If this is poverty, I wouldn't mind trying it for awhile."

At one time Lucinda would have been a little troubled by

Mike's lack of reverence. She had always believed that the bishop rightly deserved a place of preeminence, as was fitting for a man in his position of authority. But ever since Jack's revelation, all of her beliefs had been shaken. She now tended to think her father had been correct not to put one man above another in rank. Respect has to be earned.

When they knocked at the door, a tall, plain-faced woman with a thick gray bun came to answer it. She looked both kind and sensible, just the sort of woman who could be counted on to keep a place such as the bishop's residence running smoothly. She ushered them through the high-ceilinged hallway with its dark paneled walls into a waiting room, a room with thick velvet drapes dressing the windows and dark brocade furnishings.

"Father Novak will be with you shortly," she said, then briskly strode away, on to the next task in her no doubt busy day.

"I thought we were supposed to be talking to the bishop," Jack said. "Isn't that his boss? Who's this Father Novak, anyway?"

"That's who I talked to on the phone—he's the vicar general, Jack. I thought we were going to talk to the bishop, too," Lucinda said.

Mike snorted in disgust and walked over to the window. He didn't want to agitate Jack by revealing too much of his own anger. He took a deep breath and willed himself to be calm, trying to remember the AA slogans that Scotty told him to hang on to whenever he got anxious or tempted to drink. Let go and let God. Whose God, he wondered. Father Delanoit's God? The God that he was supposed to represent?

Just then, the housekeeper came back in the room.

"Father Novak will see you now," she said. "I'll take you to his office." She led them down the hallway, past the portraits of all the bishops who'd served in the diocese, to the vicar general's office, then went back to her duties.

"Come in," Father Novak said. He was seated behind a large walnut desk, and he waved his hand in an apparent invitation for them to have a seat. Lucinda sat on one side of Jack, Mike on the other, and Pappa took a seat by Lucinda. Father Novak's study had the same rich drapery, heavy furniture and thick carpeting as the other rooms. Yet somehow, the vicar looked out of place amid all the opulence, as if he would be more comfortable pitching hay or driving a combine. His broad Irish features and robust build reminded Mike of his own Irish-peasant heritage, and for the first time since they'd driven up to the diocese, he felt slightly hopeful.

"I spoke with you, Mrs. Walters, on the phone the other day, and you said there was a problem regarding Father Delanoit and a member of your family," he said. "What seems to be the problem?"

"We were under the impression that the bishop was going to talk to us, Father Novak," Lucinda said. Her lifelong habit of deferring to priestly authority made her hasten to add, "Not that we aren't grateful that you're taking the time to see us."

"No. I will be handling this matter for Bishop Groat, though be assured I'll keep him fully informed about this situation," Father Novak said. His voice sounded firm, but not unkind, less harsh than he had over the phone. "Now, you wanted to talk about a situation at St. Maria Goretti Parish in Hook's Point. What is it?"

"It's about the head priest, Father Delanoit. Father Delanoit...he took advantage of my son, Jack, here. Molested him," Mike spat out angrily. "The first time was when Jack started serving as an altar boy two years ago, when he was in the sixth grade. He'd just turned 12 years old."

Tears began rolling down Lucinda's cheeks, and Jack's eyes were fixed firmly on the floor.

"He tricked Jack, made him think that he'd get into trouble if he told anybody, and this went on for over a year," Mike continued. "Jack never said a word until he found out that Delanoit had it in his mind to go after Jack's friend's little brother. Then he couldn't hold it back any longer, and he told us. I went to the rectory and had words with Delanoit, told him he'd best never come near my son again. We'd thought that would be the end of it, but Father Schmidt told us that if Jack would report this to the diocese, he could prevent the same thing from happening to any other kids, that you folks would make sure of it. So that's why we're here today," Mike concluded.

Father Novak, his expression grave, waited until Mike was done. Pursing his lips, he released a deep breath, pushed his glasses up, and rubbed his shiny forehead with a meaty hand.

"Does anyone else at St. Maria's know about these allegations, Mr. O'Donnell?" he asked.

"These are *not* allegations," Mike replied heatedly. "These are the facts."

"I didn't mean to imply that I don't believe you, Mr. O'Donnell," Father Novak said. "I am just asking how many other people know about this…situation? I'm sure we'd all rather keep this quiet. For the boy's sake," the prelate added hastily.

Why were those the first words out of this man's mouth, Jack wondered. Jack didn't want anybody else to know about this, either, but he thought maybe the vicar would have thought to ask how Jack was, tell him that he was sorry, something crazy like that.

"Nobody knows about this. I take that back—Father Schmidt and the housekeeper at the rectory heard me confront Father Delanoit," Mike said. "Jack didn't want people to know about it. He didn't want to come here today until Father Schmidt talked him into it, told him that's the only way to keep other boys from getting hurt."

Father Novak brought his hands together and pressed them against his lips. His solemn expression gave Jack the impression that at least he did believe him and was a little concerned. The priest sat silently for a few moments, apparently contemplating. Pappa took the opportunity to broach the question he'd wanted to ask the bishop.

"To the best of your knowledge, Father Novak, has Father Delanoit ever done this type of thing before?" Pappa asked, his dark eyes closely observing Father Novak's face. The vicar hesitated, blinking twice before he responded.

"No, nobody else has accused Father Delanoit of abusing a child," he said firmly. "But you folks did the right thing, bringing this to our attention." For the first time, he looked directly at Jack.

"We will make sure that, in the future, Father Delanoit understands that he can't behave the way he did with you, and I will talk to Father Schmidt about helping him stay away from young boys. Father Schmidt can take over the altar boy duties at St. Maria Goretti's from now on." Then Father Novak smiled briefly, looking like a kindly old uncle.

"Now, my advice to you, young man, is to go back to Hook's Point and forget all about this unfortunate incident. Put it behind you," he said. "Throw yourself into sports and other wholesome activities. Don't give the devil a moment's time to torment you about all of this, and before you know it, this will just seem like a bad dream."

Unfortunate incident. Unfortunate incident. The words burned into Lucinda's brain, a brand of disillusionment from which she would never recover. Minor car accidents, broken windows, bad grades on the report card, rash words spoken in the heat of the moment, these were all "unfortunate incidents." The sexual abuse of her youngest grandson by the parish priest was not an unfortunate incident.

"Do you want to know about bad dreams, Father Novak?" Lucinda said, using that low, measured tone that her family understood instantly as dangerous. "Bad dreams have troubled my grandson for the past two years, ever since Father Delanoit first assaulted him. Bad dreams are what makes him cry out in the night and, when I go to console him, they make him jump out of his skin and beg me not to touch him. Bad dreams… no, this is not a bad dream, Father," she said, her voice rising as she stood and leaned closer to the vicar general. "This is a nightmare, and Jack's been living it for two years now, and for God knows how much longer yet. We can't go back to St. Maria's and act as if nothing ever happened. We can't receive the Eucharist from that… that man."

"So help me God, I've never raised my voice to a priest or sister before," Lucinda continued. "My mother revered the clergy; she told me they represented God, Jesus, and that I should treat them with the greatest of respect. So I did. When Father Delanoit came into our home and told me he wanted to befriend Jack, I was honored. I served the man coffee with my best china on Fridays, and then he would take my grandson, the boy I've raised from birth, and..."

At this point, Lucinda broke into tears. For a few moments, the only sound in the room was the soft intake of breath, a shaking release of subdued weeping. Father Novak had the grace to look slightly ashamed. Mike and Jack looked down at the desk, and Pappa gently stroked Lucinda's hand. When she was able to stop crying, she continued speaking.

"The worst thing that man did is steal my grandson's innocence, Father Novak," she said. "Don't let him rob us of our faith, on top of it."

"I will see what I can do, Mrs. Walters. Perhaps we can find another spot for Father Delanoit," Father Novak said. "I will call you and keep you apprised of the situation." He rose, indicating the meeting was over. The priest extended his hand to Mike, who ignored the gesture.

"You do that, Father Novak," he said. "We won't be taking up any more of your time, now." Mike walked to the door and held it open for his mother-in-law, who turned to speak again before leaving the vicar's office.

"Don't make us lose our faith, Father," Lucinda repeated. Then she walked out the door, followed by Pappa, Jack and Mike. Father Novak heard his housekeeper showing them to the door and wishing them "good day to you, now;" if they replied, he didn't hear it.

"Damn him!" Father Novak muttered bitterly, clunking himself into his chair. The vein on his forehead throbbed, keeping perfect rhythm with the steady thumping pain in his head. He swallowed hard to force down the bile that rose in his throat. Why, oh why, had Bishop Groat insisted on letting that pervert have another opportunity to serve in this diocese, especially after what had happened at St. Mary's in Chicago? Though the tragedy occurred more than twenty years ago, the priest remembered clearly the anguish on the face of the boy's mother when he'd met her at the hospital, too late to give her son the last rites, for he had been dead when the paramedics had cut down the rope he'd hung himself with in the basement of their apartment building.

"Charlie!" she had cried out. "Is my Charlie in hell then, Father? He's taken his own life… oh, my boy, my boy!" Then the woman had dropped to the floor, mercifully unconscious if only for a while. Charlie had been in hell from the first time Father Delanoit had laid his sick hands on him, the priest had thought grimly. Father Novak had walked in once and seen it for himself, Delanoit with his hands down the boy's pants: the child's expression reminded Father Novak of a deer frozen to the spot in front of the headlights of an oncoming vehicle. He'd been so repulsed that he'd turned and walked right out of the room and shut the door. Father Novak had tried to keep Delanoit away from children after that, but somehow the wily bastard always managed to finagle time alone with poor Charlie. Father Novak had reported the abuse to the bishop, who had urged Delanoit to go to confession and to ask the Blessed Virgin to help him. It was only after the boy committed suicide that the bishop decided to transfer Delanoit to Atlanta, where Father Novak had hoped he would stay.

But eventually Delanoit had been transferred back to the area, first in Peoria for several years and then to Hook's Point, which fell under the authority of the diocese headquarters in Mobile, where Father Novak then was serving as vicar general. He'd felt in his gut that it was only a matter of time before somebody called to complain about Delanoit. Since the turmoil of the sixties and the changes in the Church because of Vatican II, people were less deferential when dealing with the clergy, more likely to log a complaint than in the past. Well, the other shoe had finally dropped.

For the life of him, Father Novak could not fathom how a brother priest could behave in such a reprehensible fashion. When Father Novak had taken his vow of celibacy, he had meant it. And not once had he broken it. It was difficult, especially when he was younger, watching other men enjoy the comforts of family life, Father Novak had to admit. Some of the women in the parish were very attractive, and he had the same feelings as any normal man did. He dealt with his desires by throwing himself into his work and by praying, which somehow made the feelings manageable.

That any man would connect those feelings with a child,

though, was incomprehensible to him. That Delanoit was not just any man, but a priest, that made it all the worse. And now, he'd gotten himself roped into lying for the scoundrel. Father Novak sighed in disgust and pressed the buzzer that connected his office with the kitchen, which was usually where Hannah was this time of the morning.

"Yes, Father?" she asked. "Did you need something?"

"Hannah, would you bring me an antacid and some water?" Father Novak said.

"Certainly, Father, right away," she replied.

Now it remained for him to give Bishop Groat a full report and to contact Father Schmidt, as well as getting a hold of Father Delanoit. He'd like to get a hold of Delanoit, he thought: give me five minutes with the man and a good, sharp knife, and he'd make sure Jack was the last boy that Delanoit bothered. Calm down, he urged himself: that kind of thinking wasn't going to help the pounding in his head any. Bishop Groat knew about the incident, of course, since Father Novak had told him about Lucinda's call first thing Monday morning. Now he would be able to give him a full report, though; more than likely, the bishop would want to discuss all the ramifications with him. Delanoit had managed to make St. Maria's parish financially solvent for the first time in the church's history; traditionally, this was a parish that had to be carried by the wealthier ones in the area. Now they had been in the black for almost four years.

What Father Delanoit had done to this child, to his family, troubled Father Novak deeply. He hated the thought of those people turning away from Mother Church because of that man's actions. But he knew that many people in Hook's Point thought Father Delanoit was just what the parish had needed: a sound businessman and a strong leader. While ultimately the decision about whether or not to oust Father Delanoit belonged to Bishop Groat, Father Novak simply could not justify keeping him in the parish after this incident, especially since it wasn't the first time. A knock at the door delivered the priest from his musings.

"Come in, Hannah," he said.

“Here is your antacid, Father,” the woman said kindly. “Can I get you anything else?”

“No. Thank you, Hannah, that should help,” Father Novak said. Although, quite frankly, he doubted it.

Chapter Seventeen

Mike sat on the cold metal folding chair, clutching a Styrofoam cup filled with muddy coffee and listening to the speaker tell his story. The guy had woken up one morning from sleeping on a park bench lined with newspapers to keep him warm, a bottle of cheap whiskey beside him, his pants soaked with urine. That was when he'd decided he'd had enough, that he was, to use an AA slogan, sick and tired of being sick and tired. That had been five years ago. The guy had gone to his first meeting and never looked back, to hear him tell it.

Mike had looked back plenty. He'd looked back with disgust when he realized his failure to be there for Jack had been a major factor in his son's abuse. Father Delanoit had known exactly what he was doing, picking the son of a drunk to work his evil ways on. Mike had looked back with sadness when he thought of how he'd let Rita down and broken the promise he'd made to her when she was on her deathbed. But lately, Mike had also looked back with longing, a longing to experience the sweet oblivion that he knew alcohol could provide. Anything to turn off the screenplay in his mind, the one where the priest molested the little boy and, sorry folks, that was no screenplay, that was real life.

That's why Mike was here, sitting on an uncomfortable chair in a church basement on Twelfth Street. He had one week of sobriety under his belt now. He had kind of hated to leave his family tonight, after the troubling trip to talk to Father Novak, but Mike knew that he needed to get himself to a meeting if he wanted to stay sober.

And he did want that. He wanted that even more than he wanted the quick release that alcohol could provide. After the meeting he was going to talk to the guy he'd asked to be his sponsor, a man about ten years older than Mike and with seven years sobriety under his belt. His name was Tom Saunders. Scotty, his friend from work, had recommended that Mike find a sponsor, so Mike had asked Scotty to sponsor him, but he'd said he didn't have enough time in the program yet to feel like he could give Mike the support he needed. So Mike asked Tom, a roughneck truck driver whose gruff words revealed a simple wisdom. Like the program said, keep it simple, let go and let God, and, most importantly to Mike, one day at a time, because he truly could not fathom spending the rest of his life in this hyper-aware condition called sobriety.

At the end of the meeting, Mike joined the others while they stood in a circle and recited the Lord's Prayer, but he remained silent. Our Father, who art in heaven… these words were tainted now, triggering memories of all the times he'd prayed this very prayer while his son stood on the altar next to Father Delanoit, his guts writhing in disgust and fear. Mike's tenuous relationship with God had definitely taken a nosedive due to the recent revelations. While the prayer brought him no comfort, standing in solidarity with a roomful of people who shared a common problem did.

Tom walked up to Mike after the meeting and extended his hand. This time, Mike gladly responded to the friendly gesture and clasped the trucker's calloused hand in his own.

"Come on," Tom said, motioning for Mike to join him in a semi-secluded seating area at the back of the room, far enough away from the others, who were laughing and talking and, in a couple of cases, crying, so that he and Mike could have some privacy.

"Thanks for helping me out, for agreeing to be my sponsor," Mike said.

"That's what we're here for, to help each other out," Tom said, his voice rough and gravelly from years of smoking and drinking. He'd given up the booze, but not the cigarettes: Tom pulled a Winston out of the package in his chest pocket, lit it, and took a deep drag. "I'm willing to be your sponsor, but you've got to promise me two things."

"What's that?" Mike asked.

"You've gotta promise you'll call somebody in the program before you take a drink, and you've gotta promise you'll work the Twelve Steps," he said as he exhaled, then quickly taking another drag. "Otherwise, it's never gonna work and you might as well not waste your time or mine."

"I'm not gonna take another drink, though," Mike protested. "Isn't that what this AA stuff is all about?"

"Yeah, that's what it's all about," Tom said. "But there's gonna come a day when you want to chuck the whole damn thing and crawl right back into that bottle you just crawled out of. It happens to everybody. I don't want you to promise you're never gonna take another drink. But I do want you to promise you'll call me, or somebody else if you can't get a hold of me, before you do."

"All right," Mike said dubiously, although what the hell good that was going to do, he didn't know. "All right, I will."

"And you have to work the Twelve Steps. I'll help you, and so will anybody here," Tom said. He handed Mike a sheet of paper listing the steps and some of the AA slogans.

Mike looked at the steps as Tom read them off. Powerless over alcohol—uh-huh. Came to believe that a Power greater than ourselves could restore us to sanity? Sure hope so. Made a decision to turn our will and our lives over to the care of God... Mike grimaced.

"What's this third one? You want me to make some kind of religious vow or something? Cuz I've gotta tell you, Tom, me and the Church don't really see eye-to-eye right now," Mike said.

"Nobody wants you to make any kind of vows. It says to make a decision to turn your will and life over to the care of God, *as you understand him.* Not the God you learned about in Sunday school, standing there looking pissed off at you like you're something he found on the bottom of his shoe. It's however you understand God. Some people, it's just a Higher Power, maybe just the group. For some people, it's God like the one you hear about in church. Now me, I like to think of God as Jesus, because he always was one to hang out with the drunks. But you can make up your own God, for all I care. It's about trust," Tom said.

Trust. Now that was a tough one. But Mike warmed up to the idea that God wasn't necessarily the angry old man he'd often pictured him to be. And it's not like he was doing so hot, trying to handle life on his own. Okay, it was worth a shot. Hey, if he could do that, Mike was sure he could do the rest of them, too.

"Okay," he said, filling up with a sudden exuberance. "Okay, I'll do it. I'll take the steps."

"You don't exactly take the steps, Mike: you work them," Tom said, a smile spreading over his face, shearing years off his weatherworn features. "But that's good enough for now. You're off to a fine start, my friend." He shook Mike's hand again, and Mike felt the tension from the day lifting, and a real sense of hope that he could have a different kind of life, that he could be a different kind of man and make a better future for himself and his family.

Back at the house, Jack was talking on the phone to Kelly, ostensibly to get his homework assignments, but they'd gotten that out of the way in the first few minutes of their conversation. Now he was telling her about their dealings with the vicar general.

"He believed me, it's not like he didn't," Jack said. "But it was weird. Like it was no big deal or something. Like it happens every day."

"Isn't Father Delanoit going to be in a lot of trouble?" Kelly asked. "He ought to be. He ought to be in jail."

"I don't know what they're going to do. Maybe they'll make him leave St. Maria's," Jack said, hoping fervently that would happen. He dreaded the thought of his next encounter with the man who had abused him, yet he knew it was only a matter of time before he ran into Father Delanoit at school, and he didn't know how long Grandma would let him keep skipping Mass.

"You were really brave to go there, Jack. And I'll always remember how you stuck up for my little brother," Kelly said.

Jack soaked up the kind words, a balm in the wounds inflicted by Father Delanoit. "I'd better get going on that math assignment," he said. "I'll see you tomorrow. I love you."

"I love you, too," Kelly said. She gently replaced the receiver, assured that she had made the right decision, the decision not to tell Jack about the rumors flying around the school. Amanda Cranston had cornered her in the girls' bathroom, demanding to know if it was true that Jack had gotten picked up for smoking pot. Kelly had responded angrily, telling Amanda that Jack never even smoked pot, let alone been arrested. But she didn't think that Amanda had believed her; she saw her later in the afternoon between classes, huddled in the hallway with her girlfriends, whispering and sending pointed glances in Kelly's direction. The sad thing was, there was no way to prove the allegations were untrue. The best that she could hope for was that, as time went on and it became apparent that Jack wasn't using drugs, all the rumors would fade away.

While Jack was talking to Kelly on the phone in the main house, Pappa was taking a call on his line in the garage apartment. He had just taken off his shoes and gotten ready to stretch out on the couch when the phone rang. Pappa, weary from the trip and the meeting with the vicar general, considered not answering it, but decided he'd better take the call.

"Tony? This is Sol, Sol Martino," the caller said.

"Sol, what's up?" Pappa asked, instantly alert, adrenaline flooding his body.

"You asked me about Father Delanoit, and that got me to remembering. There was something, something really bad, I remembered, so I did some digging. Called Regina's little brother Johnny, you remember Johnny, the cop? Big brawny guy, with a mouth as big as his biceps? Anyway, Johnny said the story was that Delanoit had a thing for young boys, if you get my drift," Sol said.

"I get it, Sol," Pappa said. "Go on."

"Seems like Delanoit started in on some kid named Charles Romano, a kid who went to St. Mary's. His mother was a widow," Sol said.

Why am I not surprised, Pappa muttered.

"So Delanoit screwed around with this kid, and then the stories started to get around. Somehow Delanoit twisted it around, made it sound like it was this poor young kid's fault. Kids started to harass him, called him a faggot and a queer, then one day the kid takes a rope and hangs himself in his old lady's basement," Sol said.

"Mother of Christ!" Pappa said. "What did they do about Delanoit?"

"It wasn't long before he was out of here," Sol said. "I hear they transferred him down south somewhere, but I don't know for sure. So, does that help you any?"

"Yeah, it does. Thanks, Sol, you helped a lot," Pappa said, grateful that Sol wasn't inclined to ask a lot of questions about why he'd wanted this information in the first place.

"Good night, Tony. Keep in touch," Sol said.

"I will, Sol. Take care," Pappa said. After he hung up the phone, he tried to digest this bit of news. It was worse than what he'd expected. Pappa had thought that Novak was lying when he said nobody had ever accused the priest before, but not only had the diocese known that Delanoit was molesting children, the man was responsible for a boy's death, and yet he was still working with children, still in charge of young lives. With a gnarled hand, Pappa rubbed his stiff neck, contemplating the situation. One thing was for sure, he was more relieved than ever that he had gotten Jack away from that man.

At the St. Maria Goretti Rectory, the priests were also contemplating the situation. Under Bishop Groat's orders, Father Novak had called both of them to deliver his message. Novak's blistering words would have been enough to fill Father Delanoit with shame if he were capable of feeling that emotion. But he was able to tune out the vicar general's tirade, occasionally making a properly penitent reply, and focus on the fact that it seemed he wouldn't be required to leave the parish, not yet, anyway. Evidently, Father Schmidt would be "keeping an eye on his every move," Father Novak had said, his voice quaking with rage. This would be irritating, having to answer to that annoyingly sincere little twit. One had to make certain sacrifices, however. Father Delanoit sighed. He supposed he could become accustomed to having a watchdog again; it probably would curtail him somewhat, but he usually found a way to work around it. Those folks who were overly scrupulous like Schmidt weren't usually very hard to outmaneuver. Not that there was even anything to hide at the present time, anyway: Father Delanoit considered that this would be the time to be circumspect. Things would settle down after a while, and then he could find another young man with whom he could pursue a special relationship. In the meantime, he would throw himself into the work of the parish and earn back the bishop's good will.

Some people may have wondered why a man like himself would stay in the priesthood, Father Delanoit realized. He had to admit, he wasn't strictly abiding by the vows he had taken twenty-five years ago. (Twenty-five years ago! He wondered briefly if the parish was preparing a ceremony of some sort to honor him. That would be something to look forward to, in the midst of all this fuss.) But Father Delanoit believed that overall, he did more good than harm. Wasn't that the best anyone could claim? He raised more funds for the church than any priest did in the past fifty years. He was involved in several community organizations, putting a face to the faith that still seemed questionable to some of his Protestant brethren. He was completely dedicated to his work, other than this one small foible. And Father Delanoit knew for a fact that he was not the only priest with this failing. Why, some years back a fellow in Piermont, a priest he had met at a retreat, had actually brought the subject up to him. He wanted to know if Delanoit would be interested in a special gathering with several young boys. That type of thing was really rather revolting, Delanoit thought, somewhat judgmentally, he realized. But, my God, man! There had to be some limits.

Father Delanoit had turned him down flat, making the appropriately horrified-sounding comments and suggesting the fellow needed to make a confession, even offering to hear it for him if he'd liked. The other priest seemed a tad embarrassed and kept his distance anytime they happened to run into each other after that. But Father Delanoit knew there were others who would take the man up on his offer, just as he knew there were still others who preferred to play the lone wolf, as he did.

And, then there were those like Father Schmidt. Goody-two-shoes, by-the-books, never-cause-a-scandal Father Schmidt. More of his brethren were like Father Schmidt than like himself, he realized. Fortunately, those who learned about the little peccadilloes of men like himself were not inclined to get too excited about it. Pray the rosary every morning, Father Delanoit. Ask the Blessed Virgin to help you stop, Father Delanoit. He snorted derisively. They were as eager to avoid talking about it as he was, he had found. Father Schmidt would be no different from the others, he imagined. Don't talk about it, and it will all go away. And that suited Father Delanoit's agenda just fine.

In the room down the hall, Schmitty kneeled by his bed, his face buried in his hands. When he'd gotten the call from Father Novak, he'd felt sure the vicar general was calling to tell him that Father Delanoit was going to be removed. He didn't know if the older priest might be sent for treatment somewhere, he'd heard of that happening, but what he really hoped was that Father Delanoit would be removed from the priesthood, even sent to jail, at least one of the two. He'd been so sure that the bishop would be just as outraged as he was once he heard of Jack's horrific experience. When the vicar had sounded so… so *detached*, Schmitty had been astounded. All the prelate had said to him was that he expected Father Schmidt to keep a watch over Father Delanoit, making sure that he had no opportunity to be alone with any young boys. He was to assume all the altar boy training, and any other youth programming the parish had. Any violations of the expected standards of behavior on Father Delanoit's part were to be immediately reported to the diocese.

The only time the vicar had sounded adamant was when he

told Schmitty that he was not to speak a word of this to anyone. *No one, do you hear?* If Father Schmidt felt burdened by what he knew, well, the Lord always had a listening ear, didn't he? While he was at it, he should say a few extra prayers for his brother, Father Delanoit, that he be delivered from temptation.

"And Jack?" Schmitty had asked, his voice trembling with anger. "Should I say a few prayers for Jack, Father Novak? You know, the boy whose childhood Father Delanoit stole? That boy that was in your office today?"

"Drop the insolence, Father," the vicar had answered evenly. "I hate what happened to that boy just as much as you do. Now, do your damnedest to make sure that it doesn't happen again!"

With that, Father Novak had hung up the phone, leaving Schmitty wondering if he'd made a serious mistake when he told Jack and his family to report the abuse. Not because he'd been ordered to by his superior, but because it was his habit, the young priest sunk to his knees and unburdened his heart to the One he knew was always just, always true, always compassionate.

Father Schmidt wasn't the only one who was on his knees in prayer. Lucinda also was kneeling by her bed, clutching her rosary, pouring out her heart to the Blessed Virgin Mary. Right now talking to another woman, a mother, was much more appealing than talking to God the Father; in her mind, he was so tightly connected with the priests that she really didn't want anything to do with him. But what had sustained Lucinda through all of life's troubles but her faith? Never had she needed divine help more than she needed it now. Lucinda released her grip on the rosary and began talking to Mary, just one mother to another.

"Mary," she whispered. "They didn't care. They didn't care about Jack and what he went through, they didn't care how that man, that evil, wretched man, took such a good little boy and… and twisted him. They didn't care that Jack's life is never going to be the same again. They didn't care about the hell this family is going through. They really didn't care."

"I thought they would take care of it for us. I trusted them," she said, her voice breaking. "Mary, dear Mother, I trusted them, just like I trusted Father Delanoit. How can we ever go back to church there? How can we go on as if nothing happened? Jack's been trying to do that for over two years. Oh, Mary! Please help Jack. Ask your son to heal him, like he healed people in the Bible. Ask him to forgive me for not taking better care of my grandson. Ask him to forgive me, because I'm so angry, just so angry. Please, just help us."

Lucinda remained on her knees for a few moments before sinking into her bed, exhausted. Almost as soon as her head hit the pillow, she was fast asleep. Downstairs, Jack was finishing his math assignment. He had just closed his book and gone into the kitchen for a glass of milk and a piece of homemade chocolate layer cake when his father walked in the door. As Jack greeted him, Mike noticed the way his son cautiously looked him over. Tom had warned him that it would take a long time before his family could trust Mike was serious about sobriety. One day at a time.

"Long day, huh," Mike said, gently rubbing Jack's shoulder. Jack shuddered ever so slightly, but Mike noticed and immediately regretted touching him. What that bastard has stolen from my son, he thought ruefully.

"Is Grandma asleep, then?" Mike asked.

"Yeah, I think so," Jack said. "So how was the meeting?"

"Good. I got a sponsor," Mike said.

"What's a sponsor?" Jack asked.

"A sponsor is somebody who's been sober for a long time who helps the new people stay off the booze," Mike said.

"Cool," Jack said. And cool was how he was playing it: as great as it would be if his dad truly did quit drinking, Jack didn't dare get his hopes up too high, because he really couldn't afford another colossal disappointment right now. "Do you want a piece of cake?"

"Sure. Pour me some of that milk, too—those drunks go through a lot of coffee at those meetings. I've got a caffeine buzz," Mike said.

They took their cake and milk to the table and ate in companionable silence for several moments. Then Jack asked the question that had been bothering him since they left the diocese office.

"What if they don't do anything about Father Delanoit, Dad? I can't keep going to church there," Jack said.

"No. None of us can," Mike said. "We'll transfer to St. Augustine's if it comes down to that."

"That Father Novak today—it didn't sound like he was going to do anything about it. Maybe we shouldn't have bothered telling him at all. You had to miss a day of work, probably for nothing," Jack said, suddenly feeling deflated.

"No, it wasn't for nothing," Mike assured him. "You did what you felt you had to do, so that was worth it. It's been a long day, son. We'd both better go get some sleep," Mike said. As he got up to put their plates in the sink, Mike patted Jack on the back. He was grateful to see that this time, his son didn't cringe when he touched him. Baby steps, his sponsor had told him. It's all about the baby steps.

In his dorm room at Benedictine University, David was sitting at his desk, staring at his religion textbook. He was trying to study for the next week's test, but all he could think about was what his grandmother had reported from the family's trip to see the bishop. Phrases like "forget this unfortunate incident," and "this will seem like a bad dream," and the most ludicrous, "throw yourself into sports," kept intruding on his mind. David had spoken briefly to Jack, who seemed like he was trying to keep a stiff upper lip throughout his ordeal. But David had seen the naked pain in his brother's eyes last weekend; Jack's tough-guy routine wasn't fooling him a bit.

If David's faith wasn't shaken before, it definitely was now. He had believed so strongly in the inherent goodness of the Church that he had encouraged his little brother to take his humiliating story before the bishop, never doubting for a moment that the prelate would handle the matter justly, never doubting that his first concern would be for the well-being of the children in the Church. Now it seemed that his faith had been misplaced. For the first time since he'd decided to become a priest, David doubted his vocation. How could he become a part of an organization that treated his brother like this, he wondered. Whereas before he had felt peace regarding his decision, now all he felt was confusion and a deep sense of betrayal.

The next day was a Friday. It started out to be a mostly uneventful day, a welcome change from the dramas of the days before. Lucinda went on another cleaning binge, this time taking down all the curtains, washing them and hanging them on the clothesline, washing the windows and putting the curtains back up; Pappa got himself an invitation to Rose Canstani's for coffee and learned that she still didn't know the whereabouts of her son Alan; Mike unloaded six truckloads of frozen pies which would later be distributed throughout the state; and David attended his usual Friday classes at the university, as did Jack at St. Maria's. The two priests at St. Maria's got through the day by spending as little time together as possible; Schmitty rose early and left for the high school, grabbing a bite to eat from the vending machines in the teachers' lounge, and Father Delanoit ensconced himself in his study where he prepared for Sunday's sermon. It was a tricky text: the story of the widow's mite, where Jesus commended the old woman who gave her last bit of money to the temple and castigated those who gave greater amounts, but did it only to be seen and admired, tricky because St. Maria's liked to recognize their most generous donors quite publicly and found that practice increased giving dramatically. Father Delanoit usually strove to emphasize the fact that the widow gave all that she had and glossed over the rest of the story as quickly as possible. So that was his Friday, without the customary pleasures to look forward to at the end of the day.

Friday evening found Lucinda actually too tired to cook; for once, she felt every one of her sixty-nine years. Perhaps she'd overdone it a bit today, Lucinda admitted to herself ruefully. Mike picked up some pizzas from Tony's, and they gathered around the table to eat. They deliberately avoided talking about the trip to Mobile; yesterday they'd sliced it and diced it, and every time they came to the same unsatisfactory conclusion: the bishop was not going to do anything about Father Delanoit. So they talked about the unseasonably warm weather and about the Cub's chances at making it to the World Series, which were surprisingly good, and hashed over the latest news from Sheila about the twins. Sooner rather than later, they would need to make a decision about continuing at St. Maria Goretti's, but today they needed to take a break from the whole sordid mess.

"So, I thought I'd go over to Kelly's for awhile," Jack said as they finished their meal, asking for permission without quite coming out and saying it. Asking made him feel like a little kid, but he knew he wasn't yet allowed to come and go as he pleased.

"Do you want me to drop you off on my way to the meeting?" Mike said, by way of granting permission.

"No, thanks, Dad, I'll walk," Jack said. "It's nice out still."

"Be home by ten, Jack," Lucinda said.

If anybody in the O'Donnell house had had a crystal ball to consult, they wouldn't have let Jack walk out the door that night. But they didn't. Lucinda felt a vague sense of apprehension when he left, similar to what she'd felt when Father Delanoit would take him for the evening, but again she ignored her intuition, assuming her feelings were just leftover anxiety from the trip to see the bishop.

Chapter Eighteen

Kelly's mother was still at work when Jack arrived at the house. Kelly had heated up some leftover chicken and dumplings for Bill and herself, and applied a little sibling pressure to convince Bill to help with the dishes: if he didn't, Kelly threatened to tell their mother that Bill had broken one of Mrs. Ryan's favorite vases when he was bouncing his ball off the wall in the living room, an activity his mother had warned him against time and time again. A small piece had broken off the top of the vase when it hit the floor, which fortunately was carpeted or the vase would have shattered into a million pieces. Kelly glued the fragment back on and her mother's prized possession actually looked as good as new, but she still figured the situation would give her a little leverage. Kelly and Bill were just finishing up in the kitchen when Jack knocked on the front door.

"Hey, buddy, how's it going?" Jack asked Bill, who had raced from the kitchen into the living room to answer the door.

"Alright," he said, still sulking a bit from getting stuck with the dishes. "I got a new Nolan Ryan," Bill said, brightening a bit. "Do you want to see it?"

"Sure," Jack said. He smiled at Kelly, who had just come into the room, and followed Bill up the stairs to his bedroom, the walls of which were plastered with baseball posters. Bill carefully removed the card from his binder, holding it by the sides, and proudly showed it to Jack.

"Very cool," Jack said. "You hold on to these, and someday they'll be worth some money."

"That's what my mom said, too, but I'm not really interested in selling them. I just want to keep them," Bill said. He put the card back in the binder, and Jack started to head downstairs. "Wait a minute," Bill said.

"What is it?" Jack asked.

"I heard something today," he said, clearly uncomfortable as he studiously avoided looking Jack in the eyes. "Ryan Slater said...."

"Wait a minute. Ryan Slater—isn't he Ronny Slater's little brother?" Jack asked. When Bill nodded, Jack said, "Let me guess. The little Slater said I was taking drugs, didn't he?" Jack said, feeling his anger rise.

"Yeah. Yeah, he did. I told him you weren't and to just shut up, but Jack... you aren't, are you?" Bill said worriedly.

"NO!" Jack said, raising his voice, then immediately realizing he was letting it get to him too much. "I mean, no, no, I'm not and I never have. I've never even seen them, let alone take 'em." Seeing the worry fade from Bill's face, Jack added, "Thanks for sticking up for me, buddy."

"Anytime. You're practically like family," Bill said. Just then, Kelly appeared at the door. "Hey, are you going to marry my sister?" Bill asked with faux innocence, eager for the chance to pay Kelly back for blackmailing him.

"Bill!" Kelly shouted, grabbing a pillow off his bed and throwing it at him.

"What?" he said, throwing it back at her. "I heard you talking to Mindy about him on the phone. 'Don't you think Jack is so cute, Mindy? Isn't he a hunk?' Bill said, pitching his voice girlishly high.

"Knock it off! I thought you were going to go over to Andy's and trade cards," she said, her face reddening until it was only slightly lighter than her hair.

"I'm goin', I'm goin' already," Bill said, collecting his cards and heading for the doorway. "You just want to be alone with your boyfriend," he whispered to Kelly as he left the room, making sure he was loud enough for Jack to hear, too. Then he thumped down the stairs and out the door.

Now alone, Kelly looked at Jack with embarrassment.

"Stupid brothers," he said to cover her. But deep down, he was pleased that she'd been talking about him to her girlfriend.

"Let's go downstairs," Kelly said, eager to get past the embarrassing moment. Jack followed her down the stairs; as he did, he couldn't help but notice that she was filling out her jeans a lot more than she had a year or two ago. Now it was Jack's turn to be embarrassed. He averted his eyes upwards to her shiny red hair. She had it partially pulled back with a dark green ribbon, and he'd noticed the tiny tendrils of hair around her face. This was definitely a safer area to contemplate. Jack followed her into the living room, where they sat at opposite ends of the worn leather couch.

"Ronny Slater's little brother told Bill I was taking drugs," Jack said. "It made me wonder how many people believe that stupid story."

"Who cares?" Kelly said. "Anybody who knows you knows that it's not true. So what does it matter what the rest of them say."

Buoyed as usual by Kelly's faith in him, Jack chose to accept the encouragement and forget about the rumor mill, at least for tonight. He picked up a photo album that was sitting on the coffee table and started paging through it. The first few pages were filled with pictures of Kelly's parents early in their marriage: Kelly's dad struggling with the lights for their Christmas tree; Kelly's mother perched on her dad's knee, a bottle of beer in her hand; her dad and two other men hauling furniture into the house; Kelly's mother giving a side view of her big pregnant belly.

"Was your mom pregnant with you there?" Jack asked.

"Yep. That was just a couple of weeks before I was born, so I hear," Kelly said, sliding closer to look at the pictures with him.

In the next picture, her mother was holding an infant wrapped in a pink blanket. "That was me, on the day they brought me home from the hospital."

Jack's heart contracted, for the photo of Kelly and her mother immediately brought to mind a picture in his own family album, a picture of Rita holding him when he was a baby, one of the few photographs he had of himself with his mother. Only in that picture, his mother looked weak, unwell, the dark circles under her eyes and hollows in her cheeks a stark reminder that she was seriously ill by then. As it always did when Jack was feeling stressed, the fear tugged at him, the fear that he was responsible for his mother's death. Not wanting to get bogged down in his troubling feelings, Jack quickly turned the page in the album, where he saw a snapshot of a smiling baby Kelly, a white ribbon pulling her one strand of hair into a knot on the top of her head. She looked just like a Kewpie doll.

"Nice hair, Kelly," he teased.

"Yeah. I didn't have any to speak of until after my first birthday," she said.

Jack was suddenly aware of the smell of her hair now, fresh and slightly almond-scented. He playfully pulled on a red lock.

"Well, you kind of made up for it since then," he said. He began running his fingers through her hair, and she moved closer yet, resting her head on his shoulder. She looked up at him, her lips slightly parted, and he pressed his own lips against hers, very softly at first, gently increasing the pressure and shyly, tentatively, sliding his tongue into her mouth. Jack became aroused, and suddenly the pleasant, exciting sensation was replaced with revulsion as horrible memories intruded into his consciousness. He pulled away from Kelly and jumped to his feet.

"What's wrong?" she asked, looking at him with alarm. "Did I do something wrong?"

"No! NO!" he said. "I just… I just don't feel too good. I'm sorry," he said, struggling not to reveal his confused mishmash of feelings. How much longer was Kelly going to put up with him, he wondered. "Kelly, maybe I shouldn't have come over tonight. I think I'm just kind of worn out from everything."

"I know it's been a lot to handle," she said. "Are...are you sure I didn't do something wrong?" Since this was her first experience in this area, she didn't have a great deal of confidence.

"No," he assured her. "You're perfect." He bent down and gave her a quick, chaste kiss on the lips. "I'm sorry. I probably should go on home, get some sleep. Hey, do you want to go to the movies tomorrow? Poseidon Adventure is playing at the Orpheum."

"I've got to watch Bill until three-thirty," she said.

"He can come along," Jack said. Might be easier with a chaperone, he thought to himself.

"Well, okay then." She rose and walked him to the door, where they briefly kissed again. "Bye, Jack. Hope you feel better tomorrow."

"Yeah, I will. G'night," he said, heading out into the night.

In the brief time that Jack had spent at Kelly's house, the sky had changed from rosy dusk to almost pitch dark, a few stars and a sliver of a moon slightly illuminating the night. He breathed in deep the cool autumn air, releasing some of the tension. What the hell was wrong with him? Kelly was the prettiest girl in the class, in his eyes at least; not only that, but she was the nicest. He loved her, Jack knew he did. But when the kissing became more passionate, he'd started to freak out. Images of Father Delanoit, what he'd done to Jack and made Jack do to him blasted through his mind, ruining his joy, taking away his desire to be with Kelly.

Maybe the next time, he could try to stay focused more, he reasoned. Tonight, events had kind of taken him by surprise. Next time he'd plan things out better. He'd try harder. He'd concentrate. Maybe he could...

"There's O'Donnell, O'Donnell the dope dealer!" a raucous voice called from down the block.

"Makin' a drug deal, Jackie?" someone else yelled, evoking chortles of laughter from his cohorts. Slater! Jack's swirling mass of emotions coalesced into anger as the roving gang approached him.

It was Ronny Slater and three of his friends, out on the prowl and looking for a way to liven up their Friday night.

"I don't know where you got that stupid idea, Slater, but I'm not doing drugs. Quit saying that I am," Jack said heatedly.

"You want to score us some dope, man," Slater said, doing his best impression of how he imagined a drug deal would go down. Then his face, which Jack could see clearly now under the streetlight, took on a lewd expression. "Or maybe, maybe you're too busy scoring something else, huh, Jackie," he said, looking pointedly at Kelly's house. His friends broke out in fresh gales of raunchy laughter.

All the emotions of the past week hit Jack with a rush to the gut. The agony and relief of breaking his silence about the abuse, the raw tender feelings when his family and Kelly were so kind to him, the shock of his father assaulting Father Delanoit, the roller coaster of hopes raised and then dashed when the family reported the abuse to the diocese, the embarrassment he'd felt all week due to the rumors, and the horrible mixture of arousal and revulsion he'd just experienced when he'd made out with Kelly, all the feelings struck him with the force of a mighty wind. Jack lashed out with all the fury of that tornadic force, punching Slater hard in the face, then jumping astride him when he fell to the ground, grabbing him by the shoulders and pounding his head into the pavement. Two of Slater's friends pulled Jack away from Slater, and the third boy began hitting Jack, punching him in his stomach and face.

"What's going on out there?" demanded an angry voice. The woman who lived next door to Kelly stood on her porch, glaring at them all. "I've called the cops, you boys. You'd better get out of here." And Slater's friends heeded her words, fleeing into the shadows. But Jack and Ronny lay motionless on the cold ground.

A police siren sounded, first distant and then louder until it abruptly stopped. First one and then a second police cruiser parked in the street by the boys. A tall lanky cop jumped out of the first cruiser, appraised the scene and approached Jack and Ronny. Two officers emerged from the second vehicle and joined the first.

"Boys," the first cop said. "Can you hear me?"

Jack grunted, then rolled to his side, trying to find a position where he could breathe without wanting to scream in pain. Ronny, though, lay silent. The police officer knelt by his side, looking at his chest, watching to see the rise and fall of inhalation and exhalation.

"He's breathing," the cop announced. "But he's out cold. My guess is a concussion. What happened here, son?" he said, not unkindly, to Jack. One of the other officers went back to his cruiser to call an ambulance.

"I… hit him, and then his friends jumped me," Jack said, still writhing in pain.

"But you started it, huh," the officer asked.

"No, I mean, I threw the first punch, but he… Slater said something nasty about my girlfriend, and I… I just lost it," Jack said.

Then Ronny began to murmur and the officer turned his attention to him. Moments later the ambulance pulled up. The paramedics loaded Jack and Slater onto the gurneys, shooting off fresh waves of pain at least for Jack—Slater didn't seem to be aware enough to register much pain just yet—and put them both in the ambulance. Sirens again sounded as the ambulance sped off to the hospital.

"Friday night fights," said one of the officers from the second car, an older man with grey hair and a tired expression on his deeply lined face.

"We'll get them patched up and then see about pressing charges," said his partner. "You gonna take their info down and do the paperwork on 'em, Leonard?"

"Yeah. Stupid kids," said the lanky cop. Although it hadn't been too many years back that he was a stupid kid himself, getting into fights and rabblerousing. He hoped these kids would learn from their mistakes, like he had. There were plenty of them out there who never did.

As all this commotion went on in front of her house, Kelly lay soaking in her bathtub, surrounded by lemon-scented bubbles and singing at the top of her lungs along with the Top 40 hits which were blaring from the radio she'd set on the floor, totally and blessedly oblivious to everything that was taking place outside of her sanctuary. She had puzzled briefly over Jack's reaction to their kiss, and then decided he was just being chivalrous, not wanting to let things get carried away. Yup. She was a goner, she knew it. Kelly was in love, and she'd fallen hard.

The ambulance brought the two boys, both now fully conscious, to Sisters of Charity Hospital, where the paramedics turned them over to the care of the emergency room staff. Officer Leonard Peel arrived almost at the same time, ready to question the two combatants, call their families, and file any appropriate charges. The boys were brought into separate but adjoining cubicles. After ascertaining that neither one was in any immediate danger, the doctor delayed further treatment until their families could be notified and permission granted to treat them. Within a half an hour, Lucinda and Pappa sat in a waiting room just off the emergency room, with Officer Peel and Matt Slater sitting across from them. As soon as Lucinda has gotten the phone call, she'd scribbled a note for Mike, who was at his AA meeting, and called a cab to take her to the hospital. Pappa had insisted on accompanying her, and she was glad.

"At this time it sounds like Ronny won't be facing any charges," Officer Peel said. Relief eased Matt Slater's tense, pinched features somewhat, though the lines in his face indicated that he often wore a sour expression. Officer Peel turned to Lucinda and Pappa. "Jack will be facing charges of assault. If he can tell us who the boys were that hit him, they will also be charged. So far, he's not talking."

Relief, anger and despair battled in Lucinda's heart: relief that neither boy was more seriously injured; anger that Jack had behaved so foolishly; and despair, despair over the apparent loss of the sweet boy that Jack had been prior to Father Delanoit's intrusion into his life. Despair that she had allowed the abuse to take place, the abuse that had altered Jack's kind, easygoing personality into this angry, volatile one. She had feared that something like this was going to happen. At least it wasn't any worse. What had set him off, she wondered.

Mike walked into the room, a grave expression on his face as he looked first at Lucinda and Pappa, then at Officer Peel.

"Are you the boy's father?" the police officer asked.

"I am. What happened?" Mike asked.

"All we know at this point is, your son hit a classmate, Ronny Slater. Beat him pretty badly, actually. This is his father, here," Officer Peel said, gesturing at a grim-looking Matt Slater. "Then some of Ronny's friends teamed up on your son. He's going to be okay—both boys are," he said, seeing the look of alarm on Mike's face. "But your son will be facing charges in juvenile court. He'll probably spend some time on probation, since it's his first offense. But this goes beyond the scope of a little schoolyard fight, Mr. O'Donnell. It could have been a whole hell of a lot worse."

"I want to see my son," Mike said.

"They should be done patching him up in a few minutes, and then you can go back there," Officer Peel said. "I have a few questions while we're waiting. First, do any of you know what the reason for this altercation was?"

The four adults shook their heads. None of them remembered hearing anything about the boys' long-standing quarrel.

"Wait!" Lucinda exclaimed. "Jack did say something about getting into a fight with a Ronny Slater. That was a long time back, when they were practicing to be altar boys. He'd said something… something hurtful about our family, and Jack lost his temper."

Mike remembered with shame, then, what Jack had told them before: how Ronny had teased Jack about his father being a drunk, how Jack had reacted, and how Father Delanoit had used the situation to gain control over him. Mike swallowed hard, but the lump in his throat didn't budge.

"But you haven't heard of them having a problem any more recently than that?" Officer Peel asked.

"I heard Ronny and his friends talking about how Jack

O'Donnell had gotten into the dope," Matt Slater said, casting a look of contempt at Mike. "Maybe he was just all hopped up on that stuff. Kids on drugs, they don't need much of an excuse to go ballistic."

"That's bullshit!" Mike erupted. Then, realizing that losing his own temper could only make things worse for Jack, he struggled to calm down. "Jack has never done any such thing. Why, he doesn't even like the taste of alcohol."

"Surprising," the elder Slater said, his voice dripping with sarcasm. It wasn't hard to see where Ronny had gotten his nasty streak. Lucinda glared at him, and Pappa gently took her hand. Just then, a nurse came over. She informed them that they could see the boys and talk to the doctor about their conditions.

"You will be receiving a summons for Jack to appear in juvenile court. "You'll need to come with him, Mr. O'Donnell. That's all I need for tonight," Officer Peel said, rising to leave.

Mike, Lucinda and Pappa followed the nurse into the emergency room, where she took them to Jack's cubicle, which was separated from Ronny's by a curtain. Swelling and scratches disfigured Jack's face, and Lucinda stifled a cry. She hurried to Jack's side, Pappa beside her and Mike on the other side of the bed.

"How are you, Jack?" Lucinda asked gently. This was not yet the time for recriminations.

"I'm okay," Jack said. The medication the doctor had injected him with had eased the pain he felt in his midsection and face. And his fears that he'd done some real damage to Slater were alleviated when he heard Slater responding to the nurse's questions, sounding no more stupid than he normally did. But the pain Jack felt now, he didn't know if anything could erase. He was filled with self-loathing, worse now than anytime since Father Delanoit had first molested him, not only self-loathing, but also despair. Jack didn't know who he was sometimes. His anger rose so quickly that it frightened him. Whatever the repercussions of this incident were, Jack was less worried about any possible punishment he might receive than he was about the future. His future.

"Can you tell us what happened, son?" Pappa asked.

"I… I was leaving Kelly's house, when Slater and his friends started yelling stuff at me. They were saying that I was taking drugs…"

"Bastard!" Mike interjected under his breath, thinking more of Father Delanoit than Slater, for he realized the source of the rumor.

"But that wasn't what started the fight," Jack said. "They… Slater said something nasty about Kelly, and I just lost it and started hitting him. Then his friends grabbed me, got me off Slater, and started punching me. I think some lady called the cops. I kind of blacked out for a minute, and the next thing I knew, there was a cop leaning over me, and they put me in an ambulance and brought me here."

A tall, portly, balding doctor entered the cubicle.

"And we've patched the two of you up," he said. Addressing Mike, he continued, "Providing Jack doesn't get into any more fist-fights, he's going to be just fine. His ribs are going to be sore for a while, but they're not broken, and there's no sign of any internal injuries. Other than a few cuts and abrasions, his face is fine, too. So you can take him home. He's had a shot to help with the pain when we examined him, and if he needs some pain medication for the next few days, here's a prescription and a few pills to tide him over until you can fill it. Anybody have any questions?" They all shook their heads, exhaustion setting in now that the drama was over. "Alright then, you can go home now. Try to keep cool, buddy," he said.

"Okay," Jack said.

From the next cubicle came the sounds of the Slaters arguing heatedly.

"I've told you to keep your trap shut, haven't I? I told you, you were going to run it one too many times someday, and somebody was going to haul off and whack you, didn't I?" Matt Slater said. "You never learn, you stupid little moron, do you?"

As furious as she was with Ronny for once again baiting her vulnerable grandson into a fight, Lucinda couldn't help but feel a little sorry for the boy. If this was how his father talked to him in a public place, what was he like at home, she wondered. No wonder his son was such a jerk.

"Come on, son, let's go home," Mike said. "We'll step outside while you get dressed."

They left the cubicle and almost ran into Ronny and his father. The boy looked surly, his eyes on the ground and his mouth pinched into a frown. Matt Slater shot the O'Donnell clan another look of contempt and then led his son down the sterile corridor. After Jack got dressed, the family walked out to the car. When they got home, Mike helped Jack upstairs and into his room. He pulled down the covers, eased Jack onto the bed, and gently removed his shoes. Jack, woozy from the medication, fell asleep almost immediately. Downstairs, Lucinda, Pappa and Mike gathered around the dining room table.

"Our Jack has a problem, does he not?" Pappa said softly.

"No wonder he has a problem, after what that son of a bitch Delanoit did to him," Mike said angrily. "He was just fine until that pervert got his hands on him."

"Getting angry again doesn't help, Mike," Lucinda said.

"The anger is okay, it's what you do with it," Pappa said. "Jack is angry, very angry and who would not be? But he has to learn how to master that anger, or else it's going to master him."

"Maybe he should see a therapist, a psychiatrist even," Lucinda said.

"A psychiatrist? Jack isn't crazy, Delanoit is the crazy one," Mike said.

"I didn't say he's crazy, Mike. I just think that he needs more help than we can give him," Lucinda said. "Somebody's got to know how to help a boy get through something like this."

Something like this. Mike wondered, did you look in the yellow pages under 'help for kids who were messed up because a priest molested them?' What exactly did you do to help somebody get over *something like this*?

"What if people find out, the other kids?" he asked. "They'll make fun of him even more than they already are."

"What if we don't do anything, and the next time he kills somebody," Lucinda said evenly. "You know that Jack's had a real problem dealing with his temper ever since Father Delanoit began abusing him. Just sitting back and blaming Father Delanoit is not going to do Jack any good; we've got to find somebody who can help him. By God, I've already lost my daughter, I'm not going to lose another child," she said, finally releasing the tears she'd been holding back since she received the phone call from the police. "I won't lose him. I won't lose Jack."

Pappa stood up and put his arms around her, rocking her as gently as when she was a child.

"You're right, Lucinda," Mike said, chagrined. "I tell you what: I'll ask Tom, my sponsor, if he knows any… therapists or psychiatrists, and I'll call somebody, first thing Monday morning. We'll do whatever it takes."

Lucinda blew her nose into a tissue, and then got up for a drink of water.

"Do you really think a therapist is going to help?" Mike asked Pappa when she left the room.

"I don't know," he said honestly. "All I know is, we have a boy who's been badly broken, and we must try to mend him. In the old days, you'd take him to the Church for that. But the Church is what broke him, isn't it?" Pappa sighed.

Chapter Nineteen

Ten days after Jack vented his anger onto Ronny Slater, Mike, Jack and Lucinda walked in the door of Midstate Therapy Services, where a buxom young receptionist seated behind a shiny oak desk greeted them warmly.

"Hello," she smiled reassuringly. "Are you the O'Donnell family?"

"Yes," Mike said. "We have an appointment with Rhonda Spheres."

"I have just a little bit of paper work for you to fill out, Mr. O'Donnell," she said, handing Mike an intimidating-looking pile of papers attached to a clipboard. "You can have a seat in the waiting room and fill those out."

The family filed into the peach-colored waiting room, which was furnished with a lumpy brown couch and three well-worn chairs. Jack took one of the chairs, the one beside the door, looking as if he might bolt at any moment. He still wasn't crazy about the idea of seeing a therapist, but his family and even Kelly had convinced him that it might help him deal with the anger that had landed him into so much trouble. Mike and Lucinda sat on the couch, where Lucinda could assist Mike with the paperwork if he needed her help. A young woman with a pretty, sad face sat in the chair opposite Jack.

"Deborah?" said the receptionist, sticking her head and her formidable chest in the doorway. "Marty will see you now." The young woman put the magazine she'd been looking at down on the table and disappeared down the hallway. Lucinda noticed the cover of the magazine had an Easter theme, with a pink-frosted cake decorated with pastel candies surrounded by construction paper rabbits and chickens. Jack uncomfortably registered the fact that the receptionist had addressed the woman by name, wishing she'd just said, 'Hey, you,' or something on that order. He hoped to be as incognito as possible and desperately hoped no one he knew would see him here.

Moments later, the cheerful receptionist popped back in the waiting room. Jack wondered if she acted so cheery to counter the clients' gloominess. Whatever the reason for her gaiety, it was starting to get on his nerves.

"I'll take that if you're done," she said, and Mike handed her the completed forms. "You can come with me. Rhonda's ready to see you now."

Mike, Jack and Lucinda followed Smiling Lady down the short corridor. She opened a door and ushered them into an office where a strikingly beautiful black woman was waiting for them. When the woman stood to greet them, Jack saw that she was almost as tall as his father. She looked more like a model than a therapist, he thought.

"Hello. My name is Rhonda Spheres," she said in a voice deep and melodic. As he got closer to her, Jack realized that she was older than she'd first appeared, maybe in her late thirties.

"I'm Mike O'Donnell, and this is my son, Jack. And this is his grandmother, Lucinda Walters. She's raised Jack since he was a baby, though," Mike said.

"Hello," Lucinda said.

"Won't you all have a chair, and then we can discuss what brought you here today," Rhonda said. Lucinda, Jack and Mike sat in the straight-back chairs opposite hers. *Where's the couch*, Jack wondered, suddenly feeling giddy and close to breaking out in nervous laughter. To calm himself, he carefully studied the wall behind Rhonda, where several framed diplomas and a beautiful pen and ink drawing of a man holding an infant hung side by side.

"Jack, when your father called to make an appointment, he said he wanted to get you into therapy because of some problems you've been having," Rhonda said. "Could you tell me in your own words why you came here today and what do you want me to help you with?"

Because I want to pummel people until they're dead. Because I can't forget the feeling of his hands and his mouth and his… Because I'm afraid I'll never be able to make out with my girlfriend without remembering.

"I guess because I got into a fight and got into a lot of trouble," Jack said quietly. "I… I lose my temper too much."

"You lose your temper too much," she repeated. "Why do you think that is?"

"I… I don't know," Jack said, suddenly embarrassed to think he might have to tell this knockout lady what Father Delanoit had done to him.

"I'll tell you what it is," Mike said. "Jack was abused, sexually abused. The priest at St. Maria's molested him when he started as an altar boy, when he was just barely twelve years old. Ever since then, he's had problems. He only told us what happened a few weeks ago."

Rhonda looked concerned although not shocked by the revelation. Her deep brown eyes were warm and compassionate as she looked into Jack's.

"That was difficult," she said, somehow speaking volumes with just three short words. While Jack's family had been very kind and so had Kelly, Jack had the feeling that this woman 'got it' in a way the others didn't. Moments before he'd felt close to manic laughter, and all of a sudden he felt like he could burst into tears.

"Uh, huh," he replied, trying desperately not to lose control of his emotions.

"What I hope you will find, Jack, is that, yes, you were assaulted and yes, you are handling your anger inappropriately, but these are two separate issues," Rhonda said. "They are related, but separate. I hope you'll discover that you can handle your anger in ways that don't harm anybody, including yourself. And I hope you will learn that although you were abused, and that did harm you deeply, you can recover." She sounded so confident in what she said that Jack wouldn't have dared to disagree aloud, even though he had his doubts.

"While Jack has been through a truly traumatic experience, he is also very blessed," Rhonda said. "He has a supportive family who believes him and is willing to help him with his healing process. Many sexual assault victims don't have a supportive family, they don't receive treatment, and if they do, it's often many years after the fact. Over the course of those years, they develop many coping mechanisms to deal with the trauma resulting from the abuse. That's what I suspect Jack is doing, acting out in a violent manner in order to cope with his emotions. But Jack is going to learn new ways for handling that anger and all the other emotions that sexual abuse survivors have to deal with."

"You're also incredibly strong," she said, addressing Jack directly. "What you have survived is, very possibly, the worst thing that will happen to you in your lifetime. Once you've learned how to deal with this situation in a healthy way, there's nothing that you can't do, if you set your mind to it."

"I won't lie to you, Jack," she said, her deep brown eyes looking deeply into his. From most people such intensity would be intimidating, but from this woman it felt strangely healing, as if light was boring into the deepest recesses of Jack's soul, where pain had festered for so long. "Dealing with sexual abuse is hard work, very hard work Sometimes you may feel worse as you revisit the experience and learn how to process your emotions. But I will promise you this: I'll be right here every step of the way. And when you get to the other side, you're going to discover that you've got a strength you never even dreamed of." Then she addressed Mike and Lucinda.

"You both will need to be a key part of Jack's recovery," she said.

"When a child or young person has family backing them up, the process of healing is so much smoother. Are there any other family members that Jack sees on a regular basis who know about the abuse?"

"My father, Jack's great-grandfather, who lives with us," Lucinda said. "And his brother knows. David. He's going to college."

"What I want to do is see Jack alone, primarily," Rhonda said. "It may be easier for him to open up that way. But there will be times when I'll want to meet with the entire family, to update you on Jack's progress, if he agrees to that—everything said here is confidential—and to help your family process this situation. Sexual assault of a child violates the whole family, and especially when the perpetrator is somebody they've known and trusted, which seems to be the case here."

Mike nodded grimly and Lucinda, shamefaced, softly murmured "yes."

"Father Delanoit was a frequent guest in our home," Lucinda said. "Every other Friday afternoon, he would stop over for coffee and then he'd take Jack… he'd take Jack…" Her voice trailed off as she struggled to maintain control.

"You have permission to cry about this," Rhonda said rather sternly. "Something was stolen from you, something valuable, and you can't get it back. That 'something' is your sense of basic trust, along with your grandson's innocence. It's okay to cry, to grieve, to mourn this loss, individually and as a family."

"I thought that counseling was going to make Jack feel better, not worse," Mike said, his initial misgivings rising up again.

"It will," Rhonda reassured him. "But it's like Jack has a wound inside him that became infected, filled with pus, a wound that needs to heal. Therapy will help Jack clean out that wound, release all that infected material, the stuff that Jack's been trying to get rid of by acting out violently."

"As I said before, Jack is incredibly strong, and that's a fact he will need frequent reminding of," Rhonda continued. "What I'm going to do is help Jack release all that pent-up pain in a way that is a lot healthier and a lot safer than going around knocking other people's heads off."

"Do any of you have any questions?" she asked.

"How long is this going to take?" Jack said.

"I'm sorry, I can't answer that one," Rhonda said. "I can tell you that it will be time well spent. You are worth it, remember that. Is money going to be a problem?"

"No, we're doing okay," Mike said. "Even if it means working some extra shifts, I'll do whatever it takes to help my boy get over this."

"Get through it," Rhonda said firmly. When Mike looked at her in puzzlement, she said, "When people suffer a trauma, it's a more realistic appraisal of the healing process to say that they get through it. Okay?"

"Yes, ma'am," Mike humbly agreed.

Rhonda handed Jack a card with her name and phone number.

"What you're dealing with is tough, really tough," she said. "Don't be afraid to call me between sessions if you need to, okay?"

Jack nodded in agreement.

"I would like to see Jack back here, alone this time, in a week," Rhonda said, writing on her notepad. Jack wondered what kind of notes she would write about him, and if anybody else would see them. She looked up, and then warmly shook hands with each of them, holding on to Jack's a moment longer. Her touch didn't give him the creeps like most people did, he was surprised to discover. "I'm glad to be working with all of you," she said.

"Thank you so much," Lucinda said, a sentiment Mike echoed, as did Jack.

"Thank you, Miss Spheres," he said.

"Rhonda," she said firmly. "Nobody's any better than anybody else in this office. I have the education and experience that I do, so I can help you, but that doesn't make me more important than you are. Call me Rhonda."

"Uh, thank you, Rhonda," Jack said. It felt weird to address a grown-up that way. But what wasn't weird anymore?

When they left Rhonda's office, they stopped at the Smiling Lady's desk for Mike to write a check. Jack glanced into the waiting room, curious to see if anybody else was still there. It had to be after five o'clock. The only people in the waiting room were an elderly couple, sitting side by side on the sofa. I'm glad I'm not the only crazy person, Jack thought, and then felt a little ashamed to be happy about somebody else's misfortune.

"Bye!" the cheery receptionist called as they walked out the door. The day was a gloomy one, with rain clouds threatening since early afternoon, but Jack felt strangely buoyed. He got into the backseat of the Chevy behind Lucinda, and Mike sat in the driver's seat. Mike turned around and looked at Jack, his eyes inquisitive.

"What did you think, son? How did you like this therapist-lady?" he said.

"She's okay," Jack said cautiously. Actually, he thought she was pretty cool, but he wasn't ready to give that much away just now.

"I have a good feeling about her, Mike," Lucinda said. "She seems like a class act."

"That's kind of what I thought," Mike said as he turned the key in the ignition and shifted into drive. He turned on his headlights to combat the dark clouds overhead. They were all quiet as he drove home, each one mulling over their time with Rhonda. Finally, the rain began to fall, a steady rain that smelled of fresh new beginnings.

While Mike was driving his family home from their first visit with the therapist, Father Delanoit and Father Schmidt were sitting down to Mrs. McGrevey's Monday night special: fried ham and scalloped potatoes. By this point, the two priests were both accustomed to the awkward silences that filled the room at mealtime, actually anytime the two were forced to spend time in the same room. Occasionally, in the spirit of forgiveness and Christian brotherhood, Father Schmidt would try to initiate a conversation, carefully bringing up a neutral topic such as the high school football team's ranking or upcoming parish affairs. Father Delanoit played along, if only for Mrs. McGrevey's sake, but usually their conversations were short and desultory. Tonight Father Schmidt wasn't up to the effort. What with taking on the added burden of altar boy training and trying to keep a watchful eye on Father Delanoit, he was just too tired.

Father Delanoit, however, had never felt better. With his trimmed-back schedule, he felt relaxed and well rested. Watching Father Schmidt try to act as jail warden was proving to be most amusing. And, while he missed his little interludes with the boys, Father Delanoit was a patient man. He knew that things would get back to normal sooner rather than later. He could wait.

"Pass the potatoes, would you, Father?" he said. "Mrs. McGrevey is quite an inspired cook, you'll have to admit," he added with a wink, knowing the woman was within earshot. So far, he'd kept the bishop's irritation about his little crimes and misdemeanors away from the housekeeper, but it never hurt to keep the woman on his good side.

Father Schmidt, annoyed by the wink and the obvious flattery, sighed as he passed the bowl to Father Delanoit. Give me strength, Lord, he silently prayed.

At Rose Castani's house, a welcome home party was in the works. After almost a year with no contact with his family, Alan Castani, the proverbial prodigal son, had returned home. Rose had heard a knock at the door and told her youngest son Johnny to see who it was. She had just finished boiling the noodles for spaghetti and was in the process of dishing up; it was probably one of the kids' friends, who always just happened to appear at suppertime, knowing that Rose would invite them to join the family.

"Mom, it's some guy with dirty hair and a beard," Johnny said after peering through the window. "He looks really skuzzy."

Worried, she went to the door herself, unsure if she should even open it. She looked through the glass pane and saw a young man with dark matted hair hanging past his shoulders and an unkempt beard. On second glance, she noted his tattered jeans and flannel shirt, no match for the cold October wind and the pelts of rain now starting to fall. She noticed the man was trembling. Still staying behind the relative safety of the door, she took a closer look and almost fainted dead away.

"Alan!" she cried, finally throwing the door open and crushing her child to her bosom. "Alan is home!" she cried, tears of joy streaming down her face. The kids raced to the door to see him, then stood back as they looked at this stranger who was their brother.

"Hi, Mama," he said, his voice husky from cheap whiskey and nights spent out in the rain with only a sheet of cardboard for shelter.

"Come in, come in," Rose said, practically pulling him in the door which just minutes ago had been closed to him. "Look, your brother is home!"

The four younger Castanis looked shyly at Alan, full of questions they wanted to ask but didn't dare. Where had he been? What had he done for money? Why did he finally decide to come back? Recalling the many tears their mother had cried over him as he'd gotten into one scrape after another, they weren't sure how to feel about Alan being back. Eight-year-old Johnny was too young to have learned all the social niceties, so he was the first to break the siblings' silence.

"Are you really Alan?" he asked, eying the hairy stranger warily.

"It's me, Johnny," Alan replied, a ghost of his old smile playing on his lips. It was enough to give Rose some hope.

"You stink!" Johnny said. "Why haven't you taken a bath—did you run out of soap or something?"

"Johnny!" his mother shouted, reaching out to cuff him. "Watch your mouth!"

But Alan burst out laughing.

"Yeah, I ran out of a few things, little brother," he said. "It was time to come home."

Jenny, the sister closest to his age, then approached him for a hug. She embraced Alan, disregarding his ripe odor, and he responded by lightly squeezing her, then stepping back.

"Johnny's right, you know—I do stink. Haven't had a bath since I'm not sure when," Alan said. "Mama, can I go up and take a bath?"

Slapping her own forehead, Rose replied, "Since when does anybody have to ask to take a bath in this house?"

"I guess what I mean is..." he hesitated. "Can I stay? Can I come home, Mama?"

Rose could not hold back any of the emotion she had experienced over the past year, wondering if she would ever see her son alive again, wondering if she would ever even know his whereabouts. She answered as best she could through her tears.

"Of course you can, son. Of course, you can. It's everything I've been praying for."

While Alan went upstairs to take a bath—they were going to have to fumigate those clothes, or maybe dig something up from Jimmy Junior's closet—Rose set to work on preparing a fresh pan of noodles. The last batch sat congealing on the plates, totally beyond salvage.

"She seems pretty cool," Jack said. He had stretched the phone card as far as it would go so he could take the phone into the kitchen and have a little privacy while he talked to Kelly. "She's not very old, maybe in her thirties. But she seems to really know her stuff."

Jack didn't want a lot of people to find out that he was seeing a therapist, but he didn't mind Kelly knowing about it. In fact, her mother insisted that the only way Kelly could continue to see Jack was if he did get professional help. While she would be eternally grateful for how he had stepped up to prevent Bill from falling into Father Delanoit's hands, after Jack's last altercation Mrs. Ryan was becoming seriously concerned about Kelly's safety. Clearly, Jack had a problem managing his anger, and she did not want Kelly to wind up in the middle of something ugly.

"How did your family like her?" Kelly asked.

"They liked her. Grandma said she was down to earth. And Dad liked that she wants us to call her by her first name—said it shows she doesn't think she's all better than we are because of all her education. Pappa's coming down with a head cold so he didn't come, but he thought she sounded cool," Jack said. A thought flashed through his mind, a remembrance of how Rhonda had sounded so confident that he was actually going to be normal some day, making Jack feel almost giddy with relief. Finally, some day he could put this whole god-awful mess behind him, maybe. Put it to rest.

"So when do you go back?" Kelly asked him.

"Next Monday. She wants me to come alone next time," Jack said. He felt a little apprehensive but even stronger was his desire to get on with it.

"I'm glad you liked her. I still feel bad that you got into trouble defending me," Kelly said.

"Don't. It was my own dumb fault for letting it get to me that much," he said. After a moment, he said, "It's going to seem weird, not going to St. Maria's anymore." The family had decided to start attending church at St. Augustine's and to have Jack transfer to public school as soon as the quarter ended. Nobody wanted to deal with running into Father Delanoit on a day-to-day basis, and it seemed the diocese was not going to remove him as the family had hoped. Jack didn't really want to transfer schools: he'd gone to St. Maria's since kindergarten, and most of his friends went there, but he knew he couldn't stand worrying all the time about the possibility of seeing Father Delanoit, either.

"I know," Kelly said quietly. "We can still see each other on weekends, at least."

"Yeah," Jack said. He felt uneasy, though, when he remembered how memories of what Father Delanoit had done had broken into his mind when he'd kissed Kelly. "Well, I'd better let you go. See you tomorrow, okay?"

"Okay," she said.

Jack hung up the phone and then poured himself a tall glass of milk. Lucinda had baked oatmeal raisin cookies, and he helped himself to a generous handful of them. He took the milk and cookies out into the living room and plopped down to watch the football game with the rest of the family.

Down the street at the Castani house, Alan was neck-deep in steamy hot water. He'd washed his hair three times, scrubbed himself all over twice, pulled the drain and released some of the dirty water and replaced it with fresh hot water. This was it, he knew. His last hope. He'd blown every lousy chance he'd ever gotten so far. In the Army, he'd hoped that the recruiter's prediction would come to pass, that he'd find his niche in the discipline and the camaraderie the service offered. And, for a short time, he had. Basically, Alan had enjoyed the military life: with its structure and strictness, he always understood what was expected of him. Even when they'd plunked him down in the jungles of Vietnam, he was okay. Stalking the enemies, taking them out, it all provided him with a safety valve, a relief for the bottomless pit of rage that always seemed to lurk right below the surface of his consciousness.

But then Alan found he couldn't turn that valve off. One night when his platoon had set up camp and settled down underneath a tarp to sleep, Alan had a dream, a nightmare. He was stalking an enemy soldier, just about to move in for the kill, when the guy turned around and it wasn't Charlie after all, it was Father Delanoit from back at St. Maria Goretti's, and he was smiling in that sickening way he had. The priest's pants were unzipped and he started coming after Alan, just like he had when Alan was a little kid. Only now, Alan was all grown up, and he aimed his gun at the priest, ready to fire, when he realized the gun had turned into a rope. Father Delanoit grabbed the rope away from him and tied Alan up and it was all happening all over again. Alan woke up, stifling a scream, and discovered his sergeant had rolled over in his sleep and was lying right next to him, almost on top of him, it seemed; Alan went berserk and attacked him, beating the sergeant with his fists and then reaching for his gun. Luckily, Matt and Danny had pulled him off, or he'd have been facing criminal charges instead of getting off with a dishonorable discharge.

Alan had landed in California, where he found it relatively easy to survive on the little bit of money he made panhandling or washing dishes in dumpy restaurants. It was warm enough that he could sleep on the street or, better yet, on the beach. The sound of the waves pounding the sand settled his nerves even better than the booze and the pot and the pills did. He befriended a scroungy-looking dog whose black fur looked as matted and knotted-up as his own hair, a dog with one ear half torn off and a white muzzle. Alan named him Old Geezer. One sunny afternoon Alan and his new friend were walking down the street past the quirky little shops and restaurants when all of a sudden the stupid animal got a wild hair up his ass and ran in the back door of a restaurant when a heavy-set man wearing a white apron had just stepped outside to throw some garbage in the dumpster.

"Hold it, Old Geezer!" Alan yelled, charging after the dog.

"Who in the hell are you calling old geezer, you derelict!" the man shouted in outrage. "Is that your dog that ran into my restaurant? Get that mangy beast out of my kitchen!"

Alan hurried in the back door, the restaurant owner right behind him, and found the dog with his paws on the counter, helping himself to the contents of a large metal bowl. The dog looked up at Alan, not one bit apologetic. In fact, he seemed to be rather pleased with himself. He looked from Alan to the cook, then let out a huge, satisfied belch.

"Come on, you Old Geezer," Alan said to the wayward creature.

"Old Geezer's the dog, huh?" the man said, a smile slowly spreading over his round, ruddy face. "Don't you get fed enough, boy?" he asked. Fortunately, the dog had only gotten into some leftover stew he'd planned to throw out, anyway, or the man wouldn't have been so quite so forgiving.

"We do okay," Alan said defensively. He scrounged in the dumpsters when his earnings were too skimpy to buy food, usually finding enough half-eaten hamburgers and tacos, steak scraps even, to satisfy the dog's hunger as well as his own.

"Well, you both look a little skinny to me," the man said. He hesitated only a moment before saying to Alan, "There's a dab of that stew left in another bowl; if you wanna have it, go ahead. Otherwise I'm just gonna throw it out."

Alan's stomach started to growl at the prospect of food, and he realized he'd barely eaten that day or even the day before, though he had made sure the Old Geezer got his discarded burgers. The cook motioned toward a bowl further back on the counter, and Alan picked it up.

"Fork's in that drawer there," the cook said, pointing.

Alan took a fork from the drawer and began engulfing the stew, a savory blend of pork and potatoes and rosemary. Too soon it was gone; he could have easily eaten another portion that size and then some.

"Thanks," Alan said, wiping his mouth with his sleeve. Then he started for the door.

"So where you stayin'?" the cook asked.

"Wherever," Alan shrugged.

"You just get back from 'Nam?" he asked.

Alan nodded, wondering what was with the twenty questions.

"My boy was over there," the man said, his eyes filling with tears. "Never made it home. Died last April."

"Sorry," Alan mumbled. He had a hard time handling emotions, whether his own or somebody else's. He didn't know what to say, and if he did say something, it usually turned out to be the wrong thing, so he just kept his mouth shut.

"He used to help me in the restaurant, cookin', bussin' tables, washin' the dishes," the man said. "I bought the place twenty years ago, kept all the customers the other guy had comin' in and added more. Always thought that Myron would take over for me one day.

Not that he had to, you know. If he wanted to do something else instead, that was okay with me, too. But it was his if he ever wanted it. That ain't gonna happen now." The man released a deep sorrowful sigh, and, as if on cue, Old Geezer let out a howl.

"Arooo!" he belted out, sounding like his ancestors did when they howled at the moon.

The man scratched the dog behind his ears and patted his rump.

"You're a good dog, aren't you, boy? Maybe a little scruffy, but a good boy. Good dogs usually have good people," he said, looking Alan in the eye. "So maybe you two would like to hang around here, help me out, I was thinkin'. There's an apartment over the restaurant—it ain't much, but there's a bed and a couch and a shower, anyway. You could work here, bus some tables, do a little cooking maybe, and get your rent free. Sometimes this place gets to be too much for me, you know. I'm pushin' fifty and it's hell bein' on your feet twelve hours a day. You'd be helpin' me out."

"You've never seen me before, and you're offering me a job and an apartment?" Alan asked, surprised and more than a little suspicious.

"Yeah. I'm thinkin' maybe Myron sent you here," the man replied.

Crazy old bastard, Alan thought. But having a place to crash sounded mighty tempting. Steady kitchen work, he didn't know. He had helped his mom with the cooking quite a bit, and enjoyed it, really, when he was younger.

"Woof!" Old Geezer said, wagging his tail enthusiastically. The dog seemed to think it was a good idea, so why not?

"Okay, we'll try it," Alan said, and felt surprisingly happy. "I've gotta warn you, I haven't ever cooked before. A little at home, but not for a job."

"That's okay. We'll start you out easy, washin' dishes, peelin' vegetables, that kinda thing. Here, I'll show you the apartment and you can get cleaned up." The man opened the door and Alan and the dog followed him outside. The steps leading to the apartment were on the west side of the building. The man motioned for Alan to go upstairs, so Alan headed up, with Old Geezer and the kindly restaurant owner behind him.

"What's your name, anyway?" the man asked.

"Alan Castani," Alan replied. "And yours?"

"Myron, just like my son. Myron Delanoit."

Alan felt the hair on the back of his neck stand up. His stomach cramped violently, threatening to eject its contents, and he began breathing rapidly. He spun around on the ball of his foot, pushed past the startled Myron Delanoit, and jumped from the fourth stair, falling to the ground but quickly rising.

"Come on, Old Geezer," Alan yelled. The dog whined, his tail down, and refused to budge. What the hell, let the dumb dog stay behind, Alan was getting the fuck out of there. He ran through the parking lot, past the dumpster and toward the beach.

"Where ya goin'?" shouted the confused Myron Delanoit. Geez —ya try to do something nice, and the guy freaks out on ya. Thought maybe he could help the kid out, maybe take some of the sting out of losing his own boy. But it looks like this one is too far gone. Damn war, he thought sadly. Then Old Geezer whined again and Myron patted him absent-mindedly. At least it looked like the dog was gonna stay. He knew a good deal when he heard it, anyway.

Alan slowly sat up and pulled the plug on the now-tepid bath water. It wasn't long after his run-in with Myron Delanoit that he had decided to come home. He was sick of sleeping on the beach, getting chased by cops, scrounging for food wherever he could find it. The panic that he'd experienced when he heard Myron's last name had spiraled, fueling an even greater need for the anesthesia that alcohol and drugs afforded him. Any money Alan made off panhandling went to buying cheap whiskey and wine and dope. He spent an indeterminate amount of time in a haze, just getting sober enough to go back out and get some more change—nobody gave you any money when you were totally wasted, he'd discovered. But then he woke up one morning, sick, aching, and decided he'd had enough. He'd give it one more shot and see if he could possibly find a way to fit into this crazy world. There was only one place he could think of where he might find the space to pull himself together, and that was home. Back in Hook's Point.

So here he was. He stood up cautiously, a little weak in the knees from the hot water, dried himself off with a rough yellow bath towel, and turned around to rinse the filth from the tub. He'd hitchhiked home from California, catching rides from truckers so eager for conversation they were willing to overlook his stench just to hear another human being say a few words, from a minister set on converting him, and from a group of hippies who were heading to a commune in Ohio. They'd shared some weed with him, Alan thought that was the day before yesterday, and a couple hits of really good acid. He was going to try to get clean, though, and didn't plan to hook up with any of his old suppliers now that he was back in town. Beyond that, he didn't have a well-formulated plan for what he should do next.

Right now, the smell of his mother's spaghetti was stimulating his taste buds and even lifting his spirits. He dressed in the jeans and sweatshirt that his brother Johnny had dropped in the door, then glanced at himself in the mirror. It was clouded with steam, so he wiped it off with his sleeve and looked at the image reflected there. A mistake.

Any happiness Alan had felt immediately evaporated as he looked at the gaunt cheeks, the listless sunken eyes. No wonder his brothers and sisters looked scared of him—hell, he was almost scared of himself. He turned away in disgust. His hunger drove him downstairs, where he joined his family at the table. Four faces looked at him curiously, wanting to ask him so many questions, but they'd been sternly warned by Rose to leave their brother alone for now. Let him get used to being home, back in Hook's Point. There would be time for questions later.

Rose admitted to herself that she had mixed feelings about her second son's reappearance. While she had missed him dreadfully, once she saw him, she remembered how unsettling Alan was. She didn't understand this child of hers, this moody brooding boy. It had been more peaceful when he left, actually. Although there was never any true peace, always wondering where he was, what he was doing, whether or not he was eating right. And from the looks of him, he hadn't been, not for a long time.

That, at least, was one problem that Rose knew how to handle. Her round arms jiggled as she gave a final stir to the spaghetti sauce, savoring the smell of the basil blending with oregano and sweet marjoram.

"Need some help, Mama?" Jenny said, sticking her head in the door.

"Yes, put the salad on the table and then get the garlic bread out, please," Rose said. She dished up six servings of spaghetti and carried them out to her hungry family, placing an extra-large helping in front of Alan.

"Looks good, Mama," Alan said. "I missed your cooking."

"You're too thin, Alan," Rose said, "but we'll get some meat back on your bones. Children, grace," she reminded, as a couple of the younger Castanis tried to sneak in a bite beforehand.

The religious words and ritual caused tempestuous feelings to rise up for Alan, but he tried with all his strength to push them down. When his mother glanced at him from across the table, Alan gave a grotesque attempt at a smile and hungrily dug into the spaghetti.

My son, my son, Rose thought worriedly. *Where have you been? Where did I lose you?*

Chapter Twenty

Jack sat in the waiting room at Midwest Therapy, nervously bouncing his legs and leafing through an outdated Time magazine. At least he was alone in the waiting room today, so he didn't have to worry about running into somebody he knew. Mike had dropped him off for his four o'clock appointment and would be waiting for him in the parking lot when Jack got done at five, he'd promised.

And, Jack had to admit, his dad was becoming quite reliable, now that he had quit drinking. It used to be that Mike would drop him off somewhere, say he'd be back at a certain time, then arrive half an hour late with booze on his breath and some cockamamie story about traffic jams or something, like there were ever any traffic jams in Hook's Point. Jack was starting to dare to hope that things were really going to be different for his family, that with Mike off the booze, they could be normal, like Wayne's family. Not Brady Bunch normal, where everybody acted way too nice and all the problems got solved in a half an hour, but just normal, where nobody had any horrible secrets to hide and they didn't have to pretend all the time.

"Jack, Rhonda's ready to see you now," Smiling Lady said. Today she was wearing a nameplate that said 'Julie,' but Jack still thought of her as Smiling Lady. Her ever-present smile was actually starting to be a quite reassuring, Jack realized as he followed her down the corridor to Rhonda's office.

"Hello, Jack," Rhonda said warmly. "Pull up a chair."

Jack suddenly felt shy, being alone with Rhonda without the buffer that his family had provided. He sat hunched over in the chair directly across from the therapist and distracted himself from his fear by looking at the memorabilia on her wooden desk: a silver-framed photo of Rhonda with a handsome black man and a little boy, a small basket of scented potpourri, a blue bowl with three red apples, plus her notebook and an elegant silver pen.

"How has your week gone?" Rhonda asked.

"Pretty good," Jack said. Realizing this wasn't going to work too well if he didn't talk, he racked his brain trying to think of something to say. "We started going to St. Augustine Church last Sunday, since it looks like they're going to let Father Delanoit stay at St. Maria's."

"Uh-huh," Rhonda said, somehow conveying her disgust for the diocese's decision with two short syllables. "Are you more comfortable there at your new church?"

"Kind of, I guess," Jack said warily. "At least I don't have to see Father Delanoit anymore. But… I don't know. It's still creepy sometimes, just… just being around priests and seeing them with the altar boys. It gets to me. Too many memories."

"Those are very normal feelings for someone who's been sexually abused," said Rhonda, who had been listening intently. "Anything that reminds a person of a traumatic experience, especially an experience which they've not been permitted to talk about, those reminders trigger a lot of uncomfortable feelings. The man who abused you, his name is Father Delanoit?"

"Yes," Jack said, hanging his head.

"How old were you the first time he touched you in a way that felt uncomfortable to you?" Rhonda asked.

"Twelve years old," Jack said, his voice barely louder than a whisper. "I had just celebrated my twelfth birthday."

"And when did you feel safe enough to tell someone about it?" she asked.

"A little over a month ago. I finally told because my girlfriend's little brother, he's in sixth grade, and Father Delanoit was trying to get to him. I couldn't tell anybody before because he... Father Delanoit... always said I'd get into a lot of trouble, and that nobody would believe me anyway," Jack said, feeling defensive, afraid that Rhonda would think he hadn't tried hard enough to stop the abuse, afraid she'd think that it was his fault, like Father Delanoit made it out to be.

"Let's get one thing straight right away, Jack," Rhonda said vehemently. "There was nothing you could have done to stop this, there was nothing you did to cause this, there was nothing wrong about you that made 'Father Delanoit' choose you," she said, spitting out the name as if she were pronouncing a curse word, Jack thought. "The man who did this, the man who sexually abused you when you were a little boy—the entire responsibility for any and all actions, that was his. *He* is the one at fault here, not you, not for one minute, do you understand?"

Jack nodded and mumbled a "yes."

"Maybe you don't believe that right now, but in time you will," Rhonda continued. "Sexual abusers are predators, and they prey on people who have less power than they do. Wouldn't you agree with me that children are, by nature, less powerful than adults?"

Jack nodded again.

"And since they are less powerful, it's never a child's fault when an adult chooses to harm them, sexually or any other way. It is not their fault that the adult abuses them, and it's not their fault if they don't tell anybody after the abuser has threatened them," she said. "Do you understand that?"

"Yeah, I guess so," Jack said. "It just seems like... I always felt like there was something wrong with me and that's why he picked me. Like... I don't know, like I make bad things happen, I guess," he said, his voice getting softer as he spoke. "Like... like with my mom." Jack was startled to have that fall out of his mouth.

"What about your mom, Jack?" Rhonda said gently.

"She got a brain tumor when she was pregnant with me, and then she died when I was just a baby. It's like… if she wouldn't have had me, then maybe she wouldn't have died, and everything would have been better. Maybe Dad wouldn't have started drinking so much then. They'd all have been a lot better off without me," Jack said, his face a mask of misery. He couldn't believe all this shit was coming out of him. These were his deepest fears, thoughts and feelings that he tried to keep hidden, even from himself, and somehow this lady was opening him up in a way that brought them up to the surface and made it seem possible that he could expose them and she wouldn't hate him, she wouldn't say, how stupid to think that, or try to dismiss it like David had done the few times he'd gotten the courage to speak them out.

"So you believe that you caused your mother's cancer? And also made your dad drink?" Rhonda asked.

"Yeah. Sometimes I do," Jack said. "My brother said that it isn't true, but I just can't help thinking that way sometimes."

"The way you've thought about your mother's illness and your father's drinking, that's the way all children tend to think, Jack. They blame themselves for events they had no control over. Children think they control the world—they all do, it's a normal developmental thought process. So when bad things happen, children think that they caused them to happen. If they have a caring adult who understands this, the adult can explain to them that the bad things are not their fault, that, like in the case of your mother, people just get sick sometimes and doctors can't always cure them. Or, in the case of your dad's drinking, they could tell you that your dad is a grown-up and if he drinks too much, that's his own decision," she said.

"Children believe that when they feel bad, it's because they are bad," Rhonda continued. "They think that if something bad happens to them or somebody close to them, they are the ones who caused it. And children also think that if something bad happens to them, they deserved it. A caring adult who knew what you were going through could have told you that sometimes bad things happen to good people, and that you, Jack, are good people, and so were your mama and your dad."

"And in the case of Father Delanoit," Rhonda continued, "they could tell you that he made a decision to touch you in ways that grownups should never touch a child, and that you couldn't have stopped him because he was so much bigger and more powerful than you. They'd tell you that it's never, never a child's fault when a grownup touches them the wrong way, it's the grownup's fault."

As Rhonda spoke, her words fell on Jack's soul like rain on parched ground. All the pain rose to the surface and he began to softly weep, releasing years of anguish, relinquishing the dark fears that had tormented him for so long. She sat quietly, bearing witness to his pain, and Jack was surprised that he wasn't even embarrassed for her to see him cry. She had a box of tissues on her desk, and when Jack was finished, he wiped the tears from his face and blew his nose.

"Sorry about that," he said reflexively.

"Jack, crying is alright. Really," Rhonda said. "Crying lets the sadness out."

Jack chuckled mirthlessly.

"I didn't even know I was sad. I thought I was just angry," he said.

"Well, in our society a lot of people believe that it's acceptable for boys and men to be angry, and it's not acceptable for them to be sad, at least not to express it. But as human beings, we all have a wide range of emotions. We can't just shut them off—they're a part of who we are," Rhonda said. "When we try to do that, when we try to shut them off, they don't just go away. They come out in nasty ways we didn't plan for."

"Like pounding the hell out of people?" Jack said.

"Right. Now, I'm not saying that excuses your behavior, because it doesn't. Just like your father is responsible for his own actions and Father Delanoit is responsible for his, so you are responsible for your own choice to settle matters with your fists," Rhonda said. "Behaving violently is apparently one of the ways you've coped with all those emotions bubbling up inside of you. And, in many cases, that behavior is socially sanctioned. Tell me, how did your father respond when you first began getting into fights?"

"He chewed me out, but I could tell that underneath it, he was kind of proud," Jack said, smiling at the memory.

"Kind of a 'boys will be boys' type of thing?" Rhonda asked.

"Yeah, something like that," Jack said.

"But he is not so proud now that your violent behavior is escalating, it seems," Rhonda said.

"No," Jack replied, hanging his head again. "Now he's scared, worried." And so am I, he thought.

"One of the things we're going to do here is help you learn how to control your impulse to behave violently. You're going to learn how to make better choices on how to express your emotions," Rhonda said. "When did you first start getting into a lot of fights?"

"Sixth grade," Jack said. "Not too long after Father Delanoit started to… after he… touched me."

"What did he do to you?" she asked gently.

"Well, you know," Jack said, squirming in his seat. "He touched me. On my private parts."

"I'm going to ask you again, Jack. What did Father Delanoit do to you?" Rhonda said. "There is tremendous power in telling your story in a safe environment. I'm not going to think any less of you after I hear your whole truth, Jack, and there's nothing you could say that would shock me."

Jack felt like his face was on fire. The shame was so great and he had held on to it for so long. As much as he didn't want to tell her, at the same time the truth was just about ready to burst out of him. Words welled up and suddenly began to overflow.

"I had just started altar boy practice at St. Maria Goretti's," Jack said. "I was in the sacristy one day, and one of the other kids, one of the other altar boys, he said Father Delanoit was treating me special—he'd come over to our house for supper—because he wanted to help me, because my dad was a drunk. I punched him, and he punched me back and then Father Delanoit came in and saw it, and I was really scared. I thought I'd get into so much trouble for hitting somebody in church! I never fought a lot before then, just kidding around with my friends a little. But I was so mad about what Slater said about my dad."

"Father Delanoit was really nice. I thought I had lucked out," he said. "But then he told me to come to church the next day and make up the practice. I came after school and we did the practice in about fifteen minutes. Then..." Jack paused a moment, then continued.

"He told me to come over to the rectory. I thought he wanted... I don't know what I thought, maybe he needed help or wanted to give me something to take to my grandma, since they were getting to be such great friends. But then..." Jack ran his shaking hands over his face. "I went into his study. He was standing by the desk and he turned around and walked over to me. He started telling me how I was special, and then he kissed me on the mouth! I couldn't believe it."

"I just stood there, shocked, and then he took his... his penis out of his pants. He put his hands down my pants and started to rub me. I was so embarrassed I could hardly talk, for Christ's sake, I was barely twelve years old!"

"Then he unzipped my pants and he... he sucked my penis. It felt so...so wrong, I wanted to run, but I felt trapped—he was the priest! It felt... just so creepy and horrible, I wanted to die. He told me to do that to him, and I didn't want to do it, but he said it was okay, he was the priest so he set the rules, and if he said it was okay, well then, it was okay. I still didn't want to, so he... he pushed my head down there and... he forced me to do it to him," Jack said, unable to repress a shudder. "Then he said I shouldn't tell anybody, that it would be our little secret. He reminded me about that I had hit Ronny in the sacristy, and he said they'd send me to reform school if they found out about it, and it would break my grandma's heart," Jack said.

"When I went home, the next day—I don't even remember

walking home or anything until the next day. It's like a big blank in my mind. So the next day, I woke up and I decided I'd try to forget the whole thing ever happened; it seemed unreal anyway, like a nightmare. But then he came to my house a week later and talked my grandmother into letting him take me out every other Friday night. I tried to fight him a few times, but it only got worse—he got rougher, and he said that nobody would ever believe me, because my dad was an alcoholic and we didn't have much money, that everybody would believe him. He… he'd say stuff about my mom, like it was my fault that she'd died, and that my dad started drinking, and I'd get so confused I'd do whatever he said, just to make him shut up, just so I could get out of there," Jack said.

"How long did the abuse go on?" Rhonda asked.

"For over a year. Then, I think it was my great-grandpa who convinced my grandmother not to send me with Father Delanoit anymore. We had him over for supper and my grandmother told him, 'thank you for spending time with Jack," and at this point Jack practically choked on his words, "thank you, but she'd decided she needed me at home.' Now why in the hell couldn't she have decided that a year before?" Jack said, his voice brimming with anger.

"You feel betrayed?" Rhonda asked.

"I do! And then I feel bad, because it wasn't her fault, I know that," Jack said.

"You don't need to feel guilty about your feelings, Jack. Emotions just are: they're neither good nor bad," Rhonda said. "Emotions don't hurt us, although what we do in response to them can. But it's perfectly natural that you would feel betrayed. So, the abuse stopped at that point?"

"Yes," Jack said. "Finally, it was over."

Rhonda looked at Jack with her dark, intense eyes.

"You have done a courageous thing today, young man," she said. Jack felt as if she were pronouncing a benediction over him. "You have spoken the truth, and, with your religious background, maybe you know what they say about the truth: you shall know the truth, and the truth shall set you free."

"We need to stop for today. Jack, you've shared some heavy stuff. You may experience some intense feelings, and I want you to remember that you can call me if you need to. How are you now?" Rhonda asked.

"Relieved," Jack said. "I just feel relieved. I've told a few people—Kelly and my family, and then the vicar general—that Father Delanoit abused me, but I didn't tell them the whole story. It felt good to get it out."

"Yes, it does feel good to let those secrets out in a safe place," Rhonda said. "And everything you say here is confidential: we only will discuss with your family what you decide you feel comfortable telling them. So, next week, same time. If you need me, give a holler." She rose and extended her hand to Jack.

"Thanks," he said as he shook her hand, and then left the sanctuary of her office. Mike was waiting in the parking lot for him, just as he had promised.

"How did it go today?" Mike asked.

"Good. It was pretty good," Jack said. He was still amazed that he'd told the whole nasty story and she hadn't looked disgusted or anything, just sad, like she was sad for him. Like she really got it, how much this had hurt and how bad it had screwed everything up.

"I'm glad, son," Mike said. "Let's go home."

Chapter Twenty-one

That weekend David came home, ostensibly to do laundry and enjoy Lucinda's cooking, but primarily to check up on his little brother. During their phone conversations, David had thought Jack sounded better now that he was getting professional help, but he wanted to visit with him face-to-face, so he could gauge his brother's true state of mind. Over the phone he couldn't see if Jack was still grinding his teeth the way he had been since the sixth grade; he couldn't see if his brother's dark blue eyes would evade his own when he spoke, always a sign that Jack was lying (Jack may have become a more proficient liar over the past couple of years, maybe he could fool his teachers and his grandmother, but his brother could still tell if he was being honest with him or not); over the phone, he couldn't tell if Jack was sleeping peacefully or if he was still tormented by the frequent nightmares that had plagued him during the past two years. So David decided to come home to Hook's Point.

"Hello, uglier than I," Jack greeted him with a friendly punch to the arm and then grabbed one of the bags that David was struggling with. David thought his brother's face looked light and happy.

"Ready to have your old roommate back for the weekend?" David asked.

"Do I have a choice?" Jack said. But David could tell from his expression that Jack was glad to see him.

The brothers dropped the bags in the living room by the stairs, and Lucinda hurried from the kitchen to greet David. She had been preparing some of his favorite foods for his homecoming: chocolate chip cookies, cheese bread and roast chicken, so the front of her apron was spotted with flour, but David squeezed his diminutive grandmother, lifting her off the floor in an exuberant hug. Then Pappa snuck in behind her.

"What's an old man have to do to get a handshake from his oldest grandson?" Pappa asked as Lucinda dabbed at her eyes with a tissue.

David easily engulfed Pappa's hand in his own, but his great-grandfather's grip was still strong and steady, he noticed. Lucinda looked good, too: still stressed but not as bad as the last time David had seen her. So far, so good, he thought. The next half an hour or so passed rapidly as they quizzed David about how things were going at college and caught him up on the latest news from Hook's Point.

David was still a little concerned about his father, even though Mike had also sounded good over the phone, his voice clear without a trace of the slur that it had whenever he was drinking, which used to be most of the time. David was glad to hear that Mike was still going to his meetings. But he was relieved to see it for himself when his father walked in the front door, his gait steady, his breath free of alcohol or the telltale cover-up scent of mints.

"Hello, son. It's good to have you home," Mike said, and warmly embraced David. David, still slightly shorter than his father and thirty pounds lighter, looked up at Mike.

"It's good to be home, Dad," David said.

The food was delicious and the conversation lively at the O'Donnells' that Friday evening. Across town at the St. Maria Goretti rectory, though, dinner was a much glummer affair, with Father Delanoit at one end of the long table and Father Schmidt opposite him, both chewing morosely on Mrs. McGrevey's leathery pot roast. Schmitty wanted nothing more than to crawl into bed and pull the covers over his head as soon as he was done with dinner, but he didn't feel that he could dare leave Father Delanoit unattended. He'd noticed lately that the older priest had seemed agitated and easily annoyed, even losing his temper with Mrs. McGrevey because of the overcooked meat: normally Father Delanoit was extremely cautious not to risk losing the woman's allegiance.

"Damn it, woman, is it too much to ask that you not ruin a perfectly good piece of meat?" he'd said loudly. When the shocked housekeeper had looked as if she might burst into tears, he had tried to backpedal, apologizing profusely. "It's just that your meals are generally top-notch, Mrs. McGrevey, so when they're not, it is a terrific disappointment," he'd said with apparent sincerity. She'd accepted his apology, but looked slightly suspicious at his abrupt shifting of gears.

Schmitty decided to make an effort to have a genuine conversation with the man.

"Father Delanoit, have you ever regretted choosing the priesthood instead of marriage, family? Ours can be a lonely life, after all. Do you ever wish you'd gone in a different direction?" he asked.

The older priest was quick to answer, as if he had settled this matter in his own mind long before.

"No, I never regret becoming a priest," he said resolutely. "The call was clear; since I was a young boy, I knew that marriage and family weren't for me. I knew that I would be a priest."

"It's difficult, sometimes," Schmitty said. "We're like other men, after all. We do get lonely, we do experience longings."

"Is this some type of test, Father Schmidt?" Father Delanoit asked. "Some trap that Father Novak suggested you set for me?"

"No. No, it's not a trap, it's a simple question," Schmitty said. "No agenda, just the truth. Sometimes I have wondered why we aren't allowed to marry like our Protestant brethren do. They seem to be able to balance the needs of their families with the needs of their parishes."

"Don't question these things, Father Schmidt," Father Delanoit said, clearly tired of this conversation. "You will find your life will be much easier if you don't question." He turned his attention back to his meal. At least the woman hadn't massacred the potatoes and carrots, anyway.

Later that evening, David lay in his old bed, across the room from his little brother. He felt full in a good way: his belly full with good home cooking and his heart full to see his family doing so well. Still, he needed to ask his brother something directly.

"Jack, how do you feel about me becoming a priest?"

"Geez, I don't know, David. I can't expect you to change your whole life around because of what Father Delanoit did to me," Jack said. "Being a priest is what you've always wanted to do. I can't stand in the way of that."

"But does it bother you?" David persisted.

"I don't know," Jack said. "I haven't thought about it that much, to tell you the truth. I think it'll be okay. I mean, to me you're always going to be my brother David, no matter what you do."

"It's not like I hate all priests," he said after a moment. "Just Father Delanoit and that Father Novak the vicar general or whatever he is."

"How is it for you, going to Mass at St. Augustine's?" David asked.

"Well, it's better than staying at St. Maria's. But sometimes… sometimes it's really hard, even there. Grandma doesn't make me go when I'm afraid it's gonna be too creepy, seeing the priests and the altar boys and all of it," Jack said. "The worst part is having to get close enough to the priest to receive the Eucharist. To tell you the truth, I really don't care if I ever go to church again. When I'm out on my own, I probably won't, either."

The brothers were silent for several moments before Jack poised the question that had been bothering him.

"Do you think I'll go to hell, David?" he asked.

David heard the echo of the little boy his brother had been just a few short years ago in his poignant question, the brother who had thought he might even follow David into the priesthood.

"I mean, I skip Mass sometimes, and that's supposed to be a mortal sin. I hate Father Delanoit, I really hate him, and that's not too good, either. And I don't even want to be a Catholic anymore. It's like, when he abused me, all the faith that I had just died," Jack said. "I don't even know if I believe in God anymore."

David took a deep breath and prayed for guidance in answering his brother's question. He knew, of course, the official Church teaching on these issues: there was no waffling, no wiggle room. The rules were all cut and dried, plain and simple. But what about when life wasn't so simple?

"Jack, you are not going to hell," David said, sure at least of this much. "Anybody would feel the same way that you do, if this happened to them. Anybody would be angry, feel betrayed. I even feel betrayed, myself. I…I can see why you don't want to be Catholic anymore, when the bishop didn't even do anything to Father Delanoit after Dad told him what he did to you. I have had some doubts, myself. But, Jack, try not to blame God for what Father Delanoit did. I just think about Jesus and how he loved little kids, and said that anybody who messed with them would be better off if they had a millstone hung around their necks and were thrown into the sea."

"I just don't think God had anything to do with what Father Delanoit did, or what the bishop didn't do," David added.

"But, geez, David—the priest is supposed to be God's representative on earth! He speaks for God!" Jack said. "I just can't trust Him anymore. I can't."

David didn't know what to say. All the platitudes about God being mysterious and suffering a part of life sounded hollow, meaningless, even to him.

"Maybe nobody really speaks for God, Jack," he finally said. "Maybe just God speaks for God. Maybe, sometime, you could try just talking to God, just like you're talking to me now."

"And say I hate a priest? Won't he, like, strike me with a bolt of lightening?" Jack said cynically.

"No, he won't. God made you, with all of your emotions. God won't be surprised by anything you have to say," David said. "Trust me, if you can't trust God right now. I've given him an earful a few times, over these past few weeks, and I'm still standing."

"Well, maybe sometime," Jack said. With longing, he remembered the comfort he'd received from his faith years ago. Before. "Maybe someday."

The brothers fell silent, and soon David noticed that Jack had drifted off to sleep. His breathing was slow and regular, and David was pleased to notice he didn't seem to be grinding his teeth as much as he used to. Not once in the night did David wake to hear his brother struggling with the disturbing dreams that used to torment him, either.

It was a different story at the Castani's, however. Almost every night since Alan's return, the silence had been shattered with his tortured shouts or muffled cries. The first night Rose had run herself ragged, trying to reassure the younger children who had rushed into her room, terrified, and then going into Alan's room and trying to wake him up. She'd gently shaken him by his shoulders, and when his eyes opened, he had looked at her as blankly as if he'd never seen her before in his life. It was a scene they replayed nightly; once he almost punched her, and would have if Rose hadn't ducked so fast. She really didn't know how long she could keep this up, and considered calling Father Delanoit for help, but she didn't want to risk upsetting Alan any further, and she remembered how angry Alan had been at the Church before he'd left. When it came to dealing with her troubled son, it seemed Rose Castani was on her own.

David awoke early the next morning and went to the kitchen, where he found Lucinda and Pappa drinking coffee.

"Morning, Grandma, Pappa," he said, then grabbed himself a cup from the mug tree on the counter, poured himself a cup of strong black coffee, and joined them at the table.

"How did you sleep, being back home in your old room?" Lucinda asked.

"Pretty good, actually. And so did Jack," David said. "It seems like he's doing better, now that he's seeing a therapist."

"She's a smart lady. I think she's really going to be able to help Jack get through this whole ordeal," Lucinda said. She sipped her coffee, then said, "I saw Rose Castani at the grocery store on Tuesday, and she said Alan was home."

"Alan was another one of the boys that Father Delanoit took a special interest in, was he not?" Pappa asked. The three of them fell silent as they considered the havoc that the priest had wreaked on poor Alan's life, and how close Jack had come to becoming another casualty of one man's selfish actions and the diocese's cover-up. Each one hoped that Jack would be able to recover, and each one secretly feared what would happen if he could not.

"Maybe I'll go over and see him later," David said.

"Are you gonna say anything to him about Father Delanoit?" asked Jack, who had just walked into the kitchen.

"I don't know," David said. "I would like to know if our suspicions are correct or not. But I haven't seen the guy for years. I don't want to pry, and I don't want to shake him up, either."

"Just don't tell him anything about me, okay?" Jack said. "I don't want any more people to know than have to."

"I won't. Probably I'll just stop over and talk to him for a little bit," David said.

After he'd wolfed down a generous helping of coffeecake, taken a shower, and talked to his father for a while, David walked next door to the Castanis' house. He had spent many hours there as a child, and the comfortable two-story wood frame house looked much the same, though a bit more rough around the edges: the white paint was chipped and a board was loose on the porch steps, but the yard was raked and the windows shiny. Two little Castanis peered out the front window at him, and Jenny greeted him at the door.

"Hi, David, how are you doing?" she said, smiling shyly as she motioned him in. "How do you like college?"

"So far, so good. It's different from high school: nobody making sure you go to classes or get your work done," David said. "But I'm hanging in there. Hey, I heard that Alan is home now."

A shadow crossed Jenny's pretty face at the mention of Alan's name, and she looked vaguely apprehensive. She forced a smile, though, as if he'd been away at college, too, instead of getting kicked out of the Army and living on the streets.

"Yeah, he got home Monday. It was great to see him. He's still sleeping up there, I think," she said. "You can go upstairs and see him, though—geez, it's going on eleven o'clock.

"Oh, I don't want to bother him…" David began.

"Bother! No bother with old friends!" said Rose Castani, who had emerged from the kitchen, carrying a plate of cinnamon rolls dripping with frosting. "Here, take these and go up and see him. It's been too long since we've seen you around here, David."

Reluctantly, David took the plate of rolls and headed up the stairs to Alan's room. This had also been a familiar route years ago, but now David definitely felt awkward. He really didn't know what to say to Alan; at least the food would provide a distraction if things were too uncomfortable. He knocked at the door to the second room on the left, the one that Alan used to share with Jimmy Junior, who had graduated from the police academy and gone to work in Dubuque. Silence from behind the door. David rapped a little harder, saying, "Hey, Alan, it's David O'Donnell."

This time he heard someone stirring, then a muffled voice mumbled, "Come in." He opened the door, leading with the rolls.

"Your mom's the same as ever," he said. "She was pushing food at me the minute I walked in the door. Want a roll?"

David hoped that he was concealing the shock he felt at Alan's appearance; if the two men had passed each other on the street, David would never have recognized his childhood friend. Alan looked none too happy to have his sleep disturbed, but then a trace of awareness flickered in his eyes, and he pushed himself up on one elbow and smiled.

"Hey, man, it's good to see you," Alan said. Animation took

some of the hardness from his features, and he motioned for David to come in. "You can move some stuff and sit down over there; hey, give me one of those rolls, okay?"

David handed Alan the plate of rolls, moved the pile of clothes that were on the chair to the floor, and sat down.

"So how are you doing?" David asked.

"Pretty good, man. I was over in 'Nam, saw a lot of action, then I hung out in California for awhile," he said, conveniently arranging the facts to make them more palatable. "Then I thought I'd better check up on Mama, see how she and the kids are doing. Like you said, man, she's just the same. Everything's the same here." He took a bite from his cinnamon roll. "So how are you? Where are you these days?"

"I'm in Hays at Benedictine University," David said. He had decided not to mention that he was planning to become a priest, at least not right away. He didn't want to upset Alan by mentioning subjects that might trigger painful memories. "It's okay. Hey, did you know my great-grandfather moved in? Remember Pappa, the one who used to play poker with us for pennies?"

"I remember him! He was cool—used to let us win sometimes, but not very often. Hey, have a roll. I don't want to hog the whole plate," Alan said.

Even though he had just finished eating coffeecake at his own house, David took the offered cinnamon roll—he hadn't forgotten Mrs. Castani's cooking.

"You boys used to polish off a plate of rolls in practically no time," said Rose Castani, who had just come upstairs. She looked wistfully at the two young men: David was the same age as Alan, nineteen, but that was as far as the resemblance went. David's dark brown hair covered his ears, but it was combed and neatly trimmed, and his face was clean-shaven. His skin was clear and vibrant, his features unmarked, and he looked you right in the eye when he talked to you. Although Alan was much cleaner than he'd been when he first appeared at the door, his face still bore the marks of the life he'd been leading: an angry scar ran from the middle of his right temple halfway down his cheek, he wore a perpetually wary, hostile expression and his eyes shifted rapidly when he talked, as if he were constantly on high alert. Alan, sensing his mother's critical appraisal, shifted the conversation to David in order to deflect attention away from himself.

"So, Ma, David's going to college in Hays," he said.

"That's what I heard," she said. "You're planning to become a priest, aren't you, David?"

"Uh, yeah, so far," he said evasively, glancing at Alan to see how he would take this information. He shot David an angry glare, then seemed to settle back inside himself.

"I remember when you two were serving your first Mass at St. Maria's," Rose continued. "I can still see you both, up there on the altar by Father Delanoit. I was so proud," she said sadly.

"That was a long time ago," David said.

"Father Delanoit really did a lot for our family after the children's father died," she went on. "I'm sure you'll help a lot of people as a priest, too, David."

Alan looked at his mother with cold, dead eyes, a chilling stare that caused her to take a step backwards.

"Father Delanoit," he said. "Is he still around?"

"Why, yes, he is," Rose said. "Do you remember how he used to take you out for dinner, Alan? Why, you were one of his favorites, always."

David was becoming more and more apprehensive at the turn the conversation had taken and at Alan's reactions. But Alan's malice seemed to fade just as abruptly as it had appeared. A cynical sneer replaced the look of abject hostility, and he gave out a snide chuckle.

"Yeah, one of the good priest's favorites, that's what I was," Alan said. He stretched once, then got out of bed and slipped a pair of holey jeans over his boxers. "So, I think I'm gonna take a walk, see how old Hook's Point has changed since I've been gone. David, thanks for stoppin' over, man. Don't let that grandfather of yours take all your money, now."

It seemed obvious to David that Alan did not want any company on his walk, so he stood up and walked to the door.

"Stop over anytime, Alan," David said. "Good to see you, buddy."

"Yeah, man," Alan said, though his mind was clearly elsewhere. He had put on a pair of worn boots and a flannel shirt and stuck his pack of cigarettes in his pocket, and turned around to make his bed, a habit Rose had insisted on since he was a small boy.

"Bye," David said softly, then walked down the stairs. "Thanks for the cinnamon roll, Mrs. Castani," he said, then headed out the door and down the street to his home

"How was Alan?" Lucinda asked when he got home.

"In pretty rough shape," David said. "He was glad to see me, I think. But his mom started talking about Father Delanoit and when we were altar boys, and he got really mad. He didn't say anything, but he looked like he wanted to kill somebody—I'm not kidding. Then he calmed down and seemed like he was okay. But he looks like he's been leading a pretty rough life."

Lucinda sighed, remembering the sweet, quiet little boy who used to knock shyly on the door and ask if David could come out and play.

"It eats at you," said Jack, who had been sitting at the table doing homework. "I know there were a lot of times when I felt like I was going to explode. Guess I did a few times," he added sheepishly.

"You were carrying a heavy burden, something no kid should have to shoulder," Lucinda said. "I hate that you had to bear that alone for as long as you did, Jack."

"Yeah, well it looks like Alan's still keeping that secret," David said.

Right about that time, Alan was rounding the corner to St. Maria Goretti's. The schoolyard was empty except for the ghosts. They were swarming all over the playground. Alan could see himself standing in line, waiting to take his turn at bat, then approaching the plate. Taking a swing at the first pitch and missing it, then hitting the next one and making it to second base, his teammates cheering because the guys on both second and third made it home without getting tagged. He could see himself walking with David O'Donnell, arms around each other's shoulders, best friends. In fifth grade, the boys had taken one of Rose's paring knives and made small cuts on their forearms and rubbed them together, proclaiming themselves blood brothers forever. Ghosts from a happy childhood, unmarred by trouble until his father died so unexpectedly.

Then a diabolical figure wearing priestly robes entered the playground and all the smiling ghosts from Alan's childhood vanished. Alan instinctively stepped back and crouched on one knee, but then the evil spirit disappeared also, leaving the playground vacant except for a handful of crumpled brown leaves blowing around in circles in the cold wind. The rectory sat across from the playground, and suddenly Alan saw the evil figure appear again, standing at the doorway, ushering in the children from the playground. Alan knew they would never leave the rectory once they walked through its gaping, leering doors.

Alan fled back to his house, looking over his shoulder every step of the way. When he got home, he locked the door behind him. Nobody was in the living room: in fact, it seemed no one was there, at all. He walked upstairs and into his room, reached under his bed and pulled out his backpack. In the bottom of the bag, underneath the grubby sweatshirts and jeans he'd not gotten around to washing, was a six-inch barrel .357 Magnum revolver. Ever since he'd left Vietnam, Alan felt safer carrying a weapon. He'd gotten this one from a guy in California who'd traded it for a bag of dope.

Even in his confusion, he'd thought not to bring a loaded gun into the house with little kids. Alan had wrapped the bullets in a rag, so he took the rag out of the backpack and removed them. Carefully he placed six cartridges in the gun's chambers. He put the backpack under his bed, grabbed his jacket from the bedpost and headed back down the stairs, gun in hand. At the bottom of the steps stood Rose, carrying a laundry basket full of clean clothes which she had brought up from the basement.

"Oh, Alan, you startled me. I didn't know you were back home already," she said. Her eyes widened when she noticed the revolver in his hand. "My God, son, where did you get that thing? What are you doing?"

"It's alright, Mama," Alan said, slipping past her and heading for the door. "The enemy's at the playground, but I'm gonna take care of it."

"No, son! No! There's no enemy here, you're mixed up," she cried.

"They've got the kids, but I'm gonna get them out of there. It'll all be over soon. Bye, Mama," Alan said resolutely, then unlocked the door and walked outside, slipping the gun under his jacket.

"Alan, no!" Rose cried from the porch, but he was already halfway down the block. "Oh my God, what is he going to do?"

She dropped the laundry basket on the floor, scattering tee shirts and socks and underwear all over the floor, and ran to the phone. The police? No! How could she turn in her son, her own flesh and blood? With a shaking hand, she dialed a familiar number, the place she always called in times of trouble.

"Hello," said the rich baritone voice. "St. Maria's rectory, Father Delanoit speaking."

"Father Delanoit!" she cried hysterically. "Alan's lost his mind, and he's got a gun!"

"Who is speaking?" he demanded.

"Father Delanoit, this is Rose Castani, Alan's mother. He just came home about a week ago, and right away I knew something was wrong with him," she said. "He's sick, I know he is, but I can't call the police on him—he's my son!"

"My dear woman, please try to calm yourself," Father Delanoit said. He was starting to get a bit worried and wanted to get all the facts he could. "Alan has a gun, you say? Where is he now?"

"I don't know, he left. He was talking crazy, something about the enemy at the playground, he said the enemy was at the playground and they took the kids, but he was going to take care of it," she said. "Oh, Father Delanoit, please help my boy!"

"Mrs. Castani, I'll do what I can. Try to be calm, now, and remember—did he say anything else? Anything all about this enemy?" he asked.

"No, just that the enemy was all over the playground," she said. "That poor boy was mixed up before, and then he went over to that terrible war. Now he seems to be out of his mind, Father."

"That poor young man," he cooed. "What a shame. You just try to stay calm, Mrs. Castani, and let me handle this." With that, he hung up the phone, then picked it up again and hurriedly dialed the police.

"Hook's Point Police," a young man answered, his voice sounding bored.

"I have an emergency here," Father Delanoit said. "This is Father Delanoit at St. Maria Goretti's Church, and I've just received word that one of my parishioners, a young man with a history of being seriously disturbed, is on his way to the rectory, and he's carrying a gun."

"I'll send some officers right over," the young man said, all boredom gone from his voice. Who said nothing ever happened in Hook's Point? "Who reported this?"

"The young man's mother, a woman named Rose Castani," Father Delanoit said. "The poor young man came back from Vietnam recently and has been suffering from delusions, even before the war, I've heard."

"All right, Father, don't try to play the hero, now," the young man cautioned. "The officers will be there right away."

Father Delanoit hung up the phone, rushed to the door and locked it. Just then, Mrs. McGrevey entered the room: she had been cleaning on the second floor and just came down to take a break.

"What is going on?" she asked. "Why are you locking the door?"

"Rose Castani called. It seems that Alan has finally gone over the edge," Father Delanoit said. "He left home brandishing a gun, and he said something about 'enemies on the playground,' so his mother thought he may be headed this way."

"My God!" she said. "What could he be thinking?"

"I don't know that he's capable of thinking," Father Delanoit said. "The poor boy is suffering from shell shock, it seems."

"My God," she repeated. "Thelma Dalvey said she saw him at Castanis' in the yard, looked like hell, she said, pacing and talking to himself like a crazy man. Now he's on the way over here."

"You'd best seek shelter upstairs, Mrs. McGrevey," Father Delanoit said, more concerned about what Alan might say in front of her than about the housekeeper's welfare. They both jumped when they heard someone trying to turn the door handle, followed by a rap on the door when the handle wouldn't budge, but it was only Father Schmidt, carrying two heavy packages and looking extremely annoyed.

"Why is the door locked?" he asked as he sat his packages down on the table. Father Delanoit had opened the door and quickly relocked it once Schmitty was inside. "What's wrong?"

"Alan Castani's gone mad," Mrs. McGrevey said, her voice betraying equal parts of fear and excitement. "His mother called, said he's headed this way with a gun."

"Alan? A gun? Why would that poor boy be coming here with a gun…my God!" Schmitty said as an ugly suspicion hit him. He glared at Father Delanoit, just about to pose the question, when again the door handle shook. Only this time when the caller was denied entry, he broke the glass in the door with the butt of his gun, reached in and unlocked the door, then pushed it open. Alan Castani stood in the pile of broken glass, steely-eyed and stubborn-jawed, gun in hand. Mrs. McGrevey shrieked and ran up the stairs.

"Where are they?" Alan growled, pointing the gun first at one priest, then the other. He took another step into the hallway.

"Where are who?" Schmitty asked.

"The children. The kids—where are they?" he said again, louder. "Don't fuck around with me. I know they're in here. I saw you."

"Son, I don't know what you thought you saw..." Schmitty said, genuine compassion overruling his fear until Alan shoved the gun into his belly. Then he gasped and slowly raised his hands in the air.

"Don't call me 'son," Alan hissed. "You're not my father, you're not anybody's father. My father would never... he would never..." with that Alan's ferocity faded as quickly as it had appeared and his lips began to tremble, revealing a terrible vulnerability beneath his battle-hardened features.

Heedless of Schmitty's safety, Father Delanoit seized the opportunity and lunged at Alan, who snapped back into military readiness, shifting the gun from Schmitty toward Father Delanoit.

"You!" he spat. "It was you who took the children. I remember now!"

Father Delanoit backed up against the wall, his eyes never leaving the barrel of the gun. Schmitty looked out the gaping hole where the window had been and saw three police cars pulling up in front of the rectory. Alan's eyes twitched as he looked from the two priests to the door of Father Delanoit's study.

"In there, both of you, now!" he growled. "Get your asses in there and on the floor!"

The priests complied, walking close enough to their captor that they could smell the sour odor of his sweat.

"Get down!" he yelled. "On your knees, on the floor! You heard me!" He pointed the gun first at Schmitty's face, then Father Delanoit's. Unwilling to risk any sudden moves, the two men knelt on the floor as Alan had demanded. He stood behind Father Delanoit and pointed the gun at his head. "You! Release those children now, or I'm going to blast your head off!"

Hearing footsteps on the porch, Alan looked up. Suddenly the hallway was filled with police officers, guns drawn. Alan pointed his gun towards the new threat, momentarily forgetting his mission.

"Drop your gun or we'll have to shoot!" yelled the first officer.

"Please don't shoot him, officer," Schmitty implored. "He is a sick young man that needs help, not a criminal."

"What's wrong with you?" snarled Father Delanoit. "The lunatic was going to kill you!"

"Please, just give him a chance. Alan, put down the gun and I promise you, we'll get you the help you need. Put it down, Alan," Schmitty said, his voice almost supernaturally calm. Something in his tone reached through the cloud of madness that had engulfed Alan, and he began to falter, lowering the gun and pointing it towards the floor. The nearest police officer rushed him, knocking the gun out of his hand and pushing him down. Two of his partners joined him, and they successfully pinned Alan on his stomach, pulled both hands behind his back and handcuffed him, then pulled him to his feet.

"We'll take him in and book him," said the first officer, who seemed to be in charge of the operation. "Peel, you stay here and get a statement from the priests. Are you two okay?" he asked.

Father Delanoit had jumped up as soon as the first cop had tackled Alan, while Schmitty had remained on his knees for a moment and whispered a prayer expressing gratitude that his life had been spared and concern for Alan's well-being. Both men claimed to be just fine, though in fact they were still quivering in shock. They watched as the officers took Alan to the police car. He seemed to be cooperating with them, but just as they opened the back door and began to push him inside, Alan turned toward the rectory and lunged, straining against the two burly cops who held him back.

"I know what you did to those kids!" he yelled as they shoved him in the backseat. "I saw you!"

Officer Peel and the two priests watched as the police car carrying Alan drove away. Several other officers scoured the hallway, examining the scene of the crime. Mrs. McGrevey warily made her way back downstairs, shaking her head in disbelief.

"Who would ever think that something like this would happen

in Hook's Point?" she said.

"You'd be surprised at what goes on in Hook's Point, ma'am," Officer Peel said.

Chapter Twenty-two

Father Delanoit sat in the back of the church, waiting. If anyone saw him sitting in the back pew looking somber and reflective, they would probably think he was praying. In fact, he was mulling over the recent changes in his life since the day Alan Castani attacked him at St. Maria's just a month ago.

It had been child's play to convince the police officers that poor Alan Castani was just a disturbed, drug-addled Vietnam vet who'd gone over the edge, that Alan's attack at the rectory had been a random act of violence. Although Father Schmidt had had his suspicions about the reasons behind Alan's attack, he had no proof, and he'd had to collaborate what Father Delanoit told the police, that Alan Castani had broken the door, gained illegal entry to the rectory, mumbled a lot of incoherent nonsense and held the two of them at gunpoint. Alan continued to act bizarre while in police custody, babbling about ghosts on the playground and demon spirits and other gibberish; he'd been found unfit to stand trial and was transported to the state mental hospital at Columbia.

The diocese heard about the incident, of course; Bishop Groat had decided it was finally time for Father Delanoit to move on. He still chuckled when he recalled that last conversation he had with Father Novak. Novak had called him late Saturday evening, the same week that Alan had attacked him.

"Delanoit?" he'd said when Father Delanoit had answered the phone.

"Speaking," he'd answered, immediately recognizing Father Novak's rather guttural tone. Clearly, he was not a man of good breeding.

"What the hell is going on down there now?" he asked with an air of resignation.

"Actually, we were about to call it a day, since tomorrow is Sunday and a busy one at that," Father Delanoit said. He did like to antagonize the old man, he had to admit.

"You know what I mean. What's going on at St. Maria's, that young man breaking in and brandishing a gun? What kind of connection did you have with him?" Father Novak demanded.

"Well, we were as shocked as anyone," Father Delanoit said innocently. "We had not seen young Alan at church for years, and then I get a call from his mother, who's frantic and telling me that he is heading this way and he's carrying a weapon. I understand the poor young man suffered a total nervous breakdown—stress from the war, I'd assume."

"Oh, you would, would you?" Father Novak said rather nastily. "It wouldn't be that he was one of the boys you had a 'special relationship' with, now, would it?"

"Certainly not, Father!" the priest had said. "Why, I barely knew the young man outside of church." Father Delanoit wasn't worried about being caught telling a little fib, because he knew that the bishop never checked the validity of his statements, anyway.

Father Novak sighed. "Well, tomorrow's your last Sunday at St. Maria's," he said. "Effective immediately, you will be transferring to Holy Cross in Lexington, Missouri. Your replacement will be assigned to the parish within a month or two."

"Rather abrupt, but these things can't be helped sometimes," Father Delanoit said. He had been excepting this call, really. 'Well, this is good-bye, then, isn't it?"

"Indeed it is," Father Novak said, his tone suddenly lighter. "Indeed it is." *And good riddance*, he thought as he hung up the telephone. From now on, Father Delanoit would be somebody else's problem.

The move to Missouri had gone quite smoothly. The church was a little larger than St. Maria's and had been without a senior pastor for almost two months, since the priest who'd previously held the position had abandoned his post, left the priesthood and gotten married, totally forgetting his vows, Father Delanoit thought with a tinge of self-righteousness. The people had welcomed him very warmly, as had his associate, young Father King. Father King had been so pleased when he'd offered to take over the altar boy training. The poor young man was exhausted from trying to manage all the parish business.

And so Father Delanoit sat in the back pew of his new church, patiently waiting for the group of fresh-faced boys to walk through the door. They should be here any minute now, he thought.

While Father Delanoit was eagerly awaiting the new crew of altar boys, Jack was finishing his weekly session with Rhonda. Today they had covered a lot of territory. Rhonda had encouraged Jack to express his feelings about Alan attacking Father Delanoit and Father Schmidt. At first, Jack had been reluctant to admit what he was really feeling for fear that Rhonda would despise him if he told her the truth. He'd begun with just telling her the facts of what had happened.

"Alan Castani broke into the rectory and held Father Delanoit and Father Schmidt at gunpoint. He probably would have shot them, but the police got there in time to stop him," Jack had told her. "I heard he was talking crazy, saying something about Father Delanoit taking the children or something."

"Not all that crazy, if you think about it," Rhonda interjected.

"Well, no, not really," Jack admitted. "We kind of think… that is, my family wonders if maybe Father Delanoit did the same thing to Alan that he did to me."

"I wouldn't be surprised," Rhonda said. "Generally those who sexually abuse children have a number of victims. So how did you feel when you heard about this?"

Jack hung his head, afraid that she would somehow read his mind.

"Did it feel good to have Father Delanoit suffer through a fearsome experience, after all the suffering he'd put you through?" she asked.

"Yes," Jack admitted, feeling relieved to bring the ugly feelings to the light. "I just wish that Alan had gone ahead and killed him. I'm sorry, that's how I feel."

"You don't have to apologize for your feelings, Jack. Feelings and actions are two separate things. Maybe if Alan had been able to talk honestly about his feelings, he wouldn't have chosen such drastic action. And if your gut reaction was the desire to see someone who'd harmed you suffer, well, that's a pretty normal feeling, too."

"It's got to be some kind of sin, though, "Jack said.

"Do you believe in God, Jack?" Rhonda asked.

"Yes, I do. Sometimes I wonder, but I do," Jack said.

"And do you believe that God created us?"

"Yes," Jack said, wondering why this was turning into a religion lesson.

"Then don't you suppose God understands all of our feelings? Not just the pretty, happy ones like love and happiness, but the disturbing feelings, like anger and fear and even hatred?" Rhonda asked.

"Hatred?" Jack repeated. "Isn't that like, the worst sin of all?"

"Worse than abusing a child? I'm no preacher, but I'd have to say no. Hatred is just a feeling like all our other feelings, and, unless you spill it all over onto other people, it's not going to hurt anybody," Rhonda said. "It will hurt you, though, if you stuff it back until it corrodes your insides."

"So, then, what do you do with it? What do I do with it?" Jack asked.

"Just what you're doing now," she said. "Be honest. Admit that you feel what you feel, and don't apologize for it. Then take all that fierce energy and use it. Write or paint or make music; exercise or work out. Better yet, take it and fight to make this world a better place somehow."

"But… sometimes I just want to destroy everything," Jack said.

"It's okay to *want* to. It's not okay to *do*, get it?" Rhonda said. "You were violated in the worst way that a person can be violated. This anger, this rage, it's just an emotion that shouts, 'Hey! Get off my property!' You didn't have the ability to say that at the time the abuse took place, so now what you're feeling is backed-up emotion. You can learn to release that emotional energy in healthy ways that don't harm anybody. Do you like to write, Jack?"

"Yeah, it's okay," he said. "English is my favorite class."

"I'm going to give you an assignment, then. Go out and buy a notebook, just a regular notebook like you use in school," Rhonda said. "I want you to write some every day. Write what you're feeling, write what you're thinking about. If you want to bring it in and we can talk about it, that's fine. But you don't have to—you don't have to show it to anybody."

"You mean, like a diary?" Jack said, a little disgusted. "Isn't that for girls?"

"Yeah, it's for girls. And it's for men and women and guys," Rhonda said. "Anybody who wants to learn how to release their ugly feelings—without getting themselves arrested."

"Well, I guess I could give it a try," Jack said, somewhat chagrined.

"Okay, then. We'll stop for today. See you next Monday, same time," she said. "You're doing a good job, Jack." Her handshake, like her smile, was warm and encouraging, and Jack left her office feeling lighthearted and hopeful.

A few snowflakes were starting to fall, Jack noticed as he

stepped outside. Mike was waiting for him in the parking lot. Jack opened the door and quickly got in; the blast of warmth from the car's heater was a pleasant contrast with the chilly December air. Mike was humming along to an Eagles tune that was playing on the radio.

"So everything go okay today?" Mike asked. Since Jack had begun his weekly sessions with Rhonda, Mike had noticed that his son seemed less tense, less inclined to lose his temper. Mike was beginning to believe that this therapy business might be okay after all.

"It was good, Dad," Jack said. "Can we stop at the store and pick up a notebook?"

"Sure," Mike said.

"Jack, what would you think if I were to take a lady out on a date?" he asked suddenly.

"A date? That'd be cool, I guess," Jack said, though he actually had a hard time picturing it. His dad on a date? Whew.

"Good," Mike said. "You know, I loved your mother with all my heart. I always thought she'd be the only woman for me, and if she'd lived, she would have been. But she's been gone a long time, now, and… hey, what's the matter?" he asked, glancing over at his son.

As soon as Mike had said those words, 'if she'd lived,' Jack's heart had filled with fear, that old fear that he was responsible for his mother's death. Mike didn't know what he was thinking, but he could tell by his son's expression that something was wrong.

"I just wonder sometimes… maybe if Mom hadn't had me, then she wouldn't have gotten sick," Jack said quietly. "Maybe she wouldn't have died, and you'd all have been better off."

Mike pulled over to the side of the road and stopped the car.

"No way, Jack. That's not true. Your mother had terminal cancer. It had nothing to do with being pregnant, it had nothing to do with you at all," Mike said vehemently. "As a matter of fact, Dr. Krisdale told me your mother probably lived longer than she would have if she hadn't been pregnant, because she wanted to hang on and see that baby. You. She loved you, Jack. And I don't say it enough, son, but so do I. You've been a blessing since the day you were born." Mike hugged Jack, an awkward but heartfelt hug that vanquished his son's fear totally and completely.

They both sniffled, self-consciously wiping their eyes, and then Mike switched gears and began to drive. The windshield wipers' gentle swoosh, swoosh, dissolved the snowflakes on contact. Father and son rode in companionable silence for a few moments before Jack asked the question that had began formulating in his mind.

"So, who's the lady?"

"It's a gal I met at my AA meetings," Mike said. "Real nice gal. We always sit down and have a cup of coffee after the meeting. I'm thinking I'd like to take her out for supper, go on a real date somewhere nice."

"What's her name?" Jack asked.

"Kate. She's a real nice lady, been in the program for a year and sober the whole time," Mike said "Nice-looking, too."

"Go for it, Dad," Jack said. "David and I both, we always thought it would be kind of cool if you'd get married some day."

"Whoa," Mike laughed. "Nobody's talking about getting married. As a matter of fact, my sponsor said I really need to concentrate on staying sober now and not do anything to rock the boat, just focus on my program. So I'm not talking about getting married, son. Just taking a nice lady out on a date."

"Sure, Dad," Jack said, smirking a bit. He knew his father was never one for doing things halfway. Jack wouldn't be surprised if this turned out to be far more serious than his father was letting on. And that would be okay. Jack loved his grandmother and didn't feel any need for another mother figure in his life, but he would like to see his dad have somebody to care for, especially since in just four years, Jack would be graduating from high school and going out on his own. Yeah, he'd like to see his dad find somebody.

"Thank God, I'm a Country Boy," started playing on the radio, and Mike sang harmony to John Denver's tenor. As they drove home, the snowflakes hit the windshield and covered the ground with patches of white. Jack even found himself singing along with his dad once or twice.

Epilogue: One Year Later

"It's ready!" Lucinda shouted into the living room, striving to make herself heard over the football game and the talking and laughter. They'll figure it out soon enough, she thought, and carried the steaming pot of chili to the table, letting the spicy aroma draw them in. Slices of cheese and summer sausage and crackers stacked high on one plate and chopped carrots and radishes and celery in the relish dish rounded out the meal. Slowly they drifted into the dining room, David and Jack and Mike and Kate joining Lucinda at the table.

"Looks good, Princess," David said. Since Pappa had passed away last April, her grandsons had taken to occasionally calling her by the same nickname that he had, and somehow that helped fill the void Pappa's death had left in her heart. Pappa! Once Father Delanoit was out of their lives for good and Jack began receiving help to deal with the abuse and its aftermath, it was as if Pappa felt he'd accomplished his purpose. During the winter, he had grown steadily weaker. His legs would no longer carry him up the stairs to his apartment so he moved into the main house, making his bed on the couch. Pappa never lost his quick wit or sense of humor, but he did seem far away, as if he was more in tune with the next world than this one. He spoke more frequently of people he'd known growing up in Italy and of his wife Gina and of Rita, as if he were looking forward to meeting up with old friends. Then one morning when Lucinda had come downstairs, she walked into the living room and knew instinctively that Pappa was gone.

Lucinda felt the loss of her father keenly and she grieved for him, but she also felt his presence in so many ways. She kept his favorite red cup with the chip on its lip sitting on the counter, a reminder of morning coffee breaks they'd spent in animated conversation. She saw Pappa's expressions sometimes on the boys' faces, a quizzical tilt of the head or a proud little smile over a job well done. She remembered his wisdom when she worked through a problem, especially when dealing with people, and she remembered his humor when life got dicey. And she felt Pappa's presence in a less tangible, almost mystical way that she couldn't easily put into words, like a gentle whisper in her ear or the softest of touches on her cheek when she was blue. Yes, Pappa would always be with her and with the rest of the family, too.

And it looked like the family might be expanding soon. Mike and Kate had started dating last year just before Christmas. For the first couple of months their relationship had been casual, just as Mike had claimed it would be, but by spring, everybody could see that this was the real thing. Mike saw Kate at least three or four times a week, depending on their work schedules. Kate worked as a reporter at the local newspaper, and sometimes their schedules didn't allow them to do much more than meet for a quick bite to eat before she had to rush off for her shift. Lucinda had overheard David and Jack talking about their father's relationship with Kate, and she was glad they both were enthused about it.

Lucinda had to admit that she'd had mixed feelings in the beginning. It was hard to see another woman taking her daughter's place at Mike's side, seeing his eyes light up the way they used to do when he was with Rita, watching the two of them exchange a quick kiss or hug. Yet it had been fifteen years now, and the time for mourning was long over. Mike deserved to be happy, and Lucinda was glad for him. She liked Kate a lot, all the better perhaps because she was nothing like Rita. Where Rita had been small and dark, Kate was a tall, full-figured blonde. Rita had excelled in the domestic arena, and Kate could barely boil water, she cheerfully admitted. Although the two women were very different from each other, Lucinda couldn't help but think they would have been friends. Kate was quick and funny and very warmhearted, and the boys thought she was terrific. Yes, Lucinda was pleased.

Lucinda had told Mike that, if he and Kate did get married, she would get an apartment near by. He had promptly nixed that idea, reminding her that she was the only mother that Jack had ever known, and besides that, this was her home. She had reluctantly agreed to stay, at least until Jack graduated from high school, but she did have some misgivings. Maybe it would work out just fine, though. Kate obviously had no desire to take over Lucinda's role, and they did enjoy each other's company. It might be a little unorthodox, but so what?

As for Mike, he could scarcely believe his good fortune. To win the love of a good woman not once, but twice in his lifetime, was a blessing that he would never cease to give thanks for. To see his son gradually being restored mentally and emotionally was another great blessing. And to be sober, because without that, none of the other good things would have happened. After what Father Delanoit had done to Jack, Mike would never again be comfortable in the Catholic Church, but he felt a connection with God that went beyond the ties of religious dogma and doctrines. Still, Mike had come to the point where he fully accepted, even respected, David's decision to continue studying for the priesthood.

When David had first learned that Father Delanoit had sexually abused his little brother, he had been sure the Church officials would be just as outraged as he was, and that they would give his brother justice. But when instead they stonewalled his family and left the abusive priest in his position, essentially forcing his family to leave their parish, David had come very close to losing his faith, not only in the Church but also in God as well. He had lived through what St. John of the Cross described as a "dark night of the soul," a time so painful and full of loss that it served to drive him completely, totally into the arms of his Father. Stripped of all false pretensions and naiveté, David clung to God and God alone. As he recovered from this experience, his decision to become a priest was strengthened and solidified. But he would be the antithesis of Father Delanoit, David determined: honest and transparent, committed to serving God and the people with the love and humility modeled by Jesus. Perhaps as his brother watched him living out his faith, he could regain his own.

A few weeks after Alan Castani had been committed to the mental hospital, David had gone to visit him for the first time. Alan had been so heavily sedated that he had barely recognized David, but David had vowed to go back every month, and he had kept his vow. It pained him to see his boyhood friend shuffle down the hall like an old man, but Alan did seem pleased by his visits and the candy bars David always remembered to bring. David hoped that eventually Alan would confide in him the real reason he had gone to the rectory that day, and if, as he suspected, Alan was another of Father Delanoit's casualties, David had made another vow: that he would do his best to make sure the priest was held accountable for the trail of misery that followed him wherever he went. He just thanked God every day that Jack was gradually being restored to health and relieved of the burden the abuse had place on him.

Jack watched happily as his father and Kate bantered back and forth, being careful not to betray his feelings too much. After all, he was fifteen, too old to be overly concerned with his father's love life. Inside, though, he was beaming. Jack had never known what it was like, having two parents who loved each other, and he found it quite delightful to see his dad and Kate all wrapped up in each other. Not that he felt left out or on the outside, because he didn't. Kate seemed to enjoy Jack's company and had an easy-going demeanor that made it a pleasure to be around her. Instead of taking away Mike's time and attention, it felt like Kate added a new dimension to their family that Jack hadn't even known he was missing.

Jack had transferred to the public school and, after almost a year, felt comfortable there. Initially, it was awkward: nobody changed schools in midyear unless there was a reason. When people asked him questions, he just told them that he'd gotten into some trouble at St. Maria's and that was why he'd switched. For a while, the "good" kids kept their distance from him and the wilder element tried to get him to join their kegs and pot parties, but Jack ignored them all. He just focused on doing his schoolwork and tried not to let any of it get to him too much. Rhonda helped immensely.

He'd started writing in his notebook like she had suggested. At first, it was strange and he ended up writing something stupid, like "I'm having shrimp for supper," or "The math teacher is a jerk." When Rhonda had asked him how it was going, he told her he didn't really see that it was doing him any good.

"Write a letter to Father Delanoit," she'd said.

Jack looked at her like she was the crazy one.

"You want me to write a letter to *him*? All I want to say to him is, 'Go to hell,'" he'd sputtered angrily.

"Then that's what you should write. Whatever you've felt toward him, put it down on paper. How he hurt you, how he damaged you with his actions. Get it out, all those feelings. You ever go fishing, Jack?" she said in an apparent non sequitur.

"Yeah, a few times with Wayne," he said. "What's that got to do with anything?"

"Did you ever get your fishing line all tangled up?" she asked.

"Yeah, I think that's why I hated it," Jack said, remembering the frustration of trying to untangle the wiry mess.

"Your emotions are a lot like that tangled-up fishing line," Rhonda said. "Right now, they are so twisted together because of the abuse that you often find yourself becoming angry and you don't even know why. Then you have lashed out and harmed other people. Once you get clear on your true feelings and can associate them accurately with what caused them in the first place, you're going to find it a lot easier to keep yourself from behaving aggressively. You'll find that, once you get that line straight, your emotions are truly your friend, not your enemy."

"So, am I going to send this letter to him?" Jack said.

"That will be up to you, Jack," Rhonda said. "This is something I want you to do for yourself, though. You really have no control over his actions, but you do over your own, and that's what this healing process is all about."

So Jack had gone home and written the letter. He'd started three times, each time writing a line or two, then ripping the piece of paper out of the notebook, crumpling it up and throwing it in the wastebasket. Finally, he'd soldiered his way through and completed it. He had shared the letter with Rhonda the following week. She had listened gravely while he read it, his voice shaking.

"Mr." Delanoit,

You are not worthy to be called 'Father.'

Two years ago, I turned twelve years old and became an altar boy at St. Maria Goretti's. I was so excited to be serving God that way, I thought I might even become a priest like my brother was going to. Now I can't even stand going to Mass, and I know you know why.

You touched me in ways that no adult should ever touch a child, you stole something away from me and no one can ever give it back. When you started doing that, Louis, I didn't even know what was going on. I was just a little boy, for Christ's sake. Why would anybody want to do something like that to a little kid? I felt so dirty, I wanted to die. Sometimes I still do.

Then you came into my home and convinced my grandmother that you were going to take me under your wing. Well, you took us all in, that's for sure. You made me do things I didn't even know existed, and I will hate you for that until the day I die. (Then followed a series of expletives, stretching out over four lines; Jack had pressed down so hard with his pen that it had ripped a hole in the paper. He deleted that section when he read the letter to Rhonda.)

You were supposed to teach me about God. Instead, you gave me a pretty good glimpse of the devil himself. You are an evil, evil man and if I'm glad about anything, it's that you won't be fucking up any more kids in Hook's Point. I feel sorry for the kids wherever you are now.

You made me feel so bad about myself. I was afraid to tell

anyone because I thought they would hate me. I got so messed up from holding all this inside me that I got into trouble, started getting into lots of fights, even got arrested. Now I've got to try to learn how to live with all this.

Well, Louis, I am done. I don't want to give you any more of my time. Good riddance to bad rubbish, like my grandma used to say. Remember my grandma, Lucinda Walters? The woman who thought you were such a great guy? That's not what she says about you now.

Signed,

Jack O'Donnell"

When he finished reading the letter, Rhonda said, "That's a powerful step, Jack. You are getting straight in your mind about whose fault the abuse was, and that's going to make a difference in how you feel about yourself."

Jack sat silent for a few moments, and then asked the question that had been bothering him.

"I said that I hate him, and I do," Jack said. "Isn't that... wrong? Aren't we supposed to forgive people?"

"As time goes on and we work on helping you to heal, you may find that you lose the need to hate him," Rhonda said. "Right now, you're hurting. Who wouldn't be? Part of that hatred is a righteous indignation over what that man did to you when you were just a little boy. Another part of it is a self-defense mechanism. If you hate Louis, then you feel stronger than if you fear him, or feel hurt by how he betrayed your trust. Hate feels safer than those emotions. Over time, though, you'll discover that now it's safe to experience all your emotions, and you won't need to cling to hatred anymore."

"Are you supposed to forgive him? Well, what do you mean? If you mean, should you refrain from returning the harm that he did to you, I'd say, yes, you should forgive him. But if you mean, should you feel all warm and fuzzy toward the man who assaulted you, a man who has yet to express the slightest regret for his actions and the harm he caused you, well, no. I think down the road, you'll find you want to release a lot of the anger and hatred you're feeling towards Louis. But you'll be doing that for your own well-being, not his," Rhonda said.

And Jack was finding her words to be true. As they worked, talking about the abuse and the feelings he'd experienced as a result of it, he found a good deal of the rage and hatred was seeping out of his soul. He'd been able to avoid getting into any more trouble, and after six months, Jack had gotten off probation. He felt good more often than he felt bad, and that seemed like a genuine miracle, even to a doubting Thomas such as Jack. The writing thing really helped. Jack began to think that maybe he would become a writer when he grew up.

He'd also been able to talk to Rhonda, shyly and haltingly, about the troubling feelings and memories that sometimes crept in when he kissed Kelly, and Rhonda had helped him learn how to stay in the present moment, even when ugly stuff tried to intrude. She'd encouraged him to talk to Kelly and let her help him cope with it.

"Just don't get too carried away, though. You're both young yet," Rhonda had cautioned him.

Jack was amazed that he and Kelly were still going together, with all the drama they'd lived through, even after he'd transferred to the public school. Not only was he in love with her—and they had gotten the kissing thing pretty much worked out, he was glad to say—but she was his best friend. He realized that they were both young, just fifteen, but he had to admit that he hoped they would be together forever. Who knows? Jack shook his head a bit. Somehow, he'd engulfed a bowl of Grandma's chili as all those thoughts had run through his mind. He dished himself up another bowlful. This time he wanted to savor every morsel.

Postscript: While some abusive clergy members have been held accountable for their actions, there is still much room for improvement. On October 1, 2006, BBC aired a documentary, Sex Crimes and the Vatican. The BBC report stated that Pope Benedict XVI, then Cardinal Thomas Ratzinger, issued a secret Vatican edict in 2001, instructing all Catholic bishops to follow certain protocol for addressing the sexual abuse of children by clergy members. According to the BBC report, victims, witnesses and perpetrators should be encouraged to keep quiet about the abuse instead of reporting it to civil authorities. To prevent them from speaking out, the bishops could threaten them with excommunication.

Father Thomas Doyle, former Vatican attorney until he was fired for criticizing the church's handling of child abuse, said, "What you have here is an explicit written policy to cover up cases of child sexual abuse by the clergy and to punish those who would call attention to those crimes by the churchmen… This is happening all over the world."

Afterword

In the strange words of Rhonda Sphere, Jack was indeed blessed. Most victims of clergy sexual abuse kept the secret for years, decades even. Many of them thought they were the only ones who'd had such an experience. Many developed addictions, depression, low self-esteem, eating disorders, and other maladaptive coping mechanisms. Some did commit suicide. If the victims or their families reported the abuse, they were often ignored or intimidated by church officials.

Experts estimate that one out of four girls and one out of seven boys are sexually abused before they reach the age of eighteen. Whether the offender is a family member, clergy person, "friend," or acquaintance, childhood sexual abuse casts a long shadow. Bringing the abuse to the light is the only way to dispel that shadow and give survivors hope for a brighter future.

Resources: Organizations

SNAP: Survivors Network of those Abused by Priests
Toll-Free Phone: 1-877-SNAPHEALS (1-877-762-7432)
Mailing Address:
Survivors Network of those Abused by Priests
P. O. Box Box 6416
Chicago, IL 60680-6416

The Rape and Incest National Network
1-800-656-HOPE

Books for Survivors

Victims No Longer: Men Recovering from Incest and Other Sexual Child Abuse, by Mike Lew

Courage to Heal, by Ellen Bass and Laura Davis

Don't Tell: The Sexual Abuse of Boys, By Michel Dorais

Secret Survivors, by E. Sue Blume

Books about the Catholic Church's Response to the Sexual Abuse Crisis

Sex, Priests and Secret Codes by Thomas Doyle, Richard Sipe and Patrick Wall

Betrayal: The Crisis in the Catholic Church, by the Investigative Team of the Boston Globe

The Church That Forgot Christ, By Jimmy Breslin

Sex, Priests and Power: Anatomy of a Crisis, by Richard Sipe

Vows of Silence: The Abuse of Power in the Papacy of Pope John Paul II, by Jason Berry and Gerald Renner

Acknowledgements

Many thanks, first of all, to my wonderful husband Joe for supporting our family and allowing me to pursue my dream of becoming a writer, and also to our son Ben and daughter Sarah for their patience and encouragement. And speaking of encouragement, thanks to all my friends, and especially to Carolyn Bushman, Peggy Murphy, Val Reinholtz and Karla Rector for your priceless words of support, your prayers, your faith in this project, and in me, and to Leigh Streff, who is not only my friend since kindergarten, but also my first editor. Thanks to my sisters Marcia Mulroney and Kathy Estlund, and my mother-in-law June Clark for all your encouragement, and to my parents, now gone, Ann and Bill Mulroney, for instilling in me a love for the written word. Thanks to my furry kids, Sparky and Daisy, for all the love and laughter you give me on a daily basis.

Thank you to Steve Theisen, head of SNAP (Survivors Network of Those Abused by Priests) in Iowa and former police officer for the city of Dubuque, and Christopher Feldman, licensed private investigator and former Dubuque County sheriff deputy, for information about police procedure and for proofreading sections of the manuscript, to Father David Hitch for helping me understand the protocol for Mass preparation, to Robert Wolf for providing me with information about altar boys and Catholic tradition in the time period the story takes place, to Delia Ronconi for teaching me several Italian terms and phrases, to Dr. Mike Stitt for medical information, and to Arlene McColley Nicola, MSW, LISW, for helping me develop the Rhonda Spheres character. Any mistakes in the book are due to this writer's interpretation, not the experts' information!

Thanks to past and present Messenger newspaper editors Molly Bates and Deanna Meyer for offering Writers Workshop, and to Messenger Editors Barbara Wallace Hughes, Sandy Mickelson, Walt Stevens, and all the writers there for sharing your wisdom with me. Special thanks to first reader Peggy Murphy, whose encouragement and enthusiasm helped me believe in myself and in the project, and to Sacha Pfieffer, Robert Wolf and Sandy Mickelson for reading the manuscript and giving me many helpful insights. Thank you to my editor Tony Ellis for shepherding me through all the necessary revisions. Thanks, also, to Ed Spinoza, publisher at 1st World Publishing, and to all the team there.

And special thanks to all the brave survivors who shared your stories with me. Healing thoughts go out to you today and always.

A Conversation with Janet Clark

Q. You have said that Blind Faith is the story of the Roman Catholic clergy sexual abuse scandal as seen through the eyes of young Jack O'Donnell and his family. Would you say that Jack's is a fairly typical story?

A. I don't know that there is a typical story. Just as each person is different, so is each victim and each perpetrator. From what I've seen and the research I've done, though, I do believe many victims, like Jack, came from vulnerable family situations that made them an easy target for predatory priests. Many others came from very devout families where it would have been extremely hard for a child to come forward with the truth because the life of the family was so deeply enmeshed with the church. But many other victims don't meet either of those profiles. Unfortunately, sexual abusers tend to be equal-opportunity offenders, choosing victims from all walks of life.

Q. What was the most difficult part about writing this book?

A. Writing from the point of view of Father Delanoit, the perpetrator. I asked for prayer from my husband and several friends before I began writing that part. Well, before I began the whole project, but especially that section. When I began that process, I felt like I was entering a long, dark tunnel: inside the mind of a child molester is not a happy place to be. But through that process I discovered that, while most of us would never molest a child, virtually all of us have used our power to exploit others to get what we want. Writing from the abuser's point of view has made me very aware and very careful of how I use my own power in relationships.

Q. Did you find a need to balance the serious nature of the book's subject matter with moments of levity?

A. I did. In fact, that's why I introduced Kelly in Chapter Six. Jack was going through such a horrendous ordeal that I was having a hard time handling it myself. I needed to interject something positive into his life. Hence, as with Charlie Brown of Peanuts fame, the little red-haired girl! And bringing Pappa to live in Hook's Point brought some needed light into the situation. He is a wise character and a steadying influence for the entire family.

Q. Some people may be frustrated by how the book ends. Why did you not have Father Delanoit suffer any consequences for his behavior?

A. Because most of the time, abusers didn't. The Roman Catholic Church only began to seriously address the issue of abusive clergy and the bishops who moved them from parish to parish after the Boston Globe broke the story in 2002.

Q. Why did no one report the abuse to the police?

A. Frequently, abuse by clergy was considered a problem best handled "in house." The media has described incidents where the family did report the abuse to the police, only to find the police turned the issue back over to the church instead of filing charges. In 1974 the Child Abuse Prevention and Treatment Act was passed by Congress, providing funding to help states set up or expand mandatory reporter programs. To this day, however, many states do not require clergy to act as mandatory reporters.

Q. Is clergy sexual abuse strictly a Catholic problem?

A. No, there are similar problems in other churches and faith groups. Author Dee Ann Miller has examined the problem in her former denomination, the Southern Baptists, and found a similar dynamic with what occurred in the Catholic Church: a pattern of denial and cover-up which serves not to solve the problem, but to hide it. Blind faith, when applied to human beings and human institutions, even if they purport to represent God, is a risky business, in my opinion.

Q. Is there an autobiographical element to this narrative?

A. I am a sexual abuse survivor, yes. Other than the fact that I belong to that unfortunately large fraternity/sorority and that I live in Iowa where the story takes place, no. This is neither my story nor the story of anyone I know. The shame, pain and sense of isolation sexual abuse causes are common to all survivors, though.

Q. What kind of research did you do for the book?

A. When I was struggling to deal with my own issues, I read many books and surfed many Web sites devoted to understanding and healing from sexual abuse. Also, I participated in both individual and group therapy. In order to gain understanding about boys abused by clergy members, I interviewed male survivors, attended a conference where the speakers included survivors and their spouses, a priest who is the brother of a survivor—and this was after I had already written Jack's brother David into the story—and David Clohessy, director of SNAP, Survivors Network of those Abused by Priests. I read documents from the Bishops Accountability website, which details the paper trail that proves abusive priests were moved from parish to parish, that survivors and their families were stonewalled when they confronted church officials, and that far greater concern was shown to offending clergymen than to their victims.

Q. What's been the biggest help to you in your own healing journey?

A. First of all, realizing it's just that—a journey, not a destination. When I began therapy, I thought, okay, I'll do this for a year, tops, and then I'll be back to normal. Wrong! Like anyone who deals with a life-changing event, be it the loss of a loved one, a serious illness or disability, or sexual abuse, I discovered that I would need to adjust to a new normal. Once I accepted that fact, everything got easier. Not easy, by any means, but more manageable.

Of all the books I've read, Secret Survivors by E. Sue Blume was most helpful to me. I thought she did an incredible job of illustrating how abuse affects every aspect of a woman's life. But she also shows how a person can transcend even the most serious effects of abuse and build a meaningful, joy-filled life.

And most crucial to my healing thus far have been the many people who've helped me along the way. You really, really can't do something like this alone. I've relied on my very gifted therapist, survivors group, 12-step groups, beautiful friends, my incredibly supportive family, especially my husband and children, and God as I understand Her. Which is often and first through Jesus, but also God as Mother as well as God as Father.

Discussion Questions for Blind Faith

1. The bulk of the story takes place in the late 1960s and early 1970s. What societal changes have occurred since that time, and do those changes make children more or less likely to be abused? Are they more likely to be believed if they come forward now?

2. What is your reaction to Mike O'Donnell? Does your perception of him change as the story progresses?

3. Why does no one question Father Delanoit's interest in the boys he abuses? Is it because of his position of authority or because of the times, or some other factors? Would you have found him suspicious? What precautions do adults need to take in order to avoid even the appearance of evil when working with kids?

4. What, if any, clues did Lucinda miss that might have led to her uncovering the truth?

5. What is the difference between faith and blind faith? Is it ever appropriate to have blind faith in another person or an institution?

6. What leads Pappa to perceive that Father Delanoit may not be who he presents himself to be?

7. Why did Father Novak continue to cover up for Father Delanoit, even though he thought Delanoit was dangerous to children? Did he experience any internal conflict about his role in the cover-up?

8. Pappa's friend Vinny became angry when Pappa questioned him about Father Delanoit. Did he have any valid reasons to fear coming forward with what he may have heard about the priest's behavior?

9. Kelly is the friend that every abuse survivor needs in their corner: compassionate, non-judgmental, and clear about her own

boundaries. How does Kelly's friendship impact Jack's life? How would his life have been different if she hadn't been there for him?

10. What challenges will Jack face as an adult, and what tools does he have to help him meet those challenges?

11. Does Rhonda allow Jack to use his background as an excuse for his violent outbursts? How are his outbursts connected with the abuse? Is it still more acceptable for males in our society to show anger than sadness or fear?

12. Did you see any point at which Alan Castani could have made a better choice and created a different life for himself, or was he simply the victim of his circumstances? Do you think he ever recovered from the effects of the abuse?

13. Regarding sexual abuse by authority figures, what challenges are faced by the Roman Catholic Church and other institutions? What needs to happen in order to ensure children and vulnerable adults are safe?

About the Author

Photograph by Kim Fraher

Janet Clark graduated from Buena Vista College with a degree in education. She taught for ten years, primarily working with disabled adults, before going to work as a journalist. She has published more than 300 articles and received several awards from the Iowa Press Women. Blind Faith is her first novel. She has also worked as a waitress, nurse's aide, pharmacy technician, day care provider, field interviewer, and housecleaner, and once did a stint at a car wash as an interior cleaner.

Janet Clark lives with her husband and two dogs in Fort Dodge, Iowa. They have two adult children. Visit her website at janeteclark.com

www.ingramcontent.com/pod-product-compliance
Lightning Source LLC
LaVergne TN
LVHW090556110826
845146LV00001B/147

* 9 7 8 1 4 2 1 8 9 9 1 8 3 *